CALL OF THE VOID

A NEWEST
MYSTERY

Library and Archives Canada Cataloguing in Publication

Title: Call of the void / J.T. Siemens.
Names: Siemens, J. T., author.
Description: Series statement: A Sloane Donovan mystery
Identifiers: Canadiana (print) 20230453872 | Canadiana (ebook) 20230453902
    | ISBN 9781774390863 (softcover) | ISBN 9781774390870 (EPUB)
Classification: LCC PS8637.I27 C35 2024 | DDC C813/.6—dc23

Editor for the Press: Matt Bowes
Cover and interior design: Michel Vrana
Cover images: iStock
Author photo: Tamea Burd Photography

NeWest Press wishes to acknowledge that the land on which we operate is Treaty 6 territory and a traditional meeting ground and home for many Indigenous Peoples, including Cree, Saulteaux, Niitsitapi (Blackfoot), Métis, and Nakota Sioux.

NeWest Press acknowledges the support of the Canada Council for the Arts, the Alberta Foundation for the Arts, and the Edmonton Arts Council for support of our publishing program. We acknowledge the financial support of the Government of Canada through the Canada Book Fund for our publishing activities

NeWest Press
#201, 8540-109 Street
Edmonton, Alberta T6G 1E6
www.newestpress.com

No bison were harmed in the making of this book.

Printed and bound in Canada
22 23 24 25 5 4 3 2 1

To A.J. Devlin

CALL

OF

THE

VOID

A
SLOANE DONOVAN
MYSTERY

J.T. SIEMENS

NeWest Press

CHAPTER 1

FOR A LONG TIME, I BELIEVED THAT IF I RAN fast enough, the dead couldn't catch up with me.

I was wrong.

But it didn't stop me from trying.

Feet gliding over rock, root, and earth, my body felt so light that at any moment I might lift off the earth's surface and fly. With a fresh gust of speed, I caught up to a lanky and bearded runner, his numbered race bib reading 67. As I passed him, he gave a double take, his eyes registering shock at having been passed by a woman.

The trail rose abruptly, and I heard him huffing as he scrambled to catch me. A glance at my watch timer revealed 5:36:10 … 11 … 12 …

Crossing a wooden footbridge over a deep ravine, I glimpsed a rushing creek at the bottom.

Flash. *An ancient Winnebago abandoned in a snowy forest. A scream from within.*

Coming off the bridge, my knee buckled, and I stumbled against the mossy bark of a Douglas fir. Pushing away from the tree, I kept going, down the trail that suddenly seemed darker, full of menace. Number 67 zigzagged past on the next downhill. "Nice try," he called back, before disappearing around the next bend.

I shook it off and kept going, feeling the blood pounding in my head and the sear of lactic acid in my legs. In the minutes it took to regain my rhythm, a compact, blonde woman edged past, moments later followed by a taller brunette in a red toque. I trailed them down the steep and gnarly section leading to Deep Cove.

The echoing scream hit me again. My vision juddered and my left foot caught a root. The ground swung up. My wrist took the brunt of the fall, and my forehead smacked against another root. Rolling onto my back, I lay there, stunned and gasping, staring up beyond the spires of the trees at a patch of ash gray sky, a distant bird circling.

Touching my forehead, my fingers came away bloody. I took a deep breath and pushed up, wincing when I put weight on my wrist. If it was broken, nothing I could do about it now. Except get up and move.

Several hundred yards down the trail, the bobbing red toque disappeared where the trail ended, and wooden stairs led down to the pavement.

Adrenaline kicked in and I began to jog, quickly picking up speed until I was again flying straight down the trail. No brakes. Rock and tree blurred past. The weightless sensation returned as my feet skimmed down the stairs. Feet hit pavement and I veered right down Panorama Drive. A row of faces cheered.

Ignore everyone.

Except Red Toque, fifty yards up the road, and the blonde a little farther beyond.

Don't think, just breathe, breathe and kick.

More cheers, more bodies. Rounding the sweep of road leading to the cove, I caught up to Red Toque, passing her at the same moment as my shoes hit the grass of the finishing stretch.

"Go, Sloane, go!"

I recognized the voice as belonging to my friend Karin.

Breathe and kick, breathe and kick.

Suddenly the screams and shouts went mute, replaced by a shrill whine in my left ear, a vestige of an old injury.

Overtaking the compact blonde fifty yards from the finish, time suddenly seemed to slow, and despite my distorted hearing, my other senses heightened. I noticed the choppy blue waters of Deep Cove, people standing on boats, watching the race. Across Indian Arm, the green mountains of Belcarra rose in the distance. I could smell the smoke from the wildfires that were devastating the province's interior, hundreds of kilometres away.

The digital timer above the finish line counted: 5:48:41 ...42...43...

A sea of smiling faces mutely cheered. A gust of wind blew off the water. A flash of a blue-gray face caused my stomach to drop and my shoes to fill with cement. It was like someone had pulled the plug to my power source, slowing my sprint to a shuffle. The other two women passed me metres from the finish.

Amid the crowd in front of the announcer's podium stood my sister Stephanie, wearing a nightgown and holding her infant daughter against her chest. Charlie wore blue pyjamas and stood at her side, holding his mother's free hand.

My sister's accusing eyes pinned me to the spot. So did Charlie's.

They weren't cheering.

Because they were dead.

Two other blue-faced women stood further back in the crowd: Geri and Eva, one middle-aged, the other in her late teens. Geri's eyes carried disappointment, while one of Eva's was dangling from her mangled face, and the other was just an empty socket.

Squeezing my eyes shut for several seconds, I took a deep breath. When I opened them, all the dead were gone.

The moment I crossed the finish line, Karin rushed up. "Sloane, what's wrong? Oh my God, you're hurt!"

"It's nothing," I said, just as my legs buckled and I nearly fell.

She pulled my arm over her shoulders and led me toward the medical tent. "You almost won," she said. "You came so close."

CHAPTER 2

A BALL CAP AND AVIATORS HID MOST OF THE bandage on my forehead as I stepped from my black Jeep onto Commercial Drive. A smoky haze hung in the air, so thick you could taste the thousands of burning trees. On the sidewalk outside Prado Café, several masked-up people passed by. For a summer day, the normally bustling thoroughfare seemed apocalyptically quiet, street-front patios mostly vacant save for the odd die-hard or smoker who'd long stopped giving a shit.

My skull throbbed, and my wrist was sprained and swollen, though thankfully unbroken. My palms and knees were scraped and scabbed, and despite my best efforts, I could not manage to walk without a slight limp. The Knee-Knacker was the first race I had done in years, and it had taken more out of me than I cared to admit, and not merely on a physical level.

You think the monsters have died and the ghosts have vanished, but they're always there, waiting. They die when you die, or maybe they follow you around for all of eternity. There's a happy thought.

On the corner of Commercial and 4th, beneath a ratty blue-and-gold Corona parasol, sat seventy-two-year-old M.J., the hood's perennial busker. She strummed a half-decent "Stairway to Heaven" on her ukulele while wearing a gas mask that looked like it dated back to the First World War. Her pet skunk, Pepi, dozed on a blanket beside an open guitar case sprinkled with coins and the odd bill.

I tossed a toonie into the case. M.J. glanced up, stopped playing, and pushed the gas mask up on her forehead. Her frizzy, gray hair stood straight up above the mask, like she'd stuck a fork in an electrical outlet. She studied me for a moment. "Darlin', you keep up the rough stuff, soon you're gonna look like me."

"Then I'll take up the banjo," I said. "Give you some competition."

"Start practicing," she said.

"Start learning a new Zeppelin cover. You've been play-ing 'Stairway to Heaven' for the past three months straight."

"I only play it when I see you coming up the street. Seems to suit you somehow. By the way, you gotta be nuts to run a race with all this crap in the air. You got any idea what that can do to your lungs?"

I shrugged and feigned a hacking cough. M.J. shook her head like I was a lost cause, then gestured with her thumb at the three-storey redbrick building behind her. "You got a visitor. She's been up there about ten minutes."

Great. I hoped it was a client of Wayne's and not a walk-in. Walk-ins were a pain, typically retirees who read too many detective novels and sought to pepper you with ques-tions on sleuthing techniques. Or they were paranoiacs con-vinced that their phones and computers were being bugged by any number of government agencies. I had no patience for any of that today. What I needed were two Advil, chased with a stiff drink. The intent was to put my feet up for an hour and then get to some paperwork.

After thanking M.J., I turned the corner onto 4th Avenue and stepped beneath a blue awning that read, HARDKNOCKS INVESTIGATIONS & SECURITY SERVICES, INC.

Pulling open the door, I nearly collided with a heavyset woman exiting the building. We both apologized at the same time. Her shoulder-length, dark brown hair had an inch of gray coming in at the roots. She smelled of nicotine and her skin bore the orange hue of a tanning bed junkie. Her red and swollen eyes jittered with desperation. The kind of eyes I wanted to avoid most days. *Especially* today.

"Sloane Donovan?"

Shit.

"Yes."

"You probably don't remember me, but I'm Maddy Pike ... Emily's mother?"

Emily.

Despite the muggy July heat, I felt a shiver.

Emily Pike, gone missing 2013.

"Of course," I said. My stomach dropped. I already knew why she was here, and I wanted no part in it. If only I had come in five minutes later. If only I hadn't come in at all.

"I saw you on the news recently, where you found those runaways before the cops did? And I remembered you from the search party for my Emily ... and I thought ..." A tear raced down a crease in Maddy's cheek.

I took her arm and gently guided her back inside the stairwell. "Let's talk upstairs, Mrs. Pike."

She stopped and took a deep breath. "Please call me Maddy. And I can't go back up there."

"Why's that?"

"Your partner kicked me out, saying your agency couldn't help me, and that I ought to go to the police. The thing is, the cops won't take me seriously; they just brush me off like I'm a kook. I know you won't treat me like that. I remember the day you volunteered in the search. I could tell you wanted to help find my daughter. I was so sad to read in the papers what happened to your sister and—"

"Let's grab some coffee, Maddy."

Despite the oppressive atmosphere outside, the air-conditioned Prado Café teemed with hobo-bearded hipsters and their geek-chic girlfriends wearing vintage glasses and baggy overalls. In the East Van coffee shop, it was de rigueur to sport full-sleeve tats and facial hardware while tapping away on a laptop or tablet—while appearing disconnected, or simply stoned.

I ordered a coffee and Maddy ordered a decaf latte, informing me that her psychic friend Lilith told her caffeine led to blocked chakras. Once we managed to snag seats at the window, she also said that Lilith recently revealed to her that Emily was still alive and trying desperately to get home.

My temples began throbbing. "Did Lilith happen to say where she might be?"

Maddy wiped foam from her lip. "Somewhere close."

I wanted to inquire how much it cost to keep a psychic on retainer, but instead I removed my sunglasses and sipped my coffee.

Her penciled-in brows rose in alarm. "What happened to your head?"

"Fell down running."

"But you're okay, though?"

"Never better."

"That's why I never run," she said, then laughed. "Probably pretty obvious."

I smiled and sipped more coffee. The sooner I ditched this woman, the sooner I could go upstairs for something stronger.

Maddy tapped her long, pastel green nails on the wood of the table. Her other hand twisted a soiled tissue. "I keep thinking that if I'd been a better mother, the kind that gives their kids a ride home from work, she'd still be here. Everyone tells me not to blame myself, but when your baby drops off the face of the earth, it's what you do: you dwell on the worst. Life becomes a living hell."

She reached across the table and clutched my hand. My sore wrist shrieked, and if she was aware of my grimace, she didn't show it. She did, however, get to the point of why she had come. When she asked me to reopen her missing daughter's case, dread pooled into my guts like acid.

I looked out onto the street, where a female letter carrier strolled down the sidewalk, whistling and bending over to pet someone's golden retriever. I'd chosen the wrong profession. I hated missing person cases. Wayne had been right to reject this one.

"Will you help me?" Maddy pleaded. Looking at her was like watching an egg about to roll off the edge of a counter.

I eased my hand from her damp grasp. "Maddy, have there been other private investigators on the case?"

She shook her head. "The police always advised against it, and up until recently, I've tried to follow their orders. They do the best they can, I guess, but they got so much going on. The people at the Missing Children's Society are good for support and whatnot, but they're out in Calgary."

"Have there been any new leads?"

"Inspector Davis basically said it's a cold case. Do you know him?"

I shook my head.

"Emily's file got transferred to him four years ago when the other cop in charge of the case retired. I doubt he's even looked at the file in years."

Suddenly an ungodly fatigue swept over me. I closed my eyes for a moment and saw bones buried in the earth off some remote back road. Forcing myself to look at Maddy Pike, I said, "Those girls I found—that my agency helped find—were runaways. One of them had only been gone a week. The others, less than a month. *And* I got lucky. The police would have found them sooner or later, or they would have returned home on their own."

Maddy nodded and blinked. "Emily did take out some money from her savings account the day she disappeared. Five hundred bucks, which is so unlike her. Em was a saver. She never spent frivolously and was always on me about how much I blew on smokes and scratch tickets. In the end, she had more money in the bank than I did. Tax-Free Savings Account, the whole caboodle. So, that withdrawal really jumped out at me. Police didn't see much in it, though. Said runaways do it all the time, especially ones on drugs."

"Did Emily use?"

A frown turned her smoker's lips into a thousand tiny lines. "*God,* no. Never. And after seeing what booze did to her father, the girl never even touched a drop of liquor."

"OK. The thing about runaways is that unless they know what they're doing, they burn through money extremely fast, and it's hard not to leave tracks. Emily would've needed more cash. Five hundred on the street is nothing."

"Speaking of,"—she pulled an envelope from her purse and slid it across the table—"it's all I have right now, but I can get you more."

I pushed the envelope back. "I'm sorry."

"*Please.* Please don't say no. You're my last chance, Sloane. You know what pain is like, the way you lost your sister and niece and nephew. You realize your story was in the papers the same time as Emily's?"

"I can't take your money," I said, "because I don't think I can help you. Truth is, I'm pretty much done with missing persons."

"Please find it in your heart to make an exception." She pressed the envelope into my hands and closed my fingers around it. "I'll give every cent I have to find my daughter, even if she's ... I just need closure either way. It's killing me."

I looked up at her desperate face. Her lips trembled and her eyes welled up. Lacking the energy to deal with a melt-down in a coffee shop, I agreed to spend a week—no more—looking for her missing daughter.

CHAPTER 3

I OPENED THE DOOR TO OUR OFFICE AND WALKED across the creaky hardwood floor of the small waiting room. The previous tenant had run an escort agency that had to close up shop in a hurry, leaving behind two black leather couches and an ornate, mirrored, 80s-era coffee table that looked like it had been a set piece on *Scarface*.

Wayne's office door was closed, but I could hear his muffled voice on the other side. I went into my small office. With both windows closed to keep out the wildfire smoke, it was stifling. The western window looked down on Commercial Drive. The south-facing window revealed a black iron fire escape. White-walled and trimmed in black, the room consisted of an oak desk, two chairs, a rolling whiteboard, file cabinet, mini fridge, and a framed poster of Death Valley at sunrise. There was a faint and artificially sweet smell in the room that refused to be evicted, as though a lost box of cherry-flavoured condoms sat mouldering in a ventilation duct. I lifted the lower half of the window, letting in smoky air, along with the revs, bus belches, and honks of Commercial Drive. My head began to throb again, so I took off my ballcap and released my long, red hair from its ponytail.

In the window's reflection, my angular face looked OK. A little tired and a little beat up, but when I forced a smile all my teeth were straight and intact. A good smile could trick and disarm. My own smile even fooled me sometimes, until I looked deep enough into my own intense blue-gray eyes. Hidden just behind them were the cracks, some of which ran deeper than others. Some led straight to the abyss.

I put my sunglasses back on.

After retrieving the Advil from the top drawer of the desk, I went to the fridge, on top of which sat several glass tumblers. Opening the fridge door, I glanced in the narrow freezer, cursing to see the empty ice cube tray. I pulled out the bottle of Stoli and poured a double. Tossing back two extra-strengths, I washed them down with the fiery liquid.

The drink was gone and I was working on my second when I sat down and opened Maddy's envelope. First thing I saw was a school photo of Emily, age 15, a pretty and petite brunette with dark eyes and dimples. She wore a red sweater. I stared at the photo and felt the Stoli begin to soften the sharp edges of my consciousness.

A rap on the door. Before I could hide the photo, the door opened, and there was Wayne. When he and I first met, nine years ago, he was what you'd call husky. Now he was husky plus twenty pounds, which he tried to hide—with mixed results—under a tan, linen suit. When he needed to, he could blend into a crowd like a pro. When he didn't, he gravitated toward the perpetually disheveled bachelor look, more often than not making me the agency's "front-woman" when it came time to charm potential clients.

Wayne raised a brow and acknowledged my head bandage by tapping his forehead. Then he saw the envelope on my desk and frowned.

As I opened my mouth to speak, he cut me off with a halting motion of his hand. Then he opened my mini fridge, helped himself to a can of Pabst, and sat in the chair across from me. He popped the tab on his beer and took a sip.

"Two things," he said. "One: you shouldn't have taken that case—"

"One week," I said.

"And two: what the fuck happened in the race yesterday?"

"I got injured."

"I *see* that. Your little boo-boo doesn't explain why you went from a full-out sprint to shitting the bed twenty feet from the finish line."

"Calf cramp."

"Calf cramp my ass. I've seen you run yourself nearly to death without slowing down."

"You weren't there."

Wayne pulled out his phone, tapped the screen several times, then held it up so I could see a photo of my finish, such as it was. Using his thumb and index finger, he zoomed in on my face, enough that you could see my eyes wide with shock.

"What did you see out there?" he asked.

"Nothing."

"No phantom Winnebago in the woods?"

I didn't respond. He was referring to our first big case, to the vehicle which had nearly become my tomb—and my own personal hell. I would never be able to look at an RV the same way again.

Wayne nodded. "What about Geri and the others? Any visits?"

My late friend Geri had been the catalyst behind the aforementioned case, and the investigation into her death had led to an unanticipated wave of violence across the city, culminating in carnage on a snow-covered mountain nearby.

"You try running fifty klicks of terrain for six hours and tell me you don't see some shit. I'm at work today, and I'm good to go, and there we are."

He paused and nodded again. "I'm just glad I didn't put money down on you to win is all I'm saying. 'Cause some people were taking bets, had you at like 12-1."

I slouched back and shook my head. "Fucking armchair athlete. If you ran up a hill, you'd probably stroke out. Did you come in here just to give me a hard time?"

"No, even though it's a lot of fun. I turned down that Pike woman's offer—a *wise* decision, I might add—and yet here you are, thirty minutes later, with an envelope of cash and a photo. No contract at least. Means you can give it back."

"I told her I'd give her a week."

"You're a sucker for a sob story, and you took on the case without consulting me. We're partners; the deal is we have to agree on every case before accepting."

"Goes both ways; you're also supposed to consult me before you turn something down."

"That girl is long gone, and you know it."

I rolled the cool glass against my left temple, just below the bandage. "Everyone is somewhere," I said.

Wayne grabbed the envelope and thumbed through the money. He shook his head. "Less than half our normal retainer. We doing charity work now?"

"One week," I said. "My time, my dime."

"Case you forgot, Haley's also back in town this week to wrap up shooting. You're going to need to be with her for every event, and every day on and off the shoot."

"Frank can take some of the babysitting detail."

"She wants *you*, he said, "and that 'babysitting detail' is paying two large per diem, meaning this is the biggest thing we got going on right now. By far."

Wayne reached for Emily's photo. Looking at it, his eyes lost a little of their edge, and he slowly shook his head. "This is a mistake," he said.

CHAPTER 4

FRESH FROM SANTA MONICA CELEB REHAB, Haley Cooper was back in town to wrap up shooting of *Zyborg Apocalypse*, a film that had been delayed six weeks due to the debauched shenanigans of the star. Zypoc Productions had hired HardKnocks to bodyguard Haley, from hotel to set and back, and whenever she wanted to go clubbing, to a restaurant, or running on the seawall.

The reason we'd been hired was because Haley's team had been receiving creepy stalker mail, along with packages containing jizzed-in undies and ever-so-endearing envelopes jammed with pubic hair trimmings. Also, during her last stint in town, we had been so consumed with watching for weirdos that we had no idea that the chemically dependent actor had been taking a page from Keith Richards' playbook by having her L.A. dealer mail her rock star quantities of coke and heroin taped within the pages of screenplays.

On the first day of shooting, I picked her up from the Four Seasons, where the wasted starlet had promptly puked all over me in the lobby. With lawsuits pending, filming was paused until Haley completed her requisite stay in treatment.

I had hoped that it would be the last I'd see of the train-wreck Hollywood cliché, but there we were, on Tuesday night, in the Granville Strip's latest hotspot, The Avalon. *(I need to be able to test myself, Sloane. Plus, Woodview was such a drag. I need to let out some steam on the dance floor.)*

This time the rules were clear. In addition to keeping pube-clipping fans at bay, we were to protect Haley from her worst enemy: herself.

Leaning against a post near the dance floor, I sipped my soda with lime, and kept an eye on the incognito star, who was rocking an eclectic ensemble: chunky glasses and a dark pageboy wig to hide her blonde locks. She wore a red-checked button-down over white shorts with cowboy boots. With my jeans and black leather jacket, you'd never have guessed we arrived together, which I was just fine with.

When Haley had taken to the dance floor with her Cosmo sans vodka, I was relieved: no one recognized her. Another rule was that I had to steer her away from paparazzi, which meant bouncers and staff were never notified ahead of time that she would be arriving at their establishment.

Ninety minutes and three virgin Cosmos later, Haley had to pee, so I waited in the hall outside while she used the washroom. I sipped my drink and glanced over the railing to the more lounge-y first floor, replete with shitfaced couples making out on couches.

From my pocket, I took out the photo. The pulsing purple-and-green strobe lights lit up Emily Pike's smile. If she were alive, she'd be twenty-two now.

That girl is long gone, and you know it.

A drunk girl stumbled into me, knocking my drink to the floor and sloshing her rum & coke down the front of my jacket.

"Ohmigod, I'm *so* sorry," she slurred.

"Jesus Christ," I muttered.

She dug into her purse. "Let me buy you another drink."

Just then Haley passed by in the background, heading for the stairs. I nudged the drunk girl aside and called to Haley, who was already descending to the lower floor.

I caught up to her at the bottom of the stairs and grabbed her arm. *"Haley!"*

But it wasn't Haley, just another brunette about the same size, wearing Haley's clothes and glasses. She yanked her arm away. "Don't touch me," she said. "Haley *said* you were a creepy ginger stalker."

My eyes darted around the packed club. "What's she wearing now?" I asked.

"Fuck off," she said, smirking and turning away.

I grabbed the pinkie of her right hand and twisted her arm behind her back. The girl shrieked and rose up on her toes. *"What. Is. She. Wearing. Now?"* I yelled.

"Pink-and-white hat," she blurted. "Little black dress. Valentino shoes." When the decoy tried to wriggle free, I torqued her pinkie, making her squeal again. "Where is she?" I shouted.

"In one of the stalls doing bumps."

"Fuck." I bounded back up the stairs, pushing past the girls in the washroom line. "Wait your turn, bitch," someone said behind me. None of the women primping at the mirror were Haley, so I checked the stalls. Beneath the door of the corner cubicle stood two sets of designer heels. Whispers, followed by a distinct *chop-chop,* followed by an even more distinct snort.

I rapped on the door. "Haley, ditch the blow and get your ass out here."

A clatter of activity came from inside the stall. A toilet flushed. The door opened. I was prepared to grab my client by the back of her dumb little neck and march her out, but of the two wide-eyed powder princesses, neither was Haley Cooper.

"Where is she?"

"Who?" asked the taller one.

"You *know* who," I said.

The shorter girl's eyes widened as she turned to her friend. "I fucking *told* you that was Haley Cooper. We shoulda selfie'd with her. No one's gonna believe this shit!"

I ran from the washroom and back to the railing, just in time to see a woman in a white-and-pink fedora and a little black dress skip out the door and onto the street with a tall guy in a leather motorcycle jacket.

It took me at least a minute of pushing to get through the crowd and onto Granville Street. After midnight, the street teemed with pizza-noshing drunks, tourists, a few theatre-goers, and scores of panhandlers. No Haley to be seen.

Wayne was going to ream me royally. I had my phone out and was about to call him, when I spotted, on the next block over, the woman from before, now wearing a motor-cycle helmet, hopping on the back of Leather Boy's Triumph. As the motorcycle revved and ripped away from the curb, I saw the white-and-pink fedora clutched in her right hand.

By the time I got there, the bike had screamed off into the night and I hadn't gotten close enough to make the plate.

"That fucking bitch," I muttered.

"She can't be all bad," muttered a grizzled homeless man nearby, holding up a fifty-dollar bill. "She looked like some famous chick."

"She say anything?" I asked.

"I heard her tell buddy she wanted to party," he said, "and that guy wearing leather said something about a sick warehouse rave he knew."

Warehouse rave. Jesus. I sprinted up the sidewalk and around the corner on Nelson Street, using my fob to unlock the black Range Rover at the curb. I climbed in and paused, looking at my phone. Call Wayne? Or Amy Gardner, Haley's manager? Both would shit when they found out I lost her, only the latter would shit first, fire us second. No reason anyone had to know about this little blip.

First, I called Haley's number. Straight to voicemail. *Hey y'all, it's me. You know the drill.*

"Haley," I said, "call me and I'll come get you. No questions asked."

Tapping into the Find My Phone app showed that the GPS on Haley's phone had been disabled.

I paused again.

Warehouse rave.

Scrolling through my contacts, I found the number for Andy "Dogger" Peretti. Several years ago, Dogger had been a suspect when I was investigating my friend's murder. By occupation he was a tennis coach, but he was also a full-time party-boy and homewrecker. It had been awhile since our paths had crossed, but since I had quite possibly saved him from being beaten to death by a jealous fiancé, not to mention considerable jail time in a third world prison, he owed me one.

He picked up on the fourth ring. "Calling to fuck up my life some more?"

"You still owe me big time," I said. "Listen, are there any warehouse raves going on that you know of?"

"Warehouse raves?" he asked. "What're we, back in the nineties? There used to be a warehouse after-hours called Gomorrah, a few blocks off the skids. I haven't been in a while, but it's the underground place to be for those in the know. It's on Pandora Street in a shithole area, probably why the cops haven't shut it down yet."

"Thanks, Dogger," I said. "Buy you a drink sometime."

"I remember what happened the last time we drank together," he said, "so maybe not."

Leaving the nightclub district, I sped north on Seymour Street, heading toward the Downtown Eastside, the open-air drug and flesh market that never slept. While the surrounding neighbourhoods gentrified, this decrepit and diseased pocket of old Vancouver resolutely refused to change, and I kind of loved her for keeping it real.

The area around Main and Hastings was block after block of flophouse hotels, rooming houses, pawnshops, street clinics, and corner food marts that sold everything from roses to crack pipes. The hot summer night brought everyone out, hustling and roaming: hookers, dealers, addicts, mentally ill, burnout punks, skinheads, winos, tweakers, and kids from the 'burbs looking to score.

A dozen blocks later, the squalor thinned, giving way to empty side streets, crumbling buildings and fenced-off sites slated for demolition. I turned left on Victoria, then right on Pandora, cruising slowly with the windows down. Three blocks later I found what had to be the place: a rickety, two-storey structure next to a meat packing plant. The surrounding streets were chockablock with cars and trucks, and the building vibrated from heavy bass. In the alley alongside the building sat a matte-black Triumph motorcycle. I noted down the plate number then crouched and released the air from both tires.

A black-clad bouncer at the door mumbled something about a private party.

"I'm an investigator," I said. "My client is here. She's underage and if you don't let me in, the cops are going to be on this place inside ten minutes."

He dead-eyed me for a moment, then stepped aside. I walked up the stairs to the second floor. Graffiti covered the walls and red candles guttered inside black birdcages hanging from chains attached to the high ceiling. Despite the deafening EDM throbbing from massive speakers in the corners of the large room, barely anyone was dancing. Maybe it was too early for this crowd. I scanned the room. Maybe fifty people were spread out, on low-slung couches, random chairs, or swaying absently in the dance area, the round, crimson-painted floor looking like a pool of blood.

No sign of Haley. Off to the left, several booths were set in alcoves, separated from the rest of the club by curtains of metal chains. A skinny guy in a wifebeater exited the furthest alcove, and through the swinging chains I caught a glimpse of a pink-and-white fedora. I walked over and slipped through the chains.

A tall, runway-skinny blonde wore the hat. Two men sat on either side of her, one of them in motorcycle gear.

"Where is she?" I yelled over the music.

Leather Boy looked me up and down. "Who the fuck are you, her *mom*?"

The others giggled.

Swiping my finger across the surface of the table, it came away coated with powdery residue. I flashed my ID, and when I raised my phone to take his photo, his hands went up.

"Haley was with me," he said, "but all I had was some molly. She railed it, *right here*, all of it. Then Cutter came along, and she went with him. Said he had a better party."

"Cutter's a *bad* boy," the blonde said.

"Where'd they go?" I asked.

"I think he lives around here," said Leather Boy, "but I'm not sure."

On the way out, I asked the bouncer if he recalled seeing Haley leave. He held out a shovel-sized palm and I placed a ten on it.

He tucked it away. "Yup."

"With Cutter?"

"Yup."

"Where's Cutter's place?"

He gestured left, up the street. "All's I know is they went that way, on foot."

For lack of a better option, I got in the Range Rover and pointed it in that direction. I drove slowly up the street, past chain link fences surrounding weedy lots, a steel fabrication shop, a recycling depot, and the odd dilapidated house sandwiched here and there, the final holdouts in a neighbourhood that died generations ago.

Suddenly I felt shaky and sick. I squeezed my eyes shut for a moment, and when I opened them, I shouted and slammed on the brakes, nearly hitting a coyote crossing the street, a dead cat in its mouth. The glowing, green eyes of the coyote matched those of the cat.

I pulled over, rolled down all the windows, and sucked in the gritty industrial air that contained smoky overtones of wildfire.

That girl is long gone, and you know it.

I picked up the phone to call Wayne, but instead rang Haley again. *Hey, y'all ...*

Using a cop tactic from years ago, I cruised at a deliberate twenty kilometres an hour, concentrating on roughly thirty square blocks, Dundas and Hastings Streets representing the north and south ends, Nanaimo and Victoria Streets representing the east and west borders. I worked north-to-south first, street by street, then started east-to-west, searching for signs of life.

Time was getting on, and all houses I passed were dark or most likely vacant. Haley could be halfway across the city by now. Wayne would crucify me if we lost this contract. Out of desperation, I called Haley's phone one more time.

It answered on the second ring. Country music in the background, men whooping and hollering.

"Haley, where the hell are you?" I asked.

"Whozis?" came a female voice, but not Haley's.

"Where did you get that phone?"

"The famous chick that's here. It's hers. She said I could have it."

"Where are you right now?"

"I'm not saying shit."

"Please, it's very important. Haley has a medical condition which requires immediate attention."

"I gotta go," she said, "but I'll tell her you called."

"There's a hundred bucks in it if you tell me where you are."

"Three hundred," she said.

"Fine. Where?"

She told me and I punched it into the GPS and drove there. It was only a few blocks away, and I had driven right past it only minutes ago. The streetlights were out on the block, so had I not been looking for it, I never would have seen the sad bungalow, set back from the road amid trees. I parked in an alley across the street and killed the engine. Rockabilly music twanged from the house.

Flipping open the glove box, I pulled out what a casual observer might assume was a black, foot-long flashlight. While the device did function in that capacity, it wasn't called an Enforcer because of its ability to light up the dark.

Raindrops began spitting down from the deep roil of overcast night. A rickety, gray picket fence separated the property line from the road. I walked up to a gate, unlatched it, and entered a backyard of knee-high grass and dried-out pine trees. Enforcer in hand, I stepped up to the house and peered through a mullioned window into a darkened kitchen.

To the right of the fridge, a light spilled down a hall. From that direction came the hoots and hollers of at least two men.

I walked over and rapped lightly on the back door. Seconds later it was opened by a chunky, tattooed woman with purple hair and wide eyes. She put one finger to her lips, then extended her other hand out, rubbing her thumb and index finger together.

"Not till I know she's here," I whispered.

"She's *here*."

"How many others?"

"Cutter and two other guys," she said. "I don't know them."

"Any weapons?"

She looked at me like, *Duh*.

"Extra hundred in it if you can get her to me," I said.

She looked around nervously. "I gotta jet, man. If they find out I ratted this place—"

Over the music, there was a sudden shriek. Haley. The men laughed louder. I pushed past the woman and went in, grabbing a cast-iron pan from the sink.

The living room was half-drug lair and half-amateur strip bar. A brass pole ran floor to ceiling, and twirling rather expertly around it—wearing only her bra and underwear—was Haley Cooper.

"Holy shit! *Sloane!*" she yelled, then leaped from the pole and hugged me. The three who had been filming Haley's routine with their phones appeared dumbfounded. The big guy rising from the couch didn't require an introduction for me to know this was Cutter. Around six-four, with a shaved head and mountain-man beard, he was bare-chested under his leather jacket, and his shit-kickers looked like they lived up to their name.

His dilated eyes went from the frying pan in my right hand to the Enforcer in my left. On a nearby coffee table sat several light bulbs that had been repurposed as meth pipes, but I wasn't so much concerned about those as I was about the pearl-handled pistol jutting from his jacket pocket.

"Get your clothes, Haley," I said, not taking my eyes from his. "We're leaving."

"Aw, mom," she said, "we just got here."

"You're Cutter?" I asked the big man.

"Could be," he replied, in a surprisingly wispy voice.

"We're not going to have any problems tonight, are we, Cutter?"

"Remains to be seen, Red," he said. "Girlfriend here promised me an autograph before we were through." His boys laughed. One of them was still filming everything with his phone.

"I'm going to be needing your phones," I said.

"See," he said, "*that's* going to be a problem for me. I believe my friends will also take issue with that."

The pan was killing my wrist, so I did a quick exchange over to my left hand. The Enforcer was now in my right.

"What're you going to do with the pan," he asked. "Fry me some eggs?"

I raised the iron pan and smashed it into the side of the head of his nearest seated comrade, the one with the phone. Haley muttered *holyfuckingshit* as the druggie fell sideways and onto the floor. In the second it took for Cutter to process this new turn of events I stuck the business end of the Enforcer where his neck met his beard—and lit him up. He did a jerky dance befitting a large man being juiced with two million volts. When I released the trigger, he dropped, crushing the coffee table beneath him.

I dropped the pan, pulled the revolver from his pocket, and aimed it at the third man. Bug-eyed fucker put his hands up. "Fuckin' rad," he said.

Using my foot, I gestured toward a large Ziploc drug baggie on the floor. "I'm going to need you to collect all your phones and put them in that bag."

While he was doing that, I asked Haley where her gear was: clothes, wallet, ID.

"I gave it to some rockabilly chick?"

"Along with your phone," I said. "You know, there are better charities to get involved with."

"How'd you find me so quick?" she asked. "They implant a chip up my ass?"

"Not a bad idea."

CHAPTER 5

BACK OUTSIDE, HALEY ATTEMPTED TO RIP OFF her underwear and dance in the tall grass, but I yanked her toward the Range Rover.

A few squealing turns brought us back to Hastings Street, westbound toward civilization. I turned to her. "What the fuck, Haley? You're scheduled to begin shooting in a few days—"

She leaned over and kissed me on the cheek, eyes all skittery. "I was just testing you, you know? Seeing how long it would take for you to find me. Turned off the Find My Phone app and everything. You're *good*, anybody ever tell you that?"

I shook my head in disbelief, which she misinterpreted. "Well, they should. I am *totally* going to pass your name along to everyone in Hollywood. Every A-lister is gonna request you when they come to town."

I stopped at a red on Hastings and Clark. Haley flicked on the stereo and began hitting buttons until she came up with some EDM. She commenced car dancing, giving some guys in the next car a show. Wasted famous chick dancing in her undies. The driver pulled out his phone to take a video.

Leaning past her, I called out the window, "I'm a cop, asshole!"

He put the phone away.

The light changed and I accelerated ahead, then reached over and turned down the music.

"You *used* to be a cop, right?" she asked.

"That's right," I said.

"But now you're an investigator?"

"Very perceptive."

"How'd that happen?"

"My goal in life was always to have no job security and babysit rich, spoiled brats."

"Sarcasm comes very naturally to you, girl," she said. "I like it."

As we drove past the squalor of Main and Hastings, I said, "You know, the way you're going, in a few years, I could see you in a place like this. Not many A-listers, but your kind of people—"

"Hey, Sloane," she said, "you can insult me up the wazoo, but save the lectures, OK? Don't you think I had enough of that shit at Woodview? They took us on a scared-straight field trip to L.A.'s Skid Row, which is a fuck of a lot worse than this candy-ass strip, let me tell you."

I shrugged. All this was above my pay grade anyway. But still, I'd fucked up tonight and couldn't very well return her to the Four Seasons in her current state.

Haley turned the music up, but I was sober and too dark-minded for electronica, so I switched stations. Kings of Leon came on. "Sex on Fire". Appropriate.

"One of those guys tried to fuck me once," Haley said.

Huh. "What?"

"Yeah, he was drunk at a club one night after a gig, and he tried to hook up with me in a washroom."

"But you didn't hook up?"

"Nope."

"So, a hot rockstar you *don't* hook up with, but for a bunch of redneck tweakers you'll risk your health and your life while you lap dance for them."

"It was a pole dance," she said. "But here's the thing: I'm a tease. All show, no go."

"What about that sex tape a while back?"

"I was, like, eighteen then," she said. "Did you ever see it?"

"No."

"Bullshit," she said. "*Everyone* saw it, including my grandmother. But the guy in it was my boyfriend at the time anyhow."

"Wasn't he your forty-five-year-old, *married*, agent?"

"Seem to know a lot for someone who's never seen the tape, Sloane. Anyway—hey, where we going? This isn't the way back to the hotel."

"Little detour first."

Just before five a.m. I pulled into the underground parking lot of my apartment building, on Nelson Street, right next to Stanley Park. I managed to spirit Haley up the stairs, into the lobby, and up the elevator and into my place without being seen.

Still in her underwear, she stood in front of the large, southeast-facing living room windows that offered a full view of the city skyline, glass buildings ablaze under the rising sun.

"Wow, wicked view," she said, then turned and glanced around. My place was Spartan save for a tan couch and sofa, TV and stand, and my large, black oak table and chairs.

On the wall behind the table hung my sister's final gift: a painting of a blood red sunset over a lake. Haley said she dug the painting, then moved over to the pillar separating the living room from the kitchen. On it was hung the only other piece of art I possessed: a hand-carved multicoloured Borucan devil mask.

"Where'd you get this thing?" she asked.

"Costa Rica."

"I was raised Pentecostal," she said. "My people would be writhing around babbling in tongues if they saw this thing."

"Wonder what they'd do if they saw you in the meth den back there."

She laughed. "Half of them would fit right in."

"What about your parents?"

"I got a lawsuit pending against my folks. Haven't talked to them in years. Mom and dad *misappropriated* my money when I was a kid."

Eclipse, my massive black cat, appeared out of nowhere and followed Haley around the living room, his yellow eyes staring up in a kind of feline reverence. She leaned down and scratched under his jaw. Eclipse stood on his hind legs and rubbed chins with her. Friends for life.

Haley went into the kitchen and opened my fridge like she owned the place. She pulled out a bottle of white wine. I took it from her and put it back.

"Yeah, like a little vino at this point is going to push me over the edge," she said. "Damage has been done, sister. Fuck-it switch has been flipped."

Against my better judgement, I took the bottle out again, along with two glasses from the cupboard. I poured us each a dose and handed her one. "Not a word of this," I said.

"Got anything stronger?" she asked, grinding her jaw.

"All you get is melatonin," I said. "But hop in the shower first: you smell like a back-alley mattress."

She took her wine into the bathroom and I went into the bedroom to get some fresh clothes. I heard the shower turn on. Several minutes later, when I opened the door to the bathroom, I stopped short. Haley stood, dripping with water as she slapped some pills in her mouth. I grabbed the bottle from her. Zopiclone.

"You idiot," I yelled. "How many'd you take?"

"Only two," she said. "Don't worry, they're only zops. Jeez, I'm not out to kill myself, I just wanna keep from grinding my molars to dust."

"They're only for emergencies," I said.

"I think tonight qualified," she said, then looked curiously at another bottle in my cabinet. "Fucking hell, Sloane. You take *lithium*?"

I closed the cabinet and walked to the bedroom. Eclipse stared at me from atop the bed. When Haley entered, he stared at her instead.

I gave her the clothes and she dressed, tripping and nearly falling as she pulled on sweatpants. She had similar trouble getting into an oversized T-shirt.

"Sure you only took two?" I asked.

She collapsed on the bed beside Eclipse, who immediately curled up next to her. She grinned up at me. "Would I lie to you?" she said.

I leaned against the doorway and sipped my wine. Dawn's soft glow crept into the room. The chirping of birds outside seemed amplified, but now I needed quiet. Every time I closed my eyes, I saw Emily Pike staring back at me. It was time to take another lithium, but I could feel the drug building in me, sapping my vitality a little more each day.

The doctor said I just had to ride out the "adjustment phase," and then "we" could fine-tune the dose.

I yawned. "C'mon, let's get you back to the hotel before your manager has a shit fit."

Haley flopped back on the bed and stretched out, eyes dopey. "I don't wanna go back yet. I like it here. It's still super early. Can I stay, just for a bit? *Please?*"

Eclipse rubbed his head against her chin. "My biggest, most handsomest fan," she mumbled.

I sighed, went into the bathroom, and took my medicine. When I returned to the bedroom, Haley and Eclipse were cuddled up beneath the covers on the far side of the bed, asleep.

I took the other side, eventually falling into a tense half-sleep. Nightmares melded with the real world, where the dead were living and the living were dead, or caught somewhere in between, existing in murky twilight. I was trapped in a Winnebago, hands and feet bound. Two large shadows entered, hunched and snuffling, more animal than human. Through a crack in the curtain, I saw my dead sister and her kids, barefoot in the snow, calmly staring back. I could smell gasoline as one of the shadows grabbed me.

CHAPTER 6

I SNAPPED AWAKE, HEART GALLOPING, MY body lathered in sweat. Haley snored beside me. A beam of sunlight fell on her waxy forehead. My phone buzzed on the bedside table.

10:22 a.m. *Shit.*

I picked up the phone. "Hey, Wayne."

"Where the fuck is she, Donovan?"

"Right here," I said. "At my place. Sleeping."

"Why's *that?* And why haven't you been returning my calls? Her manager's having a conniption and has already called the cops."

"She's safe."

"What about reports of her shaking you at The Avalon? Getting on the back of some clown's motorcycle? Ending up at *Gomorrah?*"

"I lost her," I said, "and I found her. No problem."

"Yeah," he said, "except there *is*, and it's already gone viral."

I stood up and groaned. The phone. The rockabilly chick.

"YouTube 'Haley Cooper crack house striptease,' and guess what comes up?"

I glanced at Haley, deep in sleep, spooning Eclipse.

"She gave her phone to some chick," I said.

"No shit," he said. "As she has a propensity to do, which is why they hired us. All you had to do was keep an eye—"

"She's a wily little bitch, Wayne. She duped me, exchanged clothes with another girl at the club—"

"Just get her ass to the Fairmont. Paparazzi are already swarming the Four Seasons. And for fuck sakes make sure she's not all cracked out like the last time. Meanwhile, I gotta go track down her phone. Girl wants three grand for it, claims there are tons of nude shots on it. Any paparazzi would give their left nut to get their hands on those. By the way, any money I spend on this is coming outta your end."

I hung up. Haley opened her eyes and looked at me as she stretched. "Wily little bitch, huh?" she asked.

"And last night you referred to me as a 'creepy, ginger stalker'," I said. "Why did they have to choose my town to film your shitty movie?"

Haley sat up, blinking, then fell back and burrowed under the covers. "Why'd you have to remind me?" she said. "I *hate* that movie. Fucking *Terminator* meets *Walking Dead* shit. That's what happens when you're an Oscar-nominee at thirteen; it's all downhill after that. Do you have any pick-me-ups in your cabinet? I feel like a poopy diaper."

"Deservedly so," I said, tossing her the disguise of a debauched starlet: a hoodie and sunglasses.

Following a back-alley entrance into the Fairmont on Georgia Street, I received a solid tongue-lashing from Amy Gardner, Haley's wolf-in-a-Gucci-suit manager, who threatened to sue HardKnocks. I walked off in the middle of her tirade, leaving YouTube's latest strip-tease sensation temporarily in the care of Frank Shikwitz. Frank was simply too good to let what happened last night occur again. I was slipping, but what I found most disconcerting was that I didn't much care. It was probably the pills that were sapping my gusto, but I wondered if on some level, deep down, I wanted to lose.

It was another smoky, muggy day. For the better part of an hour I sat at a window seat in Prado, sipping iced coffee while staring at the mountains, trying to dredge up the desire to move. Emily Pike's photo sat on the keyboard of my Mac.

Finally, I picked up my phone and called the cops.

CHAPTER 7

AFTER KEEPING ME WAITING FOR TWENTY minutes, Inspector Pryce Davis met me in the bustling reception area of the Cambie Street VPD station. I was not familiar with him from my brief time there, but from his knowing look and begrudging handshake, he seemed to recognize me. Davis looked a little like Alec Baldwin, if you took away the good hairline, heavyset handsomeness, and any trace of charm.

Following curt intros, he said, "I'm late for something, so let's make this snappy."

I told him I was looking into the Emily Pike case, feeling the futility in my words the moment they left my mouth.

"I've received no notification of such," he said, raising his brows at several cops passing behind me. A cop's brain is attuned to facial recognition, and they tend to have long memories. Although it had been eight years since I had left this place in disgrace, a few of them were bound to recognize me. It hurt to come back, but I've always been a sucker for pain.

"I can get my client to contact you with confirmation," I said.

"You're talking about Maddy Pike?"

I nodded. "I was hoping for a little professional courtesy here. If I could just get a copy of Emily's current file—"

"You know the woman's an opportunistic con-artist, right?"

"All I know is she hired me to find out what happened to her daughter—"

"She saw you on the news and wants to milk this case some more. In the past five years, Maddy Pike's been under investigation three times for setting up bogus charities for missing kids, and she's been busted for cheque-kiting too many times to count. Only reason she hasn't served time is because of sympathetic judges."

I noticed a tall, female, South Asian cop standing to the side. Her nameplate read: CONSTABLE FIONA SADDY, and she seemed to be waiting for Davis.

"That doesn't change the fact that I've been hired to look into her daughter's disappearance," I said.

Constable Saddy stepped forward. "Inspector, I've just been notified the parents are here."

"Great," he muttered, then leaned toward me, close enough that I could see the abundance of blood vessels in his sidewalk-gray eyes. He smelled of stress and nicotine. "You want that file?" he asked.

"Only reason I'm here."

"Good," he said. "We'll get it for you, don't worry. When you open it up, be sure to take note of last year's entry, the one about the anonymous tip saying that Emily Pike was seen down in Washington. Maddy happen to mention that one to you, out of curiosity?"

"No."

"Maybe because we traced the tip back to her," he said. "Apparently her psychic pal looked into her crystal ball and told her Emily was in Blaine. Maddy succeeded in steering our efforts down there. We mobilized a lot of cross-border manpower for that bullshit. Up to me, she'd be on the hook for that, know what I mean? People should be held accountable for their actions."

"No argument from me," I said. "Still gonna need that fil—"

Davis' phone buzzed in his hand. He glanced at it, then stormed off, leaving me standing there.

Constable Saddy stepped up. Standing close to six feet, she had at least four inches on me. "We're all a little pent," she said. "An eight-year-old boy went missing from Second Beach pool on Saturday."

"I heard about that," I said. "Any leads?"

"None that are any good. If you give me your card, I'll see that you get the file."

I handed it over, thanked her, and watched Fiona Saddy walk down the hall. Despite her stature, she moved tentatively around the other officers, like someone new to the job and uneager to ruffle any feathers. Despite that, her eyes carried a determination that told me she could be a good cop, maybe even one who could get things done, if the system didn't wear her down. After she disappeared, I stood for a moment amid the buzz of the station, trying to resurrect something long gone.

Back in my Jeep and feeling another headache coming on, I reached into my satchel for the bottle of Advil. My fingers closed around steel. I looked around before pulling out Cutter's revolver from the previous night. Flipping open the cylinder, I saw eight stamped .45-calibre rounds snug in their chambers. I pressed the cylinder shut and held the weapon in my lap, feeling its weight and studying the well-worn pearl inlay. The steel of barrel and cylinder was dull and marred by scuffs and scratches. This weapon had likely passed through many hands, and odds were good that it had been used in a crime. Right then I should've wiped my prints off and tossed it down a sewage drain or off a bridge, taken it back in to the cops, or buried it in a hole. I ran through all those options, knowing I would choose none of them. Making sure the safety was on, I re-stowed the weapon in my satchel and drove away.

By early afternoon, Commercial Drive seemed even more deserted than the previous day. Even M.J. was absent from her usual spot. Wayne was out working a fraud case. The office had a too-quiet feel that put me on edge and made me feel lonely at the same time.

I sat down at my desk, eyeing the mini fridge as I called the Missing Children's Society of Canada. After explaining to the receptionist who I was and why I was calling, she patched me through to the director, Wendy Silverman.

"Sloane," she said, "I've heard about you and your agency in the news. I understand you're looking into the Emily Pike case. Have you talked to the police yet?"

"With mixed results," I said.

"They're overworked and overwhelmed," she said. "Ton of public pressure on them and so far, it's been a record year for number of kids missing across the country. Our limits are also being stretched at the moment, but we're always happy to cooperate where we can. What's your email? I'm in the middle of something right now, but when I get a moment, I'll send you what we've got."

After thanking her and ending the call, I went to the mini fridge, reached into the back, and pulled out an expensive bottle of chardonnay that had been gifted to us by a client. I hated chardonnay. I opened the bottle and filled a tumbler nearly to the top and returned the bottle back to the fridge. I drank half the tumbler of wine like it was water, then paused, closed my eyes, and drank the other half. It wasn't so bad after all. I opened the fridge again.

The chime of my Mac woke me. I was on the couch in my office. I pushed myself up. Discombobulated, I wobbled over to my desk, and opened the email containing Emily's file. It took me several moments to focus my eyes. First thing I saw was the empty bottle on the floor beside the couch. I looked at the time on the computer. Ninety minutes had passed, and I'd had no recollection of lying down. I made a mental note to ask the doctor if maybe my lithium dosage was too high.

I got back up and deposited the bottle in the recycling bin, covering it up with some newspapers. I sat down again and refocused on the computer screen. Using a yellow legal pad, I jotted down that Emily had disappeared August 14, 2013, between 4:05 and 4:15 p.m.

Last place seen: Westborough Farm.

Suspects questioned:

1. Oscar Benoit, Emily's boyfriend and the last person she was seen with.
2. Lucas Pike, Emily's father, who had abducted her when she was two, and who had a history of drunkenness and petty crimes.

Two suspects, both with records, both questioned, both passed the polygraph, both had their homes and vehicles searched, and both got to go home.

I opened a video attachment to the file. It contained footage from a convenience store ATM at a strip mall on the outskirts of Surrey. The grainy black-and-white footage showed Emily's nonchalant face and expressionless eyes as she pressed buttons and withdrew cash. The time stamp below read 5:38PM/14/08/13. I watched the ninety-second video a dozen times, and although her actions were somewhat slow, Emily showed no signs of being under duress. If she knew there was a camera positioned just above her face, she gave no signal that she was in trouble, not even a flicker of her eyes.

Her eyes.

I paused the video, then pulled out Emily's photo and contrasted the smiling, animated face to the vacant-eyed expression on the screen.

Drugs. I was sure of it. I'd witnessed those same eyes in enough street kids and runaways over the years to spot them. Other cops would, too, even though there was no mention in the file of Emily ever having a history of drug use.

I thought back to Maddy Pike's vehement protestation at the possibility of her daughter being a user. I studied her eyes on the screen again, then resumed reading the file. The $500 withdrawal from her savings account was the last transaction she'd ever made. Prior to that, the most cash she'd taken out had been sixty dollars. Until then, her spending habits reflected a frugality her mother had corroborated; aside from the occasional movie or Subway sandwich, Emily's money stayed put. Further down the page it revealed that Emily didn't own a passport, and there had been no record of her getting on a plane, train, or bus out of the city.

I pulled up a Google Map of the Metro Vancouver area, one that could be used to chart distances and travel times around the city. According to coworkers, Emily had left Westborough Farm at 4:05 p.m., gotten into Oscar's truck, where they had driven away. In Oscar's statement, he claimed that an argument had ensued as a result of him eating a McDonald's burger. Emily, a strict vegetarian, had demanded he stop the truck less than a block from the farm. At approximately 4:10 p.m., she got out and stormed off, and he drove in the opposite direction.

Several minutes later, on Celtic Avenue, near the Fraser River, Manuel Carrera, a landscaper working behind a hedge, heard a woman conversing with a man, their voices drowned out by a loud vehicle, possibly a truck with a broken muffler. Ninety-three minutes later, Emily showed up at the Surrey ATM. Given that there was no record of Emily taking a cab or bus, and that the distance between the farm and the ATM involved nearly forty kilometres and at least one bridge—too far to cover on foot—given the time it was surmised that she had been driven there.

Oscar would have been the likeliest, given that he lived in Surrey. The cops would've thought so also, except his alibi was tight—at 5:01 p.m., video footage showed him filling his truck with gas at an Esso in North Burnaby. A long way from Surrey.

After contemplating the contents of the mini fridge for a full minute, I pushed up from the desk and headed out. Back on Commercial I paused again, thinking about the liquor store several blocks away. Instead I went into Prado for a large Americano, two extra shots, along with some breath mints.

"For here or to go?" asked the girl at the counter..

"To go," I said.

CHAPTER 8

MADDY PIKE LIVED IN A TWO-STOREY TOWN-house off Boundary Road, in Burnaby. It was one of those shabby, green-paint-peeling 70s jobs you find in the suburbs of every Canadian city. She ushered me into the kitchen, one hand holding a cigarette. Her other hand clutched a can of Diet Coke with a lipstick-smeared straw sticking out from the hole. The place was a cluttered mess, with bills, flyers, and newspapers covering the table. Dirty dishes and empty soda cans were jumbled on the counter. The floor hadn't seen a broom or a vacuum in many months, and the room smelled of ripe garbage. A fat fly buzzed lazy loops around the perimeter.

"Don't bother taking off your shoes," she said. "Place is a pigsty; maid's been on strike a few years now."

Moving down the hall, we passed a living room domin-ated by a big-screen TV, where a soap opera was muted; plas-tic, over-lifted faces trying to manufacture slivers of emotion from a bad script.

On a small table to the left of the TV sat a shrine of sorts: a framed portrait of Emily, white candles burning on either side of the photo. Kind of thing you'd see at a funeral. The candles appeared new, making me wonder if they were lit for my benefit.

Further down the hall we walked past a framed family photo on the wall. Except for the same orange fake-n-bake hue, Maddy looked like a different person, slim and bright-eyed. Emily, around eight years old, stood to her left wearing a red dress and a smile that looked ready to dissolve into giggles at any second.

Maddy glanced back at me. "She was such a happy little girl."

As we turned a corner and walked upstairs, I mentioned the ATM footage showing a vacant look in Emily's eyes.

Maddy paused, using the handrail for support. "I can tell you beyond a single doubt that my daughter did not take drugs. But one thing Emily *wasn't* good at was eating properly. She was never diagnosed with anorexia or anything, but she'd get so busy with other stuff that she'd forget to eat. A few times she collapsed, once at school, and she had to be taken to the hospital. Low blood sugar. I knew when she wasn't eating because her eyes would get that dull look. When I saw the ATM tape, I thought to myself, 'my baby's hungry and not thinking straight'."

Maddy opened a door at the end of the hall and we entered a small and neat room, the walls done in soft pink and blue. On the right was a double bed, perfectly made with horses embroidered on the comforter, and stuffed animals lined up at the headboard: bear, sloth, dragon, killer whale. A dresser sat opposite the bed with a small TV on top, boxed DVD sets of *Star Trek: The Next Generation* and the original *Star Wars* trilogy beside it. Lace curtains stirred in front of an open window above a desk. Shelves beside the desk were lined with school texts, three-ring binders, and books on animals. The walls were plastered with photos of farm animals, Emily in many of them, riding horses and goofing around with other teens. Several were of her with a large redheaded girl at an amusement park. A scan of the wall showed other shots of her with the same girl, some dating back to when they were kids.

Maddy's eyes followed mine. "That's Chelsea Evans. She and Em went way back to grade three. After Emily was gone, she kind of drifted; didn't finish high school."

"And this was her boyfriend, Oscar?" I asked, gesturing to photos of her getting close with a muscular kid with dark hair and eyes.

"That's him."

"What did you think of him?" I asked.

"Oscar's a good boy. He's had some troubles, and his family is—well, he's not perfect, but he felt guiltier than anyone over Em's disappearance. He still brings me flowers on her birthday."

"Do you buy his story that he and Emily were fighting over him eating a burger?"

"Sure do," she said, waving her cigarette in the direction of the books on the top of the shelf. Some of the titles that jumped out were: *The Chain: Farm, Factory, and the Fate of our Food*, and *The End of Animal Farming*. "Em was militant about this stuff; she didn't allow any meat in the house. Even now, I feel guilty when I eat it."

She sat on the edge of her daughter's bed, near the window. Across the street, two blonde girls played hopscotch, their voices floating up and into the room. Maddy's eyes were wet as she sucked on her cigarette.

"Here I am, smokin' in her room," she said. "She'd kill me if she knew."

"Is this how she kept her room?"

"You mean *neat?* Yeah, we used to joke that Em had OCD. Check out that closet. She used to organize her clothes according to alphabetical *colour*, like blue before green, left to right, that kind of thing. Chaos used to really make her loopy. So, the only thing I do in her room is dust and wash the bedding every so often, keep it from going musty, in case she—I know it's stupid, but if a person lets go of hope, everything just fades to black."

I used my phone to take photos of the room. Maddy looked on, every so often tapping cigarette ash out the window. I opened desk drawers and found neat stacks of books, school binders, and old horse magazines.

"Did Emily compete in any equestrian events?" I asked.

"Gotta be from a money family to do that," she said, blowing a jet of smoke sideways. "My little girl wanted to be a vet. Had the grades for it, too. No, she just loved working at the farm, being around the animals and such. She loved to ride though. Tried to get me up on one once, damn thing nearly bucked me off. And her dad's deathly allergic, so no idea where she got the animal gene."

In the bottom drawer of the desk was a heart-shaped Purdy's chocolate box. Inside were some trinkets, among them a silver necklace and bracelet. I photographed the contents. Seven years ago, a forensic team would've combed over the entire contents of this room with a thoroughness outside my pay grade. Anything of note would have made it into the report. My first impression of the room was that it felt sanitized, staged, like it had never belonged to a living, breathing human being.

A siren screamed in the distance. Maddy stiffened, butting her cigarette on the windowsill. "For the first two years she was gone, every time there was a knock on the door, my heart would jump, and I'd think it was my Emily coming home. Now when it happens, I feel sick because I think it's the cops coming to tell me they found ..." Her voice trailed off. I looked away, thinking maybe babysitting movie stars wasn't so bad after all.

CHAPTER 9

WESTBOROUGH FARM WAS LOCATED IN THE tony and heavily equestrian enclave of Dunbar-Southlands. Sandwiched between two golf courses and cut off by the Fraser River to the south, the area was one of giant hedges and sprawling homes, set back from the roads that were largely devoid of traffic. Driving south on Balaclava Street, the only signs of life were the sounds of hoofs clopping as I passed several horses with riders trotting down the side of the road. A significant number of homes had "For Sale" signs outside the gates or hedges.

I parked on the street outside the farm. As I walked across a footbridge over a culvert, I looked down to see four ducklings paddling after their mother. Several stopped to peck at a floating Cheezies wrapper. Trash and fast-food containers lay strewn amid the weeds on either side of the culvert.

Pushing through a gated entrance, I was greeted by the smell of horse shit before I walked down a gravel path. In front of a dilapidated barn, a woman with short, dark hair demonstrated to several families how to shoe a horse.

Behind the barn were the stables and a paddock where other children were taking riding lessons. The horse being shoed whinnied and jerked as I passed.

"*Eeeasy, girl,*" the woman said, stroking the horse's neck.

"Sorry," I said. "I'm looking for Doc Barney. Is he around?"

She smiled and pointed to the right. "I believe he's over in the office getting a much-needed tech tutorial."

I thanked her and continued up the path, sidestepping an ornery rooster that tried to peck my Converse high-top. The fence that bordered the path looked on the verge of collapse, several posts having been knocked out of the earth at some point. Piles of horse droppings were everywhere, and as I walked up the path, my only goal was to avoid swallowing any of the thousands of buzzing flies.

I walked up the steps and onto the porch of an old clapboard farmhouse, where several teenage girls were selling eggs, cheese, and preserves. They were around Emily's age when she disappeared—too young to have worked there seven years prior. A camera was situated above the door, and a chime tinkled as I entered the house.

To the left was a small library nook, its shelves full of books on various farm animals. The walls bore photos of teenage volunteers, smiling, mugging, and mock flexing for the camera. One section was devoted almost entirely to sun-bleached photos of Emily, bordered with pink crêpe flowers. Friends and coworkers had left notes: **Come back to us, Em! We'll never forget you!**

Down a short hall to the right was a counter with an old-fashioned cash register and a 90s-era computer. I made Doc Barney as the gray-haired fifty-something behind the counter. He squinted through his bifocals at the computer screen, as a teenage girl with braces instructed him.

"Doc Barney?"

He took his time looking up, and when he did it was with faraway, washed-out blue eyes that complimented his pale complexion. "What can I do for you?" he asked in an Aussie accent.

"I'd like to ask you a few questions about Emily Pike."

Doc Barney studied me for a moment. His fingers trembled when he removed his glasses. He excused the girl, who looked at me before heading outside.

"I've answered all the police questions I ever care to about that day," he said.

"I'm not police. I'm an investigator here on behalf of the family. You were here the day Emily went missing, weren't you?"

He nodded, absently scratching his forearms through the denim fabric of his shirt. Despite the relative cool of the office, the skin of his forehead glistened with a sheen of sweat.

"How did she seem to you that day?" I asked. "Or the days leading up to it? Any unusual behaviour?"

He shook his head. "We get our share of temperamental teenagers here, but Emily was our golden child. She always showed up early for her shift, and never, ever missed one. We used to joke that if we all decided to pack it in, Emily could run the whole show by herself."

"Who do you mean by 'we'?"

More arm scratching. "Well, me, *and* my late wife Clara, who used to manage most things around here. Things have gone a little haywire around here since she passed two years ago."

"I'm sorry," I said. "Were the two of you close with Emily?"

"Emily was like our second daughter. What happened that day absolutely broke our hearts. Clara had been battling leukemia for years, and after that, it just sped up her illness."

"The police looked at the camera footage at the time?"

"We didn't have cameras back then," he said, scratching again. "Wish we had. No, the few you see around were installed after Emily's disappearance. Half the time, I forget to turn them on."

I asked if he remembered any suspicious people hanging around before Emily went missing. He shook his head. "Just the usual families," he said. "Same type of folk you see here today, only more of them."

"How about employees and volunteers? Anybody that didn't sit right with you, or someone who quit suddenly after Emily disappeared?"

"The police questioned everyone working here. As you can see, it's mostly teens. Even so, we're required to do criminal record checks on every single person who works or volunteers here."

"What about her boyfriend?" I asked. "Did you see her get into his truck that day?"

Doc Barney's brow furrowed as he ran a finger over the wood grain of the countertop. "I was dealing with a pregnant sow when she left for the day. Truth is, I only met the fellow once, when they were first dating and Emily brought him in to show him around."

"What was your impression of him?"

"Hard to tell after meeting someone only once," he said, "but he seemed nice enough. I remember them walking around holding hands, and she was showing him the horses. She seemed happy."

"How long was that before she went missing?"

"Maybe several months," he said. "It's hard to say."

"Could it have been closer to six? Emily and Oscar had been seeing each other roughly six months before she disappeared."

"It's possible. Memory is an elusive thing."

"Who else from the time of Emily's disappearance is still working here?"

"There's Loretta. She's out by the barn with a group. And then there's Willy, our maintenance guy. He was around before I took over the place over twenty-five years ago. Last I saw him, he was out behind the chicken coop. The police already questioned them, but I expect you'll be wanting to as well?"

I looked him in the eye. "Memory is an elusive thing. You never know what time might stir up."

He offered a tight smile. I let my eyes drift down to his shaking hand, before looking up at him and returning the smile. "Do you keep veterinary drugs on the farm?"

"We have a fully operational clinic."

"Opioids?"

His hesitation lasted only half a second, but it was there. "A limited supply," he said.

"Ever had a break-in?"

"Thus far we've been lucky on that score."

"And none of your employees have ever been caught pilfering your 'limited supply'?"

"Never. Like I said, everyone has to clear a criminal check to work here."

"Good thing," I said, and thanked him for his time.

Willy Diesing stood in the shadow of a weeping willow, tinkering with a tractor engine and muttering curses. He didn't hear my approach from the side. After startling him by saying hello, I apologized and introduced myself. For a man well into his eighth decade, the maintenance man's eyes were shiny blue marbles set beneath thick, white eyebrows that matched his hair.

I asked about Emily and what he remembered about the day she disappeared. Wally paused and mopped sweat from his forehead with a red handkerchief, then proceeded to tell me about how Emily used to come in on her days off and sing to the baby goats. "Those little devil-eyed buggers would look up at her as though she were the goddamn Rapture. Goats are the one creature that always give me the creeps, but people like 'em for some goddamn reason."

"Do you remember anything unusual about the day she disappeared?"

"Just that one day she was here, and then she wasn't. I mainly just keep to myself out here in the back. I'm not much for people. They probably got a pill to fix that now, but I'm too damn old."

"You ever meet her boyfriend?"

He shook his head. "Like I said, I mainly keep to myself. Life's simpler that way."

"Right. Thanks, Willy."

He nodded and resumed tinkering with the engine. As I began walking away, he said, "I hope you find out what happened to that girl."

As I approached the barn, the woman who had been shoeing the horse earlier was now tossing bales of hay over the fence. She looked strong, her exposed forearm extensors bulging above her work gloves. The families were gone. I checked my watch. It was quitting time, around the same time of day Emily would have left work.

The woman glanced up as I neared, gave a crooked smile. She removed her gloves, set them on a fence post, and wiped her hands on her overalls. "I get a feeling you're looking into Emily's disappearance," she said, extending her hand. "I'm Loretta."

"Good guess," I said, shaking her hand. "I'm Sloane."

"You look like police," she said, "and Emily going missing is the only notable thing that's ever happened around here."

"Did you know Emily well?"

"Not as well as I'd have liked," she said. "Bit of an age gap, I guess. Have there been any new leads?"

"Just trying to scare some up. Do you remember anyone suspicious hanging around the farm around the time of her disappearance?"

She paused. "Everyone seemed pretty normal. So many people come through here that they kind of blend together. The only person who never sat right with me was her gangster boyfriend."

"Oscar Benoit?"

"Yeah, I think that was his name."

"Why do you refer to him as a gangster?"

"If you ever saw him, you'd know why. He looks just like all those inked-up thugs who live in the Valley. What she saw in someone like that, I'll never know."

"Opposites attract, I guess," I said.

"I suppose. But to be honest, that day really messed with my head, because I was going to come in and pick up my cheque that afternoon, but I got busy doing other things. If I'd been around, I'd have offered her a ride. Ever since that day, I've been looking over my shoulder. I mean, if it could happen to her, it could happen to anyone, right?"

Manuel Carrera met me two blocks south of the farm, on Celtic Avenue, in front of a hedged-in property that occupied nearly the entire block. Middle-aged and balding, Manuel possessed a broad smile and his eyes radiated genuine warmth. When he asked if there were any leads in the case, I replied that I was merely looking into things for the family.

He pointed to the rampart-sized hedge to his right. "I was on the other side, pruning some rose bushes, and I hear a loud truck and voices. I think I hear a woman's voice, but I'm not hundred percent."

"Could you make out anything they were saying?"

He shook his head. "Too noisy. But the voices didn't sound mad or anything. Just people talking."

"How do you know it was a truck?"

"It sounded too loud to be a car, unless it was an old junker. I told the cops, I don't even know if it was her, but this street is quiet, and I hardly never hear anyone. When I saw on the news that she was missing at a certain time, I thought maybe it was her. I wish I had gone out to check, maybe I could help more. Please let her family know I pray for—"

Suddenly my mouth went dry, and I felt dizzy and sick. It felt like the ground was opening beneath my feet and I was falling. I closed my eyes and saw a nondescript delivery truck. A shadowy face looked down, smiling, beckoning.

"Ma'am ... ma'am, you OK?"

My eyes blinked open. Over Manuel's shoulder I could see across the street to the weed-choked lot, the woods beyond. Isolated. Opportunistic. The field had been one of the areas of the grid search years earlier.

Then I heard the screams. I saw a shovelful of dirt hitting Emily's cold, dead face.

Manuel looked at me with concern and offered me water.

"I'm fine," I said, staring at the bottle of water in his hand.

"The day she went missing, it was hot like today. One of the hottest."

In rush hour it took me nearly two hours to get to South Surrey, the last place Emily was seen withdrawing cash from the ATM. From the time she'd left work at Westborough, it had taken her roughly ninety minutes to get here. And she hadn't arrived by bus or taxi. Someone had driven her.

Here looked quite different than it would've back then.

Seven years ago, the ATM in question was located in the corner of a no-name convenience store within a blink-and-you'll-miss-it strip mall, on a once-blighted stretch of King George Boulevard. Blighted no longer, over the decade, owners of sketchy strip malls, grimy bungalows, and two-storey walk-ups had caved to large cheques presented by developers. Now it was endless blocks of the same ubiquitously bland condos that were spreading over the Lower Mainland like fungus, along with Starbucks, baby boutiques, and doggie day cares. Just like anywhere else in the city, I saw Lululemon and baby strollers that resembled ATVs on Mars. Not a liquor store in sight.

My GPS told me to pull over in front of an organic grocer on the ground floor of a condo tower, the location of the old convenience store. Consulting the file, a crack shack across the boulevard seven years ago had been bulldozed to make room for a long-term storage facility. Back then, grid searches of the area had turned up nothing. Other than on the ATM, the only other camera that had picked up Emily entering and leaving the store had been located above the entrance.

The manager, Marinder Dhaliwal (now deceased), said he remembered a girl fitting Emily's description entering the store and using the ATM. Dhaliwal also said that around that time, there had been a thin man wearing a jean jacket and ball cap standing in the shadows near the doors, just beyond camera range. The manager didn't see if Emily had any contact with the man, nor did he see her enter a vehicle. No other witnesses were listed in the statement.

I opened my laptop and pulled up the footage of Emily withdrawing cash, pausing the screen on her blank facial expression. I looked at my surroundings, at the busy thoroughfare, new buildings all around. This all happened right here. Seven years ago, this location—like Westborough— had been scouted and chosen for its minimal cameras. Back then, the types of people around weren't likely to take notice of a teenage girl entering a convenience store while a man waited outside. And despite the area's recent gentrification, the preponderance of rust-buckets continuously chugging past on the King George told me that one more truck or van sporting a rattling muffler would scarcely warrant a glance.

I looked back at the still of Emily's face.

Those eyes.

She was on something, I'd bet anything on it.

And she'd gone willingly.

CHAPTER 10

WAYNE SAT AT HIS DESK, COMPARING SIGNA-tures on several documents using a small magnifying glass. A jumbo bottle of kombucha sat on the corner of the desk.

"She knew him," I said, taking a seat across the desk from him.

Not looking up from the papers, he said, "I have to assume you're talking about your long-lost girl."

I filled him in on what the landscaper told me, then of Marinder Dhaliwal's witness report from Surrey, when he had sighted the thin man standing outside the convenience store while Emily withdrew cash.

"Weak," he said. "None of that got the cops anywhere."

"Maybe, but one thing's for sure—Doc Barney, the guy who runs the farm, is a junkie. When I was there, it was close to quitting time, and he was jonesing for a spike, big time."

"He the resident vet?"

"It would appear so."

"Vets have a high rate of substance abuse," he said. "Shitty job having to put animals down."

"I also saw the footage of Emily at the ATM in Surrey, just after she went missing, and she was drugged out, I'm sure of it."

"Maybe she'd been dipping into the ketamine or whatever. If that was your thing, you could do worse than be around a working clinic stocked with choice pharms. Between her and the junkie Doc, maybe supplies were running low and she went out looking to score."

"By all accounts, Emily didn't use."

"You just said she was fucked up."

"Yeah, but what if it wasn't voluntary? A few hours ago, Manuel Carrera offered me some water, and I'd only just met him. Maybe whoever took Emily offered her a spiked drink."

"Then she'd be fucking stupid for accepting it," he said.

"Not if it was someone she trusted. Speaking of drinks, what's up with the kombucha? Sally been bugging you about your gut again?"

He shot me a look. Sally McGrudder was a touchy subject, on account that she happened to be the cuckolded wife of a prominent local politico. Shortly after Sally had hired us to keep tabs on her husband and document *his* infidelities, she and Wayne had commenced their affair, which made the situation a pretty big professional and ethical no-no. It also meant I had something over him.

"I'm just trying to stay sharp, Donovan," he said. "Something you should be doing. Case you forget, Haley's film starts shooting on the viaduct tomorrow, and you're on it."

"I thought Frank—"

"Oh, Frank's on it, too," he said. "No more fuck-ups." He opened a drawer, reached in, and slid an iPhone across the desk. "Had to pay out three grand to that tweaker chick to get this back. Photos on this thing show Haley all kinds of naked; who knows what could be floating around cyberspace as we speak?"

"Not our problem."

"Fuckin' *right* it's our problem if our client's property got stolen on our watch."

"Except it wasn't stolen. She gave it away."

"Wouldn't have happened if you'd gotten there earlier." He took a sip of his drink and made a face. "Hey, what happened to that bottle of chardonnay our client gave us?"

I shrugged. "You tell me."

"This morning it was in the fridge," he said, "and now it's in your garbage."

"Wow, with investigative skills like those, soon you won't even have to leave the office to solve crimes."

"How often you need a drink on the job these days, Donovan?"

"Like you're one to talk, Mr. I-Got-Made-By-A-Mark-At-The-Titty-Bar-Because-It-Was-Buck-A-Shot-Night."

"Yeah, I admit I got carried away that night. But I don't come into the office early in the afternoon and polish off a bottle of wine by myself."

"Do I seem drunk to you, Wayne?"

"No, but you've always been highly skilled at hiding that shit." He paused. "Have you talked to anyone about what happened on the mountain?"

"Like a shrink?"

"Something along those lines, yeah."

"In other words, someone who will prescribe more drugs. 'Cause it's the lithium that's fucking me up, which I'm still taking, by the way."

"Pretty sure it's not meant to be followed up with a bottle of wine, though."

"Here we go again."

"Even M.J. has mentioned that you seem off."

"That old busybody is just cranky because I didn't tip her the other day."

"I'm just sayin' be careful. Shit can get outta hand. No one needs to see that happen."

I stood. "Duly noted." At the door, I turned. "Your kombucha's still lame, though."

He sighed. "Tell me about it. Replace that bottle of wine, would you?"

CHAPTER 11

ZYBORG APOCALYPSE WAS DRAWING ENOUGH dollars into the local economy to warrant the temporary nighttime closure of the Georgia Viaduct—the elevated east-west artery that connects old Strathcona to the glitz and shine of the downtown core. The smoke-filled night sky made the lights from the nearby skyscrapers seem faraway and otherworldly.

Tonight's shoot involved a scene where Haley's character crashes a Hummer to avoid hitting a group of children, who turn out to be rabid zyborgs. Haley's stunt double crawled from the flaming, overturned vehicle, where she was promptly swarmed by a horde of moaning and lurching kids.

From her position beside me at the edge of the viaduct, Karin took a photo. "Zombie kids are scarier than grown-up zombies," she said. Ever since Haley had returned to town, Karin had been bugging me to meet her. Tonight, I'd caved and brought her to the shoot.

"Zyborgs," I corrected. "Can't you see their metal exoskeletons?"

"Still scary," she said, "and twice as hard to kill."

The director yelled, "*Cut!*" and there was a frenzy of movement among the crew. The stunt double hustled away, and the real Haley arrived to be savaged by the children.

The scene resumed and Haley limped away from the horde. She issued a blood-curdling scream as a young girl latched onto her leg and tried to gnaw at her shin. Haley tripped and the girl scrambled up her body and was about to chow down on her face.

"*Cut!*" was shouted again.

I noticed a dark-haired man with a three-day beard standing in the shadows twenty feet away. He smiled intensely as he looked at Haley. I hadn't noticed him before and wasn't even sure how he'd gotten on the set, as he didn't have a visitor's lanyard and wasn't a member of cast or crew. As soon as the scene was over, he began walking quickly toward her.

I intercepted him fifteen feet from the actress, pointing the Enforcer at his ribs. "Sir, step back *now*."

His eyes widened and his hands shot up. We locked eyes and at the same time a little girl called out, "*Daddy!*"

With his arms raised, I noticed his laminated visitor pass that had fallen partly between his open, blue-checkered button-down and his T-shirt beneath.

I stepped back and saw some other parents of zyborg children watching nearby. The man's daughter ran up to him, looked once at me, then back at him. Her makeup was done so that it appeared as though half her forehead skin had rotted away, exposing shiny chrome beneath. Her blue private school uniform was partly shredded and revealed bloody gashes and dangling gobbets of mangled flesh.

"Don't I look *gross*, daddy?"

"Dis-*gusting*," he agreed. "I'm going to have nightmares now. I think it's the reason this lady came over, to protect me from *you*."

"That's dumb," she said. "She's Haley's *bodyguard*."

"Wow, I don't think I've ever met an honest-to-God bodyguard before." He smiled and extended his hand. "I'm Jim, by the way."

I shook his hand, holding his gaze a second more than I should have. "Sloane," I said.

"Great name," he said. "And *this* is Sadie the Zyborg." He made a move to pick her up, but Sadie pulled away. "Don't fudge up my makeup," she said.

Jim raised his hands in surrender again. "I can't do anything right tonight."

The scene coordinator called all the children over to the makeup trailer. I glanced over at Karin, who gave me a surreptitious thumbs up. Haley stood near her trailer, conversing with the director, a short, scruffy fellow wearing a ball cap. Ten feet to the side stood a middle-aged man with round glasses and a moustache: Frank Shikwitz. Our man Frank was so unobtrusive that had I not been looking for him, my eyes would have skimmed right past.

"So," Jim said, "what would you have done if I actually had been some weirdo?"

"Taken you down," I said.

"I believe it," he said. "You look like you can get pretty mean when you want to."

Haley and Karin were heading back to the trailer. I excused myself.

"Wait," he said, "what do you do when you're not guarding celebs and menacing innocent men?"

"Other things," I said.

"This is Sadie's last night on the shoot. I may never see you again."

"Very true."

"Or it's highly possible I see you again."

"I'm not so sure about that. For all I know you might have gotten your daughter into acting as a ruse to get on film sets."

"My *ex* got her into acting. I was against it, actually."

I shrugged and continued toward Haley's trailer.

"I run a kayak shop in Deep Cove," he called after me. "If you come by sometime, I'll give you a free rental."

I glanced back to see him wince at his desperate attempt. Some of the looky-loo parents were smirking at the exchange. I wanted to smack their cliquey little faces.

At the door of Haley's trailer, Karin shook her head. "What's your *problem*?" she asked. "He's hot, his daughter's adorable, and you're a woman who lives alone with a cat."

Haley stuck her head out the door and beckoned us in. "I totally agree," she said. "He *is* hot. If you don't move on him, *I* might."

They laughed. Despite Haley's recent night of pollutants, the girl had quickly bounced back to her charismatic self, even with matted hair and skin shellacked with fake blood.

I shut the door. "You think any guy's hot. Haley, this is my pesky friend Karin. She's a big fan of all your schlocky films, blah blah blah. Karin, this is Haley."

The women shook hands, and Karin told the star her bodyguard was rude and should be fired.

Haley laughed as she sat down in a film-set chair. "Or should be paid more," she said, as a makeup artist began removing the gunk from her face.

I pulled her phone from my pocket and set it on the counter in front of her. "We need to get that in writing," I said.

Haley winked and pocketed the device.

CHAPTER 12

MECCCHH ... MECCCHH ...

The dark-haired girl was being choked by a large man in the back of a truck, her eyes bugging out as she made horrible retching sounds.

Meccchhh ...

The retching rose to a demonic pitch and the girl projectile vomited into the man's face.

My eyes shot open to see Eclipse hacking up a furball on the white duvet. When I got out of bed to clean it up, my head felt as bleary as the sky outside. 8:02 a.m. Two hours past my normal wake-up time. I felt like hell. Even worse when I saw the empty wine bottle on the kitchen counter.

The bottle went into the recycling bin below the sink. I made a pot of coffee and fed and watered Eclipse. I took my lithium and jumped in the shower, brushing my teeth while under the spray so I didn't have to look at myself in the mirror.

After I toweled off and dressed, I poured a mug of coffee and stepped onto the small balcony overlooking the smoky haze of Stanley Park. Wilderness juxtaposed in stark relief against the cityscape. But it was wilderness in appearance only; hidden amid the thousand-acre green oasis were several restaurants, an aquarium, and dozens of trails, all of which I had explored since moving here last year. The waters of Lost Lagoon peeked through the trees and I considered hitting one of my favourite loops. But it was already too late and all the coffee in the world wouldn't summon my legs to move the way I needed them to.

I took my coffee back inside, sat down at the table, and flipped open the black file labeled **Emily Pike**.

At the time of her disappearance, her circle of close friends was small, most of them female. I ran down the list and started calling. Many of the women were now attending university out of province or in the U.S., and most of those didn't answer their phones, because who talks on the phone anymore? The few that did answer gave me nothing of use: *Emily was the best. I miss her so much. Have there been any new leads?* It was tedious, but necessary. All it took was one call to someone who, for whatever reason, had kept a piece of information to themselves at the time of the initial investigation. Maybe they were scared, or maybe it was something they'd forgotten at the time and been too embarrassed to come forward with later. That piece might not exist, but until you had exhausted all avenues, there was no way of knowing.

Next on the list was Chelsea Evans, the redheaded girl from the photos in Emily's room. She picked up on the third ring, and I introduced myself, telling her that I was looking into the disappearance of her friend.

Following a long pause, she informed me that she was pretty busy at the moment.

"Too busy to take two minutes to talk about your missing friend?"

"I already told everything to the police."

"I'm not the police."

"The last time I talked about it I had anxiety for a week."

"I understand. I'd just like to ask you—"

"I don't know anything. I have to go. Sorry."

"Let me give you my number in case you remember anything."

"I won't."

"OK."

She hung up. A computer check showed her address in Renfrew Heights, in Vancouver. I poured a coffee to go.

I parked in front of a green-and-white stucco bungalow on Lillooet Street. For several moments I just sat there, staring through the windshield. The sun looked like a white flashlight beam shining through a gray wool sweater. Due to water restrictions, all the lawns on the street were parched brown. I climbed out of my Jeep and walked up to the front door.

My head felt off-kilter and dull and my right arm felt like it weighed a hundred pounds as I rang the bell. Seconds later, Chelsea Evans opened the door, dressed in a Subway uniform. After a second of surprise, she frowned, knowing exactly who I was. "I already told you I don't know anything," she said.

"I just need a few moments."

"I have to catch the bus to work or I'm going to be late."

"Let me drive you."

Due to never-ending roadwork, traffic on Broadway was backed up and being funneled to one lane. I could've taken an alternate route, but I didn't want to arrive too soon. Chelsea stared out the window while tapping her foot and gnawing at her thumbnail.

"Chelsea," I said, "I'm going to be real with you. Emily's mother hired me to find out what happened to your friend, and I'm about ready to pack it in, because everyone is, like, *zero* help. I mean, people go on and on about how great Emily was and how sad they are that she's gone, but they're utterly useless, and frankly it's pretty fucking tiresome."

She looked at me sideways. Traffic began to move, and I inched my Jeep ahead.

"But I think you're different," I said. "I think you've actually got something you want to say."

She stared straight ahead.

"What do you think happened to your friend?" I asked.

"I don't know."

"Did you play a part in her disappearance?"

"No! Jesus."

"What about her boyfriend, Oscar? Did he?"

"Why don't you ask him?"

"I will. But right now, I'm talking to you. Tell me about the last time you saw Emily."

She exhaled and looked out the window. "It was maybe like, two days before she went missing."

"What were you doing?"

"Just hanging out. You know, fifteen-year-old shit. It was hot as fuck out, and we both hated heat, so we were just hanging in her room, listening to music and stuff."

"What were you talking about?"

"I don't know, boys, parties, the usual stuff."

"Did she talk about Oscar?"

"Not really."

"Does that mean she did, or she didn't?"

"She hadn't been talking about him as much. I think they had a fight?"

"You *think?* Emily was your best friend. You guys were fifteen, and best friends—she must've said more than that."

"You didn't know her," she said. "When Emily went into shutdown mode, no one could get through to her. Not me, not Oscar, no one."

"Why was she in shutdown mode?"

"I don't know. I don't like thinking about this." She hugged her knapsack to her chest. Traffic once again ground to a standstill.

"Help me out, Chelsea," I said. "I'm not a cop. Nothing is going on record."

"You don't know what it's like to lose someone like that," she said. "Emily was my *best friend*. I never had a lot of friends, and now I don't have any. I had to quit school because of my anxiety. After she disappeared, I remember thinking: now I'm truly fucked."

"What would Em think about the sob story you're feeding me right now?"

"I'm being honest with you, and all you do is fucking harass me? Let me out! It's too hot, I'm gonna be sick!"

Her hand was on the latch. I flicked a knob on the dash, and the A/C began gusting cold air. "I'm sorry," I said. "In your heart of hearts, what do you think happened to your friend?"

"I don't *know.*"

"Yes, you do. C'mon, Chelsea. You don't have anxiety because your friend is gone; you have it because you know something you've been keeping to yourself for the past seven years."

"You don't know shit about me."

"No, but years ago I knew something, and because of my silence, four people close to me are dead. Not a day goes by that I don't wish I'd spoken up."

"It was all a long time ago," she said. "It doesn't matter now."

"Then what do you have to lose? Tell me what happened."

Chelsea's nostrils expanded as her eyes filled with tears. "It's all my fault."

"What's your fault?"

"We had plans to meet up that day when she was done work at the farm. But then I bailed on her because this guy I liked wanted to hang out that afternoon. If I had shown up like I was supposed to, she'd still be here."

"But Oscar came to pick her up?"

"Only because I bailed."

"Tell me about Oscar," I said. "How did he and Emily meet?"

"I dragged Em to this party over Christmas. She hated parties. He was there with his boys. He set his sights on her, and she was into him too. You could just feel it. It was weird, like a scene from a movie."

"What did you think about Oscar?"

"He was actually pretty chill to be around, not like what I expected, because of his rep, you know?"

"His rep?"

"Yeah, that he was connected to stuff. His family anyway."

"Did you see any of that? Did Emily?"

Chelsea looked out the window as she chewed her nail. I saw the Subway sign a block away, but the stop-and-go traffic would give me a minute or so before we arrived. I could feel the window closing.

"You've been sitting on this a long time, Chelsea," I said softly. "It's time to let it go."

She paused and took a breath. "So, there was this one day, right? Just after school ended for the year. Oscar was driving me and Em out to go camping at Cultus Lake. He said he had to stop at his uncle's ranch in Langley. Oscar had to get buzzed in through a gate, and there were a lot of vehicles parked in the driveway, Harleys and stuff. He told us to wait and then ditched us. He was gone a long time, so Em went to check. A few minutes later they came back. Oscar was kind of dragging Em by the arm and she looked sick. I asked what was wrong and she said she wanted to go home. Oscar didn't say anything, just turned around and drove us home. I asked Em what she saw, but she never said a word about it."

An entirely new avenue had just opened up, and my mind churned to digest this information.

She turned to me. "I didn't *see* anything. So, it has nothing to do with me. It happened months before she disappeared, so it probably means nothing."

"Meant enough for you to remember in detail."

She opened the door, getting out just as traffic began to move. The car behind me honked.

"Chelsea—"

She slammed the door and walked away.

CHAPTER 13

KAI ABACON STOOD BEHIND THE BAR SLICING vegetables. At just after 11 a.m., only a few tables in the tiny vegetarian restaurant on Main were occupied. I took a seat at the bar. Kai continued to methodically slice radishes paper-thin. Only once did his eyes flick up at me.

"What's good here?" I asked.

"Halloumi cheese and zucchini."

"I'll have to take your word for it."

"Drink?"

"Just water. I'm working."

The Chinese chef working alongside Kai regarded our terse exchange with curious interest. No doubt Kai—with his laconic focus and brown wood Buddhist beads around his neck—was somewhat of a mystery man.

Kai poured a glass of water and set it in front of me.

When the chef went into the back, I said to Kai, "Heard you went to Burma."

"Myanmar," he corrected.

"Must've been some trip. Full-fledged Buddhist now?"

Kai went on slicing radishes. Had to hand it to him, his current Zen-like countenance sharply contrasted against the time, not long ago, when I'd witnessed him throw a cup of scalding coffee in someone's face. Granted, back then his actions *had* fit his job description—that of an enforcer for an organized crime ring specializing in underage prostitutes.

If people only knew what kind of guy was preparing their lunch.

"Satori," I said.

He glanced up.

"That's like a sudden awakening, right?" I asked. "I had that yesterday, sort of. Not like in the nirvanic sense or anything, but with this case I'm working on—"

"Tell Wayne the answer's still no."

"This has nothing to do with Wayne. Matter of fact, he's dead set against it."

I pulled out the photo of Emily. Kai stopped slicing. "That's Benoit's girl."

"Was. How do you know she was his girl?"

The chef returned, and Kai resumed slicing.

"When's your break?" I asked.

The chef smiled. "Right now," he said. "Before the rush."

In the redbrick alley behind the restaurant, Kai and I walked past overflowing dumpsters. Beside one of them slept a junkie couple, holding hands, heads slumped together like conjoined twins. Directly behind loomed a nearly completed luxury condo tower made of blue glass.

I asked Kai how he knew Oscar Benoit.

"We did our stretches in juvie at the same time, back in 2016."

"What was he in for?"

"Used a Louisville Slugger to collect on a debt."

"You guys ever compare notes?"

He shot me a look. "Funny."

"Let's get back to the photo I showed you."

"He had the same one on the wall by his bunk."

"Anyone ever talk about her disappearance in there? Any rumours?"

"People tended to stay quiet where Oscar was concerned."

"Because he's violent?"

"Everyone in there is violent. Mostly because of his uncle."

I thought back to what Chelsea had said about the ranch. "Who's his uncle?"

Kai glanced over his shoulder. "Travis Benoit. Full patch biker, high up enough that he doesn't wear the vest or ride a Harley anymore."

There had been no mention of this in Emily's file.

"What's Uncle Trav into?"

"He's a whole different league. I don't know the man, and I don't want to."

"You're scared of him."

"A healthy amount of fear can extend a person's life expectancy."

"I need another favour, Kai."

"I'm done. I don't owe you anything anymore."

"It's not about me. It's about a missing girl. C'mon, you need all the karma points you can get."

CHAPTER 14

AT BEDTIME I STARED AT THE LITHIUM PILL IN my hand for a full minute before letting it tumble down the drain. I imagined the collective look of horror on the faces of Karin, Wayne, and my mother. It's dumb to stop such a heavy-duty drug cold. Then again, the drug was starting to make me feel as sharp as a root vegetable.

Following two hours of shut-eye where I dreamed of being chased down a snowy mountain, I awoke with screams echoing in my head. My hands trembled as I made a pot of coffee. I sipped it while pinning index cards on my living room wall. I wrote names on the cards.

EMILY PIKE

OSCAR BENOIT   LUCAS PIKE   TRAVIS BENOIT

Beneath each of the first two names I tacked photos of the suspects. Oscar and Lucas stared back at me with sullen eyes. Both had guilty, mugshot-worthy faces, though each seemed dangerous in a different way. With a shaved head and steely gaze Oscar looked the type to take a baseball bat to someone in an alley, while Lucas Pike, with his puffy, hard-living face, looked desperate enough to do almost anything.

I Googled Travis Benoit. Amazingly, despite the man's criminal ties, there was almost nothing on him for the past decade. Back in 2008 he had been charged with conspiracy to murder a rival gang member, but all charges had been dropped due to witnesses recanting testimony. From that old news story, there was a courtroom sketch of Benoit in profile, flowing, gray hair swept back and a thick, white goatee. With his tan suit, he looked more like a southern plantation owner than a high-ranking member of a biker gang.

I printed off the sketch and pinned it to the wall below his name. I stared at the wall and made the mistake of calling Wayne and made the even *bigger* mistake of asking him about Travis Benoit.

"No, Donovan, *no.*"

"You sound like you're scolding a dog," I said.

"A dog would have better sense than you to avoid danger."

"I talked to a source today who told me that several months before her disappearance, Oscar took Emily to his uncle's ranch. Apparently, she saw something that disturbed her. A lot."

"No doubt. Benoit's bad news."

"Maybe she walked in on a killing."

"Then she wouldn't have walked out again. Think about it: you're a fifteen-year-old girl who spends your time around horses. You walk into a room full of gangsters, and they're liable to say some things that might rattle you. Kind of like waking up in the lion cage at the zoo. Better back out *real* slow."

"Gee, thanks for that, Wayne. Lion cage. Great stuff."

"I take it none of this was in the file?"

"She didn't tell the police when they interviewed her."

"But she told *you*?"

"She needed to get it off her chest. At the time she was too scared. Plus, I'm a people person, as you know."

Silence on Wayne's end.

"So, what can you tell me about Travis Benoit?" I asked. "Because there's precious little to be found on any of the usual gangster sites."

"Probably because he's gotten, quote-unquote, *legitimate* over the last decade. Auto detailing shops, I believe. Been a long time since his ass has ridden a Harley. But in the 80s, he learned Español and got tight with certain Colombian luminaries. Then when the power shift changed to Mexico, he began hanging out in Guadalajara. Now the bikers and the cartel are in business, so do the math. Also, the man has never done a lick of significant jail time, while his rivals and associates all seem to be getting dead or earning life sentences. What does that tell you? Look, I gotta get back to work, but here's the thing: legit or not, we are *not*, in any way, shape, or form, going up against Travis Benoit."

CHAPTER 15

PEOPLE HAVE SAID THAT IF YOU LACKED THE misfortune to live there, there is no good reason to go to Surrey. Denigrated by Vancouverites as the crime-ridden cesspit of the Lower Mainland, if you watched the local news, chances are you'd arrive at the same conclusion. Over the years I'd made enough trips across the Port Mann Bridge to know that the city and its environs weren't all bad. In fact, some parts were downright *nice*.

Then you come to an area that seems to be comprised of XXX stores, Money Marts, methadone clinics, bottle depots, tattoo parlours, coin laundries, and liquor stores. Every fourth or fifth home sports an overgrown lawn and is made identifiable as a crack shack by gang graffiti gracing the plywood-covered windows.

Welcome to Whalley.

Even at 10 a.m. on a sunny Saturday, the opioid and meth-addicted sex-workers plied their trade on side streets off King George Boulevard, negotiating with men in beater sedans and rust-bucket pickups.

Sitting in the passenger seat of the Range Rover, Kai Abacon eyed the surroundings with equanimity. Much had transpired between us that didn't need saying, such as him saving my life last year. I'd tried thanking him once, but he'd fixed me a look so inscrutable that I never brought it up again.

"What was Myanmar like?" I asked.

A squad of shirtless skinheads shambled up the street, checking the doors of every vehicle they passed in case one was left unlocked. "The opposite of here," he said.

"Yet you returned."

"They're strict on visas over there, but I'll go back."

I turned right at the next intersection and drove up a hill into a residential area. "Meanwhile, what are your plans? Just keep working at the veggie place?"

"I like it there."

"Putting your skills to use chopping radishes."

"That's right. What about you? What're *your* plans?"

A glance at my phone's GPS told me to hang a left at the next intersection. I did, and the street led me up an even steeper hill. The crack shacks and gang graffiti disappeared the higher we went, replaced by larger homes, many of them well maintained.

"Right now, this," I said. "Otherwise I'm babysitting a trainwreck of a movie star."

"You should try acupuncture. Help you deal with stress."

I yawned. "I'm not stressed."

"Right."

The GPS informed us that we had arrived. I pulled over at the crest of a hill, in front of a dark gray Craftsman with black trim. It was situated next to a ravine with a sign that said *No Dumping*. The other houses on the street were mostly bungalows and split-levels several decades past their prime.

We got out, approached the house, and unlatched the gate. Walking up the short and steep driveway, we passed a blue Ford F-150, mirrored rims so shiny I could see the bags under my eyes. Maybe the acupuncture was worth a shot.

A dog barked inside the house. A curtain in the living room pulled back to reveal a woman's pale face peeking out, before the curtain was yanked shut again.

The dog barked louder, scratching the other side of the door. I glanced at Kai. "He knows we're coming, right?"

"We're expected."

The door opened suddenly, stopped by a security chain. A Rottweiler's black snout appeared. The pale woman warily peeked out. Kai extended his hand for the dog to sniff.

"Mrs. Benoit," I said, "is your son in?"

"He's not talking to no cops without a lawyer."

"I'm not a cop, ma'am," I said. "I've been hired by Emily Pike's mother to look into her daughter's disappearance."

"He's not around."

"Actually, he's expecting—"

Footsteps came from behind the woman. The dog was pulled back and she stepped aside. A thick hand undid the chain and the door opened to reveal a tall, blue-eyed, bearded man in a wifebeater, full-sleeve tats on his muscular arms. On his right upper arm was a rather beautiful rendering of Emily, smiling sadly.

Oscar's eyes slid from me to Kai. The two of them bumped fists, then shook hands.

"You don't have to talk to them," said his mother in the background. "You shouldn't talk to anyone."

"It's OK, mom," Oscar said. He stepped outside, pulled the dog out with him, and shut the door. The dog was missing its left eye and scars were visible on its hindquarters where the hair hadn't grown back. "What's up, Kai?" Oscar asked.

"My acquaintance here wants to ask you some questions."

I introduced myself and extended my hand. After a moment, Oscar took it. At twenty-five, in person, his eyes looked several decades older than the rest of him.

Mrs. Benoit watched us from the living room window. "Let's walk," Oscar said, leading us down the driveway and out the gate. I asked the name of his dog.

"Luger," he said. "He's a rescue. Long as you don't make any sudden moves, he's safe. Mostly."

I let Luger sniff my hand, then scratched under his jaw. The dog limped along beside us.

"What do you want to know?" Oscar said. "I gotta be at work in ninety minutes."

"What's work consist of?"

Following a fuck's-it-to-you look, he said, "Just got my longshoreman's ticket."

Fresh out of jail and you're working the docks.

"Good benefits, I hear," I said.

"You come all the way out here to ask about my job? My P.O. doesn't seem to have a problem with it."

"Let's talk about hamburgers, then."

Oscar said nothing. Kai trailed a few feet behind, looking all around.

"The way the report reads," I said, "is that Emily is gone because of a burger. That seems really dumb to me."

"Why's that?"

"Because I don't believe it."

"You didn't know Emily."

"No, I didn't. How long after she went missing did you get her made permanent on your arm?"

"Few months."

"None of your other women since then have minded the tat?"

He shrugged. "Wouldn't matter if they did."

"OK, so back to the burger. You go to pick up your vegan girlfriend from work—"

"Vegetarian. She ate cheese and stuff."

"—and you're chowing down on some Mickey D's. You must've known that would piss her off."

He exhaled loudly. "I was hungry, I was eighteen and I had finished eating the thing anyhow. She saw the wrapper and flipped out about how I was perpetuating a society of cruelty to animals."

"And this happens as you're driving?"

"Just after, yeah."

"So, from the farm you drive two blocks south before she demands to be let out?"

"Yeah, like I said, she was pissed off. There was no talking to her when she was like that, and it wasn't the first time she did it."

"No, but it was the first time she disappeared off the face of the earth. That why you got the ink done, something to remember her by?"

Oscar turned to Kai. "Thought you said she was cool."

Kai shook his head. "I said no such thing."

"What did your uncle think of Emily?" I asked.

I sensed Oscar stiffen slightly beside me. "He never met her. What is it you want?"

"There's been a tip," I said. "I thought you'd want to know what it is."

He stopped walking. Luger squatted to take a dump on a parched yellow patch of grass, just outside the wooden fence of a rancher, a sun-bleached Canadian flag hanging listlessly above the porch. A shirtless elderly man watered his lawn with a hose, staring at us with a vacant expression from fifty feet off.

Oscar took out a green plastic bag from his jeans, shook it out, and bent to pick up the waste.

"You," I said. "You're the tip."

He stopped for a second, bent over. Then he straightened, tied the baggie, and turned to face me. "I passed the 'graph."

"So do a lot of liars," I said. "What went on between you and Emily in the days leading up to her disappearance?"

"Nothing. The usual shit."

I pulled out a photo I'd removed from Emily's wall, one of her and Oscar smiling, arms around each other, Ferris wheel in the background.

"Cute couple," I said, "but I've been trying to figure it—somehow you two don't fit. Good, animal-loving girl. She didn't drink or get high, and she chooses you—no offense. Was it the bling you bought her? It's funny though, in all the photos I've seen, she's never wearing any jewelry. She didn't even have her ears pierced."

His posture deflated as he gazed at the photo. "Em didn't care about that stuff. That was one of the things I liked about her."

Using my phone, I brought up the photos of the silver jewelry in her room. When I showed it to him, he frowned and shook his head. "Never seen them before. Even if Em *had* worn jewelry, I'd never buy shit like that."

"What about someone else?" I asked. "An old boyfriend?"

He shook his head. "I was her first boyfriend."

"That you know of."

"One thing Em *wasn't* was a liar. She told me I was her first. I believed her."

"Pity her honesty didn't rub off on you."

He turned to Kai again. "What's this bitch's problem?"

Sensing the tension, Luger growled at me. Oscar grabbed the dog's collar and made a move back toward the house. I touched his arm and he yanked it away.

He stopped and glared, jaw set. "What the fuck do you want?"

"I want to find out what happened to your girlfriend."

"She got into a car with the wrong guy."

"Someone she knew? Or would she just get into a car with a random stranger?"

"Em was dumb like that. She thought everyone was good."

An engine rumbled up the hill. Oscar stood at attention as a matte black Escalade rolled up. With tinted windows and oversized tires, it looked more Secret Service than gangster. Through the half-open passenger window, I saw the unmistakable gray mane and white beard of Travis Benoit. Even through his wraparound sunglasses, I could tell he was staring at me. Behind the wheel was a stone face with dark hair and mirrored sunglasses. As the vehicle pulled abreast, I caught a glimpse of a third man in the backseat. Sunglasses and black hair in a ponytail.

Travis Benoit lowered his sunglasses, letting me see his clear blue eyes before turning to his nephew. "What's up, Oscar the Grouch? I'm just paying a visit to your mama. You kids out for a stroll?"

"Yeah," Oscar said.

"Well, carpe diem then," Travis said, sipping from a large bottle of San Pellegrino. He flicked his wrist, and the driver pulled the Escalade ahead, where it parked in front of our Range Rover.

"You should leave now," Oscar said quietly.

"I think I'll seize the day," I said, heart hammering as I walked forward. Kai made a move to stop me. I sidestepped and kept going.

By the time I got there, Benoit stood on the sidewalk. He wore a white, short sleeve button-up over jeans. Cream-coloured loafers. His thick forearms sported timeworn blue and green tats: a biker patch logo and faded Gothic script. His driver watched me through the open window.

"Well, hello there," Benoit said. "You a reporter, darlin'? You look like you're in question-asking mode."

"Private investigator," I said.

He removed his sunglasses and smiled with very straight, white teeth. "Well, I'll be."

"I'd like a few minutes of your time," I said.

He gestured for me to walk with him, toward the ravine and the shade of the trees above. Glancing over the railing, I saw a trickle of water thirty feet below, trash strewn about. Someone had tossed an old stove down there. A green toilet lay on its side. Nearly camouflaged by the brush was a makeshift tent, with remnants of squatter's rubbish all around it.

"This is everywhere now," Benoit said, frowning. "Way of the world, I guess."

I pulled out the photo of Emily. Benoit looked at me, then removed his sunglasses, folded them up, and put them in the breast pocket of his shirt. I kept my eyes on him as he took the photo and studied it.

"Emily Pike," I said. "Did you know her?"

He glanced up the street at Oscar, who now stood near the Escalade, talking to the driver through the open window. Kai stood nearby, offering a reserved nod as introductions were made.

"Oz's old lady," Benoit said. "Sad deal. How many years ago was that now?"

"Seven."

"Seven years. Jesus."

"A few weeks before she went missing, there was a tip that she'd been out to your place and saw something troubling."

"News to me," he said. "If she was there, I was never formerly introduced. Oz is embarrassed of me, even though after his daddy died, I practically raised him from a pup."

"You were never questioned by the cops regarding her disappearance?"

"You're the first, honey."

"But you recognized her face."

"Her going missing had the boy broken up for a long time. So much so that he carries her likeness on his arm."

Benoit put his sunglasses back on and stretched his arms overhead. His scent was cologne mixed with animal musk. I imagined him pulling up alongside Emily in his Escalade, one of his crew at the wheel.

Hop in, honey. I don't know what Oscar did to piss you off so bad, but I'll have a talk with him, set him straight. Meanwhile, let us get you where you need to go.

"You OK, there?" Benoit asked. "Your colour's a little off."

I gave a small shake of my head and the sudden bout of dizziness left me as quickly as it had arrived. "I'm fine," I said.

"You coming down off something? You got that look, and trust me, I've seen it enough times. A person's got to wrangle their demons before they fly off with their soul."

"Thanks. But tell me something, how is it that you've managed to avoid a federal sentence all these years?"

He chuckled. "Last time I checked, a person's got to do something *wrong* to go to jail." He looked in the direction of the house, where his sister-in-law's spectral face watched us through the living room window. "Now, if you'll excuse me, I've got to get inside. This heat's not doing *either* of us any good."

Travis Benoit ambled up the driveway, just as Oscar climbed into his F-150. The big man stopped at the driver's window and spoke to his nephew in hushed tones. As I made my way back toward Kai, I saw the driver of the Escalade watching me.

As we drove back across the Port Mann Bridge, Kai accused me of having a death wish. I smiled. My driving reflected my inner state—heart strong in my chest, limbs light and energized, mind quick and sharp—and I pressed the accelerator, sliding the Range Rover back and forth between the left and middle lanes, passing every vehicle in my path.

"They know something," I said.

"You're not too subtle with your questions. Is that how they tell you to do it in your P.I. manual or whatever?"

"Subtlety to those guys is a two-by-four to the head," I said. "What's the deal with Benoit's driver? I saw you got an intro."

"Giller. I've never seen him before. Guy in the back was Jake Dove. He's been around awhile. He went to Mountain for armed robbery, and rumour has it he slicked a guy inside to get in the bikers' good books. Now he's riding with Uncle Trav."

"Way to move up in the world."

CHAPTER 16

THAT NIGHT'S SHOOT OF *ZYBORG APOCALYPSE* had moved to Crab Park, near the docks. A group of survivors—led by the now shotgun-wielding Haley Cooper—were attempting to escape by barge, while zyborgs of every shape scrambled up the riggings and instigated a bloodbath.

I could barely keep my mind still enough to focus on the crowd of fans, looky-loos, and paparazzi outside the barricades. Everyone's face seemed to carry potential menace.

My phone buzzed the same moment I heard the crackle of walkie-talkies. Security guards sprinted toward the barge. The half-dozen cops by the barricades directed the crowd away.

The text was from Frank:

bomb threat

I raced toward the barge, where security herded actors and extras down a steel gangway onto the dock. I located

Haley seconds before Frank joined us. We spirited her up the street to the Range Rover.

I was half in the driver's seat when Frank opened the back door for Haley. She giggled. "What the *hell?*"

Turning, I saw a reposed naked body in the backseat. Frank yelled, *"Get out!"* and pulled her away. As we sprinted from the vehicle, Haley asked what the fuck that was.

"The bomb," he said.

Two hours later, after the explosive team had cleared the area, Wayne, Frank, and I stood in the security trailer, looking down at an inflatable sex doll. Several security guards and cops stood in the background.

The doll was life-sized, but with inhumanly massive, missile-shaped tits and yellow hair, upstairs and down.

A cutout photo of Haley's face was taped over the doll's face.

And the pin-end of a defused grenade stuck from her rubbery faux-vagina.

Wayne turned to the sheepish head of security standing on his left. "How'd he get past you guys?"

"Camera picked him up at the gate," he said. "Guy tailed behind some of the makeup crew, and he was carrying a tech case. Looked the part: ball cap, glasses, medium height. Camera didn't get his face."

"And no one was checking crew ID?" Wayne said.

"Crew are coming and going all the time," the guard said. "If he was wearing some sort of pass—"

"You're fired," Wayne barked.

"You don't have the authority to fire us," he said. "Plus, we're union."

"He wants attention," I said. "He used a dud bomb and phoned it in. Real bombers don't threaten in advance."

Wayne gave a peptic grimace. "But the point is, he got in here, and he *could* have planted a real bomb. How did he get in the vehicle? Weren't the doors locked?"

All eyes went to me.

"I can't remember if I locked it or not," I said.

Wayne shook his head. I'd be catching flak later.

"OK," he said, "did we get photos of the crowd at least? Chances are, after our boy planted the doll, he hung around and watched."

Frank stepped up to a nearby desk and plugged a USB into a laptop, then pulled up photos he'd taken earlier.

A knock on the door, and a security guard stuck his head in. "Ms. Cooper is here."

"It's me, *Ms. Cooper*," Haley called out, placing a flirty hand on the guard's shoulder as she squeezed past and into the room. "Oh my," she said, taking in the scope of her admirer's gift. "Is that a real grenade?"

Wayne rolled his eyes. "No."

Haley's brows knitted together as she pulled out her phone to take a photo.

I snatched the phone away. "No *way* is this getting leaked, Haley. That's exactly what he wants."

"He was at a fan expo," she said.

"How do you know that?"

"'Cause I was doing the convention circuit, promoting *Space Cadet 3*, and that was one of the photos I was signing back then." She pointed to the photo. "Look by my right ear, you can even see part of my signature."

On the laptop, Frank pulled up a photo of the crowd. Out of at least fifty onlookers, he zoomed in on several of the male faces. He asked Haley if she remembered any from the expo.

"Dude, that was three years ago," she said, laughing huskily. "I can barely remember three *days* ago."

"No doubt," I muttered.

Wayne spoke up. "The bomb threat was called in at 10:54 a.m. The time stamp on that photo is 10:51. Let's go over all visible male faces, see if any pop out. Chances are, we're looking for a white guy between the age of twenty and fifty."

One by one, Frank focused in on each individual's face for several seconds before moving on to the next. I stopped him on the third one. "What about him? Ball cap and glasses. Patchy beard. Perv eyes."

Haley chewed the inside of her cheek. "I dunno. Half those Comic-Con geeks look like that, but he doesn't stand out."

Wayne drew his hand tiredly over his stubbly cheeks and chin. "From here on out, *no one* comes on set without a valid pass, and *everyone* gets checked coming in. I want someone focused on only the crowd at all times. Take their photos, see who gets squirrely."

"People don't like having their photos taken," another guard said.

"Fuck them," Wayne said. "Those losers all have their phones out trying to get a good shot of Haley. They can go fuck themselves."

Haley laughed. "I think you missed your calling in PR, Wayne," she said.

As if on cue, Haley's manager, Amy Gardner, entered, demanding to know what was being done. As Wayne filled her in, Amy eyed the doll on the table. "This fiasco is all over Twitter. Yippee. Now I've got to plan a press conference." Her thin lips looked like they were trying to repress a smile, making me wonder if she was secretly gleeful at this turn of events. It could only drum up more press for the film, not to mention her client. Celebrity stalkings made headlines. In the entertainment industry, headlines spelled megabucks.

Who knew, maybe Amy Gardner herself was behind the whole thing.

Wayne tossed me his keys. "Use my ride to get Haley out tonight. Frank, you tail them."

He and I were the last ones out of the trailer. Two suits stepped in our path. A tall, thin guy and a short, round guy. Like Mutt and Jeff, but wearing nice suits, minus ties, top buttons undone. Badges opened up, and under the film set lights, they appeared almost fake, though I knew better. These guys were too muted to be actors, unless they were really good ones.

"Sloane Donovan?" asked the tall cop, who identified himself as Inspector Paulsen of the Combined Forces Special Enforcement Unit. His no-neck partner was Sergeant Wingo.

I nodded and introduced Wayne as my partner.

Wingo eyed Wayne with disdain. "We know who you are."

"Good for you," Wayne said. "What's the anti-gang agency want with us?"

"We're here to talk about Ms. Donovan's visit to Travis Benoit earlier today," Paulsen said.

Wayne fired me a sharp glance.

"Your information is faulty," I said. "I went to talk to his nephew, who was in a relationship with a missing person I'm investigating. His uncle showed up there."

"And you approached Mr. Benoit and had words."

"Is that what the surveillance photos showed or what Benoit told you?"

Paulsen smiled. "We're going to do you a favour and simplify your investigation. As of this moment, Travis Benoit has been removed from your list of suspects. He is no longer on your radar. End of story."

"You can't—"

"We can. Because this belongs to something far bigger than your missing girl case, which, I assure you, he is not involved with."

"You'll excuse me if I tell you your assurances don't mean shit to me."

Wingo leaned in close enough that I could smell onions on his breath. "Approach Benoit again and we'll bust you both for obstruction." He turned to Wayne. "That'll be your second charge. Good luck getting your P.I. license back after that."

Wayne turned to me. "Well, how about that? They've looked into our backgrounds."

"That makes me feel so important," I said, looking at the cops. "But he wasn't even there. It's not his case."

"In fact," Wayne said, "I'm hating it more and more with each passing minute."

"Smart," Paulsen said. "Something that you hate that much, I say just drop it and walk away. Try and drum that wisdom into your partner's head, would you?"

"I'll do my best, but she's a little thick."

I stepped closer, appraising the lapels of Wingo's suit jacket. "No way that's off the rack. Armani?"

"Zegna."

I raised an eyebrow. "Cops must be better-paid these days."

Wingo gave me a dead-eyed stare.

"Like I said," Wayne said, taking my arm and steering me away, "she's a little thick."

I pulled free and turned back to the cops. "Can I get your cards?"

"Why?" Wingo asked.

"In case I want to call you up and engage in friendly banter," I said. "Plus, I'll bet you guys have some really snazzy ones to go with the outfits."

"Musta forgot mine at home," Wingo said.

Paulsen maintained eye contact with me as he pulled out his wallet and slid out a card. Holding it between his index and middle finger he flicked it my way. It was of fine quality and thick, with edges sharp enough to open a vein.

"Al Paulsen," I said, reading the name on the card. "Good, honest cop name."

When we were a safe distance away, Wayne stopped me. "What the *fuck* is going on, Donovan?"

"Those cops are in Benoit's back pocket," I said. "That's the reason he has never done any time. He could also be a C.I. That would explain why his rivals have been going down for the big counts. In the last five years, they've been able to put almost all of the Scorpions away for maximum sentences. Satisfies the public, makes the law look good, certain people get promoted—on both sides of the law."

"This is not news to anyone," he said. "That's how the game works."

"And how the disappearance of a fifteen-year-old girl remains unsolved."

CHAPTER 17

THE BOMB THREAT INVESTIGATION LED TO A two-day production delay, which afforded me a rare morning off. When Karin got word, she coaxed me out to Deep Cove for a hike and an early lunch at Arm's Reach Bistro. She seemed impressed when I immediately set the wine menu aside.

"This is new," she said.

I eyed a woman sipping a mojito at the next table, then at all the wine bottles racked by the bar. My foot started tapping beneath the table. "I need to be sharp," I said, and ordered a soda with lime. Karin inquired about work, and to distract myself for the next forty-five minutes, I talked about the suspects in the Emily Pike case and being approached by the two gang cops the previous night.

Lunch over, we stepped off Gallant Avenue and walked down the grassy slope of the park, which resurrected memories of my disastrous finish the previous week. I eyed the people all around, picnicking, tossing Frisbees and beach balls.

Lost in my thoughts, I followed Karin as she steered us down toward the water, even though the parking lot was further up the hill. We passed the dock and the pebbly crescent-shaped beach where a dozen or so kayaks sat, along with an equal number of stand-up paddleboards. As we walked near the awning of the Deep Cove Kayak & Surf Shop, it dawned on me that something felt off.

Then I saw the guy, what's his name, smiling and coming toward us from where he'd been assisting a couple with life jackets.

It was a set-up.

"Hello again," he said, pushing his polarized Oakleys up on his head.

"You're an asshole," I hissed to Karin from the side of my mouth.

"Well, well," she said cheerily, "if it isn't the handsome gentleman from the other night. What was your name again?"

"Jim," he said. "Good to see you again."

"I'm Karin," she said. "And of course, you remember Sloane, still as rude as ever."

"How could I forget?" he said. "I heard you had some excitement on the set last night. Kinda scary."

"Sounds like something the perpetrator would say," I said. "Where were you between the hours of ten and eleven p.m.?"

"My alibi's over there," he said, gesturing toward the open-air, walk-in office area, where his daughter was handing out waiver forms to customers. She looked up and waved. We all waved back. "I get her every other weekend," he said, "so the next one I'm free to stalk film sets at will. You ever get any time off?"

"Idle hands, devil's playthings," I said.

"I gotta go," Karin said. "You guys sort this shit out."

She slapped me on the ass and grinned over her shoulder while walking away.

"Bitch duped me," I said.

"I'm glad she did. People only accidentally bump into each other in romantic comedies."

"I hate those."

"Somehow I figured you would," he said. "That's why I'm not asking you to one. Or to coffee. That's lame. Look, in the summer, I'm basically here seven days a week. I don't date much. Truthfully, I don't date at all, so let's not call this a date."

"Call what a date? This?"

"No," he said, giving a nervous laugh. "Uh—"

"What's your proposition?"

"It'll be a surprise. You like those?"

"I guess we'll find out."

CHAPTER 18

I'D INTENDED ON PAYING LUCAS PIKE A VISIT later that day, but he'd saved me the trouble by coming to the office and plunking his drunk ass down in the chair across from my desk.

"Maddy phoned and said you'd be wanting to ask me some questions," he said. "Thought I'd make it easy for you. I don't live far from here."

I walked to the fridge. "Care for a drink, Lucas?"

"Why not? It's my day off."

I handed him a can of PBR and took mine back to my desk. I sat, opened the beer, and took a sip. Lucas opened his and drank it down like a man who'd spent several days in the desert. He made me feel like the very model of restraint.

Lucas Pike would've been a handsome man once, before the previous decade kicked his ass into the gutter. He had dark, thinning hair, combed back. High cheekbones, and for a face leaning toward boozy bloat, he still had a squared-off jawline. He wore a gray t-shirt with mustard stains, and cargo shorts containing what looked to be the outline of a mickey in a side pocket.

Finishing his beer, he said, "You don't look like a P.I."

"Thanks for that."

"Your partner does though," he said. "Fat dink almost turned me away. Told him I wasn't leaving till I talked to you."

I smiled. Wayne had been called far worse in his career. "Thanks for coming in, Lucas."

"Call me Luke," he said. "Can I have another beer?"

"Help yourself," I said. "Summer's getting fiercer by the day and they still haven't fixed the a/c in this dump."

"Let me guess," he said, going to the fridge, "the landlord's a cheap-ass who's only waiting for some condo developer to make him a sweet offer so that they can rape the block?"

"Sounds pretty accurate."

"Way of the fuckin' city," he said, giving a cynical smile. "Make that *all* cities. Soon you'll have to be a millionaire to live here at all."

He sat back down, popping the tab on the beer. After several long swallows, his face clouded over. "I came today because I can't bear to be accused of abducting my daughter again. I didn't want you coming to my work and making me look worse than I already do. I've had some DUIs, so I'm skating on thin ice."

"Where's work?"

"Currently it's night security for a development in Maple Ridge. I'll probably end up doing the same for the assholes who decide to snap this place up."

I asked him about his relationship with Emily in the six months prior to her disappearance.

"Nearly nonexistent," he said. "I tried, though. I called every month or so, see what she was up to, ask about school and things. She didn't have much time for her old man. Maybe it was the age she was at, or maybe because I wasn't around much during her younger years. I took her for lunch maybe a month before she went missing, but it was like pulling teeth to get her to say anything, like she couldn't wait for it to be over. It made me think that maybe her mother was still poisoning her against me." He took an aggressive gulp of beer, face flashing with bitterness.

"You abducted her when she was two," I said. "That had to have made things strange between you."

"You think because you read a fuckin' file you *know* anything? I took her because her mother's a crazy bitch who was trying to keep me from seeing my daughter while she was spending all the child support money on smokes and scratch tickets. I took Emily because I loved her, and I brought her back because I loved her. So don't *ever*"—he slammed his half-finished beer can on the edge of my desk, causing it to explode and spray nearly to the ceiling—"talk like you know me."

I paused, my hand on the Enforcer in my bag below the desk. "You finished?" I asked.

Lucas Pike collapsed back in his chair, hand over this face.

Wayne appeared at the door. "What's goin' on, buddy?" he asked. "Why you making a mess of my partner's office?"

"It's all right," I said. "We're cool. Right, Luke?"

Wayne folded his thick arms. I made a shooing motion, but he waited another five seconds before sauntering away. Lucas leaned forward, picked up the can and tried to wipe beer off the desk with his hand.

"Leave it," I said.

A flicker of anger shone from his eyes again, before disappearing. He sat back in his chair.

"Ever meet her boyfriend, Oscar?" I asked.

He ran a hand under his nose. "Not until after she went missing. At the time of the search, he came by to help. People say he's a bad egg, but they must say worse about me."

He stood suddenly and moved toward the door. "That's all I came to say. I'm sorry."

"One more thing," I said. "Did you ever buy Emily any jewelry? Silver jewelry, bracelets and necklaces, that kind of thing?"

He half-turned to me. "Never knew her to wear any. Gave her cash money when I saw her. How she spent it was up to her."

After he left, I sat for a moment looking at the spilled beer. Then I got up and walked to the window.

On the sidewalk, M.J. sat beneath her umbrella, wearing her gas mask and strumming "Stairway to Heaven". Lucas Pike walked up, paused to drop some coins in her case, and squatted to pet her skunk. I imagined his daughter Emily would've done the same thing.

He walked down the sidewalk and got into a rusted-out Ford station wagon. The engine coughed and spluttered as he tried to start it. Through his car window, I could see him yelling as he smashed his palm against the steering wheel. On the third attempt, the engine rattled to life and he drove away.

In the file, his alibi had stated that he'd been working at the time of his daughter's disappearance. I made a mental note to check the make and model of the vehicle he drove back then. If he lived the same lifestyle as now, chances are it was a shitbox like the current one.

I turned to find Wayne looking traumatized as he peered into the fridge. "Bloody hell, you let Pisstank Pete there drink the last of the brews?"

CHAPTER 19

"I JUST WANT TO KNOW IF YOU FOUND ANY-thing," Maddy Pike said over the phone. "It's been nearly a week, and you haven't returned my calls."

"I apologize for that," I said. "I've been busy."

"Lucas said he was coming to see you."

"He did, just today."

A pregnant pause.

"You don't have anything, do you?" she asked.

Tension crept up from my neck into my skull. I poured another thick dose of sauvignon blanc into a tumbler and looked at my wall. In addition to the four suspects, I had tacked up various photos of Emily at the farm, as well as photos of her room and its contents: books, clothes, jewelry.

"Hello? Are you still *there?*"

I drank down half the wine. Eclipse jumped on the table in front of me and meowed. I nudged him away. "Your ex-husband said Emily never wore jewelry."

"Surprised he even noticed. But no, it wasn't her thing. She barely ever wore makeup."

"So, where'd she get the silver jewelry in her room?"

Over the phone, I could hear the wet crackle of her cigarette as she sucked on it. "I always assumed it came from Oscar."

"He says it didn't. Did the police ever inquire about the jewelry?"

"No. Do you think this is important?"

"I don't know yet. Being frugal-minded, if Emily wasn't into jewelry, she wouldn't buy it for herself. And unless Oscar or Lucas lied about it, someone else bought her those pieces. I'm going to need to borrow that jewelry."

* * *

"Cool bracelet," Karin said, admiring the fine silver links connecting tiny silver bones. "Where'd you get this?"

"It belonged to Emily Pike," I said, handing over a silver necklace made of tiny interlocking horseshoes, "the girl who disappeared seven years ago."

Karin searched the necklace for a telltale engraving. I had already done the same and found none. We sat in my Jeep in the rear parking lot of Hillside Country Club, in the tony enclave of the British Properties in West Vancouver. I had worked there for five years, before being fired last year for misappropriating security footage for an investigation I had conducted. Legally, I was never supposed to set foot on club property again. Yet, here I was. I guess I was in the mood to flout rules.

"They're definitely unique," Karin said. "And they don't have any makers' marks. I'll contact some people today, find out if they're local."

I thanked her. Karin gestured with her chin to where the road dipped and disappeared below the tree line. "Is it weird being back here?"

"Little bit." I looked to the road ahead, the one that led down to a gravel lot hidden from view. It was where, last autumn, I'd discovered the murdered body of my friend Geri Harp. "But it's behind me now," I added.

"I don't believe you for a second," she said, getting out of the Jeep, just as a patrolling security guard strolled through the parking lot. "You better get out of here, before you get busted again."

CHAPTER 20

THE FOLLOWING MORNING, I PARKED MY JEEP down the block from Oscar Benoit's residence in Whalley. The F-150 was in the driveway. Aside from a few trucks and late model sedans, the street was empty. Barring the possibility of an undercover team camped out in the ravine or holed up in one of the neighbour's homes, the house was not under visible surveillance.

Construction sounds came from a building being bulldozed further up the block. Combined with the morning heat, the stutter of heavy machinery and the grinding of metal against earth and rock lulled me into a kind of trance. Slumping in my seat, I felt my eyes start to close.

A car door slammed, and I opened my eyes to see the F-150 reverse out of the driveway and onto the street. I caught a glimpse of Oscar's face in the rearview as he drove away. I waited for the truck to crest the rise of the hill and disappear before keying the ignition and pulling away from the curb.

Maintaining a safe distance behind the truck, I casually followed Oscar out of the residential area back toward the city, purposefully losing sight of him from time to time so my Jeep wouldn't always be in his rearview. Most people, if they believe they're being tailed, either dramatically speed up or slow down. The moment of discovery is very apparent—*unless* they're accustomed to it and have trained themselves to be cool cucumbers. In that case, you won't know that you've been burned, until you clue in that you're being taken on a random tour of the city—or worse, they drive out to the middle of nowhere or some other quiet, not-so-nice place that they've picked out just for someone like you.

If Oscar knew, he didn't show it.

And if he knew, I didn't much care anyhow. What was he gonna do, call the cops? His uncle? From the earlier meeting, I'd felt the tension between them. When his Uncle Trav had arrived, Oscar had told me to go, to avoid trouble. There was anger simmering in him, but not the kind of volcanic rage Lucas Pike carried around. Oscar had the same sort of mistrusting eyes as his rescue dog. It's possible that they were both harmless, but you wouldn't want to turn your back on either of them.

Just in case, the gun was in my satchel on the passenger seat.

As Oscar aimed his F-150 east on 104 Avenue, I was two cars behind, and by then I'd figured out that if he had any other surveillance on him, they were too good to be spotted by me. After exiting onto Highway 1, he picked up speed, heading over the Port Mann Bridge, all the way into Burnaby. After passing a police car on the shoulder, he slowed and signaled over to the right lane. Traffic thickened toward Vancouver and I kept at least three or four cars between us at all times.

I followed the F-150 as it exited onto the Lougheed Highway. A minute later, it pulled into the parking lot of an Earls restaurant. Driving past the entrance to the parking lot, in my rearview I saw Oscar removing his sunglasses as he walked toward the restaurant. Pulling a U-turn, I entered the lot and backed into a corner spot next to a giant truck.

Through my Nikons, I watched him join two thick-necks on the patio. Steroidal arms, shaved heads, Versace sunglasses: Vancouver thug chic. Oscar sipped a soda and did most of the talking, while his buddies did most of the nodding. I took photos.

Thirty minutes and some parting fist bumps later, Oscar stalked back across the parking lot, got in his truck, and drove away.

Imagining his hands around Emily's neck, I saw him choking her until her eyes bugged out, her face went purple and she stopped struggling, the light leaving her eyes.

I keyed the ignition but waited for the Ford to exit the lot before I pulled out.

Oscar drove west, taking the Hastings exit, where he sped up, changing lanes without signaling. Maybe he'd finally spotted me. Or maybe he was late for work. He turned right on Clark Drive, drove up the ramp and into the Port of Vancouver, a place where even an ex-con like him had access, due to his miraculous attainment of a longshoreman's ticket. Seeing as how my P.I. credentials wouldn't get me past the security booth, I pointed my Jeep back toward the office.

Although they maintained a lower profile than in years past, the bikers' stranglehold over the docks was long established. Vancouver was a major port hub for the vast pipelines of South American cocaine and Mexican and Afghani heroin. When the occasional bust was made here, it was in the neighbourhood of three hundred kilos plus; those unlucky enough to get pinched tended to be throwaway gangsters, low-level Indo-Canadian or Persian thugs. It was a multi-billion-dollar-a-year enterprise, and no matter the criminal affiliation, for that to work, a lot of palms needed greasing: local politicians, union officials, port authority, and narcotics and gang unit cops.

I drove slowly, putting something together. Seven years ago, Emily Pike witnesses something at the Benoit ranch. She disappears a month later, and the cops brush it under the rug. Present day: Travis Benoit pulls strings to get his nephew working the docks.

Because this belongs to something far bigger than your missing girl case.

I was just about to turn right onto Commercial Drive, go back to the office, and look over the files. But the day was still early and there was an itch that needed scratching. I continued east and up the hill on Hastings Street. Wayne would kill me if he knew.

CHAPTER 21

TRAVIS BENOIT NO LONGER LIVED ON A RANCH in Langley. Several years ago, he'd downsized to a three-storey, Mediterranean-style villa near the top of Capitol Hill in North Burnaby. On a clear day, the view of the city to the west and the North Shore mountains would be stunning. Today was not one of those days, with the thick blanket of forest fire smoke hanging over the city like fog.

I used the poor visibility to my advantage as I sat in my Jeep a few hundred yards from Casa Benoit. From this position, I couldn't see the house, only its spiky iron gate and security cameras on the posts above. Several black SUVs and trucks sat parked on the quiet street.

I pulled my Nikons and trained them on the house, then dropped them just as quickly. A brown Yukon appeared out of the haze and pulled parallel with me. A moustached driver smiled over, asking if there was a shortcut down to the water from here.

"Don't think so," I said, "but I'm a little lost myself."

"Well, thanks anyhow. I hope we both make it to where we need to go. Bye, now."

He drove off and turned left at the next intersection. I started to raise my Nikons again, when, in my rearview, I caught sight of a black Escalade pulling over a hundred yards behind me, two shapes behind the windshield.

I pulled back onto the street, and so did the Escalade, gliding along like a predatory beast. I reached into the satchel, grabbed the pistol and set it on the passenger seat. I drove at a steady pace, alternating lefts and rights at each intersection. The SUV stayed with me for every move. Hastings Street loomed ahead. The light changed to yellow and I slowed, watching my pursuers do the same. Just as the light changed to red, I pinned the accelerator and shot through the intersection, horns blaring as a westbound delivery truck was forced to brake suddenly to avoid hitting me. I glanced in the rearview, catching a glimpse of Giller's stone face through the window, Jake Dove riding shotgun.

Adrenaline lit up my veins as I took a screeching right on Parker and sped back toward Vancouver, thinking about how I was going to need a new surveillance vehicle, something nondescript but with guts under the hood. A text came through. Karin:

Jewelry made by company called NightShade

Forty-five minutes later, I was parked across the street from an Alexander Street flophouse. The air seemed even worse here. My eyes stung. I noticed that I hadn't seen or heard a bird anywhere in days. People walked by on the sidewalk wearing white KN95 masks over their noses and mouths.

Googling "NightShade Design" on my phone, I found an independent jewelry company based in Victoria. Each piece was hand-crafted and modestly priced. From their website, I found a list of retailers that carried their pieces. Two in Victoria, six in Vancouver, one in Whistler, one in Kelowna, two in Calgary.

I called NightShade and spoke to the co-owner, Dana Ashbury, and told her I was an investigator and that I was looking for the store that sold a necklace and bracelet of theirs at least seven years ago.

"Oh, boy," she said. "Back then, we were just starting out, and our record-keeping was spotty. My partner and I would go show our work to stores all over, and managers would buy whatever pieces they liked."

"So, no record of what stores bought what?"

"No, but at that time, we only had three stores that carried our pieces regularly. They still do."

As Dana provided the names, I jotted them down in a notebook, becoming distracted by movement down the street. Lucas Pike exited a crumbling three-storey walkup and headed for his station wagon nearby. I thanked Dana for her time and ended the call.

I followed him to the Astoria Hotel Liquor Store on Hastings, parking half a block ahead so I could see his car in my rearview. He entered the store and came back out several minutes later with a six-pack and a bottle in a brown paper bag. I watched him take a swig from the paper bag and wash it down with a beer before he got back in the car.

The engine chugged a few times as he started the car. I followed him east on Hastings and then onto Highway 1. He stayed in the right lane, driving just below the speed limit, until he veered onto the Blue Mountain exit into Coquitlam.

I followed him deeper into the suburbs, where he parked near the fenced-off skeleton of a new condo development. I parked down the street, pulled my night-vision binoculars from the glove box, and reclined the seat.

At 10:56 p.m., Lucas carried a sports bag into the portable construction trailer. Several minutes later, a burly Sikh man wearing a turban and a security jacket emerged and walked to a nearby minivan. For the next two hours, I caught occasional glimpses of Lucas shuffling around the complex. A casual observer might deem him a thirsty fellow judging from the thermos he kept on him at all times. At half past midnight, while standing by an open window on the eighth floor, he drained the last of the thermos. He hung his head and stayed like that for a long time. I thought maybe he had fallen asleep, but a look through the Nikons showed his head bobbing slightly as he sobbed and muttered to himself.

After a few minutes it became too depressing to watch, so I started the engine and drove away.

CHAPTER 22

AS SMOKE CONTINUED TO ROLL IN AND coalesce at the coast, the thick, gray pall seemed to press down, suffocating the city more with each passing day. The few people that were out moved as though they were trudging through quicksand, their downcast eyes seeming to question if things would ever get good again.

Maybe we're all living in purgatory, I thought, a drab eternity where we're forced to atone for our past sins.

I parked on Main Street. A double-decker, open-air tour bus trundled by, nearly empty save for several occupants wearing masks. Two weeks' vacation in Vancouver and all they'd have to show for it would be burning eyes and a raspy cough.

Earlier I'd checked out two places downtown that carried NightShade jewelry. The first business had changed owners several times in the previous seven years, and no one in their current employ had been around at the time when Emily disappeared. The second place had turned out to be a tiny kiosk in the rundown Denman Mall, where the elderly owner had shaken her head, claiming she'd never laid eyes on the pieces before.

I got out of my Jeep and entered the next store on the list. "A Select Few" was a popular but kitschy place with overpriced vintage duds, gaudy purses, and cases of eclectic jewelry. The manager was an ethereal-looking waif who looked like she would be at home dancing amid the toadstools. I explained why I was there and showed her the jewelry. "Gorgeous pieces," she said. "I've only been here two years, but hang on and I'll see if I can find someone."

A minute of wandering brought me to the NightShade display. Most pieces were beneath the glass counter, but the earrings were on a display carousel, with a built-in mirror. When I glimpsed the tired and bloodshot eyes looking back at me, for a second, I thought, *who the fuck is that?* When I realized it was me, I told myself I really ought to start putting on makeup in the morning.

Or change your lifestyle.

I just needed a good night's sleep. The pills were fucking with my head. Maybe my perception was distorted, and I didn't look that bad. Then I checked my reflection again. Same awful face. Why were there so many goddamn mirrors everywhere?

"Here you are," the manager said, reappearing with another woman in tow. "This is Deirdre. She's been here since the store opened."

Deirdre smiled crookedly and her bloodshot eyes had trouble connecting with mine. I smelled Clorets and weed on her breath. The manager moved off to assist another customer and I showed Deirdre the jewelry.

She gave a jerky nod. "I remember those."

"You're sure?"

She nodded. "Normally I wouldn't, but I had just split with my partner, and those pieces really suited my mindset at the time. I was thinking of buying them myself."

"Do you remember who bought them?"

"Some guy. Always paid in cash."

"What did he look like?"

"Medium height, kinda skinny." She cupped her hand and drew it demonstratively down her cheeks. "Narrow face. Moustache. Dark brown hair. Glasses. Awkward."

"Awkward?"

"Yeah, he looked uncomfortable in his own skin. And his voice was husky."

"And you remember all this after seven years?"

"No, I remember because he used to come in fairly regularly, until about a year ago."

I showed her photos of Oscar Benoit and Lucas Pike.

She shook her head. "Not even close."

Two hours later, Deirdre and I sat across from Frank at a corner table in Kafka's on Main Street, as he worked up a composite sketch. The face was that of a computer nerd with a cheesy moustache and oversized 80s-style glasses.

Sipping coffee while watching a most likely stoned woman describe facial characteristics gave me reservations. In my experience, weed did not enhance one's ability to accurately recall details.

Sketch completed, I asked how he moved. "Slow and methodical? Quick and jerky? You said he was awkward."

"He didn't say much, but he kinda ... *strutted*. Like those guys who work out and strut around like they have imaginary muscles, know what I mean?" She giggled. "If they only knew how stupid they look."

CHAPTER 23

"I'VE NEVER SEEN HIM BEFORE," MADDY PIKE
said, staring at the sketch as she smoked. Her eyes took on a
hard cast as she studied it. We sat at the paint-peeling picnic
table in her backyard. A thin layer of ash covered the wood
of the table, and the sun was a neon red hole through the
blanket of smoke.

"You think this man took my Emily?" she asked.

"I don't know."

"But it's something. You're going to look further."

"It's something."

"I can get you more money in a few days. My disability
is due any day now."

I looked at her parched, yellow lawn. I could hear the
same two girls from last time, playing across the street, their
voices murmuring through the heavy air.

"You have to follow this, Sloane," she said. "Lilith told
me you'd find something that no one else could."

"Enough," I snapped. "I don't buy into that psychic shit, and no one else does either. Has any of it helped find your daughter so far?"

"It's helped *me*," she said. "How is what I believe any different than people turning to God or the church? Or maybe it's better to turn bitter and hopeless and slide into the abyss—or the bottle, like Lucas. My belief is what keeps me alive, Sloane, so don't belittle it, don't you dare. What do *you* believe in?"

"Let's stick to the matter at hand."

"Do you believe you can find out what happened to my daughter?"

"I don't know."

"Yes, you do." She took my hand, and before I could pull it away, she held on and squeezed. "That's why you're here. You could have just given up. You've gone past the week you promised me, and now you show up with a suspect sketch. Thank you. Even if it only goes this far, thank you. But please tell me you're going to see where this leads."

I put on my sunglasses. "A few more days."

"Can I have a copy of that sketch, ask around the neighbourhood?"

I slid it to her. "I've emailed the Missing Children's Society. They'll use facial recognition software to run a check against known offenders."

"And the police?"

"They're next."

As I pulled up in front of the Cambie Police Station, I spotted Inspector Davis climbing into the passenger side of an unmarked sedan, Fiona Saddy at the wheel.

I got out of my vehicle and moved quickly. "Inspector," I called out. "A moment."

Davis looked up and swore under his breath. Before he could close the door, I handed him a copy of the suspect sketch, along with photos of the NightShade jewelry.

"What's this?" he asked.

"Jewelry in Emily's room that no one could account for. They came from a store called A Select Few and were purchased by the man in the sketch. He always paid in cash and came in regularly up until a year ago."

"They got him on camera?"

"It was too long ago. But a woman remembers selling him the pieces. You can scan this sketch and run it against your database."

He gave a mock-serious nod and passed the sketch over to his partner. "Yes, ma'am."

"That jewelry shouldn't have been overlooked during the initial investigation."

"Probably not," he said. "But someone else was lead on the case back then."

"Fair enough, but it's been dead for seven years. Now I'm giving you this, which means it isn't."

"You're doing your duty as a citizen. Reporting potential evidence of a crime to the *proper* authorities. You want some sort a medal? Your badge back, maybe?"

"I want you to run that sketch and keep me in the loop. Any more information, I'll turn it over to you."

"Quid pro quo kinda thing, huh?" he said.

That falling sensation came again. Feeling I was losing my balance, I instinctively reached out toward the open door of their car. Davis looked at my hand and frowned.

I turned quickly and walked away. "Forget it," I said.

When I was ten feet away, he called after me. "I always thought there was something sad about P.I.s: people who can't or *couldn't* make it as real cops, so they get a little license that entitles them to pick away at some leftovers."

Rage quashed the dizziness and I turned back. "I don't *want* this case. So do your fucking job and check this out, unless you'd like to keep ticking off days until retirement."

Inspector Davis glowered at me through the window. "That'll get you far."

As the car drove past, I could see Constable Saddy barely able to suppress a grin.

CHAPTER 24

DOC BARNEY FINISHED SUTURING THE ABDOMEN of a sedated goat on an operating table. He seemed much calmer that on our last visit, though when his long-sleeve shirt crept up, I caught a glimpse of track marks on his forearm.

"I've never seen that person before," he said, referring to the sketch I'd just shown him. "My wife was the one for faces around here, not me. In fact, she used to say I have that disorder where I can't tell one face from another. Not quite true, but I'd say there's something to that."

He snipped off the ends of the sutures with scissors and swabbed the site with disinfectant. "After your last visit, however," he said, "I remembered *you*."

"How so?"

He peeled off his latex gloves and tossed them in the trash. "From the day of the search. I was one of the volunteers, and you were giving directions. You had very earnest eyes then."

What do they look like now, doc?

During a mid-afternoon lull at Subway on Broadway, I approached Chelsea Evans, who had just finished ringing through a customer's sandwich. When she saw me, she mouthed a silent *fuck*.

"Got a moment, Chelsea?"

"I'm *working* right now."

"I see that." I pulled out the suspect sketch. "Around the time Emily went missing, do you recall ever seeing this man around?"

She glanced around, before looking at the sketch. A few of her fellow employees looked on curiously. "No," she said.

"What about at the ranch that day?"

She shook her head. "He doesn't exactly look like he'd fit with that crowd."

"No, he doesn't," I said, passing her the sketch, along with my card. "If you ever feel like chatting, give me a call."

Haley Cooper and I sat across from each other in a corner banquette of Notch8, in the Hotel Vancouver. Haley's hair was sleek sable, and she wore a coral dress. Sans substances, her face had lost its party-bloat, giving her the sharper, more refined look I'd seen in her movies. She sipped a cran-and-soda and alternated between checking her watch and scoping out the bar. She was here to meet some indie director who was in town.

Monotonous house music piped through the unseen sound system in the swanky lounge that was all muted light and shadow, making everyone's faces bony, vampire-like. Glass tinkled amid the upscale murmurs of people making a million dollars just for walking in the door and sitting down.

I sipped soda water and considered waving the waitress over for a hit of vodka.

"You seem different," Haley said, "like your mind is a million miles away."

I shrugged, my eyes following a tall man in a suit entering the bar. His eyes scanned the room for someone.

"Not him," Haley said, a second before the man smiled and made his way over to a woman seated across the bar. "But I wish it were," she added. "Hell, *my* admirer's probably waiting with a gun right now. Moment we step outside— *pop, pop,* baby. Lights out."

"I don't think so," I said, "or he would've done it by now."

"Know what's been on my mind lately?" She paused, and in a slightly deeper voice, said, "No, Haley, what's been on your mind lately?" Bubbly Haley voice: "Well, knowing if I were to be killed today—by some psycho, nothing so banal as a car accident—"

"Or in a meth shack."

"You're never going to let me live that down, huh?"

"It was last week."

"Whatever. Point is, that if I were to die today, my fame would last far longer than if I were to fade into oblivion by making shittier and shittier films."

"So, stop making shitty films. Or go out and adopt a kid, or head to the Congo and save the mountain gorilla, make a self-aggrandizing documentary or whatever the fuck you people do."

"You have to build up to that shit," she said. "No one would buy it. Plus, I'm currently up to my eyeballs in debt. Thus, I'm forced to keep making this schlock." She leaned in and slid a U.S. hundred across the table. Her eyes took on a mischievous flare beneath the fluted-glass chandelier. "Go get us a couple strong ones, Sloane. C'mon, I know you want one."

I pushed the money back. "That might explain your debt right there. Are you nuts? My ass is still in a sling over your last debacle."

"Fine," she said. "Then tell me what's got you so restless. You've been toe-tapping since we got in here. Is it that dude?"

"What dude?"

"'*What dude?*' The cute guy with the kid. Karin said he asked you out."

"You guys are BFFs now?"

"We text." She shoulder-nudged me. "Spill it, sister."

"I'm too busy to date right now."

"With what? You're only with me, like four or five nights a week. What else you got going on? C'mon, I can read an obsession from a mile away."

I looked at Haley, who nodded at me with big eyes. Because my mind was fixed on the case anyhow—and to get off the subject of my personal life—I reached into my bag for the file folder. First, I showed her Emily's photo. "Emily Pike. She's been missing seven years. Her mother hired me."

"Holy shit. That's intense."

"She was fifteen here. At first, I thought it was a hopeless case, but today I think I found a line on a possible suspect." I pulled out the composite sketch.

Haley took it and studied it. "Looks like my grade eleven computer science teacher," she said. "It's always the nerdy fuckers who live next door." She took a quick photo of the sketch with her phone.

A hulking man in a Hawaiian shirt with a full mane of white-gray hair sat down at the end of the bar. When he turned, I saw the goatee. My breath caught in my throat and it took me a second to realize it wasn't Travis Benoit. Not even close. I blinked a few times.

Hayley's eyes had followed mine. "Who's that?"

"I thought it was someone I knew." I chewed on the straw from my drink, then took it from my mouth and pointed at the suspect sketch. "There's something about this case that goes beyond a missing girl. I have no proof, but I feel it. Certain people are not going to talk, others are simply on keepaway status."

"Just go browbeat them," she said. "That's your style. If I were playing you in a movie, that's what I'd do."

I laughed.

"I'm serious," she said. "I've got an A-list screenwriter who's been trying to get in my pants for years. He'd write a script about you."

"Fuck off."

Haley suddenly became distracted by something over my shoulder. She stood, welcoming over a bearded man with tattoos covering his sinewy arms.

"François," she said, "you look like a fucking dog, and you smell worse. This is Sloane, my friend and great protector, who I've just decided I'll play in a movie someday. Sloane, this is François, who would have won an Oscar last year, had he not enthusiastically told the Academy to go fuck themselves."

I nodded absently, then became nearly too distracted by several more men entering the bar that I almost missed a clandestine palm exchange from François to Haley. Before she could tuck the vial of powder into her clutch, I snatched it away. "Nice try," I said, turning to François, who attempted to charm me with a crooked yellow smile.

"Out," I said. "Go peddle your shit somewhere else."

"He really is a famous auteur," Haley said.

"He looks like merde to me," I said.

François held out his hand. "To flush that down the toilet would be a travesty," he said.

CHAPTER 25

DRIVING TO THE HARDKNOCKS OFFICE THE next morning, I clocked a black Escalade that had been behind me since I left the West End. Angling left from Georgia onto Pender Street, the SUV stayed with me all the way to Gastown, following me left on Abbott, and right on Cordova. At Oppenheimer Park I pulled over abruptly, reaching into my bag and gripping the pistol. The Escalade drove past, a Middle Eastern woman at the wheel.

My hands shook and the world spun, and I opened the door, dry heaving onto the street right in front of the park's tent city.

Pulling the door shut I took a deep breath and wiped tears from my eyes, thinking about fifteen minutes earlier, when I'd deposited a dozen empty wine bottles in the recycling bin of my building's garage. A middle-aged man, dumping his garbage, had said, "Wow, must've been a good time."

I had forced a smile, thinking about the last time I'd actually had a *good* time.

Pulling back onto Cordova, I promised myself I'd do better today.

New day, fresh start.

All that shit.

As I walked up Commercial Drive, M.J.'s "Stairway" sounded faster, more jubilant. I tossed a loonie in her case. Pepi looked up and yawned. M.J. stopped playing long enough to tell me I had a visitor. "Cheap-suit-wearing Pillsbury Doughboy didn't even give me a nickel. Toss his ass to the curb, and I'll give him what-for."

I found him sitting at the top of the stairs, in front of our locked office door. In his late forties, he wore an ill-fitting, gray-checkered blazer over a red polo shirt. When he stood, he tucked in his shirt over his expansive stomach.

"Sloane Donovan," he said. "I'm Jerry Fifer, from the *Vancouver Sun*. I tried calling several times and sent you an email."

"No comment," I said, nudging past. Fifer smelled of garlic and cigarettes, and the combination sent my stomach flip-flopping again.

"You don't even know what I'm going to say," he said. "I understand you've uncovered new developments in the Emily Pike case."

I unlocked the door. "Like I said be—"

He held up a copy of the suspect sketch. "Can you confirm that this is the suspect?"

I gritted my teeth. "No comment."

"Don't you think that the public should be warned to be on the lookout for a possible killer?"

"You fucking leaked it, didn't you?" I yelled, barging past Frank and through the door of Haley Cooper's Gulfstream

trailer. In the middle of a Pilates session with a trainer, the actress looked up at me, concerned.

"What's going on, Sloane?" she asked calmly, like suddenly *she* was the rational one.

"Like you don't know. Emily Pike, the girl I told you about last night. You took a photo of the suspect sketch, and now it's out. Did you give your fucking phone to a random stranger again, or is it some weird publicity ploy because you're a washed-up sensation waiting to be killed by some fan? Or is it because I intercepted your drugs last night?"

"Sloane, I swear—"

Frank opened the door. "It's on the news," he said.

"Yeah," I said, staring at Haley, "no doubt."

"The mother is on CBC right now," he said.

The mother. I closed my eyes and flashed back to Inspector Davis warning me about Maddy Pike.

Haley touched my shoulder. "Honest mistake."

Frank stepped into the trailer and showed me the streaming news footage on his iPhone: teary-eyed Maddy Pike standing in Emily's room. Superimposed in the lower right-hand corner of the screen was a photo of Emily. In the other corner was the suspect sketch.

"Seven years ago, my daughter Emily disappeared without a trace," Maddy said, "and now, after all this time, we have a suspect. I implore the public to open their eyes along with their hearts, and help me find out what happened to my baby, and to give much-needed support to KidFind, which not only helps locate missing children, but allows parents under financial duress to continue the search long after police resources have been exhausted."

I shook my head.

"Without KidFind contributions," she went on, "I would never have had the means to make it this far in the investigation. On behalf of all the parents of missing children out there, I want to thank the public for their kindness and continued support."

A toll-free number and website appeared on the screen, along with a tip line and the number for the police.

"KidFind?" Frank said.

"Something my white trash mother would do if I went missing," Haley said.

CHAPTER 26

AS I SPED UP BOUNDARY ROAD THROUGH MIDDAY traffic, Wayne called. "Got to hand it to that scammer," he said, "she sure knows how to drum up a media frenzy. We got news vans outside the building, reporters clamoring for a sound bite. Some douche named Jerry Fifer keeps calling."

"Fucking horseshit," I muttered.

"Donovan, get your ass over here for a statement. Let's use this to our advant—"

"This is going to fuck everything up," I said, pulling a screeching right into Maddy Pike's townhouse complex. Miraculously, no news crews were in sight. "If the suspect isn't already in the wind, he's sure to be now."

I ended the call, pulled over, and opened the glove box, where I'd stashed a fifth of vodka.

Maddy hugged me at the door, cheeks over-rouged, and reeking of cheap perfume that did little to mask her chain-smoker breath. A woman with intense blue eyes and short platinum hair stood in the background.

"I'm so glad you came," Maddy said. "The Global News crew is scheduled to arrive at any moment."

"That was a mistake. You should have contacted me before doing anything. All it's going to do is drive the suspect deeper into hiding."

Platinum Hair appeared over Maddy's shoulder. "Sloane, you're very agitated, we can see that, but I've been communicating with Emily, and she's close to being found."

"Lilith, right? Wouldn't it be easier if she just telepathically gave you an address? Save us all a lot of trouble."

Lilith closed her eyes and gave a patient nod. "I wish it worked that way. Unfortunately, the messages are often vague, like a whisper in a dream, and then I try and decipher them. Somewhat like your process, Sloane. A bit of information is unearthed, and you use your skills and resources to unravel it further, see where it leads."

A haze of second-hand smoke hung in the kitchen. Maddy lit up a fresh smoke. Out the window a news van pulled up and a crew jumped out. Faces of neighbours appeared at windows across the way. Maddy seemed tremulous with excitement as she took a mighty drag off the cigarette before grinding it out in an ashtray.

On the kitchen table, a laptop was opened to the KidFind donation website. Beneath a photo of Emily flashed: $11,658. Several seconds later it was $11,718. Then it rose by another twenty bucks.

"Funny," I said, "before today, I've never heard of KidFind; you never mentioned it, and it's not affiliated in any way with the Missing Children's Society." I looked pointedly at the new gold watch on her wrist. "Where's the money going?"

"The *money*," Maddy said, "further funds the investigation. i.e., *you* stand to get a substantial cheque soon."

"Can't wait," I said. "What's your cut, Lilith?"

Maddy's eyes flared, while her psychic pal affixed me with the patient eyes a priest might give a petulant child.

"There are administrative costs," Maddy said. "It is a *registered* charity."

"No doubt," I said. "But hey, I'm sure Emily would want you to enhance your creature comforts using her name."

Her eyes seethed. "How *dare* you come in here and accuse us!"

Lilith placed her hand on Maddy's arm. It was a neat trick, like she found a switch beneath Maddy's skin to turn her instantly calm. "The thing is, Sloane," Lilith said, "I've been communicating with Emily for years now, and yes, she *would* want her mother to have a more comfortable life."

"She *said* that?"

"She *felt* it. And I felt it."

"How many dead people do you communicate with like this?"

"They don't have to be dead, and I have no control over the transmissions I receive."

"OK," I said, "but Maddy contacted *you* after her daughter disappeared, right? It's not like Emily just randomly decided to send a *transmission* to your crystal ball or whatever."

"You don't believe," Lilith said. "It's understandable, given your history. You exude painful energy. I wouldn't be surprised if your sister has tried contacting you. It is possible to lessen your burden, you know?"

My rage expanded. If I didn't get out of here soon, the room and its occupants would be too small to contain it.

"Your sister's journey is not over," Lilith said. "Do you feel an odd presence in the darkest nights, when you're all alone? Or perhaps you see things."

"You're a fucking crank," I said.

I turned and walked back down the hall, Maddy and Lilith at my heels. I opened the door, letting in the glare of the sun. The news crew marched up the walk, led by a sleek blonde in a smart, blue pantsuit.

"Stay with us, Sloane," Maddy hissed. "Think of what this could do for your agency."

"I'm done."

As I passed the crew, the newswoman turned to me. A camera aimed at me, and a microphone was thrust in my face. "Sloane Donovan, now that there's a suspect in the Emily Pike case, what's your gameplan?"

I pushed past and kept walking.

In the background, Maddy called out, "I want my baby's jewelry back!"

As I drove away, I pulled out the vodka and took a good slug. Just in case, I took another. Then I called Wayne and told him I was done with the case. When he asked what happened, I hung up. Every time I closed my eyes, I got a flash of Emily Pike's face.

CHAPTER 27

MY BUZZING PHONE WOKE ME. I WAS ON THE couch, still in my clothes from the previous night. Again. Eclipse slept between my knees. The phone buzzed again from the coffee table. I picked it up and frowned. "Hello."

"Sloane? You OK?"

"Jim?"

He laughed. "Where are you? You agreed to meet me at the Cove at ten, remember?"

I pushed myself up. My head screamed. The room spun. "Shit," I said.

"Do you remember calling me at one a.m.? You said you were up for a stand-up paddleboard lesson right then, and I suggested the morning, and now it's morning."

"Sorry. I can be there in thirty minutes."

"Listen, you obviously just woke up. We can do this another—"

"No, I'm good. I'll be there."

After climbing out of the shower, I wiped steam off the mirror and examined the bags beneath my bloodshot eyes.

I pulled on a white-and-purple bikini that kind of hung on me. Over that went cut-off jean shorts and a *Singha* beer tank top. They hung on me also. "You look like shit," I told my reflection in the mirror.

"You look great," Jim said. "I'm glad you drunk-dialed me last night."

"I wasn't drunk," I said.

We walked down to the pebbly beach where several stand-up paddleboards waited, fin side up.

"Either way," he said, "you called. I honestly didn't think you would. I thought maybe you used your P.I. wizardry and found out my entire sordid past."

"Probably would have bored me to sleep," I said.

"Ouch," he said, picking up a retractable paddle. He had me extend my right arm straight up and adjusted the length so that the handle was level with my wrist. I asked him about Sadie.

"She's at camp for the week. Want some sunscreen? It's pretty bright on the water."

"I don't usually wear it."

"If you saw the melanoma scar on my back, you might rethink that."

I took in the blue, full-sleeve surf shirt he was wearing. "Seriously?"

"I wish it were a bad joke." He pulled out a tube of SPF 45 and squirted some on his palms. I turned my back to him, and he gently smoothed the lotion into the skin of my shoulders and upper back, rubbing the excess down my arms. He lifted my hair to get at the back of my neck and I closed my eyes. He was thorough, methodical.

Keeping my eyes closed, I saw nothing and heard no echoing screams, only the lapping of water and the tinkling laughter of children. When I opened my eyes, the first thing I saw was the sky. The smoke had cleared, and not only was the sky a vivid blue, but more importantly, I could breathe without feeling the scorch in my lungs.

"It's a gorgeous day," I marveled.

He laughed. "You just noticed?"

We pulled the boards onto the water, climbed on, and paddled from our knees out into the cove. I pushed up to a standing position and teetered a bit before beginning to paddle. Fucking booze. Today would be different, I promised myself. Not a drop. Lowering my centre of gravity, I engaged my core, and found my stability. Something I was good at faking, at least on a physical level.

"*Nice!*" Jim called out. "I knew you'd be a natural on that thing."

With the marina to the left and the stilted waterfront homes to the right, we paddled out of the cove. He gave me a few pointers on stance and technique. My hangover began to evaporate as I bathed in a glow not just from the sun.

We made easy small talk for a bit, then fell into a comfortable silence. Once I turned to catch Jim looking at me. He held my gaze for a second or two, then turned to look at something else. Heading onto the choppier waters of Indian Arm, we spotted several seals cavorting nearby. He cupped a hand to his mouth and issued a surprisingly authentic seal bark. We laughed as the mammals froze and gave us bewildered stares.

Jim did a headstand on his board, then pushed up into a handstand. I called him a showoff, and he promptly toppled and splashed into the water. At that moment a boat cruised past and its wake caused me to lose my balance and fall in. We climbed back on our boards and just floated, dawdling our feet in the water, and enjoying the sun splintering off the water, the green hills of Belcarra, and the tiny woody islands on Indian Arm. Several herons took flight, wings skimming the water.

"It's gorgeous here," I said. "I've run all the trails on either side of the Arm, but it's not the same."

"Just wait till you see my second home. It's coming up, right around this bend."

At first all I saw was the island, a hundred yards from the mainland. As we paddled closer, a house appeared, nearly camouflaged amid the trees. Above the house, a Jolly Roger flag snapped in a sudden gust of wind.

"You *live* here?" I asked. "On an island?"

"Well, I paddle around here often enough to know there's never anyone at the house. But the beach belongs to whoever happens to be on it." We coasted toward the tiny, secluded cove. Jim leapt off his board and pulled mine up onto the sand. "Right now," he added, "that would be us."

From behind a tree he fetched a picnic basket and a blanket. He spread out the blanket and glanced up.

"Not bad," I conceded.

For the next ninety minutes we ate the chicken, cheese, and pickle sandwiches he had prepared, along with a small bag of potato chips, and washed it down with chilled sauvignon blanc. Sobriety could wait one more day.

After several glasses of wine, Jim's eyes changed from hazel to sea green. He talked openly about his life, how he'd competed in the semi-pro ranks as a surfer and catamaran racer, spending any money he'd made from endorsements as fast as it had come in. When he found out his girlfriend Annie was pregnant, he did the wrong thing and married her. They bought a place, Sadie came along, and he and Annie quickly grew to hate each other, finally splitting when their daughter was two.

"I was stressed, depressed, and living in a shitty little basement suite," he said, "when my doctor noticed an ugly mole on my back. I had it removed, and when it came back as cancer, I saw my whole life flash before my eyes. All I could think was that I was going to die, and Sadie was going to grow up without me."

Our shoulders touched and his skin was warm. He smelled like sweat and salty sea. I wanted to force him down on the sand. I wished he'd brought more wine.

"They carved a big chunk of flesh from my back, then tested my lymph. It hadn't spread, so I took it as a wake-up call to make some changes. I scraped together every cent I had and bought the kayak shop. I'm still in debt, but who isn't these days? Sorry, I'm babbling. You look like you want to say some—"

"Take off your shirt."

Jim paused, then peeled off his surf shirt, and sat back. He had surfer muscles: defined chest and abs, and a broad upper back.

And several dozen scars.

He stiffened as I ran a hand over his chest, my fingers pausing at a few of the small, round scars. The one in the centre of his back was more ominous; four inches across and an inch thick, carved into an inverted V, like an angry, purple brand. I traced it with my fingers.

"I used to tell people I was attacked by a shark," he said. "Makes for a better story."

I kissed the back of his neck and goosebumps immediately rose on his skin. He was salty, and I ran my tongue up to his ear, leaving a wet trail. We grabbed each other at the same time; me pushing, him pulling, until I straddled him.

We kissed, devouring each other's lips, faces, necks. I was dimly aware of the drone of boats in the background, people out there, doing things, but on this beach, on this island, there was only us. My past drifted away and sank into the ocean, and the future was an irrelevant abstraction. There were only our bodies and our wine-enhanced passion and the sun on our scars. Jim ran his hands up the sides of my thighs and clenched my ass. He was hard in his board shorts and I ground myself into him as we kissed and kissed.

My bikini top came off and we awkwardly wriggled out of our bottoms. I had just climbed on again when I felt a stab of pain. The echoing scream. The smell of gasoline. A bloody, naked body face down in the snow.

I pulled off and rolled to my side, reaching for my bottoms. "I'm sorry."

"What's wrong?"

"I'm fucked up." I stood and ran naked into the ocean, where I dove down, down, down, to the rocky bottom. I squeezed my eyes shut and held my breath. When I came up, maybe I would be reborn a different person, hopefully on a different planet. As long as I stayed in this body, in this place, I was doomed.

A tap on my shoulder. I opened my eyes to see Jim looking at me underwater. He waved and pointed up to the surface.

We rose and swam back to the island, where we sat naked for several minutes. "I keep my lifeguard certs up to date," he said, "so any time you feel the need to test my skills—"

"I'm fucked up."

"Is it déjà vu, or didn't you just say that?"

"No, really, I'm—"

"We're all fucked up, Sloane," he said. "We've all got baggage."

"Not like me."

"I think you're being too hard on yourself. You've got a cool job that you seem pretty good at. You're beautiful."

"I'm bipolar," I said. "I'm supposed to be taking my meds regularly, but I don't, because they make me feel slow, and I fucking hate feeling slow. But when I don't take them, I drink like a fish and do all kinds of stupid shit."

"Like calling me?"

"I don't remember doing that. For all I know, you called me this morning and took advantage of my blackout."

He nudged me with his shoulder. "Maybe I did."

I laughed and some seawater came out of my nose and my eyes welled up. Then I got mad at myself and stifled the tears before I embarrassed myself further.

"I'm sorry about your family," he said softly.

I looked over to see him offering a small, apologetic smile. "I Googled you," he explained.

Of course you did. "Was it entertaining?"

"It was really sad," he said. "I'm sorry, Sloane."

I nodded. "So now you know I have a mental illness and that I was kicked off the force for lying about it—*after* my mentally-ill sister killed her entire family, then herself? Man, no wonder you wanted to date me so bad."

"I wanted to date you because you're different."

I laughed and shook my head, feeling that tightness in my throat again.

"And you're a survivor," he said. "You're cynical and you're tough, but you don't roll over and play dead for anyone."

"Wow, Google is getting more and more informative all the time."

"Smart ass," he said. "I could see that in you the first time I met you."

"Maybe it's all just a façade," I said.

"I doubt it. I've hung around enough film sets to recognize good actors, and you're not one of them."

"Ouch."

"That's a compliment. My ex-wife was a good actor—not necessarily *on screen,* but she knew how to tweak her emotions to manipulate people. You're real, and I find that unbelievably attractive."

"Believe me," I said, "I've done my share of lying. I got pretty damn good at it, so much so that I beat lie detectors. Not that different from manipulating people into getting what you want."

"But you wouldn't have been able to have become a cop, had they known."

"Yeah, God forbid they ever have any mental defectives on the force."

"When were you first diagnosed?"

"Seventeen. But I knew I was different much earlier."

"How?"

"I began acting on my uncontrollable impulses."

"Such as?"

Grabbing the emergency pack lashed to the webbing on the front of his paddleboard, I unzipped it and rooted around, pulling out some tide table papers, held together with a paper clip. Jim watched curiously as I removed the clip, straightened it, then squeezed the ends together so that it was thin yet sturdy.

"Sloane MacGyver," he quipped.

I motioned for him to follow me. At the front of the house, the door showed a scratched-up brass Eversafe lock. Crouching down, I inserted the paper clip into the lock.

"What if there's an alarm?"

"We'll deal with that when we come to it. Got any money in your bag?"

"Maybe twenty bucks."

"Go get it."

By the time he returned, I had the door open. I wiped my sandy feet on the doormat and walked naked across the creaky living room floor.

"What if they come back?" Jim asked.

"Then we apologize profusely and paddle our asses home," I said, taking the twenty from him. A wine rack in the kitchen held only reds. I was a seasonal red wine drinker and right now it was the wrong season. I opened the fridge and found a bottle of mid-range white. I left the twenty in its place and closed the door.

Jim leaned against the doorway wearing a half-smile as he looked me up and down. I stood beneath a skylight, the thrill pulsing through every cell in my body.

I twisted the cap off the bottle. "What?" I asked innocently.

"You're beautiful," he said for the second time today, "and I feel like this is going to go down as one of the defining moments of my life."

I pulled him in and kissed him hard. We drank straight from the bottle, then kissed again, tasting the cold wine on each other's tongues.

"Don't suppose you have any condoms in your emergency pack outside," I said.

"Damn. I knew I forgot something."

"Let's go see what they have in the bedroom."

"We could *so* get arrested for this."

"Are you in or out?"

He kissed me again. "What do you think?"

Thirty minutes and a bottle of wine later, we neatened the kitchen counter and locked up.

Back on the beach, Jim fell asleep spooning me, while I stared into space and listened to the wind in the trees and tried not to think about all the ways I could flush this down the toilet.

CHAPTER 28

TIME SLOWED AS WE SLID INTO AUGUST, AS temperatures kept rising and the provincial wildfires renewed their fury. Some days the smoke returned like a vengeful spirit, clouds the colour of cast iron massing to the east, reminding us that close by, the world was on fire, and it was only a matter of time until it was our turn in the furnace.

Meanwhile, I was healing. On the surface, anyway. I was working steadily and sleeping more or less regularly. I wasn't taking my pills, but I wasn't drinking to the point of oblivion anymore either.

Jim lived in a ground floor suite on South Granville and we saw each other nearly every day, if only for an hour or two in the evening, after Sadie had gone to bed.

When flowers arrived at the office, Wayne teased me mercilessly. *Christalmighty, Donovan's in love. I never thought I'd live to see the day.*

Air quality be damned, we even managed a Sunday picnic in Deep Cove, with Jim providing kayaks and paddleboards. Wayne arrived with Sally and Theo, his eight-year-old son from his first marriage. We spent the afternoon paddling, playing bocce and laughing as we ate hot dogs and chips. Sally—who instantly became my hero when she arrived with two boxes of wine—was the life of the party, infecting everyone with her boisterous energy and laughter. It was fun to watch this plump, middle-aged ex-socialite wearing a leopard-print sundress chase the kids across the park with a squirt gun as they squealed and fired back at her. As the sun went down and a cool breeze rippled off the water, the laughter quieted down, and the kids began to yawn. Jim pulled the kayaks and boards back into the shop. I moved to the box of white plonk, filling up my cup when Wayne leaned over. "You driving, Donovan?"

"We all are, aren't we?"

"Well, Sally's not. Your boyfriend hasn't had much to drink, and I've switched over to Coke."

"Good for you. I'm not the one who brought two boxes of wine."

"Doesn't mean you have to drink it all in one day. Just sayin'."

"Thanks for the tip, Wayne," I said, taking a gulp of the wine and flinging the rest into the dead, yellow grass by the picnic table. Chucking the cup into the garbage, I marched toward the washroom just as Sally was exiting.

She stopped me and gestured down the slope to where Jim was hosing down the equipment, his back to us. "Good going snagging the hunk," she said, and giggled. "You could bounce a quarter off that ass."

I laughed. "Thanks, Sally, I'll be sure to try that later."

As I entered the washroom, I heard her call out. "Who's going to help me drink all this wine? Wayne?"

"I'm *driving*, darling."

Hoping that he was watching me, I raised my arm over-head and extended my middle finger.

The following day, *Zyborg Apocalypse* was in full swing, wrap-ping up a night shoot in the grittiest alleys of the Downtown Eastside. The alley between Hastings and Cordova was barricaded and I was on creep detail. That evening, every-one—except Haley's diehard teenage fans—looked off. Greasy, homeless trench coat guy? Check. Beady-eyed, wifebeater-wearing dude? Check. Obese woman obses-sively checking her phone and looking up into the sky? You never know.

On a wooden telephone pole to my right, someone had jabbed three used hypes, blood coagulating over the needles. But what drew my attention was the Missing Person poster below. Old and tattered, it showed a brunette teen with dark eyes. AMBER SEBASTIAN, First Nations from the Mission area, last seen in Downtown Eastside on August 4, 2000. D.O.B. 12/09/85, Height: 5'4", Weight: 112 lbs.

Listed at the bottom were numbers for the police and the Missing Children's Society.

Using my phone, I logged onto the MCS website and located Amber Sebastian's profile. There was also a digitally aged photo of what she might look like now: a little heavier, with downcast eyes.

The profile stated that Amber had hitchhiked into town to search for her mother in the DTES. Witnesses had seen her talking to people on the streets prior to her disappearance.

Amber was thought to have possibly been a victim of infamous serial killer Robert Pickton, who was respon-sible for the deaths of up to fifty women in the Downtown Eastside. But during the largest murder investigation on

Canadian soil, none of Amber's DNA was ever found on the kill site of his Coquitlam pig farm.

She disappeared twenty years ago, at the age of fifteen. Not a trace.

After pulling up a photo of Emily on my phone, I looked up at the poster of Amber Sebastian again. Then back to Emily. With their features, smiles, and long, dark hair, they could have been sisters. My head spun.

"Is *that* her?" someone said from behind the barricade. I looked up at the crowd. An excited murmur rippled through the fans as they raised their phones. I turned to see Kiersten McKay exit the makeup trailer, wearing a tattered singlet, her face and chest covered in fake blood and zombie goo.

One fan lowered his binoculars in disappointment. "It's only her stunt double."

Twenty feet beyond the crowd, in the shadow of a flop-house hotel stood a lone figure. Pink light from a neon sign around the corner illuminated his glasses and moustache.

The suspect from the sketch.

Filming me with his phone.

I moved forward, steady, as though trying to keep from spooking a wild animal. The suspect backed up a few paces, still filming, then suddenly turned and bolted down the alley toward Hastings Street.

After leg-scissoring the barricade, I pushed through the crowd. The suspect darted onto Hastings, where he zig-zagged across the busy thoroughfare, nearly getting hit by a motorcycle, before pirouetting out of the path of a city bus. Horns blared.

I used the pause in traffic to sprint across the street. The suspect booked it up the sidewalk and veered into another alley. Each time I'd arrive at where he'd just been, I'd see him tear down another street, another alley.

Two more turns and I emerged smack in the middle of a night market, with vendors, food stalls, and hundreds of people milling everywhere. Firecrackers exploded nearby. Dogs barked.

I turned around and around until I grew dizzy. The suspect was gone.

CHAPTER 29

AFTER GETTING HALEY BACK TO HER HOTEL, I made it home just past four. I opened a bottle and filled a glass, then took the glass and the bottle out onto the balcony and sat down, looking out over the dark treetops of the park. Eclipse followed me and jumped into my lap.

The suspect had outrun me, plain and simple. My ego could accept that some people were faster than me, but realistically there weren't many. The average person just didn't move with that kind of athleticism. I thought of all the male runners I knew on the local scene, but no faces drew a match. I finished the wine and lugged Eclipse back inside.

The remainder of the bottle fuelled an online search of the top finishers in local marathons, full and half, noting names of men who had times that would beat or rival mine. I did the same for other local cross-country races.

I placed the suspect sketch beside the computer, then penciled in a light beard. Then I pulled up photos of the names I had jotted down. Most high-caliber male runners had lean faces, to the point of being gaunt. Some had chiseled jawlines. The suspect had a narrow face and resembled none of them.

Maybe he was simply fit and fast. A serial killer wouldn't get his kicks from winning races, although some methodical murderers were known to keep themselves in immaculate physical condition, part of the classic narcissist profile.

The bottle of wine disappeared as gray light filtered into the room. I pulled up the Missing Children's Society site and went back to Amber Sebastian's photo, then Emily's. I couldn't get their physical similarities out of my head. I printed off Amber's photo, then began scrolling over the hundreds of missing children and teens who had disappeared over the past several decades. All those smiling, innocent faces, girls and boys of all ages. It was overwhelming, sickening. All those kids with mothers and fathers and sisters and brothers and friends, people for whom life was on perpetual pause, waiting for that phone call or knock that might allow some bitter closure in their forever tainted lives.

"I am so done with this shit," I muttered.

And then I came across Sarah Downie.

A petite, smiling, fifteen-year-old brunette, Sarah had last been seen hitchhiking on the Fraser Highway in Surrey in 2000. If you visually subtracted the eyebrow and nose rings and the heavy eyeliner, she bore more than a passing resemblance to Emily and Amber. After studying her face for a long time, I hit print.

I kept scrolling. The faces kept coming. Too many. It reminded me of the depressing statistical truth that the majority of these children were *never* going to be found. Just as I began to get weary and despondent, it occurred to me that these kids stayed lost due to lack of leads.

I had one.

I'd chased him last night.

I kept scanning down the faces of the missing, nearly skipping past Brittney Vogel's profile, because at the time of her disappearance in 2006, she could've passed for thirteen instead of her sixteen years. Homeless, she was last seen at a tent city in Haney. Another tiny thing, the girl stood five-nothing and weighed 98 pounds. But she had dark hair and eyes and was the right age for our man. Print.

I hung the printed photos on the wall in order of their disappearance. Sarah, Amber, Brittney, Emily. Standing back, I saw four pretty, smiling pixies that could easily have been related.

I found a large map of the Lower Mainland and tacked it to the wall beside the photos. I pressed coloured pins where the girls had last been seen. Sarah—Surrey. Amber—Downtown Eastside. Brittney—Haney. Emily—South Van. I stood back, waiting for a pattern to present itself. It didn't.

My phone chirped. Jim:

Sleep well, babe?

Babe? Were we at *babe* already? Is anyone *ever* ready to be called babe? I smiled.

Then I looked at the empty bottle, and at my project on the wall. The kitchen clock said 8:42 a.m. What the hell was I doing? I could feel the obsession building, taking on a life of its own, like a separate entity within me. The pills in the bathroom would fix that. Problem is, the obsession *was* my fix.

I texted back:

busy night...BABE

A moment later he texted back:

lol how bout today?
Me: **crazy busy**
Jim: **Tonight? I'll make it worth your while.**
Me: **you better!**

I took a photo of the other photos lined up on the wall, then attached it to an email I sent both to Wendy Silverman at MCS, asking if anyone had ever linked Emily's disappearance with the other three girls—and if it would be possible for me to have a peek at their files.

After some deliberation, I sent the same email—minus the file request—to Inspector Davis. Due to the strong possibility he'd delete it, I cc'd Fiona Saddy in the email.

I stood and stretched, then brewed a pot of coffee and hardboiled some eggs.

Fifteen minutes later, my phone buzzed. Wendy was in top form: she'd attached the files on the three other girls, informing me that to her knowledge no one had ever linked the cases together. She asked me if I had any new evidence to support this.

I typed back: **Just a hunch.** A few moments later, she sent another email. **That's better than nothing, which is all we have on those particular files. Keep me posted.**

Looking at the list of file attachments, I noticed Brittney Vogel's had an AVI video file link. I opened hers first. I clicked it and saw grainy CCTV footage of Brittney in front of an ATM. Both her brows were pierced, along with her nose and her black-painted lips. It took her a minute and twelve seconds to withdraw five hundred dollars from the machine.

My heart began to race.

I skimmed the file. According to her mother, who had deposited the money the day before, she initially believed

Brittney withdrew the money to score drugs. It wasn't until a week later, upon visiting the tent city in Haney, that she learned that no one had seen her daughter in over a week. It was then that the police were contacted, and the footage was obtained from a convenience store camera.

Replaying the footage again, I watched Brittney blink slowly and seem to look into the camera.

Dead eyes.

Same as Emily Pike.

CHAPTER 30

INSPECTOR DAVIS DIDN'T SEEM HAPPY TO SEE me. Then again, he never looked happy about anything, certainly not the mess of files and paperwork spread around his desk. There were photos of at least a dozen children and teens of various ages pinned to the left wall of his partition. Some were school photos, others showed them smiling and playing. One of the girls on the wall had been all over the news for months last year; a blonde teenager named Kaylee Green, who had gone missing while walking home from a public pool in East Vancouver. I recognized several other photos from last night's study of the MCS database. In the next cubicle, Fiona Saddy took notes while on the phone. She glanced up at me.

"You got two minutes," Davis said.

"I believe the suspect showed up to where I was working last night. I chased him, but he got away."

Davis sighed, rubbed behind his ear, and flipped open a black notebook on his desk. "This would be the suspect identified by Deidre Maxwell?"

"Correct. I—"

"A few days ago, I paid a visit to Ms. Maxwell," he said, not looking up from a form he was reading. "She's a stoner. No judge I've ever met would consider her a credible witness."

"Maybe you didn't hear me. I *chased* the suspect."

"And where was this?"

"Downtown Eastside. Main and Hastings area. He lost me at the night market."

He raised an eyebrow. "Approach nearly anyone on skid row and they're gonna get squirrely."

"This guy was different—and he was filming me with his phone."

"Why? You're off the case, aren't you?"

"Maybe he doesn't know that," I said, my voice rising. A few cops in the bullpen looked up, eavesdropping. They'd all have a good laugh once I left.

Fuck them.

I leaned over his desk and lowered my voice. "Look, did you get the email I sent you?"

"Yeah." He still didn't look up. I wanted to sweep all the shit off his desk, grab him by the tie, and choke him until he listened.

Reaching into my satchel, I came out with more photos of the four missing girls. One by one I placed them in a row, face up atop the work on his desk.

"All of them disappeared from the Lower Mainland, same age, same looks, same body type."

Inspector Davis stopped what he was doing, looked up at me, then down at the photos. He took his time, giving each one care and attention, and I caught a flicker of sadness in his eyes. When he looked up at me again, I watched the sadness in his gray eyes solidify back to cold concrete. "I am familiar with each and every individual in that database, and I do not see a pattern here. If Emily Pike had been overweight and fair, you would have printed off a stack of heavy blondes who'd disappeared over the past twenty years, 'cause there's just as many of them. Lot of kids go missing in this country every year. Most of the runaways get found, but the others rarely do. That's the unfortunate fact of policing around the world."

"Wow, that mantra must really pep you up in the morning."

"Works better for me than the booze I can smell on your breath."

I felt my cheeks flame. Fiona Saddy made eye contact with me and immediately looked away.

I handed Davis a red USB drive.

"What's this?"

"The last thing I'll ever ask from you, Davis."

He sighed and inserted the drive into his computer. Fiona Saddy stood and craned her neck to see. Sausage-like fingers fumbling with the mouse, Davis clicked on Emily's ATM video. At the right moment, I leaned over him, grabbed the mouse and paused the video on Emily's dead expression. Davis looked like he was about to smack me. From the sheets on his desk, I pulled one of Emily's smiling face and held it up for comparison.

"Check out her eyes in this video compared to her photo."

No one said anything.

Next, I clicked on Brittney's video. Hit pause. Side by side with Emily, they shared the same dead eyes. I pulled the photo of her in better days: a happy and smiling young teen.

"Same same," I said. "These girls were about to disappear from the face of the earth, and look at their expressions."

"Brittney Vogel had a history of drug use. We go for a walk on the Eastside and I'll show you a hundred hypes with eyes like that."

"Emily was different. She didn't use."

"Says her scam-artist mother. Her boyfriend had gang ties and has been busted for possession." He gestured to the paused video. "My theory is that the girl had a fight with what's his name ... Oscar, so she went and got fucked up, then needed money for more. She went to a machine in a shitty area of town. Someone took advantage of her. Maybe she OD'd in some crack shack out there—"

Agitation building, I stepped back and folded my arms. "Her body would have been found, and you know it. C'mon, Inspector, these girls' disappearances were not accidental *or* crimes of opportunity. I believe they were chosen and followed, and were either unwittingly given drugs or had drugs forced upon them."

Davis leaned back in his chair. "What I *know* is that these videos are many years apart and all they show are two stoned-looking girls withdrawing money from ATMs. No one else appears on camera. Not only is it not enough, it's not *anything.*"

Around us, the station buzzed with the ringing of phones, the murmur of voices, and the clack of fingers pecking out reports on out-of-date keyboards.

Fiona cleared her throat. "What about Renay Burris?"

Davis frowned. "Who's that? Not a missing person?"

"*Attempted* abduction in Mission. Some years back." Fiona sat back at her computer and typed in the name. A few seconds later, she nodded her head and read, "In twenty-fifteen, Renay was walking home from a party when two men in a dark SUV pulled up and tried to take her. Witnesses said that they interrupted these guys as they were trying to lift an unconscious girl into the vehicle. The wits yelled and the men dropped her onto the street, jumped in their vehicle and sped off. Wits were too far away to get a plate."

"Any descriptions of the men?" I asked.

"One was bigger than the other," she said. "Both wore dark clothes and had dark hair, and at least one of them wore latex gloves. Residue was found on Renay's skin."

"And this was in Mission?" I said.

"Just outside."

Davis looked annoyed. "Mission is R.C.M.P. jurisdiction. How is this relevant?"

She turned her computer screen, giving us a view of a dark-haired girl wearing too much eyeliner. My breath caught in my throat. Saddy's eyes went from me to Davis. "Because she's a skinny little thing, like the others," she said. "I remembered because I happened to be up there doing a prisoner drop-off the day she came in with her grandmother to make a statement. I overheard the cops say it was a waste of time, because she didn't even remember enough to corroborate the witness statements."

"Probably blocked it out," Davis said. "Classic PTSD."

"Maybe," she said, reading on, "but her tox report also showed a weird drug in her system, a rare version of scopolamine."

"My ex-wife used to take it for motion sickness," he said.

"Probably not *this* brand," she said. "It originates in Colombia and down there they call it Devil's Breath."

"Never heard of it," he said. "Maybe she took it at the party she came from."

"She claims she only had a few drinks," she said. "She was on antidepressants and she said she left the party early because she was feeling sick."

"Someone probably slipped it into her drink," he said.

Something clicked in my head. "Colombia. Travis Benoit has ties to Colombia. One of Emily's friends said Emily saw something at the Benoit ranch a month before she disappeared. There's a biker clubhouse in Mission. What if the girls were all given this drug—"

"I think maybe *you're* on something. You come in here babbling about a pattern, but there's no pattern, just a bunch of girls who look vaguely similar."

I reached over and pulled the USB from his computer, in the process knocking some files on the floor. He flashed me a warning—a *don't-make-me-take-this-shit-to-the-next-level* look. "I'm actually surprised Maddy Pike fired you. You seem like two peas in a—"

"I quit the case."

"Right. Then what you're doing is actually illegal. This is *police* business, and your little crackerjack P.I. license doesn't mean shit. Now get out of here while I'm still in a good mood."

CHAPTER 31

SPEEDING EAST ON HIGHWAY 1 TOWARD Mission, I called Kai to inquire about Devil's Breath.

"It's called that," he said, "because it supposedly steals your soul—temporarily, at least."

"Lovely. Ever hear of anyone using it up here?"

"It's one of those urban legend-type drugs. I've never heard of it up here, but with the shit on the street these days, anything is possible. In Colombia, apparently it's more common for women to use it on men in clubs. They mix it in his drink or give him a bump of what he thinks is blow ... next thing he knows, he wakes up naked in a Bogotá gutter, robbed blind. Stuff completely kills your free will and wipes your memory at the same time."

"Like Rohypnol?"

"No. Roofies make people seem drunk. To outsiders, Devil's Breath makes them seem *normal* and lucid, while they're withdrawing money and handing it over to the people who did it to them."

"How come you know so much about it?"

"It's a big, bad world and I've got an inquisitive mind."

"Travis Benoit's got the Colombian pipeline. Think he could be the one bringing Devil's Breath into the country?"

"I'm not *that* inquisitive."

"Fair enough. Did you look over the photos that I sent you?"

"I've never seen any of them before, although they all look a little like Emily."

"I'm glad someone thinks so."

Renay Burris didn't look like Emily. At least not anymore. Unrecognizable from the photo Fiona had shown me, the new Renay sitting before me was not merely big, but obese. At just over five feet, she had to be at least two-hundred-and-fifty pounds. She wore black tights under a black dress. Her dull, brown eyes were made duller by the gold crucifix around her neck, which she kept touching as though afraid it might vanish at any moment.

Her living room window overlooked a tiny backyard with a chain-link fence and train tracks beyond. Flickering glimpses of the churning, gray waters of the Fraser River could be seen between gaps in the graffiti-covered railcars steadily chugging by.

An oscillating fan in the corner pushed warm, stale air around the wood-paneled room. Ida Burris, Renay's stooped but spry grandmother kept scuttling into the room to refresh our drinks and deliver more chocolate chip cookies. I quietly munched on one, the first food I'd had all day. Cookie crumbs fell to the floor and suddenly a fat, black dachshund was at my feet, gobbling them up.

"Pepper, *no!*" Renay shouted from her position on the La-Z-Boy recliner. "Nana, he's going to get sick again!"

"Maybe if you didn't keep dropping food all over," the old lady said. She leaned down, grabbed Pepper by his collar, and dragged him toward the kitchen.

"Sorry," I said. After Ida left the room, I pulled out the suspect sketch and showed it to Renay. "Aside from the news recently, have you ever seen this man before?"

"You mean that night?"

"Or the days or weeks leading up to it. Do you remember anyone strange hanging around? Anyone who may have followed you, gotten to know your habits?"

Renay took a bite of another cookie. I watched crumbs fall to her chest, roll past the crucifix, and disappear into the bosom of her dress. "I don't think so. Everything was a bit foggy back then, and that night I was really out of it. I had a few drinks and blacked out."

The old lady appeared in the doorway, Pepper in her arms. "The drinks went straight to her head because of the medications she was on."

Renay rolled her eyes. "That's not what she's asking, Nana."

"But it's pertinent," Ida said. "Irresponsible drinking leads to repercussions, it's just that simple."

"Whatever."

I rubbed my eyes. There was an artificial air freshener smell in the room, and I could feel a headache coming on. I asked, "Do you remember if the men drove up to you that night, or if they were already parked there?"

She stopped chewing her cookie for several seconds and her facial muscles tightened. "I don't know."

Ida stroked Pepper. "They say blackouts from drinking can cause irreparable brain damage."

"Renay," I said, "do you feel like going for a walk, getting some air?"

"The air quality is atrocious today," Ida said.

I kept my eyes on Renay, who was chewing her lower lip. "Renay?"

She looked up.

"Just a short one," I said.

"What for?" Ida said.

"I'm not familiar with your town," I said. "I thought your granddaughter could give me a little tour."

Renay nodded.

"Make sure you wear your face mask," Ida said, "or your asthma will put you back in the hospital."

After we were out of sight of the house, Renay removed her mask.

"Your grandma cares a lot about you," I said.

She laughed. "She's a hypochondriac who drives me nuts. But she's too old to change." She looked down the street in the direction of the river. "Where do you want to go?"

I opened the door of my Jeep. "Let's just see where the road takes us."

Driving through town felt like stepping back in time forty years. Highlights of the main drag consisted of tattoo parlours, pawnshops, and greasy spoons. The gun store appeared to be the only thriving enterprise on the strip.

We cruised around and Renay pointed out the bell tower of the Benedictine Monastery in the distance, informing me that she and her grandma sometimes went there for services. When she asked me if I believed in God, I stayed silent, thinking of the best way to respond.

"It's OK if you don't," she said. "I have days where I don't know what I believe in."

"I don't know either," I said. "I think it's good that people can take comfort in something out there."

"But you can't?"

I smiled. "Ever since I was a kid, people told me I was wound too tight. Comfort has never been something I've sought out, I guess. I do like big, old churches though. I went on a trip to Italy once, and some of those thousand-year-old cathedrals made me feel *something*. Reverence, maybe. I've felt the same thing in nature, too."

Renay smiled. "Maybe it's God."

"Maybe."

After looping back onto the Lougheed, we passed Rocko's 24-Hour Diner, which, she assured me, had "the best milkshakes in the world".

"Want one? My treat."

She shook her head. "For years, food has been my drug of choice, so I'm trying to cut back. Plus, some of the meds I'm on keep me fat," she said. "You're so lucky to be skinny. You probably don't have any bad habits, do you?"

"I've been known to carry a few monkeys around," I said. "I take pills too. Sometimes."

"Have you ever seen a shrink?"

I smiled. "By the time I was your age, I think my mother had sent me to every psych doctor on Vancouver Island."

Renay seemed impressed. *"Seriously?"*

"Yup."

"How did you get better?"

Nearly unable to restrain my laughter, I said, "I just keep faking it till one day I hopefully make it."

She paused and nodded. "Must be cool to drive a Jeep. One of my shrinks saw to it that they took away my license."

"Why was that?"

"Call of the void," she said. "Have you ever stood somewhere really high and felt a weird impulse to jump, like something was pulling you over the edge?"

I remained silent.

"It's not the same as suicidal thoughts," she said, "but it's actually really common. Some people get it when they're standing on a bridge. I used to get mine when I was driving; I'd get a sudden thought of steering into oncoming traffic. But I didn't actually want to *do* it; I didn't want to kill myself. But the doctor said that that, combined with my PTSD and the meds, meant I shouldn't be allowed behind the wheel. Believe me, once something like that goes on your record, it stays there; people will never trust you again."

I pulled over and killed the engine.

Renay looked confused.

Handing her the keys, I said, "I trust you."

"But ... I don't have my license."

"I won't tell anyone if you won't."

She looked at the keys, a slow smile transforming her features.

For the first five minutes, Renay drove slowly and in silence, both hands clamped firmly on the wheel. "How's it feel?" I asked.

"Super cool."

"You look good behind the wheel," I said. "I feel safe. Do you?"

"Mmm, so-so. But thanks for doing this."

"No problem."

A few minutes later Renay pointed out a homeless encampment beneath the Murray Street Bridge. As we passed, an emaciated woman wearing a halter top and red track pants stood with her thumb out, fixing us with a jittery stare.

"You have a lot of this in the city, huh?" she asked.

"All over," I said.

"I think if people stopped doing terrible things to each other, then other people wouldn't be in such pain, and wouldn't have to live like that."

"Do unto others ..."

Renay gave me a quick glance. "See, hang out with me for an hour and already I've got you quoting Jesus."

"God help me," I said, and we laughed.

A few minutes later, we drove past what looked like a small, nondescript warehouse surrounded by a chain-link fence. Half a dozen Harleys were parked in the gravel lot. I asked Renay if she'd ever been inside. "The biker clubhouse?" she asked. "Yeah, right."

"Never back in the day?"

She shrugged. "If I'd been invited, I'd probably have gone, who knows? Those guys are all over the place around here."

I asked if she'd ever heard of Travis or Oscar Benoit. As we stopped at a red light on the Lougheed Highway, I showed her photos of both men. She looked at them and shook her head. Just outside Mission, I told her to turn left off onto a quieter side street. Renay stiffened and looked over. "You tricked me," she said. "You didn't really want to see the sights."

"Sure, I did. But this is one I'm interested in most."

"I already told you everything I know."

"I know. But can you show me exactly where it happened?"

She drove another two blocks, pulled over, and shifted into park. After taking a deep breath, she pointed to the other side of the street. "That's where they found me. Right on the corner, by that hedge. If they'd taken me, I'd be dead now."

"But you're not. Other girls weren't so lucky."

"You're trying to find them?"

I nodded. The tall and overgrown cedar hedge loomed over the street, looking like the unkempt cousin of the one near Westborough Farm the day Emily disappeared. The houses on either side of the street looked beaten down and dilapidated, with aluminum foil-covered windows and junker automobiles rusting away on oil-stained, yellow lawns. The kind of neighbourhood where crimes tended to go unreported and witnesses stayed hidden.

Renay closed her eyes and took deep breaths. Perspiration had soaked the armpits of her dress. "I have nightmares every night," she said, "that they're going to come back and find me."

I reached over and turned off the ignition. "They won't," I said, opening my door and stepping onto the street. A moment later, she did the same.

"I know that," she said. "Because I'm fat now. One of my shrinks said that I gained all this weight as a defense mechanism, that deep down I want to make myself ugly."

"They didn't say that."

"Not those exact words, but she was right ... if I'd looked like this back then, they wouldn't have tried to grab me. Pretty much the only benefit to being super fat is that no one will try to abduct you."

"There are probably easier ways to avoid abduction," I suggested.

"Like not getting wasted and walking down a sketchy street in the middle of the night?"

"That would be one."

We stood in the spot where it happened.

"I used to take this route to school all the time," she said, "back when I lived just down the road. A lot of kids use this as a shortcut, 'cause there's not much traffic."

"What do you remember about that night?"

She paused and frowned. "I don't know if what I'm remembering is real. They told me that when you have trauma and black out, you can get, like, flashbacks later ... but it might just be your mind making up stuff to deal with what happened."

"That makes sense," I said.

"I was walking down this hill. I always walked on the right side. I think they drove up from behind me and pulled over up ahead—right here, and when I passed the passenger window, they talked to me and offered to give me a ride. I don't know. I don't know if it's all just my imagination. My head is messed up."

"It's OK," I said. "Just tell me everything that comes to you. There's no right or wrong."

"I'm sure I said no to the ride, because back then I lived just around the corner."

"Then what happened?"

"I think they offered me a beer. At first I said no, but then I heard a can open, and I know it's really stupid, but I think I took a drink. That's when everything got really hazy, like I was about to pass out. But before I went under, I remember one of them said something—I think it was the driver."

"What was it?"

"I thought I heard him say, 'My wife could use a friend like you'."

"Anything else?"

"That's it. I never told this to the police, because back then it was all a black hole. Even now, I don't know if any of what I just told you was real or if it was just my imagination. Some days I feel like I'm going crazy, that none of this is real. That they killed me that night and I'm not even alive right now. That I followed the call of the void, and I'm there now."

Driving home over the Port Mann was slow going due to traffic. I replayed the conversation with Renay.

Devil's Breath. Two men. A dark SUV.

My wife could use a friend like you.

Wife? What did that mean? Most serial killers were unmarried. Unless his wife was dead, and he sought to add another body to the hole in his backyard. There was also a good chance that Renay's theory was valid, that she had dreamt up the whole scenario, her psyche's way of rewriting the script into something that made sense.

Except it didn't.

CHAPTER 32

WHEN SADIE ANSWERED THE DOOR, ALL DARK hair and eyes, I felt my heart stop. My mind flashed a montage of all the missing girls.

"You look tired," she said.

"Thanks a *lot*," I said, handing her a bottle. "I brought you a root beer."

"Thanks!" She took me by the hand and led me into the house.

Jim smiled as he sipped his beer and flipped burgers on the backyard grill. Sadie and I tossed a Frisbee in the small backyard.

Sadie aimed with great care, then launched the Frisbee far to my left, where it sailed toward the top of a wooden fence separating the properties. I sprinted, leapt high, and snared it. Jim clapped and I took a bow.

"Take it easy on her, Sadie," he said. "She's almost as old as your old dad."

"Hey," I warned, giving her an easy toss. She caught it, fumbled, and dropped it. Then for the next fifteen minutes she had me running back and forth across the backyard like a whippet. "Sloane's *way* faster than you, dad," she said.

Sadie and I sat across from Jim at the picnic table and we ate burgers and corn on the cob, and had lime popsicles for dessert. I was somewhere into my second beer, and a happy warmth flickered in my chest and spread through my limbs. From time to time, Jim's eyes lingered on mine as his bare foot played with mine beneath the table.

Apropos of nothing, Sadie asked me why I didn't have any kids.

"Sadie, c'mon," Jim said.

"I have a cat named Eclipse."

"Does he like kids? Can I come see him sometime?"

"Of course," I said. "I'll have you guys over next time."

"Do you have any brothers and sisters?"

A faint scream echoed in a deep corridor of my mind. I shook my head. *Not anymore*, I thought.

"OK," Jim said, "time to get ready for bed."

"I still have a half-hour," Sadie whined.

"Whining reduces the prisoner's time in the yard," he said. "C'mon, kid, help me with these plates."

"Sloane promised me she'd read me a story," Sadie said, shooting me a quick look that said, *just play along*.

In the bathroom, I popped an Ativan. My heart pounded double-time, my head spun, and it felt like I was leaving my body. Every time I blinked, a sickening image came: Emily's mutilated corpse in a shallow grave, maggots crawling from her eye sockets. A Winnebago in the woods. Blood in the snow. My sister dying as she read her two dead children a final story in bed. Sadie being yanked into the rear door of a van.

I sat on the toilet for a long time with my head in my hands. I took another Ativan, then stood and opened the door.

Sadie stood there, dressed in her pyjamas.

I can't do this, I thought. *I'm not ready.*

* * *

I awoke to Jim gently shaking me. Sadie snored softly beside me. I set the dog-eared copy of *The Little Prince* aside and eased out from her small bed. Jim leaned down to tuck in his daughter and gave her a kiss.

He grabbed two beers and we sat on lounge chairs on in the backyard. The night felt as warm as the day. The sky was still and dark, the moon and stars shrouded. The city lights teased from beyond the crest of Mount Pleasant.

"You look like you've seen some shit today," he commented.

I took a pull of beer. "Let's just say I'm glad you're not a cop, and that we don't live in Mission."

He laughed. "Too much of a stoner growing up to ever think of becoming a cop. And Mission? I could never live anywhere that isn't near the ocean."

Raising my bottle, I said, "I'll drink to that."

Jim raised his, and we drank. The beer felt good on my throat.

"Sadie really likes you," he said. "She talks about you all the time."

"She's an awesome kid, but she doesn't know me that well."

He pulled his chair over so that he faced me. His eyes seemed to glow under the dim light. He leaned forward, took my right foot, and began to massage it. I smiled, closed my eyes, and tilted my head back.

"True enough," he said. "You could simply be winning by default. I haven't really dated much since the breakup, and even though I know it's poor form to slag your exes, her mom's a bona fide psycho."

You should have seen me in your bathroom an hour ago.

I killed the last of my beer and opened my eyes sleepily. "I'll take what I can get."

He nodded to my empty bottle. "Guess this means you're sleeping over."

"I didn't detect a question mark at the end of that sentence."

"What can I say, I like having a bodyguard in my bed."

"Not a bodyguard currently. Haley's out of town, so I'm temporarily off duty."

"What are you working on right now?" he asked. "Or is that top secret?"

I'm trying to track down a phantom who is making young girls disappear.

"Go grab me another beer," I said, "and I'll tell you all kinds of sordid secrets."

Jim kissed me and went into the house. I smiled and looked out at the city. For a moment I felt a warm comfort, something approaching peace. Then I closed my eyes. The peace dissolved as one by one, the faces of the girls returned, and I knew that there wasn't enough booze or pills in the world that would make them go away for good.

CHAPTER 33

DRIVING THROUGH THE METHANE STINK OF Fraser Valley farmland, my phone buzzed. It was Wayne checking in to tell me about an insurance fraud case that needed some legwork. I made the mistake of telling him where I was.

"Your boyfriend taking you out on a date to milk cows?" he asked.

"I'm following up on something."

"Amber Sebastian."

"Need to talk to the mother," I said, glancing to a pasture on the right, where a dozen horses grazed. My mind flashed to Westborough Farm, to photos of Emily on horseback. Moments later, the tires of my Jeep hummed across the bridge spanning the Nicomen Slough.

"How many other parents have you talked to?" he asked.

"None. But yesterday I spoke with a girl named Renay Burris, who was nearly abducted after being drugged with something called Devil's Breath."

"How'd you come by her?"

"The cops," I said.

"Wow, I can't believe you're getting friendly with them all of a sudden."

"I wouldn't go that far. But even Kai thought the whole Devil's Breath angle was pretty heavy."

"Oh, *Kai's* advising you now? Little prick's too good to help me with some legitimate computer hacking but he has all the time in the world to give you the lowdown on an obscure drug?"

"I think he's out to atone for past crimes, not get cajoled into committing more. Anyway—"

"Anyway, Amber Sebastian's been gone twenty years," he said. "Plus, she's First Nations, *and* she was hanging out on the Downtown Eastside when Pig Man Pickton was running large."

"Her DNA was never found at his farm."

"None of the other girls on your list were First Nations."

"But Amber *looked* like them," I said. "Or they looked like Amber. Her father was white anyhow."

"Fuck sakes, just do this thing and get your ass back to the city. The Valley gives me the willies. People go missing out there all the time; an over-inquisitive ginger P.I. would be no exception."

Turning onto Taylor Road, I forced myself to slow down before I drove into a ditch. I cursed myself for not taking my meds this morning. Inconsistency with the pills threw my system into a tailspin that was almost worse than not taking them at all. Then there were the two Ativan and the booze from the previous day: not exactly a recipe for success. I promised myself no drinking that night. No drinking the whole weekend. Do what I came here to do, go home.

Simple. Maybe when I got back, I'd go for a run, then pop in and see Jim. Surprise him and take him out to dinner.

Jesus, what was happening? I thought of how good it felt to cuddle up with Sadie and read her a story. My heart swelled as I pictured the three of us together, along with some sort of future.

A family.

My sister dead in bed with her two blue-faced angels.

A horn blared. I woke, eyes snapping wide as I swerved out of the path of an oncoming pickup. My Jeep fishtailed, nearly going off the road. Tires spitting gravel, I regained control and pulled over.

A tiny voice told me to turn around, go home, get a life, shoot for stability, find some sort of contentment, however mundane that might seem. I entertained that notion for about three seconds. Then I saw the two teenage girls several hundred yards up the road. They were slim, fifteen at most, with long, tanned legs and wearing jean cut-offs and T-shirts.

A sedan passed me from behind and slowed down for the girls.

They smiled and stuck out their thumbs. One was slightly taller, cockier. The front of her shirt was bunched up and tied off to reveal her abdomen. Her cut-offs rode low on her hips. The car slowed and the passenger window lowered.

I rolled my Jeep up right behind the car and hit the horn. The driver jumped in his seat before peeling away from the curb, arm and middle finger extended out the window. The girls looked wary as I drove forward.

"Where you guys off to today?" I asked.

"Van," the cocky girl answered.

"Long way away," I said. "What's in Vancouver?"

"What's it to you?" Cocky asked.

"You know hitching's illegal, right?"

The girls snickered. "You a cop?" Cocky asked.

"Do I look like a cop?"

"Pretty dope undercover ride if you are."

"Tell you what? I'm out here to talk to someone, but I'll give you a ride to the city after. Hop in."

They looked at each other and exchanged a *why not* expression. Cocky rode shotgun and her friend climbed in the back. I started driving. During introductions, I discovered their names were Tanya and Ashley, or Tan and Ash. Tan was the cocky one. I told them I was going to see Dee-Dee Sebastian and was informed by Ash that Dee-Dee was her auntie.

Reaching into the file I kept in the door panel, I slid out a photo of Amber.

"My cousin," Ash said. "I never met her."

"You're too young," I said. "She went missing before you were born. Tan, could you reach into my bag on the floor there? In a yellow file folder is a stack of sketches. At the bottom they say: *If you see this man, call Crimestoppers.* Yeah, those ones. Take one out and give it a good look."

She did, and Ash leaned over the seat. I asked if they'd ever seen the man before and they said no.

"Looks like a nerd," Tan said.

"I agree, but he's the guy who took Amber when she was your age."

"We're only thirteen," Ash said.

Tan glared back at her. "*Sixteen,*" she corrected.

"Doesn't matter," I said, "'cause when this nerd pulls up, he's not going to ask to see your ID."

"Amber disappeared from skid row," Tan said. "Not out here."

"You two nearly got in some stranger's car a few minutes ago. It could have just as easily been the nerd in the sketch. You'd never know. Maybe he gives you a drink of something, and next thing you know, you wake up somewhere else. Or maybe you don't even wake up."

Tan looked at me. Cockiness stripped, she suddenly appeared thirteen, maybe less.

"Where do you think the girls end up?" I asked. "I say *girls* because Amber is just one of a series. Where do you think he takes them? If he buried them, it would have to be a long way away, because bodies eventually have a way of being found. But the fact is that most killers are lazy; they tend to toss their victims in a ditch or rock quarry. Or the bodies are found in the bush a hundred yards from the road. Turns out, dead people—even small women—are tricky to move around."

"Maybe he takes them to his house," Ash volunteered.

I nodded. "Maybe, but unless he lives someplace remote, he runs the risk of being seen bringing the victim inside. And the reality is: after you rape, torture, and kill someone, once again you've got that body to contend with. In a very short time, bodies begin to stink. You don't even *know* how bad they stink. But let's say he kills them at his house, after he does all the sick shit he wants, does he bury them in the back-yard? Run their bodies through a woodchipper? Feed them to the hogs out back?"

"Like that Pickton guy," Tan said, "who fed all those women to the pigs on his farm."

"He gutted them and cut up the bodies," I said. My tires squealed as I took a tight corner. "Some went to the pigs, and a lot of the guts went to an animal rendering plant."

In the rearview, Ash's face had gone the colour of her name.

"Those women were hookers," Tan said. "That's why they got killed."

"They got killed because they had their thumbs out and climbed into a stranger's car."

I spotted a rusty mailbox stenciled with the word SEBASTIAN and turned right up a gravel driveway. A small house with an attached cabin-like structure came into view. I parked beside a yellow Datsun pickup. We piled out. Tan pulled the knot from the front of her T-shirt, and suddenly she was a kid again. "Don't tell Dee-Dee we were hitching," she whispered.

A short and plump First Nations woman limped around the side of the house. She wore gardening gloves and her long, black-and-silver ponytail emerged from the opening in the back of a Blue Jays ball cap. An old black Lab ambled up to her side, a red bandana around its neck.

I removed my sunglasses. "I'm Sloane Donovan. We spoke earlier. I've recruited Tan and Ash as assistants."

"Probably 'cause these dummies were out hitchin' again," Dee-Dee Sebastian said, frowning at them. She took the glove from her right hand and when we shook hands, I saw the scars on the inside of her wrist and forearm.

She turned and motioned for us to follow. "Come on and have some lunch. I'm starving and you look like you need some food. You girls come help me."

Dee-Dee served tuna, pickle, tomato, and lettuce sandwiches on her small back porch. Tan and Ash took their food and ate on a small hillock thirty feet away, the dog lounging nearby.

"She was the mother, you know?" Dee-Dee said.

"Pardon me?"

"Amber. She was only fifteen, but she had to be mother to her sister and brother. Bebe was ten, and Wally was eight at the time. I would be gone weeks and months at a time, and she knew that if she didn't take care of them, they'd go to foster care. I came out of that system, and my parents came out of the residential schools. Amber always said that she'd be the first generation to break the cycle. Every time I'd relapse, that girl would prop me back up. 'Mom, where are you? I'm coming to get you. You're going to beat this.'"

She looked at the girls chatting on the hillock. "Ray—that's Amber's dad—killed a guy outside a bar and ended up in Mountain Institution. Before she went missing, Amber used to hitch out and visit him, bring him presents."

Mountain. I'd read something about that in the morning in Amber's file. "He died in prison, right?"

She nodded. "O.D. Six months after Amber disappeared. When Ray heard the news, he couldn't handle it. Those prison shit-mixes… It's worse than what's on the street. I always had a feeling that the only way Ray would make it out was in a box."

"Did Amber use?"

"With me being the world's worst junkie mom?" she asked, giving a gravelly chuckle. "She used to say that drug dealers should get the death penalty. You've seen her file; you know she'd never been in trouble with the cops. She never even missed a day of school—unless she was out looking for me."

I nodded.

"I got the same file from the cops and the Missing Children's Society," she said. "It's pretty thorough, but it doesn't explain how come Amber was heading out to look for me in the Downtown Eastside, my old stomping ground. The file doesn't mention how I hadn't been in contact with my children in over a month because I was turning tricks up in Edmonton and living with a pimp. No one knew where I was. When I finally got the news, Amber had been gone for weeks and Wally and Bebe were in foster care."

"You say she was *heading* to the Downtown Eastside," I said. "I thought that's where she was last seen."

"Witnesses had seen her down on Hastings in the days prior, but not on that particular day. Everyone assumes that's where she was headed and ended up, but people down there are unreliable. Half of them don't even know what day of the week it is. Back then, I didn't even know what *month* it was."

I pulled out the suspect sketch. She took it and studied it and shook her head. "I seen this on the news," she said. "I've never seen this goof around that I know of. Do you think Amber's disappearance has to do with the other girl?"

"I don't know," I said. "I really just came out here to tie up loose ends."

"You came out here because you're determined to find out what happened. I see it in your eyes. No one's come to talk to me about this for many years now, and I want to thank you for that."

I nodded again and asked if she had found any unusual pieces of jewelry among her daughter's possessions. Dee-Dee told me to wait, then stood and went back into the house.

On the hillock, Tan texted on her phone and Ash looked on, bored as her fingers tore hunks of grass from the earth and scattered them over the dog. My eyes burned and I closed them. I wanted a beer. I wanted this to be over. Go back to the city, pop a pill, take all the shit off my living room wall, and earn a tidy living doing insurance fraud cases, spousal surveillance, and personal security. Grow to a ripe and complacent old age, hopefully with enough brain cells remaining to tell the grandkids some doozers.

Dee-Dee stood beside me holding a shoebox, a concerned look in her eyes. "You're shaking," she said. "Are you coming down off something?"

I took a deep breath and forced a smile. "I was about to ask if you had anything stronger than iced tea."

"My house is a dry reserve," she said. "I've been clean almost since the day I came back." She sat down. "No one would take her disappearance seriously, because she was Native and had a junkie for a mother and a dad in jail. They thought she had run away from a bad home. Even most of my people had no time for me. I felt so guilty I nearly killed myself with a hot dose, but then I imagined what if she finally got back home and found me dead. It was like a moment of divine intervention. I went to a meeting, and I kept going, and I got clean. I still go to meetings at the hall. They tell me I've got to do it for myself, but every time we do the prayer I think of Amber, and I hope that she's found serenity, wherever she is."

Together we went through the contents of the shoebox: children's moccasins, beaded friendship bracelets, a Winnie-the-Pooh doll, photos of friends and family. A small picture frame showed a very young and beautiful Dee-Dee holding infant Amber in her arms.

No unusual necklaces or bracelets like those found in Emily's room. Significant time and distance separated Westborough Farm from the Fraser Valley, if in fact Amber disappeared from this area. Emily worked on a farm; Amber lived near farms. The girls shared similar looks but had completely different backgrounds. Both Wayne and Davis were right; it wasn't nearly enough to mount a serious investigation. I was wasting everyone's time and giving people reason to question my credibility.

But there was something, a fluttering sensation in my gut and a quickening of my pulse that told me I was close to uncovering something that people would kill over. Just push it a little more and something will crack and break through, and the picture will become clearer.

Or maybe I was just plain fucking delusional.

After giving Dee-Dee a stack of sketches to distribute in the area, the girls climbed back into my Jeep. Dee-Dee hugged me, then fixed me with a serious look and told me there was help available if I wanted it.

I nodded and mumbled thanks.

Back on the road, Tan asked me if I found anything.

"Nope. Where in Vancouver are you guys headed?"

The girls glanced at each other. "You can just drop us at the community centre," Tan said. "We don't really need to go to Van today."

Ten minutes later, the girls hopped out of my Jeep at the entrance of the centre. I handed each of them my card. "No more hitching," I said, "and if you ever need any help, I want you to call me right away, got it?"

Back home I stared at the wall of teenage girls and sipped from a can of Steigl Radler. Only 2.5%. Baby steps. I sat down with a yellow legal pad and jotted down three pages of notes from my conversation with Dee-Dee. I compared it against Amber's files for any discrepancies and found none. As I re-read my notes, something skittered around the edge of my mind.

I wrote the word MOUNTAIN PRISON on a card and stuck it on the wall. I located the approximate location of the prison on the map of the Lower Mainland and Fraser Valley and marked it with a red flagged pin. I stood back and looked at the map. Mountain was north of the town of Agassiz, which was only about thirty kilometres from

Dee-Dee Sebastian's home in Deroche. Ten minutes further was Mission, where the attempted abduction of Renay Burris had occurred. All of these places were located near the Lougheed Highway, which, if I traced it west, ran right past Haney and the homeless camp where Brittney Vogel was last seen. Following it further, the highway spanned the Pitt River into Port Coquitlam, before veering south, back toward the Trans-Canada Highway. *But*, if you didn't veer south, if you kept straight, where it became the #7A, you'd eventually end up on the Barnet Highway, which skirted around Port Moody and into North Burnaby, and then became Hastings Street, and only a few blocks from Travis Benoit's Capitol Hill home. It felt like a game of connect the dots, except I remembered that at the time of Amber and Emily's disappearances, Benoit didn't live in Capitol Hill. He had the ranch in Langley, which, although east of the city, was nowhere near the Lougheed. Westborough Farm was also a deviation in the trajectory. Maybe that was intentional. Maybe the man—or men—doing these crimes also had a map on the wall.

CHAPTER 34

THE NEXT MORNING, I WOKE UP AT FIVE, clear-headed, having spent a solid four hours in a dreamless void. No screams. No dead girls. While making my bed, I felt such an uncharacteristic peace that it made me feel almost guilty. Eclipse followed me to the kitchen, meowing to be fed. I smiled when I saw no empty bottles left out from the night before. Zero damage done. When I saw the blue sky out the window, I pinched myself to make sure I wasn't, in fact, dreaming. For good measure, I also took my pulse to make sure I was still alive.

After removing the collage of missing young girls and suspects from the wall, I went for a run on the seawall, floating past the marina at Coal Harbour, then picking up speed as I passed the totem poles and continued counter-clockwise around Stanley Park. By the time I reached Prospect Point Lighthouse, I got sick of dodging tourists and veered up past the restaurant and into the trails. From there it was a clean sprint down Bridle Path, and I finished with a quick loop around Lost Lagoon before heading home to shower.

I'd just finished dressing in a white jean skirt and a blue-and-white sleeveless top when the downstairs buzzer sounded. Jim and Sadie.

Experience has shown me that when things begin to look up, that's when I really ought to worry. In all likelihood, it means that I am ascending toward a manic phase, meaning that my wellbeing is nothing more than an illusion caused by a poorly-wired brain. Even so, when I opened the door and Jim gave me a kiss and Sadie wrapped her arms around my waist, it felt different. It felt real. I swallowed the lump in my throat.

After becoming fast friends with Eclipse, Sadie carried him into the living room. As I brewed coffee in the kitchen, Jim came from behind me, placed his hands on my hips and kissed my neck. I felt him become aroused the same time I did. "You look great," he whispered. "Smell great, feel great."

I turned my head to kiss him. "Your kid's in the next room."

"I'm one quiet sonofagun," he said. "You'll never hear me coming."

I laughed and slapped his shoulder.

"What's so funny in there?" Sadie called out.

The day was spent at Playland. We screamed ourselves hoarse on the ancient and rickety wooden roller coaster, got soaked on the log flume, jarred our bones in the bumper cars, and nearly lost our lunches (hot dogs and cotton candy) on the pendulum-like Pirate Ship. As the day buzzed into late afternoon, a sudden summer rain forced us to duck into the shooting range, where we discovered that Jim had shit aim with the air rifle, leaving it up to my marksmanship to win Sadie the gigantic stuffed elephant she would happily tote around the rest of the day. She clapped and giggled as each of my shots pinged the bullseye of the evil clown's gaping mouth each time his jaw lowered.

We bought mini-doughnuts and ate them on the covered Ferris wheel. At the apex of the ride, a shimmering rainbow appeared over the North Shore mountains. Sadie gawped and took photos with her phone.

Jim used the moment to wipe some sugar from my chin, before stealing a kiss. He gave me a look, squeezed my hand, and when he smiled, his eyes shone with the words each of us were too scared to utter. It was a moment of truth—beyond mental illness, beyond booze and drugs—where you know what you're feeling is real, because someone else feels it, too.

It scared the shit out of me.

A dozen rides later, Sadie and I laughed as our bodies slammed together on the Tilt-a-Whirl, while a puke-faced Jim leaned against a post near the exit. After the ride, Sadie needed to pee, so I took her to the ladies' room. On our way out, a middle-aged woman told me I had a cute daughter. I smiled and Sadie looked up at me, shrugged and grinned.

As we left the park, the rain stopped, and the sun was setting over the city. After weeks of smoke, the effect on the sky was dazzling, with melting layers of peach, orange, and yellow. When Sadie took my hand as we crossed Hastings Street, I was reminded that we were possibly on the route that connected a series of crimes. I considered how over the many years, criminals had driven past this very spot, fresh on their way from committing evil or on their way to do it. I gripped Sadie's hand tighter.

"I want to come again tomorrow," she said.

Jim laughed. "Your wimp dad has to work tomorrow. But Sloane looks like she's good for another hundred rides. I'm sure she's game."

"*Yes!*" Sadie shouted.

"Maybe next week," I said, voice drowned out by a rattling vehicle behind us. I turned to see a yellow-and-green, 70s-style VW van pull out, the side panels of the hippy-mobile hand-painted with peace symbols, hearts, sunflowers, and Namaste symbols.

The vehicle chugged past. Something jarred inside me. I sprinted across the parking lot and caught up to the vehicle just as it was about to exit onto the street. The passenger window was down and a woman with long, black hair and John Lennon sunglasses peered out. I triggered the recording app on my phone. Over the engine's rattle, I yelled, "I really dig the sound of your ride. Rev that baby for me!"

When I jogged back, Jim looked confused, and I told them I had to take a rain check on dinner that night.

CHAPTER 35

AT HOME I PULLED EMILY'S FILE, FLIPPED through several dozen photos, and found the one I was looking for. In it, Emily sat on a brown horse, giving riding instructions to several children also on horseback. It wasn't Emily I was interested in, but the yellow VW van in the background, parked beside a fence. The photo was slightly out of focus, and the vehicle was far enough away to make it impossible to see if anyone was inside. I flipped over the photo to see, printed on the back, AUGUST 2, 2013.

Two weeks before she disappeared.

It was full dark when Manuel Carrera met me on the same street outside the same hedge as before. Thirty minutes earlier, I had interrupted him at home where he had been enjoying dinner with his family. After explaining that I needed some assistance in a matter dealing with the Emily Pike case, he eagerly agreed.

I thanked him for coming and waited for a siren in the distance to drift further away before playing him the recording. After hearing it, he frowned and asked to hear it again. This time he closed his eyes when I played it. When he opened them, he said, "That's how it sounded, the vehicle."

"You're sure?"

"I've been hearing it in my dreams for the past seven years. The sound has never left me."

Westborough Farm was closed, but as I drove past, I glimpsed a light coming from a small window in the building directly behind the office. I pulled a U-turn and curbed the Jeep across the street from the entrance, then got out and stood on the road for a moment.

My mind transformed night into day. I saw a black truck, Emily and Oscar inside, fighting. She got out and stormed off down the road. Oscar pounded the wheel in frustration, unaware of the rattling VW van cruising slowly along the road behind him, in the direction his girl had headed.

Reality resumed. I walked over the footbridge and toward the gate, which was locked. A split-rail fence circled the property. The moment I climbed over it, I felt the immediate rush of heat that came with trespassing. My Chucks crunched softly on the woodchipped path. As I walked past the stables, a faint whinny came from inside. I paused. Hearing nothing except the faint strains of blues music coming from the direction of the office, I walked up the creaking steps and rapped lightly on the glass-paned door. I waited, bringing my face close to the glass and cupping my hands around my eyes. All I could see were vague outlines of the shelves and counter. Wind chimes tinkled faintly by my head. Realizing the music was coming from the building behind, I stepped off the porch and walked around back.

The blues music grew louder. Stepping past a curtained window, I could also hear the low murmur of men's voices. At the rear of the building, moths fluttered and smacked into the single bare light bulb above a green-painted door. I knocked, and a second later, the music went silent and an Aussie voice on the other side of the door yelled, *"Who's there?"*

"Sloane Donovan," I said.

The door opened and Doc Barney peered out, dull-eyed and disheveled. "How'd you get in here?" he asked, craning his neck to look over my shoulder, as though someone might be hiding behind me.

"Gate was open," I lied. "I was driving past and I saw the light on. I just have a quick question. Can I come in?"

Doc Barney frowned. "The gate was open?" he asked slowly, smacking his lips several times.

"It was," I said, "but I closed it behind me. I assume that's what you wanted."

"I locked the gate," came a gruff voice from inside the room.

"You forgot again," Doc Barney said over his shoulder.

I slapped at a mosquito on my forearm. It left a bloody streak down to the wrist. "Can I come in?" I repeated.

The veterinarian and owner of Westborough Farm paused, smacked his lips again, and opened the door. He ushered me into a small space that at one time had served as a work shed, with a long workbench running the length of the entire right wall, right below a pegboard half full of tools. On an old sofa pushed against the adjacent wall, sat Willy, the maintenance man, a can of Wildcat beer in his hand. The room had the depressing sour stink of aging males and unwashed socks.

Doc Barney moved in an odd, floating manner toward a giant wooden spool that served as a table, using a stack of old newspapers to conceal a syringe and rubber tubing. Trying to look nonchalant, he continued smacking his lips while arranging the newspapers into a neat pile.

"I'm pretty sure I locked that gate," Willy said, looking at me.

"You've been at this awhile," I said, staring back at him. "Mistakes happen."

I pulled out the photo of Emily with the VW bus in the background and held it in front of Doc Barney's face. "That VW van in the background," I said. "Whose was it?"

"I've no idea," he said.

"The area where it's parked," I said, "behind the stables—that's not part of the visitor's parking lot, is it? It's part of the farm."

He kept looking at the photo while running his tongue around his gums. "It was a long time ago," he mumbled. "I don't remember."

"Loretta drove that clunker," Willy said. "I even worked on it for her from time to time."

I thought back to my notes. "Loretta Houston? The woman who works with the horses?"

Doc Barney mumbled something unintelligible, looking like he might topple over at any moment.

I nodded toward the covered-up drugs on the spool. "How long have you been using, Doc?"

He looked at me blankly before slumping into a nearby folding chair. Willy shook his head and chuckled. "Why I stick with my tallboys."

I stood in front of Doc Barney. "I don't care about the fact that you're a junkie who is running your farm into the ground, but if the police don't take an interest in how you get your drugs, the press will. And when you lose your license, your opioid pipeline will go bye-bye as well. You'll be forced to score your shit on the street, and before you know it, that's where you'll be living."

He gazed up at me with the haunted eyes of a man completely at the mercy of his addiction.

"Tell me about Loretta," I asked.

He blinked as though trying to will himself to focus his eyes. "She quit."

"When?"

"Few weeks ago."

"Why did she quit?"

He shook his head, mumbled something, and gave a small shrug.

Willy spoke up. "Something about an illness in the family, ain't that right, Doc?"

"She called and left a message," Doc Barney said.

"Never heard her mention any family before," Willy said. "But she wasn't from around here. I think she was from the States someplace. Had a bit of an accent."

"She worked here for over seven years, and she just up and left *now*? I want to take a look at her employee file."

"'Employee file,'" Willy parroted, giggling.

I went to the wooden spool and pushed aside the newspaper. Blackened spoon, syringe, cotton ball. I used my phone to take a photo. Doc Barney started to object.

"Shut up and get me the fucking file," I said.

Sitting in my Jeep, I turned on the overhead light and looked at the sheet of paper in my hand. Loretta's "file" consisted of a single sheet of paper containing her name, address, and phone number. Her date of birth was listed as 18/11/84. The space for emergency contact was blank. Photocopied to the upper left-hand corner of the sheet was an image of Loretta's driver's license, showing a face that looked thinner than I recalled from our recent encounter. I closed my eyes and drew up her face from our meeting. I remembered her somewhat masculine face. It was the same woman in the photo, no question, but the differences were striking. The newer version of Loretta was well-muscled, perhaps enhanced by steroids. Doc Barney may not have been the only one shooting up on the farm.

I picked up my phone and fired Kai a text, letting him know I was in need of his computer expertise.

Then I called the number listed on Loretta's file. *The number you have called is out of service,* said the tinny recorded voice. I stared at her photo and my mouth went dry, and my heart rate quickened. The rush spread from my head and chest and through my limbs, filling me with the kind of electric excitement that could keep me going for days.

The address listed in Loretta's file was a ground floor suite of a shabby Vancouver Special on 17th Avenue, a block east of Main Street. As I drove past, I saw a shirtless and overweight bald man leaning over the upstairs balcony railing, joint in one hand, beer can in the other. He followed me with his eyes as I drove past.

I swung around the block and pointed the Jeep south on Main.

Parked half a block from the red-bricked Seaview Apartments on Wall Street, I raised my Canon Digital SLR with a 500mm lens and photographed Sally McGrudder emerging from her baby blue Mercedes convertible and sashaying up the stairs. I snapped shots of Wayne greeting her at the door with a kiss, a hug, and a grab of her ample cougar booty. He looked both ways before inviting her inside.

Oh, Wayne.

After transferring the photos to my phone, I sent them to him, with a message: **what kind of private dick are you? From now on, you do what I say. Come outside, loverboy.**

Less than a minute after I'd parked beside the Mercedes, Wayne climbed into my passenger seat. "I'm not going to apologize for having a dick, Donovan."

"No, but you should apologize for being a sloppy dick. What if Mr. McGrudder decided to hire our competition to tail the wifey, which he undoubtedly *will* when he realizes he's about to lose half his net worth to Gold Digger there."

"Hey," he warned.

"Oh, he's *defensive* about his Gold Digger. You guys planning on running off into the sunset together with hubby's money?"

"Not a bad idea," he said. "Sal's a fine woman, but up until now she's had shit taste in men."

"This conversation is being recorded, by the way. So, when this comes back to bite you—bite *us*—on the ass, I can give you a big, fat, toldya so."

"You had eyes on my place all evening?"

"No, but I'm going to be putting eyes on someone else, and I need your ride. My Jeep's been compromised."

"You're not heading back to the rez."

"Closer to home this time. I may have found something in the Emily Pike case."

About to hand over his keys, they paused in mid-dangle. "For fuck sakes."

"Nope. You do *not* get to be Naysayer Wayne this time. Just listen."

He sighed and I snatched the keys from his hand, then told him about what I'd discovered about the VW van and Loretta Houston. I showed him her file and he used his phone to snap a photo. He waited until I was finished and said, "If we sat here for a couple hours, I'll bet we see at least one or two of those VW hippy-mobiles rattle past. Believe it or not, those pieces of shit aren't *that* uncommon."

"What about Loretta terminating her employment at the farm right after I came poking around?"

"Women don't abduct and kill teenage girls."

"Not without a male partner they don't. Speaking of, I may need you as backup if I decide to approach the house tonight."

"Fuck that noise. This is my first night off in three weeks. We're gonna head up to Whistler tomorrow."

"I'll do it on my own then."

"Not to belabour a point, but you're off the Emily Pike case. You honestly believe there's something here, dump it on the cops. Let them do an honest day's work."

We got out of my Jeep and I walked over to his Pathfinder.

"Where are you going?" he asked.

"Thought I'd just go bang on her door. I get my kicks from fucking up other people's downtime."

Wayne swore, put his hands on his hips, and looked up at the sky. "Hold off on that, for tonight at least. Come back here at 9 a.m. tomorrow. Not before."

CHAPTER 36

THE NEXT MORNING WAS ASH GRAY AND MUGGY, and just breathing the air felt like the most dangerous thing you might do all day. Curbing the Pathfinder in front of the Seaview Apartments, I was just in time to see Wayne escort Sally out to her Mercedes. I popped a couple of breath mints. Sally saw me and waved. I raised my hand. Wayne leaned in and kissed her through the window, then turned and walked over.

"What's with the sunglasses?" he asked as he climbed into the passenger seat. "You sleep at all last night?"

I handed him a triple shot Americano. "Like a baby," I said, watching as Sally backed out and blew Wayne a kiss. "How about you? Did Sally's midnight vocals earn you any more noise complaints from your neighbours?"

Wayne returned the air-kiss to his girlfriend. "I get some scowls in the elevator. Fuckers are just jealous."

I pulled onto the street and headed south on Nanaimo Street, crossing Hastings Street and taking a right on Broadway.

"This has gotta be a morning job at best," he said. "Like I said, we got plans later."

"Whistler. Right. Aren't you worried about being seen?"

"She and I talked about that last night. She said, 'if it happens, it happens'."

"Wow, that's a different tune."

"Turns out she's not as pissed off at her soon-to-be-ex-husband anymore."

"So, are you saying she's no longer a client of ours?"

"I didn't say that. No, she's still gonna hose the bastard for some serious loot; she's just not as emotional about it as she was when she first walked into our office."

"Probably because she hadn't had her pants charmed off yet," I said.

"Whatever," he said. "Listen, I was planning to take Sal and Theo over to Galiano Island before the end of summer. You and Jim and the kid should come."

"Wouldn't that be cute," I said. "The kid's name is Sadie, by the way."

"Right. Things are going good on that end?"

I thought of the previous day spent at Playland with Jim and Sadie, of holding her hand and being mistaken for her mother.

"We're taking things slow," I said.

"Slow is good. Still, you should think of coming out to Galiano. Be nice to switch gears and get away from the city for a few days."

I nodded. The thought of switching gears made me feel physically ill. "Relaxing" getaways were the joyful equivalent of sticking sharp sticks in my eyeballs. I hung left on Fraser Street and a right on 12th Avenue. Several blocks later I turned south on Main.

"Give it some thought," Wayne said. "I got a line on a waterfront place over there. So cheap it's practically free."

"Uh-huh," I said, pointing to a storefront on the east side of the street. "Check it out."

Wayne looked toward the store. "A Select Few," he said. "Isn't that the place where the jewelry came from?"

"Less than four blocks from Loretta's address," I said.

"You sent the cops this info, right?"

At the next block, I turned left and parked near the corner of 17th and Sophia. "Inspector Davis has the file," I said. "He's an apathetic prick who has a hate-on for P.I.s, me in particular. His partner, Fiona Saddy, seems a touch more receptive."

"Make sure you get this through to *her* then. Otherwise, it's withholding, and since we're not even getting paid—"

"Let's just see what we got here first."

He sighed. "Alright, I checked housing records this morning, and this place isn't even listed as a rental anymore."

From down the block, we watched as the same fat man from the previous evening emerged onto the balcony, disheveled and smoking a joint.

"Yeah," I said, "and something tells me that guy isn't the owner."

"Definitely not," Wayne said. "The slumlord who owns this shitbox—along with a dozen more around town—is a guy named Gujral Singh. I also made a casual inquiry into Mr. Singh's past, and it appears that before he became a slumlord, he did a stretch for attempted murder. He didn't like his daughter marrying into the wrong caste or whatever, so he tried to whack her. Sweet fella."

"No doubt. Any idea where he served his time?"

"Nope. Probably one of the medium security pens out in the Valley."

"Amber Sebastian's father spent time in Mountain."

"Lotta scumbags have done time for various things," he said. "But let's keep on target. Namely Loretta Houston, who, other than working at Westborough Farm and being in possession of a driver's license, has absolutely zero footprint in the world, internet or otherwise. Whatever she's driving isn't registered under her name."

"Someone operating under a fake name."

"Or several. We know from the Richmond scams that procuring a driver's license in this province is a piece of cake." He checked his notebook. "Hers is set to expire later this year."

"Licenses expire every five years, and they get mailed out, so we know that five years ago she lived here."

He nodded. "No sign of any ratbag VW van parked anywhere. How about the alley behind the house?"

"Nope. And there's no garage, either."

"You've been here all night, haven't you?"

"Not *all* night."

"Jesus."

I shot him a look. "I just watched. No one went in or out from the lower suite, unless they left in the time it took me to pick you up. Lights went out at just past midnight and I left."

"Back entrance?"

"Gate to the alley."

We climbed out of the Pathfinder. Wayne pointed toward the alley running between the blocks. I nodded and he walked towards it, circling behind the house. I approached the front of the house.

The fat man was gone from the balcony. What had looked like a curtain covering the only ground floor window was really a stained yellow sheet. A rusty mountain bike was chained to a post near the door. An old barbecue and several withered plants sat on the concrete slab that served as a patio. The carport attached to the left side of the house was barren except for a shovel leaning against a post. Weeds grew where the pavement had buckled and cracked.

I held my ear close to the door, but all I heard was a TV on upstairs, some sort of game show. As I rapped on the door, droplets of sweat slithered down my sides. I thought I heard a door creak open, but it was immediately drowned out by a dump truck driving past behind me. I knocked again, louder this time.

A screen door slid open, and a creak came from the balcony above. "Help you?" a voice said.

I stepped back and looked up. "Do you know who lives here?"

The man now wore a wifebeater over his boxer shorts. From below, the view of the underside of his prodigious and hirsute gut made me turn away.

"Guy goes by the name of Bob," he said, "but his real name's some sort of unpronounceable gibberish starts with B, so I just call him Bob."

"Ever see a muscular woman with short brown hair around here?"

He shook his head.

"Teenage girls?"

"Nada. Just a lotta brown dudes who never stay for long, but they're pretty quiet generally. Hey, you a cop?"

"Investigator. Looking for some—"

From the right side of the house came sounds of splintering wood, followed by a yelp of pain and muffled curses. I turned to see a flimsy gate door come off its hinges and clatter to the walkway. Wayne emerged, dragging a thin South Asian man wearing board shorts and nothing else. The man's knees were bleeding.

"I'm just a worker ... I'm just a worker ... please, sir ..."

"This slippery sonofabitch almost knocked me down trying to escape," Wayne said, breathing hard.

"Please sir—"

"Shut up," Wayne barked, looking at the collar of his shirt. "Fucker tore my shirt."

"Bob," the fat man said, "why'd you have to run? Pretty sure they're not looking for you."

Bob looked baffled.

"Landlord is running illegals through here," Wayne said.

"Not all of the tenants are illegals," said the fat man. "Some of us are just getting a sweet deal. Ol' Gujral's like a hero. You're not going to report him, are you?"

"Depends on what ol' Gujral has to say," I replied. "When you started renting here, did he run a credit check, anything like that?"

"Just took the cash I gave him."

I nodded. "Wayne, let Bob go."

"What about my shirt?" he said.

"You made him bleed," I said. "I think you're about even."

Back in the Pathfinder, Wayne readjusted the driver's seat and lit up a cigar. I mock coughed. "You really get off on that, huh, tackling an illegal immigrant half your size?"

"He fuckin' ran. Could'a been our guy for all I knew."

I sighed. "You got Singh's number handy?"

He pulled out a notepad and flipped through it. He gave me the digits and I called them. A woman answered and I asked to speak with Mr. Singh. She asked what it was regarding, and I introduced myself as Kristi LeDuke, of MacDonald Realty. Injecting an obnoxious lilt to my voice, I added, "I have a client who is *very* interested in one of his properties on 17th Street. Money is no object and Mr. Chang advised me to make an offer."

"One moment, please."

I put the phone on speaker. Within seconds Singh was on the line.

"Hello, Mr. Singh," I said, shifting my voice back to normal. "I'm inquiring about one of your properties. You know, the dump on 17th that you rent to people who pay cash in order to remain untraceable. Which saves you come tax time, so I suppose it's a win-win, right?"

A pause. "Do you have an offer, please?"

"I need information on someone who lived there seven or eight years ago. Since I'm guessing your record-keeping is spotty, I'm hoping your memory isn't. For your sake."

"You're not a realtor?"

"Brilliant."

"You lied to me."

"My name is Sandra Davenport. I'm a cop working a murder investigation, and I don't give a rat's ass about your properties or that you prey upon desperate people, many of whom might be criminals as well as yourself."

Wayne's brows rose.

"I need to speak to my lawyer," Singh said. "This is harassment."

"Buddy, you don't even *know*. But we can avoid all that if you just tell me about a woman who lived here, a Loretta Houston."

He sighed over the phone. "There was a tenant with that surname a while back, but he's been gone some time."

"He?"

"Yes."

"You're certain?"

"Yes, but I only saw him several times. Once to show him the suite, and then when he came to pay rent—he paid six months in advance."

"Do you remember this man's name?"

"It was Larry. Larry Houston. I remember thinking that it was an odd name for him."

"How so?"

"Because it sounded like the name of an athlete or movie star. This fellow was wimpy-looking."

"What else?"

"Average. Dark hair, moustache."

I pulled out the suspect sketch. "Glasses?"

"I believe so, yes."

"Was there a *Mrs.* Larry Houston?"

"I believe he was living alone. I never saw anyone else at the house."

"No teenage girls?"

"Not that I saw."

"And how long did Larry reside at that address?"

"From the summer of 2013 until sometime in the following year."

I did the math. Loretta started work at Westborough around June of 2013, only several months before Emily went missing. Loretta's photo sat on my lap, beside the sketch of the suspect. Feeling suddenly lightheaded, I forced myself to take a breath.

"Do you remember what kind of vehicle Larry drove?"

"Some type of old van."

"A Volkswagen?"

"I don't know. I only remember it was loud and thought neighbours might complain."

I ended the call. The hairs on my arms stood up as my heart pounded double time. I found a pencil in my bag and used it on Loretta's photo, doodling in an enhanced jawline and shading in her upper lip.

Wayne watched. "It's a stretch," he said.

"Same pointed chin, same nose," I said. "This photo is seven years old, but I saw Loretta only a few weeks ago. She's gained weight and thickened through the neck and jaw. I think she might be on hormones. Or steroids." I slapped the sketch. "Loretta and Larry are the same person. I'd bet all the money I have on it."

He shook his head. "I still don't see it."

"Because *you* didn't see her. I did. But look at the time-line. Loretta starts working at the farm. Emily disappears several months later. A witness hears a loud vehicle. Loretta drove a loud vehicle. And *Loretta* isn't who she pretends to be."

Wayne puffed on his cigar. "And Loretta keeps working at the farm for another *seven years* after Emily vanishes?"

"Would look pretty suspicious if she did the deed and just up and quit after abducting an employee."

"Still, seven years."

"She's gone *now*. Right after I came around and started asking questions."

"Cops would have asked *a lot* more questions than you. All the employees would have been taken in for statements and grilled."

"Yeah, but back then they had other suspects who were a better fit, and she would have been ready for the questions. But seven years go by and she believes she's in the clear, gets complacent, and then I come nosing around."

"She *seem* squirrely the day you talked to her?"

"Not especially. But she tried to steer me toward Oscar Benoit as the suspect, referring to him as a gangster. She said that to this day, Emily's disappearance frightened her."

He tapped Loretta's photo with his pinkie. "She prob-ably *was* scared. Girl's got doe eyes. I think you're seeing what you want to see here. Anyway, it's a job for the cops now. Besides that, we've got no authority to pursue this. Even what we just did could constitute breach of privacy—"

"Not to mention assault on your part."

"He tripped and fell. But whatever, we're done now."

"Like hell."

"Donovan, you know the deal: we *both* agree on a case, or it gets dropped. It's in the contract for fuck sakes. I'm not going down over this stupid shit."

"We may have found out who took Emily Pike," I said. "*One* of the people, anyhow—and *that's* what you have to say? I think you're fucking scared."

"Bullshit—"

"You know as well as I do there's something here, only you're too much of a coward to take this to the next level."

He exhaled slowly, looking at me like he wanted to extinguish his cigar in the middle of my forehead. "Lest you forget, we've been in nearly exactly this predicament before. So go home and take your fucking pill. That's all I'm going to say."

I shoved the photos and files into my satchel and opened the door. I got out, slammed the door and began walking back toward Main Street.

"Quit being such a drama queen," he called out the window. "Would you just get back in the car, please?"

"Why don't you take your stinking cigar and shove it up your fat ass?"

Wayne stuck his head out the window as he drove past. "Don't accept rides from any trannies driving VW vans."

I flipped him off as he drove away. His laughter lasted until his vehicle disappeared around the corner.

CHAPTER 37

THIRTY MINUTES OF FAST WALKING BROUGHT me to Funky's, where I sat alone at the bar, working on a glass of house white. It was repulsive plonk, made even more so from the double shot of tequila which had preceded it. The War on Drugs played from the speakers, a moody dirge perfectly suited for a depressing dive bar on the edge of skid row. I downed the wine, wincing at the rancid taste, but closing my eyes as the warmth trickled down into my chest, spreading, spreading. It would slow things down, make my mind right. I opened my eyes and motioned at the bartender, letting him know I was switching to G&Ts. It was just past eleven a.m.

I fished my phone from my bag and made a call.

Cyrus Ghorbani picked up on the second ring. "I was hoping to never see or hear from you again," he said.

"That any way to greet the person who furthered your career? Maybe being promoted to sergeant of the Gang Squad has gone to your big, bald head."

"What do you want?"

"Loretta Houston. Also goes by Larry."

"Never heard of her. Or him."

"I need you to check if she's got a sheet, both here and in the States."

"There are safeguards. I can't just—"

"I don't need a file, just if she was charged with anything. Known associates would be swell, too. Just say a C.I. passed you a name and you need to verify it."

"You got all the answers, huh?"

The bartender set down my drink, and the medicinal scent of the gin wafted up to my nostrils. I gave him the thumbs up and he took away my wine glass, raising his brows and smirking as though amused by my drinking whims. Dick.

"You there?" Ghorbani asked, just as I was taking a sip of the drink.

"I'm going to send you Loretta's photo," I said. "According to her driver's license, her D.O.B. is 18/11/84. Could be bogus, but the age would be about right."

"I do this for you, we're done."

"Last time I called, you ended up with the collar of your career. C'mon, buddy, I know you like breaking rules almost as much as breaking bones."

"I'm not your buddy," he said, and ended the call.

CHAPTER 38

HEADING INTO THE OFFICE THE FOLLOWING morning, I tossed the daily toonie in M.J.'s ukulele case. She stopped strumming "Stairway" long enough to inform me of some "interesting visitors upstairs."

"They look like good guys or bad guys?"

M.J. gestured toward a five-dollar bill in her case. "One of 'em gave me that fiver, so they're good guys in my book. You look like roadkill. Lean down here a moment. C'mon, now."

M.J. procured a small bottle of perfume and spritzed my face and neck.

"How long do you think you can keep this up?" she asked me.

"What do you mean?"

She sighed, shook her head, and resumed strumming.

Dee-Dee Sebastian locked eyes with me as I entered the office. She sat on a chair in the waiting room, along with another woman and a man, all of them First Nations. The man looked to be in his late sixties, with a salt-and-pepper ponytail halfway down the back of his navy suit jacket. Wayne poured coffee, while Frank stood nearby, hands clasped in front of him like a butler.

Dee-Dee rose and gave me a hug. Her knowing eyes triggered my shame, deepening the pit I felt in my gut. "Hello, Sloane Donovan," she said. Over her shoulder I saw Wayne appraise my sorry state. With my eyes I gave him a quick *fuck you*.

"Hello, Dee-Dee," I said, trying not to breathe on her.

She turned back toward the group and made introductions. The suit was Chief Tobias Baker, who leaned in and greeted me with a warm handshake. The other woman was Hilda Wolfe, who had lived down the road from the Sebastians for many years.

"After your visit," Dee-Dee said, "I passed out those suspect sketches, and Hilda said she remembered something from around the time Amber went missing."

Hilda's elfin face gave way to a shy smile. In a voice I had to strain to hear, she said, "It was a long time ago, but when I saw the drawing, I remembered a guy that talked funny. And he was younger."

"How much younger?"

She thought for a moment. "Less than twenty maybe. And I think he had a little moustache, but I'm not sure."

"You spoke with him?" I asked.

"My late husband did. I was watching from the road when Chuck walked right up to the truck and asked them what they were doing there. The guy said he was lookin' for work, and Chuck told him he was on Indian land and that he should try Chilliwack or Mission."

"There were *two* men in the vehicle?"

A tentative nod. "I think so, but I couldn't see the driver."

"And it was a truck—not a van?"

"A pickup—I think." Hilda gave a slight frown, as though doubting her own memory. "But now that you mention it, it might have been a van."

Wayne and I exchanged a glance.

Chief Baker stepped forward and fixed me with a steady gaze. "Dee-Dee told me about your desire to help find out what happened to Amber. I also heard that you picked up two young girls who were hitchhiking—and scared the crap out of them with some horror stories. So much so that they'll probably never hitch again for the rest of their lives." He smiled. "Tanya, the precocious one, is my granddaughter, and I thank you."

"Any time I can scare a kid straight," I said.

"Do you think you can find out what happened to Amber?" he asked.

I held his gaze for several long seconds, feeling my heart swell in my chest. My eyes flicked over to Wayne, who gave me a look of warning. Turning back to Chief Tobias Baker, I nodded once, and said yes.

He reached into his inside jacket pocket and handed me a cheque. "We'd like to hire your agency. That's for your retainer fee plus twenty percent, and we expect to be billed for every expense."

Wayne stepped forward and shook hands with everyone. Then he turned to Frank and told him to bring three chairs into his office.

"Might as well bring them into *my* office, Frank," I said. "That's where everything is."

Everyone filed into my office, Wayne and I taking up the rear. At the door I turned to my partner. "You're a fucking suck," I whispered.

He snatched the cheque from my hand. "Money talks, baby."

CHAPTER 39

NELSON THE SEAGULL IS A CAFÉ ON CARRALL Street, on the ever-fuzzier border of Gastown and skid row, where hipster and crackhead alike share the sidewalk with relative amicability. A decade ago, the area was comprised of piss-reeking, blood-soaked alleys, needles, and rampant lunacy. All of that was still intact, only now it was cool to exist down on the fringes, sipping pricey Americanos spitting distance from Pigeon Park, whose denizens sleep on benches and preferred their drinks in brown paper bags.

The second I opened the door to Nelson, I spotted Cyrus Ghorbani. Seated at a table near the rear—with his shaven head, hard face, and massive arms stretching the limits of his tight black tee—Ghorbani looked about as inconspicuous as a Hells Angel in a flower-arranging workshop. The espresso cup, held daintily with his pinkie in the air, made the picture even more absurd. His glowering eyes picked me up as I walked across the worn hexagonal tile floor of the airy brick-and-beam room. I pulled up a seat at his table.

"Never would've pegged you as a hipster," I said. "Next you'll be sporting a handlebar moustache and a monocle."

"I picked this place because no self-respecting cop would be caught dead in here. I can't risk being seen with you. Word is getting around that you've been hanging out at the station."

"Yeah, trying to get help on this case. So far, your pals don't want to do much to solve this crime." I nodded toward the gym bag on the seat beside him. "What do you have?"

"You're not getting any hard copy from me," he said. "Two criminal record checks were done on Loretta Houston in 2013, only a few months apart. Both came back clean, and there's been nothing since."

"What about in the U.S.?"

"That took a little more digging. Get your notebook out."

I fished it from my bag, along with a pen.

"Back in 1999, a fifteen-year-old by the name of Loretta *Lessard*, aka Loretta Houston, disappeared from her foster home near Boulder City, Nevada. She had been shuffled around from five different homes, earning her the designation of *troubled youth*. Though I couldn't access it, you can bet she has a significant juvie record."

"Did you get a photo, at least?"

"Check the Missing and Exploited Children database in the States."

Back in the office, Wayne sat beside me as I scrolled down the alphabetized list of missing children and teens from the United States over the last fifty years. Compared to Canada, the sheer volume of disappeared youths was staggering. Row after row of young faces, many only toddlers—gone.

"Jesus Christ," Wayne muttered. "All those kids."

The statistical truth was that most were dead. Only perhaps one in twenty profiles had the word FOUND printed in bold red below their name, date of birth, and date of disappearance.

A quick scroll through the Ls brought us to a photo of a sullen, androgynous teen with bad skin and a lank, brown bang sweeping over her right eye. If the name below the photo hadn't said Loretta Louise Lessard, she could just as easily have passed for a Larry.

Her more current photo sat on the desk, along with the sketch. "It's her," I said.

"Fuckin' A."

I read the profile. "Born in '84. Last seen hitching north out of Boulder City."

"She hitch all the way up to Canada?" he mused. "Or did someone bring her up here?"

"The border was easier to cross, pre-9/11," I said. "Pacific Crest Trail runs right through. Northbound would be a breeze."

A few feet away, a wheel-mounted whiteboard held Amber's photo, the suspect sketch, and a blown-up photo of Loretta Lessard. To the left of it was a large map of the Lower Mainland. I stood up and pressed a small, red sticker into the approximate location of the most well-known trail that crosses the border in Manning Park, about a hundred kilometres east of Mission and Deroche.

I placed a call to the Center for Missing and Exploited Children in Alexandria, Virginia. Identifying myself to the receptionist, I asked for the number of the caseworker assigned to Loretta Lessard. Wayne inserted small, numbered, yellow stickers corresponding with Amber's last known whereabouts: Deroche and the Downtown Eastside.

The receptionist got me the number, and I thanked her and ended the call.

I called the new number, and it was answered after one ring. "Carson Humphreys," said a man with a Midwestern twang.

After introducing myself, I asked if there had been any tips on Loretta Lessard over the past twenty years.

"Loretta Lessard," he said, drawing out the syllables as though trying to remember the name. "I believe that was one of the files I took over when my predecessor passed a couple years back. Let me pull the file. One moment, please. Got a computer here dating back to the Jurassic era."

During the wait, Carson Humphreys asked me about the wildfires he kept hearing about on the news.

"If they keep going," I said, "in a few more years we'll live in a desert like you."

He guffawed. "Come spend the summer down here," he said. "See what hell on earth feels like. You probably already know this, but a lotta runaways end up in places like Seattle or Vancouver. Easier climate to live outdoors, and they believe that folk there are more tolerant to street kids. So, we get a lotta sightings in the Pacific Northwest—ah, here we are, Miss Loretta Lessard. Last known whereabouts was her foster home on the night of June 5, 1999. She'd only been there six months. Looks like she'd been skipped around pretty good. Avid hitchhiker—and shoplifter; big surprise."

"Any family members that she might have fled to?"

"None listed. Mother, father, brother, all deceased. Nothing in Canada, that's for sure. Zero reported sightings since she was reported missing. What's this about? Have y'all found her?"

"She's up here," I said, "but right now we don't know exactly where."

His voice brightened. "I'll send you the file right away. This job can get depressing; it's nice when we can stamp *found* on a case."

"She's not found yet," I said. "I'm pretty sure that's the last thing she wants."

After giving him my email and ending the call, I sat back and idly flipped open another file. Emily Pike's photo looked back at me.

Wayne watched me. "Remember that Amber's our focus."

"I know. Loretta's the connection though. Or Larry."

"Let's just call her Lola for short." He stood and moved to a second whiteboard, where we'd created a timeline in blue ink. "Here's what we got so far. In 1999, Lola goes AWOL from foster care, hitches north, maybe some guy picks her up, maybe she makes it on her own. Either way, somehow she ends up here."

"And two years later," I said, "Hilda Wolfe sees her in a truck with a mystery man, casing a reservation, shortly before Amber Sebastian disappears."

"She would've been seventeen then," he said. "I'm a little skeptical about Hilda's recollection. Twenty years is a long time to hold a memory of someone you saw inside a vehicle for a few seconds. But let's say it's something, and that Lola had hooked up with some guy and they're out trolling for girls who fit a certain profile."

"A profile Lola herself could've fit at fifteen."

"She was waif-ish enough," he conceded, jabbing his red marker toward where her Missing Person's photo was still on the computer screen. "But she's either androgynous or ugly, I can't decide which."

"Give a girl a chance, Wayne," I said. "If Loretta can become Larry—and vice versa—convincing people she works with for years, she could also doll herself up a little.

Remember when we were looking for that runaway from Maple Ridge and we drove right past her when she was hitching on Old Yale Road?"

"She was wearing so much makeup that she looked ten years older."

"Exactly. We have to assume that Lola goes to great lengths to change her appearance. The day I saw her at the farm, she was at *least* thirty pounds heavier than in this photo. She was jacked."

"Self-administered hormone therapy through the use of horse 'roids," he said.

"That's why she was so damn fast that night I chased her."

"Better living through chemistry," he said, stretching. "I'm gonna run and grab a sandwich from La Grotta. Want anything?"

Stoli on the rocks.

"I'm good."

As Wayne left, the email icon on my laptop popped up. Carson Humphries had sent Loretta's file. I opened the PDF and scanned down. Near the bottom was the name and number of her last foster parents in Boulder City. I called the number and after half a dozen rings, a young boy picked up. "Jeffries residence," he said.

I asked to speak to his mother or father and several moments later a man came on the phone. He introduced himself as Eugene and I told him I was an investigator from Canada looking into Loretta Lessard.

A pause, then, *"Loretta.* Is she alive?"

"I believe so," I said.

"In Canada? That's where you said you're calling from?"

"Yes. Did she have any friends or contacts up here that you can remember? Anyone she might have mentioned? A long-distance number that showed up on a phone bill?"

In the background came the sounds of children squabbling. A young girl shrieked. I could hear Eugene cup the phone and shush the kids.

"Hang on," he said, "I'm just going to take this on the other line."

A few moments later he came back on, someplace quiet. "We got five kids here now," he explained. "Scaled down from what we used to have, but still, sometimes I have to lock myself in a closet to hear myself think."

"Impressive. Even more so that you remembered Loretta after two decades."

"I always had a soft spot for that girl," he said. "Lot of our kids come from real rough backgrounds, but Loretta's was especially bad. Trailer park meth family—before it became a cliché. I'm pretty sure all her kin are dead or dispersed, which is probably a blessing. The girl took her share of ass-whuppins along the way, and she was sexually abused by an uncle at a very young age. You asked if she had any contacts in your neck of the woods, and I don't recall, but I don't see it either. She never got any letters, and the only phone calls we ever got were from school when she cut class—or from the law, when they'd find her hitching on the I-93."

"Do you live on a farm, by any chance?"

"No," he said. "I'm a sales manager for a department store downtown. But we do live right next to a farm. When she wasn't running away, Loretta used to be over there with the horses, every chance she got. The neighbour said she was a natural around animals, and I'd have to agree. She used to sneak out at night, saddle up and go for rides. Surprised she never tried to run away with one of the beasts. A couple times I had to talk the owner out of involving the cops."

"Did Loretta have a boyfriend? Someone older, maybe."

He gave a chuckle.

"Girlfriend?" I asked.

"Don't think so," he said, "but I'm a little naïve when it comes to that. My wife thought she was ..."

"Transgender?"

"I suppose. Seems so much more common now than twenty years ago. Personally, she just struck me as a tomboy. When she took to thievin', she sure did give those boys some exercise."

"Come again?"

"Loretta was a high school track star," he said. "Could've been, anyhow. Her coach said she could've gone to Nationals if she'd had an ounce of discipline. She wasn't big on showing up come race day, so they wrote her off. Real shame. But I'll tell ya, when she did go, she cleaned *up*."

"No doubt."

After promising to contact him if we located her, I ended the call. I sat for a moment, then stood and retrieved a beer from the fridge. I stood by the window and drank it quickly. Smoke hung over the tops of the skyscrapers downtown. Looking down on the street, I saw people coming and going. M.J. strummed her tune, as people stepped past, ignoring her. I watched a mother texting on her phone as her two young children dawdled behind. Wayne sauntered up the sidewalk from the other direction, eating his sandwich and pausing to chat with M.J.

I finished my beer, put the can in the recycling, and covered it up with a newspaper.

It was like a switch flipped in my brain and I rushed to grab another beer from the fridge. I opened it and began drinking. Hearing Wayne enter the waiting room, I sat back down and placed the can on the floor beneath my desk.

Wayne entered, went to the fridge and removed a bottle of water. "Want anything while I'm up?"

I shook my head. "I'm good," I said, then filled him in on my conversation with Eugene Jeffries. He sat on the edge of the desk while he ate and listened.

"So, she's fast," I concluded. "A natural-born runaway. She skips out of the Jeffries residence in Boulder City, hooks up with an older guy, who takes her north. Or maybe she just keeps on hitching, sleeping under overpasses, stealing and hustling along the way."

Wayne nodded and got on his laptop.

"What's up?" I asked.

"I'm sending this intel to VPD. The cop's name is Davis, right?"

"He's going to do fuck all with it."

"His partner then. What's her last name?"

"Saddy. But I don't see what good it'll do. Lola's sketch has already been all over the news."

"But we know who she is now. We know where she's from. They can issue a BOLO, we can't. They can get cross-border police cooperation, we can't."

My phone buzzed with a text. I checked it. "Let's hold off on that."

CHAPTER 40

THE BARTENDER AT FUNKY'S GAVE ME A WARY eye as he came over to take our order. "Everything going to be OK this time?" he asked.

Heat rose up my neck. "Of course," I said.

We ordered a pitcher of lager and the bartender left.

"What was that all about?" Wayne asked.

"No idea," I said.

I truly had *no idea.* All I know is that I had zero recollection of leaving the bar the other day, and that a patron's behaviour had to be sufficiently egregious to warrant getting called out by a bartender in Funky's.

Before Wayne could inquire further, Kai sat down at our table. A moment later, our beer arrived.

After ordering a soda and lime from the bartender, Kai said, "I'll never figure out what it is about this dump that you guys like so much."

"Dark place for dark deeds," Wayne said. "Why is it that when I reach out, you ignore me, but when *she* calls, you come running? Should I start working out?"

"I know how to appeal to his humanitarian side," I said.

"Yeah, right," Kai said. "Consider yourself lucky I'm here at all."

"Fair enough," I said. "What did you find?"

"A peek at Westborough's pharmaceutical inventory showed they don't stock any drugs containing scopolamine. But yes to the horse steroids and opioids. *Especially* opioids. For comparison's sake, I accessed Alderwood Farm, over in North Van—whose records are *way* less sketchy, by the way. Similar-sized farm, same animals, yet they go through *half* the morphine that Westborough does. Not only morphine, but fentanyl, hydromorphone, oxymorphone, and ketamine."

"How does that *not* raise any red flags?" Wayne asked.

The bartender arrived with Kai's drink. After taking a sip, he said, "Lotta junkie M.D.s are methodical about their use—until they're not. He probably knows *exactly* how much he can order without raising suspicion."

"Any other drugs on the list that caught your eye?" I asked.

He nodded. "They place intermittent orders for horse anabolics, like Equipoise and Winstrol, which are used more commonly on racehorses. Not so much on kiddie farm horses."

"And people use them?" Wayne asked.

"Big time." Kai glanced around the bar. "You know, vet clinics get their supplies jacked all the time. They have all the good stuff people want, and security is way more lax than your average pharmacy."

"No surprise there," I said.

"There's something else," he said. "When you called me to look into this place, I remembered something one of my colleagues mentioned back when I was still in the game."

Wayne chuckled. "I love how you guys call slinging dope a 'game.'"

"Yeah, well, I gave that up. I guess it's been harder for you to give up being an asshole."

"Too deeply ingrained," Wayne replied.

"No shit."

"Go on, Kai," I said.

"A few years ago, when I was picking up, I overheard a conversation about the best clinics in town to hit. One guy mentions this farm out by Kerrisdale, kind of in the middle of nowhere. And my supplier says no way; that it's off limits. Like a no-go zone."

I looked at Wayne. "Like the Benoit family. A no-go zone."

CHAPTER 41

WAYNE DROVE AND I SAT STARING OUT THE passenger window. Somewhere past Langley, I saw a woman walking her dog in a field, an Irish setter, same kind of dog we had growing up. His name had been Barney, which made me think of Doc Barney. My mind danced over to Loretta. Then Lola. A rattling VW van. Dead-eyed teenage girls.

As we sped toward the Fraser Valley on Highway 1, sporadic raindrops began splattering the windshield. Wayne craned his neck to peer up at the purple-black thunderclouds above. "Shitty weather is good. More people will stay home."

"Uh-huh."

"What's up with you? I thought you'd be overjoyed to be back on this case. Or do you only get your thrills from pro bono work?"

"No, it's all good."

I kept my eyes on the passenger side mirror. Minutes ago, a dark SUV had been behind us for several kilometres. Traffic had thickened since then, and I couldn't tell if it was still back there. Wayne looked over at me, then back at the road. *Deep breaths,* I told myself. Everything's going to be fine.

"Paint It Black" came on the stereo and Wayne turned up the volume, cooked the gas, and passed several semis chugging uphill. In the grassy median, someone had erected a cross and an accompanying photo of someone who had been killed there.

In this line of work, you can't have a problem with knocking on a hundred doors, a *thousand* doors if need be. You have to be prepared to ask the same questions to what seems like the same apathetic faces, over and over and over again. Some faces will seem nervous, their manner evasive, because they've got something to hide, even though that particular something may have zero to do with why you came knocking. You have to cross-reference people and their statements against old notes, checking for any discrepancies. If there are, especially after several decades, this can usually be chalked up to faulty memory, but you also need to have your bullshit meter finely tuned. In the not-so-unlikely event you come across someone who doesn't like *anyone* knocking on their door, it also doesn't hurt to have a fully charged Enforcer at your side.

What we had to work with was Amber's Missing Persons police file, which we used as a point of reference while we spent the bulk of the morning canvassing homes on either side of the Sebastian residence. After that, we were focusing on the residences approaching the highway, presumably the direction Amber would've hitched.

Rural folk aren't accustomed to strangers knocking on their doors. Several didn't answer, even though we could hear TVs droning in the background. In those cases, we made a note to try again later. Others opened the door in either fear or hostility, until we told them who we were and what we were doing. After dropping the name Dee-Dee Sebastian, we watched their demeanors change as they became immediately willing to help. Some of the original residents from 2000 had either died or moved on. Unfortunately, the people who tend to talk the most often prove the biggest waste of time. Start them jawing and they never shut up. Over the course of the day, we were offered coffee and cookies and beer and homemade elk jerky and an invite to stay for lunch. Meeting a private investigator would carry immense cachet out in the sticks; providing these people with a conversation starter for years.

Early afternoon brought a full-scale thundershower. Long before we had canvassed all the homes in a ten-kilometre radius, our shoes and socks were soaked from tiptoeing through the unavoidable pond-sized puddles. At lunchtime, we sat in the Pathfinder outside the general store, windows fogged up as we ate sandwiches and drank coffee. I was wishing we'd accepted the offer of the beer. We had a map of the area on the seat between us. I looked through the rain-beaded windshield, to vast stretches of farmland blurring into the green hills that rose to meet the mountains beyond.

"They're out here somewhere," I said.

"Somewhere's a big place," he said. "Could take forever, and we don't have that kind of manpower."

I stared out the window, as though trying to find a pattern in the chaos of droplets that came together and formed rivulets down the glass. The drumming on the roof was hypnotic, trance-inducing. A black Ford truck pulled up beside us. I sat bolt upright and reached for the Enforcer in my bag. An older couple got out and walked into the store, the woman using a magazine to shield her head against the rain.

I took a breath and closed my eyes.

"Pretty jumpy today, Donovan," Wayne said. "Everything OK?"

I opened my eyes.

"I keep wondering what Emily saw at the ranch that day."

"What am I about to tell you?"

"That we're off they Emily Pike case."

"Thank you."

"But the two disappearances are connected."

"Even if they are, any roads that lead to Benoit are closed." He started the engine.

"Fair enough," I said, checking the time. "We're going to be done out here in a few hours. I say after this we hit the Downtown Eastside, show Lola's photo around."

Wayne started the Pathfinder, shifted into reverse, and backed out onto the street. "Skid row will still be there tomorrow. Plus, Sally and I have tickets to see Beyoncé tonight. Get a life and go see your boyfriend. Get laid."

"Thanks for the sage relationship advice, pal."

CHAPTER 42

STEAM ROSE OFF THE STREETS AS I WALKED from Commercial Drive to the Downtown Eastside, fueling myself with frequent sips from a vodka-filled water bottle. I checked the alleys and beneath graffiti-coated, piss-stinking overpasses, places I knew runaways congregated, street kids with names like Skreech and Prettyboi and Trixtress, with ill-planned tattoos running like diseased vines up their necks and onto their prematurely weathered faces.

Climbing up to their concrete encampments, I asked questions and showed the sketch of Lola along with Amber's photo. A few times predators and perverts cruised slowly past, their leering eyes searching out those desperate enough to climb in their vehicles.

Sometime near the end of my bottle, I vaguely recall yelling at a man in a dark van, kicking the side of his vehicle as he raced away. I screamed and swore until no one was around me anymore and I was alone on the street. My foot hurt.

Without remembering the route I'd stumbled, I was dimly aware of limping around near Main and Hastings, being offered drugs. I drained the last of my bottle while looking up at roof of the derelict Balmoral Hotel. Hordes of homeless, addicted, and mentally ill people swirled around me.

When I closed my eyes, I saw a woman fly off the roof, arms flailing, screaming as she dove toward me with terror-filled eyes.

Black.

The girl was face down on the sidewalk, dark hair splayed out, a lake of blood spreading. Shadows swayed and whispered in the background. I bent and turned the woman over. My heartbeat seemed to come from outside my body. I saw a face that wasn't, just a crushed, pulpy mass, one blood-filled eyeball lolling out, mouth full of shattered teeth.

Someone spoke in the background, but I couldn't make out the words. What? I said, turning my head.

The woman's hand reached up and gripped my wrist. I looked down to see her lolling eye, focused on me, her ruined lips moving, voice a raspy gurgle. She pulled me closer.

Too late, she said. You're too late.

Black.

"Sloane."

Black.

"Sloane, are you OK, sweetheart?"

My eyes snapped open to sunlight. Man smell. A bed. Above it, a black-and-white photo of a surfer riding the tunnel of a wave. A digital clock that said 9:03 a.m. Jim, holding me from behind, saying, "Wow, babe, can you ever dream."

I pulled away and blinked at him, at his tousled hair, tired eyes, and expression of uncertainty. I shut my eyes, taking stock. I was covered in sweat, my temples throbbed, my mouth was dry and filled with a sour, puke-y aftertaste.

"How did I get here?" I croaked.

"You don't know?"

Eyes still closed, I shook my head. Mistake. The roaring in my head multiplied. Jim moved in bed, and I opened my eyes. "Exhibit one, Your Honour," he said.

He held up a pair of mud-caked Chucks. "My guess is you traversed a swamp en route here."

"Oh Jesus," I groaned. "At least I didn't drive here."

"Well, *yeah,*" he replied. "Though you *did* scare the hell out of Sadie when you broke into the house through her window."

I jolted upright, searching his face for traces of a lie. Finding none, I sat on the side of the bed with my head in my hands. I was wearing an oversized white T and nothing else, except for a bandage on my right big toe that had not been there the previous day. My stomach flip-flopped and the room spun. Jim's warm hand on the middle of my back only made it worse. From the living room came the sounds of a kids' show on TV: animated squealing followed by an explosion.

"I'm sorry," I said, my voice a pathetic nothing. I wanted to disappear. Worse, I wanted another drink.

"Not gonna lie," he said, "you were some sight when you came in last night. I had to clean you up and couldn't understand a word you were saying. Do you do that a lot, get shitfaced and wander the streets in the middle of the night?"

"Only on special occasions."

"Packing a gun?"

My breath caught in my throat as I watched him open the drawer of his bedside table. There it was, the pearl-handled Colt.

"Did Sadie see that?" I asked.

"She knows you're an investigator, so it seems perfectly natural for you to be carrying a weapon. Plus, ever since the night on the movie set, she idolizes you."

"*That's* a mistake," I said.

"Remains to be seen," he said. "I wasn't aware P.I.s in Canada are allowed to carry firearms."

"It's kind of a souvenir." I chanced a look at him, surprised to see him grinning. My heart lightened and despite myself, I had to smile. Our eyes caught, connected, and for just a moment, the world and all its problems stopped. He kissed me.

I pulled back. "My breath."

"Fuck it," he said, craning his neck forward to kiss me again. He grabbed me by the hips and pushed me down on the bed.

"Guess it's too early in the relationship to get out of this by pulling the I-have-a-splitting-headache card."

"That's your own damn fault."

From behind came the loud clearing of a throat. Twisting my head, I saw Sadie in the doorway. Jim slid off and yanked the sheets around us.

"Sadie," he said, "you can't just sneak up on us like that."

"Like Sloane snuck in *here* last night?"

My cheeks heated like toaster elements. "Sadie, I am so sorry I scared you. I just—"

"Scared *me*?" she said, jumping on the bed. "I thought it was a raccoon at my window and when I saw it was you, I helped you open the window. When my dad heard it, he thought someone was trying to break in, and practically pooped his shorts."

"Did not," Jim said.

Gesturing to the open drawer, Sadie asked, "Have you ever shot anyone?"

"No. It's just for protection."

"In case you run into bad guys?"

"That's right." *Idiotidiotsloppydrunkfuckingidiot.*

"You were drunk last night."

I nodded slowly.

"You shouldn't drink so much," she said. "It's bad for you, and we like you, so we don't want anything bad to happen to you. Right, dad?"

"Right, Sade."

I nodded again. An egg formed in my throat. Sadie wrapped her arms around my neck and gave a tight squeeze, before skipping out of the room and announcing that she was off to make waffles.

Jim hopped out of bed and shut the door, then sat back down on the bed. He looked at the wall in front of him, then at me.

"Here it comes," I said.

"You can't do this again, Sloane," he said. "I know that you're on medication, and that your job is stressful, but—"

"Jim, listen—"

"Hear me out," he said. "I really like you. I mean, I *really* like you, and Sadie adores you. But I gotta admit, I'm concerned."

"I understand," I said, feeling my brain shift into hyperdrive as the squirrels started running. "Maybe we moved into this too fast. I didn't want to date anyone anyhow and you pursued me, and I told you everything on that beach. To be honest, I don't know what I'm doing. I fuck up, Jim. I do that a lot. If I stay, it's a pretty safe bet, I'm going to fuck up your life, too."

He frowned and extended his arms, palms down. "Keep your voice down ... and maybe *sit down* while you're at it."

Not realizing I'd stood, I complied, feeling like a chastised kid. I ran my hands though my knotted hair and wanted to tear it out. My heart grew hot and my ribs seemed to vibrate, and the pressure grew, and I knew that soon I wouldn't be able to stand it and that I would need to drown myself in something.

Jim sat down and put his arms around me and told me it was going to be OK.

I shook my head. "I call bullshit on that."

"When was the last time you took your meds?"

"A few days ago. Maybe longer. I don't know."

"I'm not an expert, but I'm pretty sure you've got to take those things regularly for them to work."

"So they say."

"And Sadie's right about the booze."

"Mm-hm."

Jim turned my chin, forcing me to meet his eyes. "Let's stop drinking for a while. You and me. Sober summer, what's left of it anyhow. Boring as shit, but no more hangovers."

A panic raced through me. I tried to think back to the last time I'd tried to stay dry. It was a long time ago and hadn't been a resounding success. Since I hated to fail, I simply hadn't tried since. But then I thought of me, blacked out and in possession of a stolen firearm, climbing through a little girl's bedroom window. If that isn't a wake-up call ...

"What do you say?" Jim said.

"I guess that means no hair of the dog in our morning coffee today?"

"I'm serious."

"Game on, then."

We shook on the deal, then he pulled me back down on the bed and pinned me. "Since we've been somewhat tipsy since our first date, now I'll get to see if you're actually into me or were just exhibiting drunken lust."

"True enough. But I *know* you're into me."

"How's that?"

"I heard someone calling me 'sweetheart' just before I woke up."

"You were having a horrific nightmare from the sounds of it. Probably just part of the dream."

"That must've been it," I said, reaching into his boxer shorts, just as the smell of burning waffles wafted under the door.

After killing two partially-blackened waffles drenched in maple syrup, four strips of bacon, and half a gallon of coffee, I began to feel somewhat restored, if not strangely relaxed. My clothes from the previous night's debacle were in the wash, so I wore the same oversized white T and a pair of Jim's board shorts. We ate on the small patio overlooking the backyard, chatting and cracking jokes like the night before was just a silly prank. Jim and I exchanged playful glances and his bare toes found mine beneath the table. I imagined a period of sobriety, and yes, I would do it. Not just for him and Sadie, but for me, for this, for what I had at that moment. Sitting at that table with these two people made me feel like I belonged, and suddenly the world didn't seem quite so hostile and shitty. There was more to life than this obsession with solving cases, with putting the world right. I vowed to take my meds and check in regularly with my doctor, maybe wean myself off them over time. A year from now, I could be a whole different person. Get back to running races. Take a trip to Patagonia, maybe with present company. Sadie caught me smiling, and she smiled back, mouth full of waffle.

"I almost forgot," she said, pushing back her chair and running into the house. Thirty seconds later she returned and handed me my phone. "It fell out in my room."

The battery was nearly dead, but I could see that the Vancouver Police Department had tried calling. Wayne had been calling as well, before sending a text telling me to check in ASAP.

Scrolling to an earlier text, I felt my heart lurch.

I KILLED MY DAUGHTER AND OTHERS AND CAN'T TAKE IT ANYMORE

I sat stunned and heard Jim asking me what was wrong.

I stood. "I have to go. I'm sorry."

"I'll give you a lift," he said.

My head spun and I grabbed the back of the chair for balance. Lucas Pike. My mind flashed to his volcanic rage in my office, then seeing him drinking despondently on the job, staring into the abyss.

Jim stood behind me. "Maybe you should just sit down—"

My phone rang. Wayne. I ignored Jim and moved to the corner of the backyard facing the hedges.

"Where the fuck you been?" Wayne asked. "Last night I got a call from your buddy, Inspector Davis. Guess who hung himself from a rafter at a construction site last night?"

Sadie and Jim watched me from across the yard. I lowered my voice. "He said he killed his daughter. And others."

"They already found a body in a ravine in Coquitlam. Not far from where he had been working."

CHAPTER 43

I CLIMBED INTO WAYNE'S PATHFINDER, WEAR-
ing the same attire from breakfast, along with flip-flops
three sizes too big. Jim and Sadie waved from the doorway
and Wayne waved back before pulling away from the curb.
"What most women do," he said, "is stake a claim by leaving
a bunch of clothes, makeup, and other assorted shit at the
guy's place. Handy in times like this. But not you?"

"Call me atypical," I said, setting a plastic Army & Navy
bag containing the pistol on the floor.

"No shit," he said. "What happened to your foot?"

"Stubbed my toe."

Wayne cut through side streets, right, left, right, left,
and it wasn't until he sped up that I realized we were east-
bound on Grandview Highway. The sky was blue and cloud-
less, yet the world felt off. Everything was out of sync.

Wayne merged onto the Trans-Canada Highway and
stepped on the accelerator.

I asked, "Why?"

"Why *what?*" he said.

"Why would Lucas Pike kill his daughter? And 'others'?"

Wayne pulled into the left lane, passing several dawdling vehicles. "You saw him in the office that day. He was totally fucking unhinged. I expected him to go postal right then."

"He practically broke down after."

"Yeah, well, no doubt killing young girls takes an emotional toll on you over the years."

"He came to *us*, though."

"Cry for help. Lot of these guys *want* to get caught."

"Lucas was a run-down alky," I said. "And he passed the polygraph seven years ago."

"So did *you*, back in the day."

"That was different. I wasn't a suspect in my daughter's disappearance."

"No, you just lied about your past to get on the force. Point is, we know polygraphs are flawed. We also know that Lucas Pike was an angry, unstable man. Failed marriage, failed life. Maybe he felt rejected by Emily, maybe she said something to hurt him, maybe he didn't like her choice in boyfriends, who knows?"

"OK, but why now? Why text *me*? We've been off the Emily Pike case for weeks now."

"Maybe the re-opening of the case woke up his guilt, and he snapped."

"I don't like it."

"*Nobody* likes it when a body shows up in a ravine. But at least it might bring some closure."

"You know there's no such thing."

A news helicopter hovered above the wooded ravine just north of Miller Park in suburban Coquitlam. The moment we turned from Clark Road onto Seaview Drive, we hit a police barricade.

Wayne did a three-point turn and pulled over down the block with a clear view of the action. Several news vans were parked nearby, crews hustling to get the best background shots for the breaking story. A half dozen police vehicles were on the scene, and behind the barricades, two crime tech vans bustled with white-clad forensic cops.

Twenty or so rubberneckers milled about on the street. Several older men stood to the side, looking through binoculars. Front and centre of the action stood a teary Maddy Pike, being interviewed by a well-coiffed female reporter I recognized from the news. Maddy's hand went to her forehead and she shook her head vigorously. As if on cue, Lilith materialized from the crowd and stood behind Maddy.

Opening the glove box, I removed Wayne's binos and put them to my eyes. Fifty yards past the barricade, serious-faced cops and members of the forensic team came and went along a trail leading through the trees and down to the ravine.

"That's a well-used trail," I said. "That body can't have been down there long, or it would've been found by some dog walker."

"Who knows," he said. "This whole Burquitlam area's been under heavy development in recent years. Seven years ago, this ravine may have been no-man's land."

On the business side of the barricade, I spotted Fiona Saddy, wearing a gray pantsuit and a grim face. She spoke with a forensic cop, him doing most of the talking and she most of the nodding. Nearby, Inspector Davis spoke with another officer.

I opened the door and hopped out. Ignoring Wayne's protestations, I limped forward, circling the crowd while taking note of the two stone-faced cops manning the barricade. The one on the left kept checking his phone, so I used his distraction to approach that corner of the police sawhorse. Fiona Saddy had finished her conversation and was heading over to join Davis.

"Fiona," I called out.

She turned to me the same time the distracted cop did. "Ma'am, I'm going to need you to step back."

"I'm an investigator," I said, "I'm working this case."

He regarded my attire with amusement. "Where's your badge?"

Fiona approached warily, making a motion to the cop that it was OK.

"I need to talk to you," I said.

"We tried contacting you earlier," she said.

"Lucas Pike texted me last night."

"We know. We got his phone."

I nodded toward the ravine. "Is it her?"

She looked around as she stepped closer. "You know I can't say anything. You're not on this case anymore. And even if you were—"

"So, if he knew I was off the case, why bother contacting me?"

"I don't know."

"He mentioned that there were others. Is there more than one body down there?"

Fiona moved around the barricade and pulled me aside, out of earshot of other cops.

"The remains were badly burned," she said. "It's a job for a forensic dentist to prove, but there were articles of clothing nearby that belonged to Emily. Do the math."

"Was she found in a grave or in the open?"

Fiona hesitated.

"Fiona, you know this isn't right. Remember the day I came to the station, wanting a little cooperation? Remember how your partner brushed me off, told me I was wasting my time? Cold case. No leads. Then I go rattle some cages, and guess what, a couple weeks later, Lucas Pike texts a confession and kills himself."

"Not only to you."

"Who else?"

"His ex-wife."

"How'd you know to come here?"

She looked around again. "In his vehicle we found a map marking this spot."

"That's handy."

Twenty feet away, Inspector Davis looked up and saw us. Fiona turned away. "I've got work to do," she said. "Time to move on."

I grabbed her arm. "I didn't get your help before, and now bones and ash are being bagged and taken from that ravine. How long has she been dead, Fiona?"

"You know how long coroners' reports take—"

A series of high-pitched sobs erupted from the right. We turned to see Maddy Pike looking down at the tatters of what appeared to be a white blouse. Inspector Davis had moved over and was doing his awkward best to comfort the woman while maintaining a camera-friendly expression somewhere between sad and stoic.

"It's over, Sloane," Fiona said.

She turned and marched back to the other side of the barricade. I watched Maddy Pike sobbing and speaking to the cameras while clutching the blouse. "I just want to say to my beautiful baby girl that I love you so much, and I'll miss you every day of my life."

Behind her, Lilith stood, slowly nodding. The psychic looked up, and we made eye contact. A murmur of voices rose from the crowd, their attention diverted by several for-ensic investigators carrying a gurney bearing a black body bag containing a few lumps.

The news crews swarmed closer to the barricade. A wide-eyed Maddy Pike appeared to be in a trance as she moved toward the remains. Inspector Davis attempted to restrain her. She struggled to pull away, but then Lilith whispered something into her ear that reduced Maddy back to a sob-bing shell.

I found Wayne in the Pathfinder, seat partially reclined and smoking a cigar while watching the circus. On his lap sat his camera and telephoto.

"Anybody suspicious out there?"

"Besides you? Just a lot of seniors and assorted busybod-ies. No Lolas or men who fit the profile."

Up ahead, we watched cars and trucks slow, the occu-pants goggling the crime scene. "How about vehicles?"

"You mean like old VW jalopies? Nada. A corrections van drove past, a few delivery trucks, shit like that."

"You get photos?"

"Of every frigging vehicle passing by? Not bloody likely. Look, we need to face the very real possibility that Lucas Pike is the one who killed his daughter, burned her, and put her in that ravine."

"What's his connection to Lola?"

"All we have on her is that she's a cross-dressing runaway who happened to work at the same farm as Emily—"

"And was spotted in the area near where Amber went missing"

"Maybe."

We watched as Maddy Pike nearly collapsed and was set on a gurney. A paramedic attached an oxygen mask to her face. The crowd outside the barricade was building. "Search party will be setting up soon," he said. "Maybe they'll find more bodies."

"Fiona Saddy said they found a map in his car, giving directions where to find Emily."

"But he mentioned others?"

"That's what the text said. It could have originated from a person who wanted Lucas Pike to take the fall, which would effectively close the book on this investigation."

Wayne rolled his cigar between his thumb and index finger. "Almost noon," he said. "This death shit is getting to me. I could use a drink. Not to sound like an enabler, but I'm sure you could, too."

"Taking a break," I said.

"Come again?"

"Don't sound so incredulous."

"You went over to Jimmy's place blotto last night, didn't you?"

"No."

"Bullshit. Surfer boy probably gave you an ultimatum."

"We're doing this together."

"Ain't that sweet," he said, starting the engine and pulling onto the road. As Wayne turned the vehicle around, I saw Maddy Pike, still on the gurney, oxygen mask around her head, neck craned up, gazing at the chopper overhead. Her eyes held an odd, bemused expression, as though thinking, *All this for my little girl.*

CHAPTER 44

DENTAL RECORDS PROVED THAT THE CHARRED remains found in the Coquitlam ravine belonged to Emily Pike. Despite Lucas' claim to have killed others, an extensive two-day search of the surrounding area turned up no other remains.

The day after her body was found, I went to the Coquitlam detachment of the R.C.M.P. to meet with two cops from I.H.I.T., the Integrated Homicide Investigative Team. They turned on a recorder and took my statement, focusing on my meeting with Lucas Pike. When I mentioned my suspicions that it might be a setup—alluding to something bigger going on, namely involving the Benoit organization—their eyes went dead. But at least it ended up on record. Wayne would be placated.

For three days after the remains were discovered, all local and national media outlets ran with the story of her twisted alcoholic father murdering his daughter seven years ago. Demonizing exposés were cobbled together based on his petty problems with the law, his temper, and the abduction of Emily when she was a toddler. The worst photos were dredged up: a snarling and deranged mugshot, and another of him drunk and shirtless, his eyes dull and vacant. As far as the law, the media, and the public were concerned, a killer was dead by his own hand and a case was closed.

Despite this, Maddy Pike, with her innumerable teary-eyed TV appearances—witch-faced Lilith hovering at her side—seemed determined to milk the grief mill as long as possible. "I want to turn my pain into something that will help others, which is why, more than ever, I'm focused on KidFind, which assists other parents of missing children in keeping the search going when resources are exhausted and police run out of leads. I want to thank everyone for their amazing support in all this. Children disappear every day. They need your help. *We* need your help."

"She could've mentioned us, at least," Wayne groused, a can of Pabst in hand. We sat in his office, watching the flat screen on the wall. "We got the ball rolling, and that bitch barely flipped us a bone."

"Where is your empathy?" Frank said, sipping a cup of tea while sitting on the edge of Wayne's desk. "The woman's about to bury her child."

Wayne flicked off the TV, took a sip of beer and let loose a belch. "And here's to her capitalizing on it."

"You're just sore it's not us," Frank said.

"It's no way for a mother to behave, that's all."

"She behaves how she behaves," Frank said. "It's rough no matter what."

I sipped from a Mason jar filled with soda and lime.

"More pressingly," Wayne said, "we got zip in the Sebastian case. We've talked to all her old friends, teachers, neighbours. Anyone who she might have had contact with in the Downtown Eastside is either dead or AWOL themselves." He finished his beer, crumpled the can and tossed it toward the trashcan by the desk. It bounced off the rim and ended up beneath the open window, leaking its dregs onto the hardwood. A hot and polluted breeze trickled into the room.

I turned to Frank. "How'd those farms in the Valley go?"

"Nothing," he said. "No one has seen Lola. Also, I hate farms."

"Everyone hates farms," Wayne said. "Why do you think we sent you?"

"She's in the wind," I said. "Something she seems to be good at."

CHAPTER 45

ON A HOT AND BREEZELESS MORNING, NEARLY seven years to the day that she went missing, over two hundred mourners gathered at Ocean View Cemetery to witness the burial of Emily Pike. News crews were on hand, focusing chiefly on Maddy Pike's tear-streaked face as she sat in a folding chair, dabbing a tissue to her eyes beneath her sunglasses. Behind her stood Lilith, surreptitiously checking her watch.

Doc Barney stood to one side, sunglasses on, wearing a charcoal gray suit that hung on his bony frame. Chelsea Evans was in the crowd, her face pale beneath her sunglasses, looking like she wanted to crumple and sink into the earth. Every so often she glanced to her left, to where Oscar Benoit stood, wearing a dark suit, sunglasses, and a hard expression. He held a bouquet of white roses between his folded hands.

I stood between two large tombstones on a small hillock removed from the crowd. Feeling a presence to my right, I looked over to see Fiona Saddy in a black pantsuit.

"Nice of you to show up," I said. "Where's Davis?"

"Got a tip on a case."

"Right."

We listened to the drone of the minister's voice, the words barely reaching where we stood. In the distance, a siren wailed.

"Emily's grave was less than a week old," Fiona said, "and her body was burned recently."

My heart began to race. "When was she killed?"

"Inconclusive. There's nothing but bones in that box down there. Badly burned ones at that."

"Emily Pike didn't die seven years ago, did she?"

"I don't know."

"You're a cop," I said. "Speculate."

"We think that once the investigation was re-opened, Lucas dug up her body, burned her, and re-buried her in the ravine."

"Why? She'd practically have been a skeleton anyhow."

"Not if he kept her in a freezer. Lots of—"

"He lived in an SRO hotel. He'd have been lucky to have a mini fridge in there."

"Emily's jeans and underwear were found in his car."

I closed my eyes briefly.

"Seven years ago," she went on, "Pike was doing night security at various developments out there. We think maybe he had her buried near one of the sites."

"It's too neat a package," I said. "Travis Benoit is linked to this somehow."

"I've seen no evidence of that in any of the documents."

"That's because he's been granted keep-away status."

Down below, the minister wrapped up his spiel. People stepped forward to set flowers on the casket. Oscar Benoit placed his bouquet at the head of the box. Maddy Pike went last, setting down another rose. She kissed her fingertips and pressed them to the casket, just before it was lowered into the earth.

Oscar hugged her, and she clutched onto him and sobbed.

Fiona's phone buzzed. She checked it and said it was time to go. I thanked her.

"None of this came from me."

"Fair enough. Just tell me, why'd you pick Missing Persons?"

She stared down the hill. "I've got a five-year-old daughter. That's motivation enough, you know?"

I nodded.

"And for some reason," she added, "there always seem to be openings in that section."

"Can't imagine why."

Oscar Benoit walked slowly between the headstones, hands thrust in his pockets. Parked on the road fifty yards further up sat his blue F-150, sunlight bouncing off the rims as two thick-shouldered young men with buzzed skulls stood outside, passing a blunt back and forth.

I jogged up beside Oscar.

"Not in the mood," he said, not slowing or turning.

"Shitty day," I said. "But Lucas Pike did not kill his daughter."

"Why'd he hang himself and leave a note then?" His voice was low and raw. Before I could respond, he added, "It's because he's a guilty fucking coward who didn't want to get caught and rot in prison."

"No, he died because someone else didn't want to get caught and rot in prison."

He stopped. Over his shoulder I saw his boys on the hill eyeing us with interest.

I tilted my head toward the fresh grave. Most of the mourners had dispersed. Maddy Pike and Lilith were being interviewed by Global News.

"Your girl is being buried, Oscar," I said. "I want you to help me find out who did this to her. Your uncle—"

"My uncle didn't do it," he said. "I'd know."

I pulled my phone and showed him the uploaded sketch of Lola, alongside the older photo of Loretta.

"That's the chick that worked at the farm with Em," he said.

"Loretta Houston. What else do you know about her?"

He shrugged. "Nothing. I just remember seeing her around the farm from time to time."

"Emily never mentioned her? Like that Loretta maybe had a crush on her? Bought her jewelry?"

"First I'm hearing about it."

"And you never saw her around your uncle's ranch when he lived in Langley?"

"No way. I'd remember. He's had the same people working for him for years."

"I'd like you to give me the names of the people who were on the ranch that day you brought Emily out there."

Oscar Benoit paused, his brows knitting together. "You have no idea what the fuck you're doing," he said, before he turned and stalked up the hill.

"Emily didn't die seven years ago, Oscar," I called out.

He stopped.

"The coroner's report showed that Emily's body was burned and buried less than a week ago."

He slowly turned. "Are you fucking with me?" he asked, voice cracking.

I shook my head. "Still think her dad did it? Think he had the means to keep his daughter captive somewhere all these years?"

He chewed on the inside of his cheek and stared at a tree line at the edge of the cemetery. "I always felt it, y'know, like a gut feeling. Not like that freak over there with Maddy, but I *felt* it. That's why I haven't had another serious girlfriend since; I always hoped she'd come back."

"What's eating *me* is that if this thing had been handled differently, she might still be alive."

His face was pained. "Where was she kept?"

"That's what I'd like you to help me find out."

His posture deflated as he looked at me.

"Sleep on it," I said.

One of his boys laughed at something. Oscar looked up at them as he climbed the hill, and whatever that look said, it killed the laughter.

CHAPTER 46

SADIE WAS AT A SLEEPOVER THAT NIGHT, SO given our newfound sobriety, Jim and I decided to watch some Netflix and enjoy a nice quiet night in. It sounded good, but lacking a drink in hand, turned out to be interminably boring. I didn't make it ten minutes into *The Irishman* before my hands were in his shorts. He was ready.

"Whoa," I said. "Talk about a quick rise to the occasion."

Kissing my neck, he murmured, "Must be one of those gifts of sobriety they talk about."

Without the benefit of sensory-dulling libation, our first bout of couch-coitus lasted almost as long as it took DeNiro to deliver his first beating. "I can do better," Jim said.

"Glad this is a long movie," I said, continuing to grind against him until I came ten seconds later.

An hour later we cuddled on the couch watching Al Pacino rant and rail. I tapped my foot, twitched, and chewed my thumbnail. My heart raced and I wanted to go for a run, right then, barefoot, out the door and into the night. I caught

Jim studying me and forced myself to sit still and take deep breaths.

"Everything OK?" he said, pausing the movie. "You seem a little wired, and you barely ate dinner. Have you been taking your meds?"

"For fuck's sake," I said, pulling away. "No, I'm not taking my pills. One thing at a time. I'm not drinking, and that's enough right now."

"OK, it's just you've got this look in your eyes I haven't seen before."

"What look?"

"Reminds me of a caged panther in the zoo. Like you're pacing back and forth inside a cage. Only that cage is in your own head."

I grabbed his Oakley sunglasses off the coffee table and put them on. "Can you see my eyes now?"

"Not really."

I remounted him. "Problem solved then."

Following a sleepless night, I waited for the sun to rise before easing out of bed. I carried my clothes into the hall and geared up for a run. I was almost out the door when he called my name and stuck his head around the corner.

"What's up?" I asked. "Wanna join me for a run?"

He shook his head. "Sadie's grandma was supposed to pick her up from the sleepover and take her for the day. But she's sick. Today's going to be the biggest day at the shop—"

"Say no more. I'll take her."

He smiled. "She'll love it."

Sadie plugged her phone into the car stereo. We drove with the top down on my Jeep and listened to Taylor Swift and

Ed Sheeran. I smiled as she belted out the tunes, knowing every word by heart.

The smoke had dispersed, the sky was blue, and it was a good day, like summer was starting afresh. Spanish Banks Beach was busy with sunbathers, people playing volleyball, hacky sackers, potheads, and leather-skinned neo-hippies. We spread a blanket in front of a large log near the ocean. A strong wind rolled off the water, whipping our hair.

The tide was out, and we jogged through several hundred yards of warm, ankle-deep water before it was deep enough that we could dive and splash around. We did underwater handstands and had swimming races and floated on our backs. From the east, a gray wall of cloud marched slowly, almost menacingly, toward the sun.

"Go away, clouds," Sadie said.

We waded back to shore and ate the turkey, cheddar, and pickle sandwiches Jim had prepared. Sadie told me she was auditioning for a speaking role in a Disney film.

"Do you get nervous?" I asked.

She shrugged and finished chewing. "There are always other roles. That's what my acting coach says. And Haley told me not to get too famous when I'm young, because it's all downhill from there."

"Sounds like something she'd say."

Lunch finished, we used buckets Sadie brought to build a sandcastle, complete with moats and turrets. Several other younger kids wandered over and soon we had a sprawling city filled with lopsided and crumbling structures.

Leaving them to it, I went back to the blanket and observed the simple pleasure of children playing. I couldn't help but think of Emma and Charlie, and how they never had a chance to experience any of this. Aiming a bolt of raw anger toward my dead sister, it immediately backfired into my own chest.

I hadn't even realized that Sadie had plunked herself back on the blanket. "Can I please go get an ice cream?"

"Sure," I said, reaching for my bag. I gave her a five-dollar bill and she folded it into her small, pink purse.

"Do you want anything?" she asked.

"I'll just have a bite of yours."

Sadie hotfooted it through the sand toward the concession, pausing at the gravel path for several passing cyclists. She crossed the path.

"Stay where I can see you," I called out.

I sat on the log and watched her queue up in the long line. She waved and I waved back. A cold wind swept off the ocean, making me shiver. Gulls screamed overhead, their cries nearly sounding human. Children laughed as they kicked and stomped, demolishing the sandcastle Sadie and I had started. Things that take time and care to build crumble so easily. At the concession line, Sadie had moved ten feet ahead.

Tiny raindrops began spitting on my arms and the screen of my iPhone. The sky darkened and someone said, *Oh, shit.*

I stood, gathering our towels and bags. I would meet Sadie at the concession and beat the deluge. Only a few people were ahead of her in line. Something twenty feet to the right drew my attention: a muscular woman wearing a tank top and ball cap walked on the gravel path, her back mostly to me. She turned to glance over her shoulder and my breath caught in my throat.

Lola.

I jogged barefoot across the sand. Sadie was next in line at the concession. By the time I made it to the path, Lola was fifty feet ahead, walking in steady, metered strides. Beneath the ball cap her hair was cut short, and from the rear, she could easily pass for a man.

I began to run, dodging walkers and joggers. My phone suddenly buzzed in my hand and a glance down at the incoming text stopped me cold. Photos. One of Sadie and me frolicking in the water. Another was of her alone, playing in the sand.

Turning back toward the concession, I thought I saw Sadie, but when the girl turned, it wasn't her. Sprinting back toward the concession, I entered a panic tunnel, where the only thing I heard was my own frantic breath.

At the concession, Sadie was gone.

Turning round and round, my eyes skittered, searching everywhere. I was dizzy and my heart seemed to pound outside my chest.

Our spot on the beach was deserted. Suddenly very few people were around.

Looking back down the path, Lola had disappeared.

"Sadie!" I screamed. Heads swiveled. *"Nonononono ..."*

I frantically asked the remaining people in line at the concession if they'd seen a little girl with dark hair and eyes. They shook their heads. *Sorry, I'm sure she's around here someplace.*

I asked the teenager at the register if a little girl had bought an ice cream with a five-dollar bill. He shook his head.

I ran into the ladies' room. *"Sadie? Are you in here?"*

Nothing.

I ran back and forth along the path, searching, calling her name, asking random people, getting the same response. Lola had been heading west, and I did the same, but Sadie hadn't been with her. It had been a ruse to lead me astray, and it had worked.

In a nearby parking lot, I ran up and down the rows of vehicles, calling her name. A hundred yards to the right, a white Econoline van with blacked-out rear windows sped through the lot before screeching left onto Northwest Marine Drive. I sprinted diagonally across the lot, over a swath of grass, and onto the street, right in the path of the oncoming van. The bald and heavyset driver wore sunglasses, and the top of a child's head poked above the dash of the passenger side. The driver cranked the wheel, skidding the van into the rear bumper of a parked truck. Ignoring the driver bellowing curses at me, I looked past him to see the startled face of a little boy in the passenger seat. I apologized and took off again.

Back on the gravel path, I checked my phone again. The text had come from a blocked number. Just as I was about to punch in 911, my phone rang.

Jim. *Fuck.*

I answered. "Jim—"

"Sloane, what the fuck is going on!"

"We're at the beach. Sadie—"

"Some man just phoned me from Sadie's phone—"

"I was just about to call 911."

"I just did. The guy told me where she is. He said he was a friend of yours."

"Where is she?"

"On the sand behind a log about a hundred feet east of the concession, near the garbage cans. When I asked to speak to her, he told me she wasn't in any shape to talk!"

Running to that log was like living a slow-motion nightmare. The sky had opened up and people were fleeing the beach in droves, as though they had witnessed something horrible.

I spotted the trash bins to my left and veered in that direction, leaping over a log. Aside from several crumpled beer cans and sand studded with cigarette butts, the area was empty. I called out her name again as I searched log after log. Jim's voice was still coming over the phone. *"Sloane ... Sloane, talk to me!"*

Up ahead, partly obscured by tall beach grass and weeds, was a larger log. As I got closer, a small shape became visible through the weeds. My heart pounded like a death drum in my skull.

"Sloane! Are you there?"

A split in the weeds revealed a child's foot.

"Sloane!"

I kicked through the weeds and there was Sadie, blank-faced and sitting in the sand, her skin so pale she looked like a porcelain doll.

I fell to my knees beside her and said her name while I checked for a pulse. I picked up a steady beat. "Sadie, can you hear me?"

She stared right through me. Checking for injury, I ran my hands lightly over her head and neck, then down her arms, torso, and legs. Her swimsuit seemed intact.

I picked up my phone that I'd dropped in the sand. "She's here, Jim. I think she's OK."

"You *think?* What the fuck does that mean, Sloane, that you *think* my daughter is OK?!"

"She's been drugged ... I think."

"I'll be there as soon as I can," he said, and ended the call.

In the background, two police cars entered the parking lot.

CHAPTER 47

PULLING INTO THE PARKING LOT OF VANCOUVER Children's Hospital, the first thing I saw was Jim sprinting toward the emergency entrance. I parked and hurried in, finding him in the hallway talking to a tall female doctor and two cops, a male and female. When he saw me approach, his look of disappointment told me things would never be the same.

I wore a T-shirt over my swimsuit, but my hair was plastered to my face from driving in the rain with the top down.

"How is she?" I asked.

"Are you the mother?" the doctor asked.

"I was watching her when she went missing," I said, glancing at Jim. He looked away.

"Sadie appears unharmed," the doctor said. "We're running tests to determine what substance she was given."

"Devil's Breath," I said. Everyone turned to me.

"What?" Jim said.

I turned to the doctor. "Scopolamine. Not pharmaceutical grade, but an illicit form. It's used in Colombia."

"There was a powdery residue around her mouth and nostrils," the doctor said.

"I believe other missing girls in cases we've been working were given the same drug," I said.

"What case is this?" asked a stocky male cop to my right.

"I'm a private investigator," I answered.

Jim's eyes were frantic and angry. "He used my daughter to get to you," he said. "I talked to the bastard on the phone. You put her life in jeopardy."

"I had no idea something like this was going to happen."

"Who is he, this man you're investigating?" asked the other cop, pulling out a notebook.

"I don't know," I said. "But his partner's name is Loretta Lessard, but she also goes by the surname Houston. She lured me away from Sadie, and he took her."

Jim turned to the doctor. "Is my daughter going to be OK?"

"Her vital signs are fine," the doctor said, "and she's up for a CT scan within the hour. Once the lab results come back—"

"I want to see her."

"Of course."

I followed after them. Jim turned, stopped me, and shook his head. "No," he said, then turned and walked away.

"You need to come with us to make a statement," said the female cop.

"Jim," I called out, watching as he trailed the doctor down the corridor and through a door at the end.

I felt a hand on my arm. "Ma'am, come along with us, please."

I pulled away. *"I'm not leaving here until I know she's all right, do you fucking understand?"* Everyone in the hall—nurses, patients, and visitors—stopped and stared. Both cops tensed and hands went to TASERs. The corridor spun and faces blurred. I was guided to a chair in a waiting room. Their voices bled together, a jumble of nonsense. I ended up sipping a cup of apple juice and nibbling a cookie a nurse brought over. A doctor also checked my blood pressure and shone a light in my eyes.

After he left, the cops asked me some perfunctory questions and advised me that I'd have to make an appointment to come in for a full statement. After they left, I threw their cards in the nearby trash.

An hour later, Jim pulled up a chair and sat in front of me. "Sadie's coming to," he said. "There was only a tiny amount of that stuff in her system, and the scan showed nothing wrong."

"Thank God. Can I see her?"

"She's still a little out of it, and they're going to keep her overnight for observation. The police are coming back in the morning to ask questions."

I nodded. Our eyes met and his were sad, and resolute.

"I can't do this, Sloane. I'm sorry, but I just can't—"

I opened my mouth to say something, but everything I'd rehearsed in my head sounded like bullshit. I knew the moment I saw him in the hospital that we were done, and I didn't blame him.

He placed a hand on my bare knee. His touch was cold, and goosebumps rose to the surface of my skin. "I know you didn't mean for this to happen," he said, "and I know you care about Sadie, but I have to do what's best for her. That monster or murderer, or whatever he is, took my daughter, then called me up on her phone and used one of those voice altering things."

"What did he say?"

"He said that he had to run but wished he could stay around to get to know *you* better. He said, 'maybe *next* time'."

"That's all?"

"No. He also told me I had a beautiful daughter. His words were, 'Too bad she's so young'," Jim made a face like he wanted to spit something foul. "Those are the kind of people you go after and we can't be part of that."

"I'll drop the case."

"Yeah, but will he? I can't risk that. The police said they'd put a patrol on our house, but that's not good enough. We can't live like that. When Sadie gets released tomorrow, we're going back east for a while, stay with my folks."

"I'll get a different job."

"No, you won't. This is who you are, Sloane, and if I didn't have Sadie, things might be different, but you and I ... we have to end things."

I stared numbly at the floor and gave a small nod. Jim took my chin in his hand, and as we made eye contact, he kissed me on the lips. "Promise me you'll be careful, Sloane. I really do care about you."

The same doctor as before approached from the side. Jim stood and went to her and they talked in hushed tones. Neither of them noticed me leave.

CHAPTER 48

"... DONOVAN, PICK UP YOUR GODDAMN PHONE. *I got your message, such as it was. What the fuck happened today? Talk to me. I need to know you're OK. I don't want to find you running a hundred klicks out of town again.*"

As I listened to Wayne's message, I looked through the windshield at the dark house at the end of the street, before my eyes locked on the ravine beside it. At first, I thought it was the same one from where they pulled Emily's body. But no, that was Oscar's truck in the driveway, and I was in Whalley. It was past midnight and the drive had occurred in a rage-filled fugue. I put the phone on the passenger seat beside the half-empty water bottle filled with vodka and the vial of coke I'd stolen from Haley's director pal.

And the revolver.

I grabbed the gun and got out of the Jeep, closing the door as quietly as possible.

The blue F-150 sat at the end of the driveway. Quashing the impulse to shoot out the tires, instead I walked up to the vehicle and scraped the barrel of the gun down the length of the driver's door. The truck's alarm began shrieking and I stepped into the trees at the top of the ravine.

A dog began barking inside the house. Ten seconds later, I heard a window slide open and *chirp-chirp,* the alarm fell silent. A man's voice shushed the dog. A woman's voice said something, and the man responded, "It's just raccoons again, ma. Go back to sleep."

The moment the window slid shut, I picked up a small rock and lobbed it against the side of the truck. The alarm began shrieking anew and the dog resumed barking. A light went on in the house and, less than a minute later, a door opened and closed.

Through the trees I watched Oscar pad down the driveway wearing a wifebeater, pyjama bottoms, and flip-flops. In his hand he held a baseball bat. In his other hand was the fob, which he used to kill the alarm. He saw the dent in the side of his ride and cursed loudly, looking all around. He spotted my Jeep parked across the street. "I'm gonna kill you, motherfucker," he said, starting in the direction of my parked Jeep. As he moved toward it, I stepped out of the shadows and pulled back the hammer on the revolver. The click turned him in my direction. His eyes lost a bit of their fury when he saw me holding the gun on him from ten feet away.

"Get in the truck," I said.

"Go fuck yourself."

I stepped closer and raised the pistol, sighting it directly between his eyes. In the light from the streetlamp overhead, I could see they were glazed and bloodshot.

"You're drunk," he said.

"And you're stoned," I said. "I also got top points for marksmanship back in the day, and at this distance I can't miss. Get in the truck." Another light went on in the house, and I told him to hurry. "You don't want your mother to look out and see her only son get gunned down in the street."

Oscar opened the door of his truck. I walked around the passenger side and climbed in. After he got behind the wheel, I relieved him of the bat and kept the gun trained on him. I told him to drive. He keyed the ignition and reversed onto the street.

"What the fuck do you want?" he asked.

"Just drive. Get on the 1 heading north and drive."

"My mother's gonna worry if I disappear. She's got issues."

"We all have issues. She'll live."

A shrill voice came from the house. Looking past Oscar through the driver's window, I saw a woman with a drawn face under frizzy, blonde hair at the open doorway. "Oh, Jesus," Oscar said. "See?"

I lowered the gun but pressed the barrel near his groin.

"Where are you going, Oz?" his mother called out.

He stuck his head out the window. "I'm just going to the store to get some chips, ma. I'll be right back."

"I know you smoked up earlier," she said. "Cops are checking for that now with all these new laws."

"I'll be careful."

"Don't dawdle."

Oscar drove south on Bridgeview Drive, then merged onto King George Highway heading toward the lights of the Pattullo Bridge. A police cruiser passed us heading in the other direction. He stiffened.

"Nervous around cops, Oz?"

"No, but you should be, being that you're the one holding the weapon. This is straight up kidnapping."

"Kidnapping? Fuck *you*! Today a little girl close to me was taken and drugged, and believe me, if I thought you had something to do with that, I might just leave you dead on the side of the road."

"I don't know anything about any kid."

"Your uncle does. And don't give me that shit about how he's not involved. The type of people he knows dump bodies in barrels of acid and call it a day."

"Why do you think I'm not giving you a list of names? I don't have one anyhow. He keeps me in the dark. After I got out the last time, my mom made him promise he'd keep me out of trouble."

Coming off the Pattullo into New Westminster, he guided the truck north on McBride Boulevard, driving past Queen's Park. He put down his window, letting in warm night air. We passed by a group of drunk teenagers, laughing and shouting their way up the street.

"Tell me about what Emily saw that day," I said.

Oscar stayed silent as his eyes flicked all around. He reached out and rooted around in the ashtray, pulling out a tiny roach. His movements caused his vehicle to swerve partially into the oncoming lane.

"Eyes on the road, Oscar."

He sparked up the roach with a lighter and took a hit. "I'm not saying shit to you. Shoot me if you want."

"I'll save that option for later."

CHAPTER 49

A BLACK SUBURBAN WAS PARKED AT THE TURN-
around at the end of Highfield Drive. The headlights of the
F-150 picked up a ponytailed shadow behind the wheel—
Jake Dove on lookout. I slid low in the seat and out of sight
as we approached the gate. Oscar stretched his arm out the
window and hit a button on the console.

Ten seconds later, a man's voice, thick with sleep,
answered, "Whaddya want, Oz?"

"I just need to talk."

"For Chrissake. This can't wait till morning?"

"No."

Murmurs came over the intercom, one of them a
woman's voice.

The gate silently slid inward, and we rolled through.

Silhouetted against the indigo sky, the Benoit home
looked vast and imposing; a sleeping giant. As we climbed
the steep concrete stairs leading to the front door, I kept the
pistol pressed to the back of Oscar's neck. He stank of weed
and stress sweat.

The door opened upon our arrival and I locked eyes with Giller. If he was surprised to see me, it didn't show. If he had just woken up, it didn't show either, unless he slept in a T-shirt, jeans, and shoes, all of them black. No gun was visible.

"What do we have here?" he asked, glancing at the gun in my hand, before locking onto my eyes.

"Step back five feet and keep your hands where I can see them," I said.

Giller complied but did so in an exaggerated slow motion. "Yes, ma'am."

Using Oscar as a shield, I moved into the house, using my foot to close the massive wood door. It made an echoing boom through the broad foyer. In the gloom, I bumped a tall, skinny table and a vase atop it wobbled.

"Break it, you buy it," came a deep voice from a hallway to the left. I smelled spicy cologne and cigar a moment before Uncle Travis Benoit emerged out of the darkness like a black-robed apparition, gray hair swept back, intense blue eyes looking me up and down.

"Dumb place for a vase," I said. "It's begging to be shattered."

"Tell it to the boss of the house," he said, in a low voice. "I just live here. That being said, I do have a few house rules. One of them being: no guns. The second"—he looked pointedly at Oscar—"I don't allow idiots to bring trouble into my house. Oz, you truly are your father's son."

I felt Oscar's neck tighten and saw his jaw muscles twitch. Removing the pistol from his neck, I leveled it between his uncle's eyes. Benoit smiled and gave a small shake of his head as he slowly walked up to me. "Sloane, is it?"

"You know it is. Stop right there."

Another step. And another. Oscar's head was turned toward his uncle. Giller stared impassively at the scene, his eyes going from the gun to his boss. There was no fear in Benoit's eyes. I might as well have been holding a water pistol.

"You ready to use that thing, Sloane? It's been my experience that when you draw on someone, you better be prepared to pull the trigger, otherwise there's a very high probability that they will come back—"

Stepping up to him, I squeezed the grip of the pistol in both hands, imagining splattering him all over the Renaissance-style canvas behind. "If you or any of your crew ever come near the people I love again, I will fucking *kill* you."

"*Travis?*" came a woman's voice from above and to the left. I dropped the pistol to my side, just as a beautiful 50-something Black woman in a housecoat leaned over the balustrade of the landing, concern on her face. "Everything OK, Travis?" she asked, her voice heavily Latin-accented as she looked directly at me.

"Muy tranquilo, corazón," he said. "A little late-night company. You know how much I love that, man of my age and all."

"Oh, shut up about that," she said. "Hello, Oscar. How are you?"

"Just fine," he said.

"And your mother?"

"She's good."

"You should come over for a barbeque soon. Let's make some plans. I haven't seen you guys in forever."

Travis Benoit forced a smile as he locked eyes with me for a second before directing them at his wife. "I'll be up real soon, Mari."

She frowned, studying the scene below her for several seconds. "OK," she said, and disappeared.

Travis lunged in, pinning my gun arm to my side as his other hand wrapped around my neck. I kneed him in the groin. He made a face, grunting away the pain as he squeezed harder, walking me backward and pinning me against the wall. Air supply cut off, sparks danced in my vision. Giller stepped in and took the pistol.

"You gonna play nice?" Benoit whispered in my ear.

I nodded. He let go and I fell back, gasping.

He glanced up toward the landing, then leaned in again, whispering, "You're lucky I don't hurt women. Did you *actually* come here to threaten me?"

Giller released the cylinder on the revolver and looked in. "Three bullets."

"All I would've needed," I said.

"She's an expert marksman, apparently," Oscar said.

"Shut the fuck up, Oz," Benoit said. He pushed me down the darkened hall, past more large canvasses, giant vases, and tropical plants. We passed by a kitchen and dining room and through a great room with a vaulted, octagonal ceiling, and massive bay windows. He instructed Giller and Oscar to remain inside.

We stepped through French doors onto a granite patio overlooking an infinity swimming pool, complete with a ten-foot waterfall and a hot tub. The pool gave the surroundings an unearthly, green pallor. Beyond the pool was an unobstructed view of the darkened Burrard Inlet leading up to Indian Arm. Lights from homes on the Dollarton Highway twinkled across the water.

"Start talking," Benoit said. "What's this about?"

"Missing girls."

"Already made it clear. Not my thing. Turns my stomach to even read about it in the papers. Messed up situation, her own father killing her like that. He took the coward's way out."

I looked into his eyes. "Someone killed him."

"And you think that someone is me?"

"If not you, then someone you know."

"Well, *I* know it's not me, because it's not. But let's just suppose that what you're saying is true, and that I happen to know this person who abducts and kills a girl seven years ago, and more recently, murders her father but makes it look like a suicide. So we're clear, that *is* what you're saying?"

"Pretty much."

"OK, first off, if any of my associates conducted business is such a fashion, they wouldn't be in business long, if you catch my drift."

"Bad for business."

"That's right."

"OK then, what about Devil's Breath?" I said.

Benoit blinked once but stayed silent.

"Not going to act all surprised and ask what that is?" I said.

"You tell me."

"It's a Colombian thing," I said. "Rare up here, but used to abduct teenage girls."

"I wouldn't know."

"I think you *do*," I said. "Your Colombian connections are well-known. You bring in one type of powder, chances are you bring in others."

"There you go with the insulting accusations again." He motioned me back toward the house. "Time to get."

I reached into my pocket and before he could stop me, I pulled out a photo of Lola. Benoit stared hard at me for a moment, then reached into the pocket of his robe, pulled out glasses and put them on. He took the photo, studied it, and shook his head and handed it back.

"Her name's Loretta Houston," I said. "Also goes by Larry. Works with horses."

"I've never seen this person before," he said.

"She never worked on your ranch?"

"I had the same people working for me for twenty years."

He pushed me back toward the door. I stopped.

"I need names of people who were at your ranch the day Emily was there."

"You *need* to lay off the booze, honey. I don't even recall the day in question, but times were wilder then. What can I say?"

"How about the truth?"

Travis Benoit stepped close, his eyes cold and reptilian. "I can see that you're a little whacked out tonight, which is why I'm going to cut you some slack. But you come around here again, and you're going to see a whole other side of me." He grabbed my arm and shoved me toward the door. "Time to go."

He followed me through the door and immediately went to Oscar, who stood leaning against the massive stainless-steel fridge in the kitchen. "Stoned again, Oz? Don't lie."

Oscar huffed out a laugh, his eyes going to various objects in the room, but meeting no one's eyes.

His uncle stepped closer to him. "Stoners fuck up," he said. "*You* fucked up, boy. Or you're a simply a fuck-up. Which is it?"

Oscar looked at him, nostrils flaring and shrinking.

"Get out," said Benoit. "Both of you, get the fuck out. Now I'm in a bad mood, goddammit."

With that, he stalked off down the hall.

I looked over at Giller, who held a cup of steaming tea to his lips.

"What are the chances of me getting my gun back?" I asked.

He raised an eyebrow. "Not good," he said, taking a sip. "Man told you to go, you better go."

CHAPTER 50

AFTER BACKING DOWN THE DRIVEWAY, OSCAR Benoit laid rubber on the street in front of his uncle's house, leaving a smoking trail in our wake. "He's gonna love that," I said, making eye contact with Jake Dove, who sat stone-faced inside the Suburban across the street.

"Whole thing's your fucking fault," he said, flipping down the sun visor and pulling out a joint. "Forgot I had this thing in here," he said. Taking a hard-screeching right down the hill, he sparked up and took a hit.

"I wanted answers," I said.

"Did you *get* any? No. He's not going to tell you shit, but he's going to shit all over me till the end of fucking time."

"It's what he *didn't* say, like about Devil's Breath."

"The fuck is that?"

"See, now, your response I believe. Some people are born liars. You're not, because you keep your heart on your sleeve." I reached over and took the joint from him and took a hit. Pot was never my thing, but I was wound way too tight and needed something to make me feel differently.

Moments later, the world softened around the edges and my shoulders dropped away from my ears. I still wanted a drink, though.

Oscar turned onto Hastings Street and the first pink rays of dawn crept up over Burnaby Mountain. As we drove, the dark outlines of downtown skyscrapers seemed to grow and expand. It felt like we were sinking into the street and that the city was swallowing us.

"This stuff keeps getting stronger and stronger," I said. "They sell this in stores now?"

"You fucking kidding? This comes straight from Chico's op in White Rock."

"People still have grow-ops?" I asked. "Even though it's legal now?"

"Shit *he* grows ain't legal. Can't get this in a store."

Hooking left on the Cassiar Connector, Oscar accelerated steadily and remained in the right lane after merging onto the Trans-Canada Highway. Stoner speed.

"A shrink once told me," I said, "that we're only as sick as our secrets."

"I suppose you don't have any secrets."

"Not really. Only deep-seated regrets."

"And what do you do about those?"

"Live with them. Make better choices in the future. Try to, anyway."

"Like come over to my place drunk and point a gun in my face? You have no fuckin' idea how close you came to getting yourself killed tonight."

"Is that what Emily saw that day? Someone getting killed?"

"If she did, do you think she would've left there?"

"If not that, then what? If you loved your girlfriend like I believe you did, what did she see?"

He gripped the wheel tighter. "They don't even go on anymore," he mumbled.

"What don't?"

Oscar checked his mirrors, even though he stayed in the same lane and traffic was sparse. "The dogfights."

"Dogfights?"

"What're you, a goddamn parrot?"

"Were they always held at the ranch?"

"Only sometimes, usually when Mariana was out of town. There's basically a circuit and people come from all over. After Em saw it, I had to convince her not to go to the cops."

"Did anyone hear her say this?"

"I don't know."

"Think, Oscar. Did she say anything about seeing someone in particular who might have spooked her?"

"If she did, she didn't say anything. There were like a hundred people there, mostly rednecks from the Valley. Half of them spooked *me*. Look, Em was so disgusted by the whole thing she didn't speak to me for weeks after. I thought she was going to break up with me."

"Why would you bring your girlfriend to a dogfight?"

"My mom's on this crazy expensive drug for her rheumatoid arthritis, and my uncle procured some. I was just coming to grab it. Bad timing."

"Should've called first probably."

"No shit. To Em the dogfights were *worse* than someone getting killed."

"Where are they held now?"

"No idea. My uncle's done with that. Mariana told him she'd divorce his ass if he ever went near one again. She makes him donate a shitload to the SPCA every year as penance."

"Were Jake Dove or Giller there that day at the ranch?"

He shook his head. "They weren't around back then."

My head began to pound from the inside, like there was a little man with a hammer trying to get out. I closed my eyes, feeling sick and pasty-mouthed.

"Do you have anything to drink in here?" I asked.

"I'm not much of a drinker. I prefer the herb. Not so toxic on the liver."

"Your generation sucks," I told him.

CHAPTER 51

FAIRMONT PACIFIC RIM LOBBY. THE WRAP party for *Zyborg Apocalypse* was a tedious exercise in schlocky, cinematic self-congratulation. Statuesque servers bore trays of fluted bubbly and canapés, gliding through the throngs of actors in black ties and slinky dresses. Bearded crew members, uncomfortable in their suits, stood at the perimeter and drank too much.

At the single entrance, everyone's laminated passes were double-checked. My job was to shadow the effervescent and glowing Haley Cooper as she made the rounds, hugging, bussing cheeks, her tinkling laughter mellifluously melding with the jubilant swing era music from the white grand piano on the dais above the murmuring crowd.

Haley insisted on personally thanking every person in the room, from the A.D., to the script coordinator, to the grips, and it surprised me—though it shouldn't have—that she knew everyone's name.

They loved her, this beautiful, talented young woman who radiated charisma, exuded charm, and had the strength and courage to bounce back from a potentially fatal addiction.

I thought back to this girl a month ago, dancing in a meth den on the Eastside.

Maybe people really *can* change.

Haley caught me looking and pulled me aside. "Karin texted me what happened with Jim the other day. Are you OK?"

"Now's not really the time to get into it, but all is good."

"Bullshit. You can tell me over a drink in my room later. Well, *you* can have a drink. Me, I'll just stick to my soda lime with imaginary vodka. I've been doing really well. Day thirty-six. I got a sponsor and everything."

"It shows. I'm really proud of you."

Haley hugged me. Her eyes were damp. "Thank you, Sloane. We've been through a lot, haven't we, sister?"

"More than you know," I said, glancing over her shoulder, to where Wayne stood near the hallway to the washrooms. With his suit and earpiece, he looked like a bulky Secret Service agent. Frank was somewhere in the crowd, but he would be next to invisible. Goran, our newly-hired Serbian muscle, towered above the other security guards near the door, glowering at anyone who dared make eye contact. He had an even more menacing cousin, Valki, who, at that very moment, was parked outside my condo in case my abductor friends decided to pay a visit.

Haley continued her rounds and I followed casually behind, never letting her get more than ten feet away. For the remainder of the night, I forced myself to keep eyes on the crowd, for anyone who looked out of place. Minutes crept by like hours.

At 11:45, Haley yawned into her wrist. "This girl's about to give the wrap party a wrap."

I drove her in the Range Rover back to the Four Seasons. Trailing behind in a white Lexus sedan was Goran. In front of us was another Range Rover, driven by Frank. Wayne had gone on ahead to do a creep sweep of the Four Seasons lobby.

Just as I swung the Range Rover into the parking semi-circle, Wayne's voice came through my earpiece. *"We got a guy trying to get up to Haley's floor. Freak had his zipper down and was saying he just wanted to meet her. We got him in the lobby now. Cops are on their way."* In the background I could hear a man wailing: *"I'm a big fan! I came a long way for this!"*

"They got somebody," I told Haley.

"Who?"

"I don't know. Some guy yelling with his zipper down."

She laughed. "That describes almost every guy I've ever known."

Wayne: *"Cops are here. Guy's in tears. I almost feel sorry for the pube-clipping freak."*

The man wailed, *"All I wanted was an autograph."*

Wayne: *"All clear. You guys can head up. Service elevator will be ready for you."*

As we stepped off the elevator onto the 24th floor, Haley brought up Jim again.

"I'm not going there, Haley. I'm serious; it's over. Doomed from the start. The moment I found out he had a kid, I pretty much knew it wasn't going to end well."

"Bullshit. You love Sadie! Way to cram your feelings into a little box. Maybe it's why you drink so much—"

"Thirty-two days sober and you're telling me how it is, huh?"

"Thirty-*six*," she said. "But yeah, I really think it's going to be different this time. I've had what they call a profound spiritual experience."

"I'm very happy for you," I said, waving the key card over the sensor. It flashed green, and I pushed open the door.

She walked into the suite and kicked off her high heels before heading for the open bedroom door. Over her shoulder, she said, "I'm still a long way away from Step Nine, but at some point, I'm going to owe you an amend—" She stopped cold.

Stepping up behind her, through the open door of the bedroom, I saw what at first looked like splashes of crimson on the white duvet. Thousands of rose petals. "What the *fuck?*" she asked.

From the walk-in closet stepped a naked man, tall and skinny.

Eyes wide, yet calm.

Revolver in his hand.

"Hey, Haley," he said, "you going to make amends to me, too?"

I stepped in front of Haley and reached into my bag for the Enforcer.

"You probably don't even remember me," he said.

"No, Sloane," Haley said, stopping me. "It's OK. It's OK, right ... Jacob? We went to high school together. Of course I remember you."

Jacob looked surprised, then his eyes flashed to anger, before quickly settling on sadness. "You were nice to me in high school, and then you weren't."

"Put the gun down, Jacob," I said. "Everyone's friendly here."

His eyes turned enraged and he raised the gun. "*This has nothing to fucking do with you!*" he screamed. "*It's between me and Haley.*"

"I'm sorry if I hurt you, Jacob," Haley said. "I was a different person then."

"Different ... *different,*" he muttered, then looked up at her sharply. "Did you like my gifts, Haley?"

"They were ... unique," she said.

He took a step forward. I yanked Haley back behind me.

"So were you, Haley Marie Schultz," he said, taking aim and pulling the trigger.

Click.

"Oops," he said, turning the gun around and putting it in his mouth.

Haley screamed.

Jacob pulled the trigger, spraying blood and chunks of tissue out the back of his head.

His body collapsed on the bed full of roses, his dick flopping to the side.

The gun thumped to the floor, and I kicked it back into the hall. As I pulled Haley toward the door, I saw one of Jacob's clutch hands feebly at the bedspread. I stopped and made her stay at the door while I stepped closer. Jacob's eyes fluttered as we made eye contact. Blood burbled from his mouth as he tried to speak.

"He's alive," I said, taking out my phone to call 911.

CHAPTER 52

THE SMOKY MORNING SKY TURNED THE RISING sun a white ember, as Wayne and I exited the Cambie Police Station, having just spent the last three hours giving a statement. "Every suicidal idiot knows to aim up when you eat a bullet," he said, clicking the fob to open the doors to the Range Rover parked nearby, "otherwise you end up like that poor bastard, with an extra breathing hole in the back of your neck."

"For Haley's sake, I'm glad he's not dead."

"You get a chance to talk to her?"

"Briefly."

"How is she?"

"In shock. She blames herself, saying that if she'd treated him nicer in school, none of this would've happened."

We climbed in and Wayne started the engine. "Horseshit," he said. "Everyone and their dog is pulling the 'oh, poor me, here I am, all fucked up because someone called me a loser turd fucker back in grade nine.' And they *did* call me a loser turd fucker back then. Look at me now. Don't see *me* stalking movie stars."

"You go tell her that, Wayne. I'm sure it will be super effective."

Wayne slipped on his aviators, put the vehicle in drive, and pulled a screeching U-turn right in front of the cop shop. Pointing the car east, he said, "I just might."

"You'll have to be quick. Her flight is in two hours. She had to get out ahead of the media shitstorm."

"It's gonna follow her there," he said. "While you were being questioned, my phone's been ringing nonstop. And Frank says we got a news crew camped outside the office."

"How did Amy Gardner take it? She must've shit."

"Surprisingly, no. She sounded almost elated. Event like this'll probably bump up Haley's star value, so ultimately, more dinero for her. Fucked up business."

"Speaking of fucked up, what's the word on Jacob?"

"Jacob B. Delacroix, now missing most of his palate and a good portion of his neck. Miraculously, the bullet missed his spinal column."

"Lucky bastard."

"Yeah, when he gets out of the loony bin, he'll probably get some sort of book deal or they'll make a movie of this shit. Not that he needs the money. He's a failed actor and trust fund brat from one of Little Rock's richest families, which is the reason he has the wherewithal to chase an actress all around North America, and bribe cleaning staff to get into her room—not to mention the guy who created the diversion at the hotel. Good thing that first chamber of the gun was empty."

"He planned it that way for effect," I said. "He wanted to scare Haley."

"Hm. I'm hungry. You wanna go for breakfast?"

"I wanna go home and have a shower."

"You OK to drive?"

"Of course."

He paused, looking at me sideways.

"What?"

"We never really talked about what happened the other day."

"It happened. It's over. Jim was right. I fucked up."

Wayne swung a left onto Main Street. "This job is hard on relationships," he said. "But I know how much you liked him."

I put on my sunglasses and chewed the inside of my lip as I looked out the window.

"Any chance of fixing it up with Jimbo," he asked, "after things cool down some?"

"Because of me, a murderer abducted his daughter. So no, I don't think so."

"Sadie was unharmed," he said.

"Except for the potentially lethal narcotic she was given. Yeah, like that's not hard to overlook down the road—'*Hey, dad and stepmom, remember the time that creepy guy stole me for a bit and drugged me up? Whatever happened to that guy?*'"

After a pause, Wayne and I glanced at each other. "Whatever *did* happen to that guy?" he asked.

"We are going to fucking well find out."

Wayne made a left onto Hastings Street. A block later, he paralleled into the next available parking spot. A couple of passing tweakers wearing hooded jackets peered at me through the tinted passenger window. I asked what we were doing.

"I'm hungry," he said, "and you're looking skinny enough to fit in with the crack-a-lacks down here." When I began to protest, he added, "*and* I still want to know where you went after the shit went down the other day."

We got out the vehicle. A police cruiser ripped past, lightbar flashing and siren on. We walked down the sidewalk, sidestepping addicts who were doing the nod while propped up against the crumbling wall of a pawnshop.

"I went and got shitfaced."

"Understandable," he said. "But why do it in Surrey?"

"You tracked my Jeep?"

"Which was parked outside Oscar Benoit's home for over three hours."

"I needed to have a word with his uncle."

Wayne stopped outside the Ovaltine Café and gave me a hard look.

I held up a hand. "You want me to be honest or not?"

He fired me a look and pulled open the door, gesturing for me to enter the busy diner.

CHAPTER 53

OUT OF THE PAST SEVENTY-TWO HOURS, I'D slept for maybe four of them, yet when I finally got home around noon, I was mentally wired yet emotionally numb. I fed Eclipse and washed three ibuprofen down with a tumbler of white wine. I poured another and took it into the bathroom with me while I had a long shower. When I closed my eyes, I was greeted with the new image of Jacob Delacroix blowing his mouth out the back of his head to the accompaniment of Haley's million-dollar scream.

I toweled off and dressed in shorts and a loose T-shirt. Pouring more wine, I looked at the clock. I'd nearly killed a bottle in under an hour. I looked out the window to see a white Lexus sedan parked on the corner of Nelson and Chilco Streets, a bulky shape behind the wheel. Goran. At Wayne's insistence, from here on out, I would have eyes on me at all times, in case Lola or her partner made an appearance, or if Benoit paid me a visit.

I looked at the wall, to the large and detailed map of Metro Vancouver. To the right of it, I'd hung another map of the Fraser Valley, similar in scale, which included Mission and Deroche. Red flags were inserted in South Vancouver, the Downtown Eastside, and Deroche—spots where Amber and Emily may have been last seen, along with the other missing girls with similar features. Flags also went up in Coquitlam, where Emily's remains were found, and in Mission as well, to represent the botched abduction attempt on Renay Burris. Black flags went up in Langley and Capitol Hill, representing Travis Benoit. The only known address of Lola, off Main Street, earned a black flag. Another went up in Whalley for Oscar, not because I still suspected him, but just so I could step back and check for a geographic pattern.

As I finished the wine, I stared at the map, my eyes drawn toward two pins: Mission and Deroche.

Marching into the bedroom, I pulled on jeans and a black T. Then I called Wayne. "I'm heading back to the Valley."

"You got something?"

"Maybe. I need to check something. You in?"

"I've got to take Theo to soccer camp today. You OK to do this?"

"Absolutely."

"'Cause it's no problem for you to take another day. I can join you tomorrow."

"I'm fine." The walls were closing in, and the bottle in the freezer was calling out to me. "I'll let you know what I find."

CHAPTER 54

ROLLING INTO MISSION, THE SKY WAS THE COL-
our of cigarette ash and the air smelled of burned rubber.
Even at ten a.m. the town gave off a doped-up vibe, the few
people out looking like they only had the vaguest notion of
where they were headed.

By eleven, my shirt was stuck to my body as I rapped on
doors up and down Stave Lake Street, working the blocks
north and south of Renay Burris' near-abduction. I sucked
breath mints and displayed Lola's photo and sketch to anyone who opened a door. I also showed Amber's photo. Half
the doors didn't open, and of the ones that did, all I got
were headshakes. Many of the old timers who had lived on
the street for decades took a long time studying the sketch,
asking questions, and bemoaning the state of a world where
young girls could simply vanish.

More than a few of the residents were also distracted by
the pristine, white Lexus parked on the street, and its hulking
driver behind the wheel. When I reentered his vehicle and
grabbed my water bottle, I told Goran to park further away.

He shook his head. "When out of your home, you are to be kept in sight at all times. Order number one."

"But half the time people peek out the window and when they see your car, they won't even open the door. They probably think you're a realtor. Why are you driving a white Lexus anyhow?"

"Engine three-point-five litre V-6, same as Toyota. Will last forever. Yet unlike Toyota, this car runs like dream and greatly enhances my chances of quality female companionship."

"I'm sure," I said, taking a sip of my water bottle. It was filled with water. I nearly spat it out. "What the fuck is this, Goran?"

"Water. Order number two: no drinking on job."

"Did you dump it?"

"Yes. When my uncle began drinking vodka in the morning, he was dead in two years. Life is hard. Why make harder by being addict?"

"Says the guy who lives on fast food and doughnuts."

"Point taken. When is lunch, by the way?"

"Fuck your lunch."

In Rocko's Diner, thirty minutes later, I watched Goran devour a cheeseburger, fries, and a chocolate shake. I nibbled an onion ring and looked at the map I'd spread out on the table.

"Lots of places to hide out here," Goran observed, pushing the last of his burger into his thick-lipped mouth.

I sipped a coffee.

"Could take forever," he said, "and you still might find nothing."

"I know," I said, looking up at him. "Listen, Goran, the people we're after, they came after me once to send a message. Because I haven't backed off, they'd probably be inclined to do it again. But you know what's keeping them from doing that?"

"Me."

"Correct. Now let's just say you were to hang back, make it appear like I'm alone—"

He shook his Kodiak bear-sized head. "Order number three: don't let Sloane give orders."

"It's a mere suggestion, not an order. If we can lure them out—"

"Not going to happen. Too risky. Besides, my job is bodyguard, not to catch bad guys. You will not persuade me."

An elderly waitress came by to freshen my coffee. I declined and asked for the bill. When she returned with it, she nodded to Amber Sebastian's missing persons photo on the table.

"For a second I thought that was Angie," she said.

"Her name is Amber," I said.

"No, I know, but she looks a lot like Angie. Angie Fromme."

The hairs on my forearms rose. "Who's Angie Fromme?"

"She disappeared a long time ago. Forty years ago, I think. I didn't know her, but I used to see her around all the time. After she went missing, her photo was up everywhere, and in the paper and whatnot. I can't remember what I had for dinner last night, but I remember that face. Angela Fromme."

After paying the bill, I pulled out my Mac and tapped in the diner's Wi-Fi password. Pulling up the Missing Children's website, I entered Mission, B.C. into the database and immediately found Angela "Angie" Louise Fromme. Date of disappearance: August 1, 1980. Born in '65. Fifteen years old when she went missing. Clicking on her tiny photo to expand the size, I held up Amber's photo for comparison.

I stopped breathing for a second.

Goran craned his head to see. "Could be sisters," he said.

CHAPTER 55

IN THE MISSION LIBRARY, I ASKED THE MATRONLY librarian how far back their archived newspaper files went.

"Depends on the paper," she said. "Some go back a hundred years."

"I need to check local newspapers from 1980, when a young girl went missing from the area."

The librarian's face was grave. "Angie," she said.

"Did you know her?"

She shook her head. "My sister went to school with Angie's mother, who used to come in from time to time. Poor woman. She's passed now."

I told her I was an investigator working a missing persons case, and she led me to a row of microfiche machines. After bustling about in a nearby cabinet, she returned with several boxes of film. She asked me if I knew how to run the machine, and I said yes.

"You look familiar," she said. "Have I seen you on the news?"

"It's possible," I said, taking the boxes and thanking her. Removing the film, I fixed the red spool and threaded the film through the viewing window, moving it forward and back before adjusting the focus.

She snapped her fingers. "I *have* seen you on the news. You were guarding Haley Cooper when that stalker almost killed himself in her hotel room. Were you there?"

Across the room, several elderly men looked up from where they were playing a quiet game of chess.

I told her I was, then turned my focus to the film.

"That's just awful," she said.

I didn't respond.

"Well," she said, "I'll leave you to it, then."

She walked off and I began scrolling through archived editions of the Vancouver Province for the month of August. I stopped at the headline:

NO CLUES TO MISSING GIRL'S WHEREABOUTS
By Sy McDuggan, Staff Reporter, August 4, 1980

Fifteen-year-old Angela Louise Fromme was last seen leaving her job as youth coordinator at Camp Jewel on Friday August 1, at approximately 3:30 p.m. After saying goodbye to friends and coworkers, she boarded the bus, which dropped her off at the stop on Dewdney Trunk Road. She was last seen near the Cedar Ridge Golf Course, walking west toward her home on Keystone Avenue. This was something she had done hundreds of times, only this time she didn't make it home. Her current whereabouts are unknown. Angela has been gone for three days and her parents, Patricia and Brent Fromme, are worried for their daughter's safety.

"It's not like Angie to not come home," said Patricia. "Angie would always call and let us know if she was going to be late. She is a very responsible young woman, and we are worried sick. We are pleading with anyone who may have seen anything or know of the whereabouts of Angela to please contact the police. Our daughter is an intelligent, sweet, and caring person, and she is our only child."

Tomorrow, on Saturday, August 9, volunteer search parties, led by police, will set out to scour the area around Dewdney Trunk Road and Keystone Avenue. Posters have been distributed to local businesses and government buildings, and police have asked that if anyone has any leads in the case to please notify the authorities.

Over the next several weeks, the paper ran five more stories on the disappearance of Angela Fromme and how the police were doing all they could. Angela's family, friends, and coworkers had all been questioned, but no leads had been generated. As all news stories do, in less than a week, front-page headlines of the missing girl petered out to several uninspired paragraphs on page five.

I looked up to see the librarian restocking books on a nearby shelf. After striking up a conversation, I quickly discovered that her name was Lucy, and she was a Mission lifer. I asked her if she recalled any odd occurrences in the area in the time before or after Angela went missing.

She shook her head. "Nothing like that had ever happened out here before. It changed the community. Suddenly folks weren't so carefree anymore, and I remember that for the rest of that summer, you hardly ever saw any kids playing outside. But that was certainly the first—"

"My Molly disappeared back in '79," said one of the chess players in a phlegmy voice.

"His dog," Lucy said, rolling her eyes.

"She was our golden retriever," the man said. "But they found her."

"That's fortunate," I said.

"They found her *dead*. Dead in the forest with a bunch of other dogs. Some sonofabitch chained them to a tree and left 'em to starve to death. Eventually they killed and ate each other."

I paused. "Did they ever find out who did it?"

The old man shook his head. "Lots of pets went missing in those years. Local legend was that a band of Satan worshippers were doin' sacrifices in the woods. But there was never no sign of that."

"And this was 1979?"

"Yep, summer of. I know because it was just after my son's tenth birthday, and the boy bawled his eyes out when he found out. We told him Molly ran away, but he heard stuff at school."

"I'd forgotten about all that," Lucy said. "It didn't really make the papers back then, did it?"

"Nope," he said. "It's wasn't really investigated either. Even today if someone butchers a pet, they never get more'n a slap on the wrist."

"Fuckers should be castrated," mumbled his even more ancient chess-mate.

"Sir, do you know where the spot was that your dog and the others were found?"

"My name's Mike, young lady, and you bet I do."

"Castrate the sonofabitch," the other man repeated.

"Easy now, Charlie," Mike said. "You give yourself another stroke, I'm gonna need to find a new chess partner."

"Feel like taking a ride, Mike?" I asked.

Goran looked bemused to see me leading Mike toward the Lexus. I helped the old man into the passenger seat and climbed into the back.

"This a senior's bus transport now?" asked Goran.

Not hearing him, Mike looked suspicious at the behemoth behind the wheel. "You Russian?" he asked.

"Serb."

"Hm. Well, you drive a nice car anyhow. Same engine as Toyota? V6?"

"Oh, Jesus," I muttered.

"Correct," Goran said, starting the engine. "Like a purr. Will run forever."

"OK, where to, Mike?" I asked.

"Head up toward Stave Lake. It's about twenty minutes from here."

The trail that led into the woods felt like we were entering a cave, with little light making its way through the forest canopy. The air was humid and thick with decay, as though the scent of death had failed to dissipate even after all these years.

"Forty years ago," Mike said, huffing as we ascended a rocky slope, "it was a hunter and his bird dog who found what was left of my Molly and the other pups. As you can see, the trail's miles from any homes, which is why no one heard the barks. Hang on, I gotta catch my breath and have a smoke."

While Mike lit a cigarette and puffed away, I checked my phone. No bars. Although I couldn't see them, I heard the buzzing of insects. Goran looked warily from side to side.

"Nature creep you out, big guy?" I asked.

"Not a fan," he replied, swatting a no-see-um from his club-like forearm.

"This is bear country," Mike said, stubbing his cigarette against a tree and pocketing the butt. "Cougars, too. And Sasquatches."

Ten more minutes up a narrow switchback brought us to the trunk of a giant, dead cedar, ten feet across. Winding round the tree was a rusty chain, affixed by a heavy padlock. From the chain hung framed photos of the dogs that had met their fate here. Several crosses were staked to the ground.

"When they were found," Mike said, "there were signs that they'd been fed for a while, because there were empty tins and dog food bags around, along with empty buckets for water."

"He took care of them up to a point," I said, "and then he didn't."

"If you can call chaining seven dogs to a tree 'care'," Mike said. He spat and lit up another cigarette. "The dogs had gone missing over a span of four months. It was a hot summer, like this one."

"Molly was taken from your home?"

"Yep. She was an outside dog, mostly, but we let her in when weather got rough. Country dogs are brought up different. I see big dogs penned up in apartments and it seems cruel to me."

"Was Molly taken from the backyard?"

"Hard to say. She was free to roam and had different spots she liked."

"And how far are we from your home right now?"

"*Now* I live in a home a couple blocks from the library you found me at, but back then we lived in a rancher about five miles up the road."

"The same road we parked on?"

"Just off it. This neck of the woods hasn't changed a whole lot since. A few homes torn down, and a few new ones.

Give it another forty years and it'll likely be all condos and Starbucks. I ain't gonna miss what's coming, that's for sure."

"Did you know the owners of the other dogs?"

"Some yes, some no. Woman named Yolanda lives the closest to here. They all came from this general area though. I recall the police at the time saying there was no pattern to where they came from."

"He had a vehicle and knew the area," I mused, walking around the tree and taking in the surroundings. I saw a young man with haunted eyes, maybe a teenager, leading the dogs up here, one at a time, bringing them food and water, and then suddenly stopping. Or maybe it had been a slow, methodical starvation process over a period of months.

Or maybe he forgot about the dogs and moved on to bigger and better things.

Like Angela Fromme.

CHAPTER 56

YOLANDA MILLER COULD'VE AUDITIONED FOR A role as a hobbit in *The Lord of the Rings*, if hobbits were Black, cursed like truckers, and spat long streams of chewing tobacco. We'd found her sitting on a rocking chair on the wide porch of a clapboard house that looked like it had never been maintained in its hundred-plus years.

I told her I was here to ask about the dogs that were found near her property forty years ago.

"I was just a little kid when it happened, but my dog was one of them found up there. I got photos of me and Sic from when I was a kid."

"I hear you go up there on a regular basis," I said. "Have you ever seen anyone else up by that tree? Someone who didn't seem to belong, who may have felt off in some way."

"I seen a few hikers stop and check what it's about, and going back a few years, some of the other dog owners would come leave stuff. Old Mrs. Keller used to bring flowers, which I thought was a fuckin' ridiculous thing to bring a dog, even a dead one."

Beside me, Mike bristled with geriatric agitation. "That was my wife, you little sawed-off—"

I put a hand on his bony shoulder. "Easy, Mike."

Yolanda turned her head, and from between a large gap in her two front teeth, jetted an impressive brown arc, missing the front tire of Goran's Lexus by inches. From the look on my bodyguard's face, I half-expected him to growl.

Beside the Lexus was a gray rust-bucket of a Volvo with a *For Sale* sign on the windshield.

"What about your neighbours?" I asked. "Any of them strike you as strange? See anything weird going on?"

"This is Mission," she said. "Whole place is fuckin' strange. I suppose if someone were actually *normal*, they'd stand out more."

"Who is still living in this area now who would've been around back then?"

"What, you want names of people on this street?"

"That would make my life easier," I said, pulling out my notebook.

She spit again, pointed right, and began rattling, "Over there you got the Henriksens. The kids have taken it over and are raising fuckin' llamas. Across the street and east a ways used to be the Busbys, but they're dead, and some other citizens live there now, Schneiders, I think it says on their fence. They run some sort of eco-bullshit B&B. Never met 'em. They weren't around back then."

"What about on the other side of the forest?"

"There's Hillbilly Bill, a recluse whose wife died a long time ago. My mom used to make him food sometimes."

"Bill McCurry," Mike said. "Comes into town once a month by bicycle. He's even older than me."

"Any children?"

"Nope," he said. "Guess that's the sad part, huh? Growing old and having no kids to come check on you."

I ignored him and asked Yolanda if she remembered anyone else in the area.

"Next place after old Bill belongs to the Reifers. Their son and his family are there a lot. Joe. He's about thirty-five. Too young to have done those dogs, unless he did it in a past life. Across the street from them were the Dankos. The mom's dead, and the son moved away a long time ago."

Before we left, Yolanda asked if anyone wanted to purchase the rust-bucket Volvo. "Only half a million miles on the counter-thingy. Looks like shit, but it'll run for fuckin' ever."

"Tempting," I said. "How about it, Goran? Ready for an upgrade?"

After dropping Mike back in town, Goran and I returned to Stave Lake Road. The balance of the afternoon was spent talking to other families: the Henriksens, the Schneiders, and the purported recluse, Hillbilly Bill, who served me a warm can of Lucky lager on his back porch and said that the dead dogs still haunted him.

"I heard 'em baying some nights, and I thought they was coyotes. Poor buggers were up there starving, and I didn't do a damn thing."

I showed him Lola's photo and asked if he'd ever seen anyone suspicious in the area.

He shook his head, and I thanked him for his time. As we walked back to the Lexus, he said, "You want the truth, I think you're hunting for ghosts. I used to think about that girl, Angie. I knew her folks from around town, and I think we all wanted to believe she was out there somewhere, living her life. But deep down, we knew she was gone. I recall drinking with her old man one night. After a few too many, Hal told me he knew his daughter was no more. Said he felt it in his gut. Maybe that's what gave him stomach cancer years later. He died young. So did his wife, Mary."

Back in Mission, the air was full of electricity as a thunder-head rolled in over the mountains to the east. I spent the next hour at the R.C.M.P. station, talking to Constable Glen McCordick, who had been assigned to the area twelve years ago and knew most of the locals. I asked to see the file on Angela Fromme, and he was happy to oblige. It consisted of a thin manila file, showing photos of her and the area she was last seen. Also in the file was a list of family members and friends, along with pages of witness statements, many of them hand-written.

"Amazing how people just *vanish*," McCordick said. "Her photo's still up in the high school. My wife is principal over there."

I asked him about the murdered dogs in 1979, and he reiterated that although he knew of the spot in the woods, it was before his time. He then asked if I thought the crimes were related.

I replied that I didn't know. Just then, rain suddenly began pelting on the window to the right, distracting us into glancing over.

I thanked him and was about to leave when I thought of something. "Say, how long has your wife been principal of the high school?"

CHAPTER 57

PRINCIPAL VICKI MCCORDICK AND AN ELDERLY man with vivid blue eyes met me at the entrance of Mission Secondary School. The man introduced himself as Rob Piteau, the principal from 1980. His hands and speech were shaky, but he recalled Angela Fromme well.

"She was one of the school sweethearts," he said, as we walked through the empty halls toward the office. "For me, and for many others, after she went missing, this school was never the same. It was like we lost our innocence."

We entered the office, where Vicki flipped on the lights. After leading us down a short hall and unlocking another door, she ushered us into her office. Rob and I took seats in front of the desk, while Vicki went to a shelf and ran her fingers over the spines of old yearbooks.

I asked Rob if he recalled Angela having a boyfriend.

"Angela was one of those girls who was friends with everyone," he said, "but I can't recall her singling anyone out as special that way. She was an honours student and a member of student council. Very focused, very bright. Despite the fact that she skipped grade nine, she was mature for her age. The kind of kid who you knew was going to go places." He shook his head. "I remember that time so vividly. The whole town was on edge. 1980. It seemed like that's when everything started to go to hell around here. Crime. Drugs. Senseless, brutal violence. I've lived in Mission my whole life, and it's always been a bit rough around the edges, but now ... it's anything goes out there."

"Things have certainly changed," Vicki agreed, making eye contact with me as she handed me the yearbook from 1980.

* * * *

Driving back on the Lougheed Highway in rush hour, I leafed through the yearbook while Goran drove. Near the Haney Bypass, Wayne called to see if I'd gotten anywhere. I recounted my day.

"No one hired us to find Angela Fromme and look into some dead dogs from forty years ago," he said. "It's too far off the mark."

"We got nothing else, Wayne. I'm going to send you Angela's photo; she looks like the others."

I heard him mumble a curse.

"OK, Wayne," I said. "What did *you* find today?"

"That soccer moms are hot. I'm in a relationship now and suddenly I'm getting frigging *swarmed*. Sal's lucky I'm the monogamous type."

"Is she ever," I said. "Check out Angela's photo. I just sent it."

Back home I put on Metric's *Art of Doubt* album on the stereo, poured a glass of wine, and stood on my balcony, staring out over Stanley Park. A heron flew past, screeching as it disappeared into the forest. A brief chill raced through me, followed by a feeling of deep dread. My heart began racing. I held my hand up and willed it to be steady. Nothing was wrong. I gulped the wine and went back inside.

After printing off a black-and-white photo of Angela Fromme, I hung it on the wall next to the other girls. 1980. A twenty-plus year gap until Amber disappeared. Maybe Wayne was right; I was reaching, seeing something that just wasn't there. Then again, the killer may have moved away for a time, which explains how he came to know a teenage Loretta. He could have been travelling in the United States and picked her up when she was hitching. I stared at Lola's photo. He didn't kill her. Instead, he made her co-conspirator in other abductions, like Paul Bernardo did with Karla Holmolka.

I sat down with the Mission Secondary yearbook. Working back to front, I began with the grade twelve class, methodically scanning each face and name. In grainy black-and-white yearbook photos, it was difficult to discern if the young men sporting deadened eyes were of the psychopath variety or were merely stoned. None stood out. In between the individual grades were several pages of candid photos taken throughout the year. Angela was in a handful—and with her bright smile and engaging eyes, was always easy to spot amid her peers. There were shots of her working on the school paper, in student council meetings, decorating a gymnasium for a school dance, and playing field hockey. Among the classmates in her grade, no one jumped out— just a sea of floofy eighties hairstyles, bad skin, braces, and typical adolescent awkwardness.

Eclipse jumped up and flopped down on the book. I nudged him aside and he indignantly swatted my wrist before repositioning himself a foot away.

I was about halfway through the grade tens when Wayne called to let me know about some last-minute security work.

"Can't do it," I said, still studying the faces in the book.

"Not asking you to," he said. "This client is requesting some size and intimidation factor, so I immediately thought of Goran. You OK with that? The big guy said he hasn't spotted anyone suspicious all week."

"I think I'm in the clear," I replied.

"Any word from Jimbo?"

"No."

"Well, you never know. Give the guy some time."

I poured more wine. "Thanks for that, Wayne. Now I can stop sitting around waiting for that phone call."

"Listen, Sal and I are celebrating tonight. Looks like her ex is ready to settle. We're gonna dine at Parq and hit the casino to celebrate. Wanna join?"

"Nah, you kids have fun. I'm already settled in. Hey, did you check out that photo I sent?"

"I did, and you're right, she's a dead ringer for the others."

"I told you. I'm just combing through her class yearbook now."

"Let me know what you find tomorrow. Just make sure you get some sleep tonight, you hear?"

"You too, dad."

I finished my drink and yawned. I poured more wine. Angela Fromme as a person was gone. She existed as photos and hazy memories in the minds of those who remembered her. Same with Amber Sebastian. Emily Pike was in the ground. Everyone was either gone or getting gone. At that moment, children the world over were disappearing. Girls, boys, babies. Pop. Pop. Pop. Bye-bye. No one could do anything about it. I sat back and closed my eyes, listening to the melancholy chords of "Underline the Black".

Fuck Wayne for bringing up Jim. Now he was in my head too. His eyes, his smile, how his body felt pressed against mine. How we laughed. How, for such a brief time, I felt I belonged.

A tear rolled down my cheek. I kept my eyes shut and drank.

When I opened my eyes, I thought to call him, reach out, tell him that I'm done with all of this, that I'm ready to throw myself into something new.

That I love him.

I was about to slap the yearbook shut when my eyes settled on a name.

Danko.

I grabbed my phone and scrolled through the photos I'd taken earlier that day. I found the one I was looking for. It was of a dented aluminum mailbox on Stave Lake Road, the lettering stenciled on the side faint but unmistakable.

D A N K O

Looking back to the yearbook, if not for the name, my eyes would have slid right past the broad, bland face of Paul Danko. With his prematurely receding hairline, large, square glasses, and wispy excuse for a moustache, he looked more like a substitute teacher than a student. Behind his glasses, his eyelids were half-closed as he calmly stared into the lens of the camera.

I felt a twinge of familiarity and for a moment I stopped breathing.

Pulling out my Mac, I Googled the name and got back nothing. That, in and of itself set me buzzing. Logging into the investigator database, I found three people belonging to the name Paul Danko across Canada, and a quick cross-reference proved that they were the wrong age. I checked deaths and obituaries. Nada. There was no phone number listed to him. It's possible he had changed his name or had moved abroad. It's also possible he was a criminal operating under an alias, one who had taken steps to avoid being detected by people like me.

I poured the last of the wine and called Wayne. It went straight to voicemail. I ended the call without leaving a message and then looked up the number for Rob Piteau. After picking up on the fourth ring, the former principal sounded pleasantly surprised to hear from me the second time in one day. I asked if he remembered a student named Paul Danko.

"He graduated in 1980, I believe. Big lad; knew how to throw his bulk around in a rugby game."

"Any idea if he knew Angela Fromme?"

"I've no idea. I do know that for many years the family ran a slaughterhouse on the back of their property, until it was permanently shut down when some folk got virulently ill. The father became a bit of a shut-in. The mother went on to drive a school bus. They're both long gone now."

"Do you remember anything else about Paul?"

"Not really. He would've been questioned one-on-one with the police," he said, "as was every single student and teacher."

I thanked him again and ended the call.

Then I called Kai.

"Let me guess," he said. "More missing girls?"

"More like a missing fifty-eight-year-old man. His name's Paul Danko, and he used to live in Mission. There's zero on him in the database."

"I'm not hacking into CPIC," he said.

"I'm not asking you to. I just need to know if he's still around here, and if so, why he's off the grid."

"I'll get back to you in a few hours. Wayne's not behind this, is he? 'Cause I'm not working for him."

"So far he knows nothing," I said. "This is between you and me."

"Good," he said, and ended the call.

I dumped the rest of my wine down the sink and grabbed my keys.

CHAPTER 58

THE COYOTE SCAMPERED ACROSS STAVE LAKE Road, staring down the headlights of my Jeep as I rounded the corner. The animal disappeared into the ditch on the side of the road, and I turned into the next driveway, driving past the *For Sale* sign next to the rusty mailbox that bore the hand-painted red letters: D A N K O.

I steered down a rutted driveway, tall grass and weeds brushed against the undercarriage of my Jeep. Around a corner and past some stunted trees, my headlights illuminated the boarded-up farmhouse and the dilapidated and sagging outbuilding behind. I parked near the house and killed the lights. A large coffee and a fast drive into the Valley had sobered me up. I clipped my running headlamp above the visor of my ball cap and turned it on. After climbing out, I buckled on my utility belt which held the Enforcer, pepper spray, and the satchel containing my picks. I pulled on latex gloves and climbed the three steps onto the creaky porch. The front door was secured by an old padlock attached to a hasp and staple. The padlock keyhole was so thoroughly rusted that experience told me my tools would be a waste of time. A quick look around made me doubt anyone had set foot here in many months, if not years. Stealth was not of paramount importance. I walked back to the Jeep, opened the back, and removed a pair of long-handled bolt cutters.

After snipping the lock and letting it clunk onto the porch, I set the bolt cutters outside the doorframe, opened the door, and entered the home. The air inside the home was heavy and dank with the smell of rot. The floorboards creaked as I moved across the kitchen, the beam from my light playing across dusty cupboards and ancient appliances. Mice darted across the floor and disappeared beneath the ancient, green stove.

Brushing aside cobwebs, I entered the living room, which was stripped bare except for some empty boxes on the floor. Looking behind me, I saw that my shoes left tracks in the thick layer of dust that coated everything. A quick search of the two bedrooms showed that aside from rodents, the house had been empty for years.

As I walked back outside, my light illuminated green animal eyes in the tall grass and brush surrounding the house. A warm breeze rustled the branches of the tree by the porch. I picked up the bolt cutters and headed to the rear of the house.

Walking up a short concrete ramp to the outbuilding, I snipped the chain that held the handles of the two sliding doors shut. The chain clinked to the ramp as I slid open the door to the right. From the direction of the road across the field came the rumble of a truck. I paused, waiting for the headlights to pass by in the distance. With a quick glance behind, I entered into darkness. Motes of dust danced as the beam of my headlamp illuminated the hooks in the ceiling.

I smelled the coppery tang of old blood that had soaked into the floorboards.

A flapping sound behind me made me whirl and jump back as a bat nearly grazed my cheek on its way out the door. Several of the hooks swayed in the breeze, making a sound like chains clanking. My heart began to gallop in my chest.

My phone buzzed in my pocket, making me jump again. I pulled it out. Kai.

"What do you have for me?"

"Why are you whispering?" he asked.

"'Cause I'm in a haunted fucking slaughterhouse," I said, stepping back outside into the humid night.

"You might consider going vegan," he said. "Check your email. I just sent you what little information there is on this Danko guy. If it's the same guy you're looking for, all I could find was an old address on Stave Lake Road—"

"I'm there now."

"It's been on the market for twelve years. Property taxes are all paid up though. Guess it's not exactly a hot market out there?"

"Place is just oozing with untapped potential. Any other residences listed?"

"Nope, but he was married a long time ago. And divorced—also a long time ago. His ex remarried. Lives in Chilliwack."

"Address?"

"It's in the email I sent you. Oh, and one more interesting thing."

"What's that?"

"This guy's credit score. Despite owning the property, it's pretty much non-existent. No credit cards, no mortgages, no loans. Which means, unless he's dead or living completely off the land, he's a cash only guy. Makes him almost impossible to track."

"He's got money to pay the property taxes. Has he filed a return recently?"

"Hey, I'm strictly amateur now. My present operating system won't let me peek into government institutions. Plus, with all the CRA scams, they've really upped their cyber-security game. Be thankful I found you the ex."

"I owe you one, Kai."

"You can pay me back by not calling me again."

"Yet you keep picking up the phone."

"Yeah, well. Just be careful. This guy is taking pains to cover his tracks, and he's doing it really well. For whatever reason, he doesn't want to be found."

CHAPTER 59

AFTER COMPLETING A ROUGH WALKING TOUR of the property, I got back in my Jeep and drove south, over the Mission Bridge and past Matsqui Village. Ten minutes later, I was driving past strip malls, car lots, and storage facilities on the outskirts of Abbotsford. It was nearly three in the morning and other than cops, the only people out were those on something or looking to score. Though my eyes burned with fatigue, with every beat of my heart, the thrill of pursuit pulsed through my chest.

Back at the Danko home I had discovered no graves, no abattoir jumbled with human bones, no Mason jars packed with formaldehyde-preserved organs, no shreds from victims' clothes. For that matter, I had also not seen any sign that a human being had set foot on the property in a long time. Yet, there was something, an ineffable sense of something that was once there, that kept me pushing to the next step.

I thought to call Wayne again, at least text him what I was doing, but he would only tell me—and rightfully so—to get my ass home.

Approaching the turnoff for the highway, for one second I considered heading west, back home to bed.

I yawned, and pointed my Jeep east, toward Chilliwack.

TOCK-TOCK-TOCK. A drop of water hit my cheek and my eyes snapped open to see an overcast sky. Another raindrop hit my face through the open window. I was parked on a hill, across the street from what looked to be a new townhouse development.

TOCK-TOCK-TOCK.

The sound came from the roof of my Jeep. Craning my head out the open window, I peered up to see a crow pecking at something on the metal, maybe the shit of another bird. Reaching my arm out, I slapped at it, and the bird flew away, cawing.

It was 7:27 a.m. I didn't remember falling asleep. My mouth tasted sour and my stomach burned. I popped a breath mint and got out of the car. As I climbed the steps of the townhouse, a curtain in the living room moved, but I didn't see a face. I knocked, and a man in his early sixties answered. Lanky, bald, and wearing round glasses, he was definitely *not* Paul Danko.

After apologizing for the intrusion, I introduced myself and asked to speak with Shirley Beckett. He said she was his wife and asked what it was regarding. I flashed my credentials and told him it was a missing person case.

"Who is it, Don?" said a woman's voice.

"A private investigator," he answered over his shoulder. "Wants to ask you some questions."

When Shirley Beckett appeared in the hall, my main question was answered. Though in her mid-fifties, she was a petite, dark-eyed brunette wearing glasses and a housecoat.

Once again apologizing for the unannounced arrival, I said I had a few questions regarding her ex-husband, Paul Danko. At this, her current husband made a face and retreated into the background, letting her know he'd be in the kitchen.

Shirley invited me to have a seat in the living room, which looked out over nearby Mount McFarlane, its peak wreathed in fog.

"I heard something about a missing person?" she asked.

"*Persons,*" I said, taking photos from my satchel and placing them face up on the coffee table in front of her: Angela Fromme, Amber Sebastian, Emily Pike, Loretta Houston, and the sketch of Lola. "Only the first two women are missing."

"I've never seen any of them before," she said, her eyes going from one photo to the next. Her face was getting paler by the second, perhaps recognizing a younger version of herself in some of the images.

"You were only married to Paul for a short time," I said.

"We got married young. Too young. I was twenty-two, he was a few years older."

"Can I ask how you met?"

"At work. You know, groups of us would go out to the pub after work and he and I, we hit it off at first."

"What kind of work?"

"I was an addiction counselor. Used to go into various prisons. Back then he was a guard at Mountain. Heard he moved on to Kent later. Worst of the worst, that place."

My head felt light as my brain worked overtime to process this new information.

"Are you all right?" she asked.

I stared at her. Before my eyes, she morphed into a younger version of herself, before becoming Angela, then Amber, then

Emily. I blinked and she was back to being a fifty-something woman in a housecoat again. She looked apprehensive. I asked how long it had been since she saw him.

"At least thirty years," she said, leaning forward and speaking in a quieter tone. From the kitchen, a kettle began to sing. "I ended the marriage. Paul was a strong, stable man; and for me back then, it represented everything that men in my life *weren't*. I felt safe. But then it grew stifling. He wanted me to stay at home more, wanted me to quit my job. I was only just starting out. I also wanted to go out with my friends. He didn't like that. It made him mad."

"What did that look like, him getting mad?"

"When Paul was mad, he'd just kind of simmer, grow distant and cold. A few times, near the end, he'd take off, sometimes for a few days."

"Do you know where?"

"His family cabin, up near Stave Lake. His dad's place, somewhere off the grid. Would you believe, I never met his father? And I only met his mother at the wedding. She was an odd duck, too. Barely left the house."

"This might seem an odd question, but did you ever have any pets when the two of you were together?"

She nodded. "I had a shih tzu. She went missing shortly after we were married. Paul said it was probably coyotes."

CHAPTER 60

"DONOVAN, YOU'RE NOT SUPPOSED TO BE OUT *there alone! I need you to get the fuck back home!"*

As I drove through the Chilliwack farmlands, the morning rain came down harder. I flicked the wipers onto the highest speed.

"He's a prison guard, Wayne. Our guy. His name is Paul Danko—"

"For the love of fuck—"

"Just listen. According to his ex-wife, he may work at Kent Prison. Before that he was a guard at Mountain, which also housed Amber Sebastian's father Ray. Correctional officers are considered law enforcement, which is why information about him is scarce. Even Kai couldn't find out much."

Dead air. For a moment, I thought our connection was broken. I hooked left on a roundabout and pointed my Jeep back toward the highway. Then Wayne asked, "Are you coming back here or not?"

"I'm already out here, Wayne. I just need to check—"

"I think it may be time to revisit our contract, because I'm pretty much through with this. I need a reliable partner."

"Wayne, please, just find out what you can about Kent—"

The phone went dead.

Kent Pen. The government euphemistically called it a federal correctional institution, but it was really just BC's one and only maximum-security prison, and it housed over four hundred of the country's worst offenders. To earn your place among the gangsters and serial killers and ultra-violent psychopaths out here, you had to have unleashed a good dose of pure hell upon society.

Even a lawyer or a cop would require pre-authorization before waltzing into a place like Kent. Given that fact, it didn't seem wise to enter the front doors flashing my P.I. license and making inquiries regarding one of their C.O.s, so I sat in my newly acquired Volvo in the parking lot, waiting and watching the entrance.

Several hours ago, I'd pulled into Yolanda Miller's driveway to find her once again sitting on her porch, spitting tobacco into her yard. Over several mid-morning vodka coolers and some amiable conversation, she agreed to rent me her Volvo for three hundred dollars. I'd left my Jeep as a security deposit.

Now I watched as a steady trickle of people exited the building, carrying the collateral damage of violent crime in their haggard and hard-living faces. Mothers and fathers, wives and girlfriends—even some of the young children looked like they had just viewed a horror film, an ongoing one they'd carry with them for the rest of their lives.

Studying my surroundings, I counted at least six cameras situated on light posts around the parking lot. To my left was a 30-foot watchtower in which I could see the faint silhouette of a guard through the tinted glass. Surrounding the compound were tall chain-link fences topped with hula-hoops of hurricane wire. Every few minutes, gunshots echoed off the mountains nearby. At first, I thought the sounds were coming from the prison, but then remembered the gun club I'd passed on the road in. Hearing continuous gunshots must be a good way to keep inmates on their toes. Or maybe it was like a lullaby to them.

An hour went by. Ninety minutes. Sitting in a beater for an extended period of time in the visitor parking lot of a prison made me feel exposed. That very moment a camera might be zooming in on my face through the windshield. Knowing my luck, Paul Danko could be the one on camera detail. No matter who it was, a vehicle sitting for too long would arouse suspicion.

Separated from the main lot by a gate was a smaller lot that appeared to be staff parking. I could see rows of parked vehicles, mainly trucks and SUVs. Remembering back to my cop days, I had heard that correctional officers worked 12-hour shifts, but when those shifts began and ended, I had no idea. With no other corroboration, I was operating on the word from a long distant ex-wife that Danko *might* be working here. It also seemed a bad idea to call the prison and inquire about a specific guard. Word would travel pretty fast within those walls. Problem was, even if he was here, I had no current photo and no idea what type of vehicle he currently drove. For all I knew, it could have been his day off.

I checked my phone. No further response from Wayne. Which meant he was still pissed. I cursed myself for being such a stubborn bitch and once again considered starting the engine and driving away.

But I couldn't.

I called Fiona Saddy. She was just going into work.

"I have a person of interest named Paul Danko," I said. "He's a correctional officer, possibly at Kent."

"What do you want me to do about it?"

"Look him up, Fiona. Because I can't find anything about him, but I think he's connected to the missing girls and the murder of Emily Pike. He used to work at Mountain, which is where Amber Sebastian's father—"

"Hang on," she said. "I'm just heading into a meeting. I don't have time to deal with this now."

Movement to my left drew my eye and I turned to see a brown Yukon drive past and exit the parking lot. The profile of the driver froze the air in my chest.

My mind flashed back to the man asking for directions near the Benoit house. Balding, moustache, glasses, smiling as he asked if there was a shortcut down to the water.

Don't think so. But I'm a little lost myself.

Well, thanks anyhow. I hope we both make it to where we need to go. Bye, now.

"Fiona," I hissed. "It's him. I just saw him."

"Calm down, Sloane. Where are you?"

"At Kent Prison, in Agassiz."

"Don't do anything. I'll let Davis know—"

"No—"

"He's on your side, Sloane. I'll run a check as soon as I can and get back to you."

"I'm following him," I said, and ended the call.

The Volvo coughed several times before starting. By the time I pulled from the lot, the Yukon was several hundred yards down the road. In the hills north of Agassiz, traffic was sparse, but hopefully the rain hampered visibility sufficiently that my gray vehicle would blend with the landscape.

The Yukon drove at a steady seventy kilometres per hour, passing the town before turning west onto the Lougheed

Highway. He picked up speed to pass a slow-moving flat-bed carrying a backhoe. I hung behind the flatbed for a minute. When I finally edged into the oncoming lane to pass, I immediately jerked the wheel back to avoid getting in a head-on collision with another car. After a seemingly endless succession of vehicles travelling the other direction, I was finally able to pass. The Yukon was gone. I stepped on the accelerator and sped along the highway, the Fraser River to my left. The squeaking wipers on the Volvo were pathetic, merely moving the water from one side of the windshield to the other. I drove as fast as possible, passing slower moving vehicles, and receiving honks for cutting it close against oncoming traffic.

It wasn't until I'd crossed the bridge over the Harrison River that I saw a smudge of brown in the distance. The Yukon. Slowing down to a normal speed, I hung back, and despite the weather, kept my headlights off. Fifteen minutes later I saw a sign for Deroche. We were close to the Sebastian home. The Yukon kept going.

I called Wayne and left a message: "I am following Paul Danko west on the Lougheed, past Deroche. He's in a brown Yukon and it looks like he's heading for Mission. His ex-wife said he has a cabin up in the mountains. I can't get close enough to get a plate. I know you're pissed, but I could use your help here. There's a good chance I may be out of cell range soon, but my GPS will be activated."

I put the phone down and raised the Nikons. It was raining too hard to make the plate on the Yukon. An old pickup pulled out from a driveway in front of me, forcing me to slam the brakes. Up ahead, the Yukon's right signal light flared, and Danko turned right and disappeared. The GPS told me it was Sylvester Road, and when I got close, I turned right as well. The Yukon was again a blip in the distance.

The distance between homes grew further and further apart and vehicles became sparse on the narrow road. He drove at a steady, measured pace. No other cars were in my rearview, so if he had good eyes and had been paying attention, he'd have seen a gray Volvo clocking him for kilometres. When Sylvester Road became an unpaved service road, my heart rate quickened even more. He was heading away from Mission, and we were already many kilometres north of the derelict family home I had visited the previous night. The road twisted and steepened, and several times Danko's vehicle disappeared around corners.

As soon as I caught a glimpse of the Yukon, the road curved sharply to the right, and once again it vanished. Coming around the corner, suddenly there he was, pulled over on the side of the road about a hundred yards ahead.

My breathing stopped and my muscles tightened. If I kept going, I'd be forced to pass him, and he'd see me. If my tail wasn't already burned, it was about to be. Using the lamest of evasive tactics, I pulled into a driveway on the right, nearly smashing into the propeller of a powerboat parked beneath a carport.

Through the trees and brush to the left, the brown SUV sat on the road, idling. A few moments later it slowly drove away.

On the patio above the carport a tall, shirtless man stepped out and frowned down at me. "Help you with something?"

I stuck my head out the window. "I'm a little lost. How far is the lake from here?"

"Not much of a lake in this direction," he said. "More like mud flats."

"Know of any cabins nearby?"

His eyes narrowed. "They're a ways up. About as far as you can go. And they're not exactly the kind of places you go rent for the weekend. I was you, I'd turn around, head back to the highway, keep going till you get to Harrison. I doubt there's much up this way you'd want to find."

"You never know," I said, reversing the Volvo and backing down the driveway.

Continuing slowly up the road, the rain continued unabated. Homes were few and far between, the driveways sufficiently long that many houses weren't visible from the road. I checked my phone. One tiny bar.

Hearing the roar of an engine, I looked to the rearview to see a massive, mud-caked 4x4 with roll bars and fog lights riding my bumper. Grabbing the Enforcer from my bag, I slowed and pulled to the side. The monster truck tore past and continued up the hill.

Soon the road leveled off but turned into washboard, with mud-filled potholes. My progress slowed as I attempted to weave around the larger holes, occasionally bottoming out the Volvo and making an ugly scraping sound as the undercarriage met rocks. I had a premonition that this would be the last vehicle I ever drove.

After thirty minutes, the road forked. I stayed right, where the narrow road continued to climb. After a series of switchbacks, the road grew even steeper. The bald tires of the Volvo began to slip and lose traction. Second-growth trees grew dense on either side, forming a thick, green canopy that felt like driving through a tunnel. There hadn't been a home for several kilometres. The rain stopped momentarily. I rolled down the window and slowed. Silence. No birdsongs. No breeze.

After several more minutes of climbing, the trees thinned as the road widened and leveled off. I pulled over and got out, finding myself standing at a cliff face, looking down on the steep cut of a misty, wooded valley below. The silence carried the sensation of being watched and I kept turning to look at the trees behind.

I sat on the hood of the car and trained the Nikons on the valley, sweeping them slowly left to right. Steam rose from the earth around me, mingling with the growing fog. Visibility worsened by the minute. I didn't know the terrain, and I cursed myself for picking up such a shit car.

In the valley, about a kilometre to the left was what appeared to be a clearing. It could've been an old logging clear-cut, or it could've been nothing. Minutes later, the fog crept in and obscured it all.

Overhead, dark clouds obscured the sun. A low rumble of distant thunder.

From inside the car, my phone rang. I hopped off the hood and reached through the open window and grabbed it. Wayne.

"Where are you?" he asked.

"The mountains."

"No shit. I *know* that. Have you found the house?"

"No, but I'm close ... I think."

"For Chrissake, Donovan—"

"Listen," I said, "you can threaten to rip up the contract tomorrow, but are you going to get your ass out here or not? 'Cause I don't see the cops coming any time soon."

"I'm en route. Don't move until I get there."

"I have to get off this road. I'm a sitting duck out here. But I think there's something in the valley."

"Satellite map shows something in the forest; a cabin maybe, hidden among the trees, with a clearing beyond. Head back to where the road forks and take the other road for about a klick or so. There's a place where the two roads nearly converge again. I should be there in just over an hour."

I ended the call and got back in the car. In the time I'd spoken to Wayne, the valley below had become enshrouded with fog. I turned the car around and drove back to the fork in the road and hooked onto the even steeper logging road. After locating the area Wayne had mentioned, I found a spot where I could pull off and reverse snugly between the trees. I ate a banana and drank some water. From my bag in the backseat, I grabbed green camo running tights and a matching pullover. I changed in the car, then tucked my hair beneath a black toque. After texting the coordinates to Fiona Saddy, I turned on the car's engine again, and plugged the Enforcer into the cigarette lighter.

I looked down at my hands. They were shaking, and not from fear. I reached beneath the seat for the water bottle. Empty except for a trickle at the bottom. I unscrewed the cap and swallowed the warm vodka dregs. It wasn't enough to do anything, but the burn was familiar, comforting. My hands still shook.

When I looked up, the rain started again.

CHAPTER 61

AT 2:12 P.M. WAYNE'S PATHFINDER PULLED UP in front of the Volvo. I climbed into his vehicle and saw the shotgun on the seat. "Case we run into a bear," he said. Several sheets of paper printed off Google Earth sat beside it; an aerial view of the surroundings.

Wayne chewed on the inside of his cheek. It was his tell. He had something to say but didn't necessarily want to.

"The cops know we're here," I said. "I texted Fiona Saddy just before you arrived."

"She reply?"

"Not yet, but I gave her the GPS co-ordinates."

Cheek-chewing silence.

"What is it?" I asked.

"After you called and told me about Kent, I did a little quick research and found some news stories going back four, five years. It's a place they prefer to keep hush-hush, but there was an exposé on the amount of drugs getting in, along with cell phones, weapons, even guns."

"Guard corruption," I said.

"No different than any other prison in the world. It's a no-brainer; those guys get paid shit wages to do a shit job. But there's something else. I cross-referenced a few ODs and they turned out to be UN gang members."

"OK."

"Same guys who put several of Travis Benoit's crew in the morgue a few years earlier."

"Danko's in Benoit's pocket," I said. "He's bringing in hot doses."

"Some of the victims also had traces of scopolamine in their systems."

"Devil's Breath," I said.

"Yup."

He opened the door and stepped into the rain, then reached back and grabbed the Remington.

"First hike we've ever been on together," I said. "Sure you're up to it?"

"Yeah, I thought we'd just stroll up all casual-like,"—he tucked the butt of the shotgun into his armpit and pulled his blue windbreaker around it—"and pretend we're Jehovah's Witnesses."

We stepped into the woods leading downhill to the original service road. Several minutes of walking brought us past the place I had pulled the car over earlier.

A few hundred yards further, the road descended steeply. The sound of a revving truck came from up ahead and we cut into woods on the right side of the road. Seconds later, another mud-caked 4x4 roared past, too fast to see who was at the wheel. Coming out of the woods, we continued down the road. If we'd been driving—even if we'd been *looking* for it—there was a good chance we wouldn't have spotted the entrance. Only travelling on foot allowed us to see the tire tracks turn sharply off the road into what initially appeared to be impenetrable brush and forest. A closer look showed that several large, broken branches and loose bushes all but completely obscured a dirt path leading between two trees, just wide enough for a vehicle to pass through. Leaving the camouflage intact, we entered the woods ten feet to the right of the path. Maneuvering around stumps and deadfall, we moved parallel with the path. The trees grew dense and tall as skyscrapers, largely blotting out the sky above. The sudden darkness was disorientating, making me feel like it was suddenly nighttime.

Wayne held up his hand and we stopped. The only thing I heard were his heavy breaths, blending with the hiss of the rain in the trees. He pointed to the Nikons on my utility belt and I handed them over. After peering through the binoculars he passed them back to me and I took a look. "Ten o'clock," he said.

Following his direction, I saw the makeshift driveway a hundred yards to the left, and a padlocked metal gate blocking it. "That's not an official forestry gate, I can tell you that," he said.

Several more minutes of creeping brought us within sight of the corner of a log structure ahead. I was so focused on it that I nearly tripped over a foot-high metal post. My eyes counted more of them to the right, situated every ten or fifteen feet. I snapped my fingers and pointed, alerting Wayne.

"Dog collar sensors," he said, as raindrops slithered down his face. "Got your zapper juiced up?"

I patted the device at my side, and we kept moving forward. Through a dense stand of pine, the log cabin appeared. Low and sturdy, with a stone chimney, it seemed bigger than your average cabin. The earth rose up over the stone foundation, and the structure was so thoroughly covered by moss and lichen that it looked as though nature was reclaiming it. Three wooden steps led up to a small porch with two rocking chairs. A black-painted door was built into the centre of the structure with a window to its left. If it weren't for the small, gray satellite dish, and the series of black solar panels on the roof, seeing the cabin was like stepping back in time more than a hundred years.

A steady humming sound came from behind the cabin.

No brown Yukon in sight.

Wayne pointed to a small camera situated beneath an eave, aimed toward the door. Well-worn ruts from vehicle tires ran around the right side of the cabin to what looked like a clearing behind.

"What's that sound?" I asked.

"Generator," he said. "This is not a weekend warrior's place. I've seen shit like this before, with those off-the-grid Sovereign Citizen whack-jobs. That fucker is built *into* the ground. No normal person would build a cabin like this in the middle of butt-fuck nowhere."

"Papa Danko was a purported recluse. Maybe this was his Shangri-La."

Something flitted by the window, vaguely female in shape. Too far away to make out features.

"Somebody's home," Wayne muttered.

"Danko's not here yet."

"We don't even know for certain if this is his place."

"There's nothing else around."

"We don't know that either. In fact, we could write a book on what we don't know."

"We know that this place is sketchy as fuck."

"That much we can agree on. Check your phone, see if your cop friend got back to you."

I did. "Nope. Still no bars."

Wayne removed his phone and took several photos of the cabin and the surroundings. "Let's go back and wait at the vehicles. Frank knows where we are, but I told him I'd check back within the hour."

"Look, we're here now. Let's get a little closer, take a quick peek, and jet. There's only one way for a vehicle to get in here, and if it comes, we'll hear it a mile away. We get something solid to give to the cops, then let them do the heavy lifting."

"Fuck that," he said, turning. "I got sandwiches back at—"

From the cabin came the sounds of faint crying. The backdrop of rain gave it a haunting quality, and it disappeared so quickly that we were left blinking at each other.

"That was a kid," I said.

"Ah, shit."

"You're not going to leave a helpless child up here are you? You won't be able to sleep at night if you do."

"I hate you, Donovan."

I unholstered my Enforcer. "How 'bout it?"

He adjusted the Remington beneath his jacket. "Quick one."

We moved out from the cover of trees. The rain had turned the earth surrounding the cabin to mud, making our feet sink several inches with each step. I pointed to a series of large, water-filled boot prints leading away from the porch. Wayne nodded and led the way up the steps and onto the porch. I winced as the wood creaked beneath our combined weight.

With my back to the log wall, I looked through the window. The exterior glass was normal, but an inch beyond was a translucent sheet of plexiglass, which gave the objects in the room a blurry, indistinct look. At the top of the plexi-glass pane was a row of small air holes.

Wayne saw it and swore under his breath. From inside the cabin came a muffled thud, followed by the faint but unmistakable sound of a baby wailing. Then it was gone, replaced by the rattle of the generator.

A chill ran through me.

Wayne tried the door and it didn't budge. He looked at me and raised his eyebrows. "Got your religious pamphlets handy?"

I holstered the Enforcer and nodded, removing a small satchel from my utility belt.

He hammered the door three times with his fist. "Hello? Anyone home? We're lost and need directions."

It was my turn to raise my brows. He shrugged and hammered again. A commotion sounded from inside, fol-lowed by the sudden shriek of a child, in fear or in pain.

"Everything all right in there?" Wayne called out.

Through the window, I caught a glimpse of someone moving from one room and disappearing into another. Wayne stepped aside and I crouched in front of the door with my tools. The door was solid and heavy, but the lock was old.

My fingers shook a little as I went to work with the ten-sion lever and pick, focusing on my breathing and blocking all thoughts, allowing muscle memory to take over. With the pick I lifted the pins one by one, placing them in the same position as if a key were in the lock. I turned the lever.

Click.

I nodded up at Wayne, tucked away my tools, and picked up the Enforcer.

The baby screamed.

Wayne turned the knob. "We're coming in!"

He pushed open the door and a shrill, ear-piercing alarm cut through the air. It was more of a screeching sound, like something an animal might make if tortured. Wayne yelled something, but I couldn't make it out over the alarm.

Shotgun ready, he entered the cabin, and I followed. Scattered over the brown carpet were large, multicoloured, plastic building blocks. Beanbag chair. Sagging couches. An ancient box TV with a DVD player on top. *Finding Nemo* played on the screen. The air was thick with a musky animal smell. Not pets, but like savage beasts living in a cave. In the far-left corner of the room, a trapdoor was open in the floor.

To the right was the bedroom, empty and windowless except for an unmade double bed and a small vanity and stool. Makeup and skin products. Jewelry. Similar to the pieces in Emily's room.

Just off the living room, an open doorway connected to the small kitchen. The open back door swung on its hinges as a muscular figure with buzzed hair, tank top, and camo shorts sprinted away, past an attached shed and into an open field on which sat an old tractor and a yellow VW van.

Lola.

Wayne was already through the door and I was close behind when something flashed in my periphery. I whirled to see a small brunette in a white dress scampering through the trapdoor in the living room. The girl turned and looked at me with large, vacant eyes, just before she disappeared beneath the floor. Though her hair had been dyed dark, I recognized her from the photo in Davis' cubicle. It was Kaylee Green, who had vanished last year.

CHAPTER 62

"KAYLEE, STOP!" I SHOUTED, THE WORDS MUTE against the alarm as I ran to the opening in the floor. A steel ladder led down to darkness. Clipping the Enforcer to my utility belt, I climbed down after her. Eight feet down, my feet hit concrete. Floors and walls and ceiling, all concrete.

In the gloom of the narrow hall, I could make out a steel door a few feet to my right. It was ajar. I pushed it open and stepped through into an even narrower hallway lit by a string of small bulbs hanging amid exposed wires from the low ceiling. Behind me, the door swung nearly shut, muffling most of the alarm from above.

Then the lights went out, plunging the hall into blackness.

"I'm here to help you, Kaylee!" I called out.

Nothing.

Then came the baby's cries again, now muffled and faint. Triggering the flashlight function on my phone, I aimed it down the hall. A door on the left was ajar. I pushed it open, and the room was the size of a closet, with a folding chair and a shelf containing four CCTV monitors covering various angles of the cabin's exterior. The top-left monitor showed the open front door. In the corner of the screen, a vehicle pulled up close to the cabin, and a moment later a large, stooped man shambled out wearing a black corrections uniform. Looking all around, he warily approached the open front door and stared directly into the camera.

Paul Danko.

He pulled his phone from his pocket, tapped the screen a series of times, and the alarm died. With calm deliberation he put the phone back, turned, leapt nimbly off the porch, and disappeared around the left side of the cabin.

Leaving the closet, I ran back down the hall. The door I'd come through was now closed and locked, and there was no handle on this side. Sprinting back to the surveillance closet, movement on the lower-right monitor caught my eye. The camera showed part of the muddy field, the rear wheel of the van in the background. The edge of the frame showed what appeared to be the muscular hindquarters of a dog, moving side to side as though trying to pull something.

The dog backed up, dragging Wayne into the frame. The dog's teeth were sunk into Wayne's calf. With his free leg, he kicked at the animal. Lola suddenly stepped into the frame, using the stock of the shotgun to smash him in the head. Flipping the gun around, Lola aimed the weapon at Wayne's head.

The dog renewed its attack, latching onto the inside of his knee.

I ran from the room and further down the hall, holding up my phone for light. A door to the right was open, and I slipped into another room. This one had a dirt floor and stank of urine, excrement, and chemicals. Somewhere back down the hall came the child's crying and a girl singing in a soft and tremulous voice.

Shining my light around the windowless room revealed old Mason jars and cracked plastic children's toys, some half-buried in the dirt-floor. Littered everywhere were paper plates, fast food wrappers, and plastic forks and spoons. In the far-right corner, flies droned above a white bucket, wads of toilet paper all around.

Breathing shallowly against the stench, I searched the room for any sign of an exit. In another corner was a blood-encrusted mattress. Handcuffs hung from a chain attached to a metal bracket in the ceiling.

Turning back into the hall, the first thing I saw was a glowing green dot.

The second was the head of a shovel arcing toward my skull.

Ducking too late, an orange starburst exploded and I fell, dropping my phone. Black. Covering my head with my arms, I rolled to the other side of the hall. My back hit a wall and the shovel smashed my shoulder, my hip, my leg. Reaching out, I grabbed ahold of the tool. With a sharp yank, I wrested it away and rose to my feet.

She was on me, moist breath rancid in my face. She bit my neck, just above the collarbone. I yelled and head-butted her in the mouth and nose.

She fell back, muttering, *"Fuckingbitchfuckingbitch fuckinbitch."*

Grabbing the handle of the shovel with both hands, I used it to press her against the wall.

"Listen to me! I'm a friend. I'm going to get you out of here."

Dim lights from the monitors in the closet glinted off her dark eyes, reflecting back a demonic intensity. Her arm fought loose, and she clawed at my face. Using the shovel's handle, I slammed her hard against the wall several times, then released the tool and grabbed her wrist. She cried out when I twisted her arm behind her back.

Wrestling her into the surveillance closet, there was enough light to see that the woman before me wasn't Kaylee. Older by at least twenty years, her matted black hair had been haphazardly cut, hacked down to the skin in spots, and she wore a ratty wifebeater and men's blue athletic shorts. A snug-fitting metal collar circled her neck, with a flashing green sensor. Scars crisscrossed her wrists. She looked up at me with eyes that were vicious and vacant in equal measure. My breath caught in my throat.

"My God," I whispered. "Amber."

She gazed at me, the muscles around her bloodshot eyes twitching.

"Your mother's alive, Amber. She hired me to find you."

She shook her head, furiously blinking her eyes. *"I'mnotI'mnotI'mnot ..."*

"What *is* your name?" I asked.

"Angie."

I paused, studying her again. There was no possible way. This was Amber Sebastian. "OK, Angie," I said, "we need to get you out of here. Do you know the way?"

"Baby," she said.

"We have to get out now. We'll come back for the baby."

"No!" she screamed, struggling to free herself from my grip.

I pointed toward the monitor where Wayne had been. He and the dog and Lola were now gone, along with the van. "Listen," I said. "My friend is hurt. We need your help or we're going to die. Angie, please."

She ceased fighting and I released my grip. The baby began crying again. Like a zombie she walked from the room and down the hall to a closed door. She pounded on it once and gave a strange trilling whistle.

The door opened a crack and Kaylee's terrified face peered out. She wore the same collar as Amber. The baby in her arms started crying with renewed vigor.

Kaylee stared at me.

"Kaylee, I'm here to help you and your baby escape," I said.

"It's not mine," she said, in a soft, faraway voice.

"What's the baby's name?"

"Eli Paul," she said. "He's Emma's."

The baby cried louder. His eyes were crusted and goopy. Amber reached and took the screaming infant from her. It was then I noticed the swelling of Kaylee's belly.

"Who's Emma?" I asked. "Do you mean Emily?"

She nodded. "She died."

"He killed her," I said. "Paul or Loretta or both." I turned to Amber. "Your mother—"

"*You're a liar,*" Amber hissed. "My mother is dead."

"She lives an hour from here," I said. "In the house you grew up in. Your brother and sister are grown up. They all miss you. Your people miss you. And Kaylee, your parents are looking for you too. Right now."

Kaylee stared, stunned. Amber's head shook violently from side to side. Tears spilled from her eyes as her face contorted in a rictus of inner agony. She was missing several front teeth and many others were black with rot. "You're a liar," she said again, this time with less conviction.

"The liar is outside," I said. "He's a killer, and if we don't get out of here, he's going to kill you, too. How do we get out of here?"

"We don't," Kaylee said. "We're locked in."

"Eli is sick," I said, locking eyes with Amber. "He has an infection and needs a doctor."

Hugging the boy tightly to her chest, she marched past me down the hall. She pulled a ceiling cord in the far corner. The lights flickered back to life.

Holding Eli in one arm, Amber bent to retrieve the shovel with the other, before heading for the door at the end, the room with the bed and chains and the stench of hell.

She stepped over the lip of the door and was swallowed by the shadows. I followed and turned to see Kaylee halt at the doorway.

"I can't go back in there. I can't! I can't!"

I made a grab for her, but she pulled back and turned and ran back to the bedroom. I called to her, but the steel door slammed with an echoing clang. From outside in the distance came the sounds of a barking dog and shouting voices. Entering the cesspit, I spotted the white of Amber's shirt as she stood near the toilet area and used the shovel to pry a board loose near the ceiling. Eli wailed in the dirt nearby. I picked him up and he squirmed hotly in my arms.

Wood splintered and broke as Amber rammed the shovel against the top of the wall. A board fell. Looking at the extent of the damage, this attack on the wall had not been the first. I wondered if Emily had tried to escape this way—and been killed for it.

Amber pried another board, dropped the shovel from her hands to pull the wood free. She pointed toward the hole she'd made: a small portal to deeper darkness.

"You go first," I said. "I'll hand Eli through."

She shook her head and took Eli from me. "You."

Squeezing through the gap, I wriggled into another room. Water dripped on my scalp as I pulled my legs through and stood, right beside the rattling and vibrating metal generator. From chinks in the wood walls, thin shafts of light illuminated enough of the space to let me know I was in the small, attached shed, about six by six and windowless.

All was silent except for the barking of the dog, seeming much closer now.

A gap beside the door revealed a padlock and hasp on the other side. Amber grunted something and handed Eli up to me. The boy took great tremulous sucks of air as tears and snot streamed down his face.

Amber Sebastian set the spade on the floor of the shed ahead of her as she wormed through the hole. She stood, picked up the tool, and immediately began chopping away at the boards to the left of the door. The wood cracked and broke under the shovel's edge, allowing in more light. I reached into my satchel for the picks. She looked at them and shook her head and returned to chopping at the wood.

I shouldered her out of the way. "We don't have time."

Sticking my hand through the gap in the door, a quick feel of the padlock revealed it to be basic and cheap. I could have done it drunk and one-handed using a paper clip. The problem was working from a bad angle. After several fails and nearly breaking the pick in the keyhole, I felt the click.

I popped the lock off and kicked open the door. Amber rushed past with Eli under her arm. I was right behind her. From the right came a flash of movement. She gasped and dropped the child, stumbling backward into me. Over her shoulder I saw a small hatchet imbedded in the right side of her abdomen.

CHAPTER 63

BEHIND HIS GLASSES, PAUL DANKO'S EYES went wide as he loomed over Amber. A moment later, she fell sideways to the ground. "Angie, no, no, no," he said.

As I pulled the Enforcer, he grabbed me and flung me against the side of the cabin. Another bright burst of pain in my head as I fell to my hands and knees in the muck. For a second, everything went black. I could smell blood.

When my vision returned, it was like seeing through a filmy lens.

Danko wiggled the hatchet free from Amber's stomach.

Blood drained from her face as she grasped for Eli, his face filthy as he screamed in the mud.

Distracted, Danko turned to the boy. My eyes searched for the Enforcer. I couldn't see it anywhere, so I grabbed a fist-sized rock. When Danko leaned over Eli, I lunged, smashing the rock above his ear. His head snapped to the side as he reached out and snared my shirt with his free hand. I kneed his groin. The rock tumbled from my grip and I raked my fingers down his face, lodging my fingers into his eye sockets. He roared and dropped the hatchet. As my fingers dug deeper, he wrapped his hands around my throat and lifted me off my feet, squeezing so hard it felt like my eyes were going to explode. The fight was being choked out of me, and I let go of his face. My blurred vision blackened around the edges, like a photograph melting.

He stopped and looked down, blood running freely from one eye. The pressure on my throat released. I followed his gaze to see Amber, plaster-faced, pulling on his leg and mouthing the words *please, please*. He dropped me and I landed in a heap near Eli. The hatchet sat five feet away. Danko bent over Amber. "It was an accident, sweetheart," he said. "You're not supposed to be out here. You knew it wasn't safe."

Blood burbled from her mouth. Danko cradled her head.

"You've got to get her to a hospital," I gasped.

"She's gone," he said, voice hollow.

"No, she's still alive. We can stop the bleeding, get her up the road—"

With sudden speed he reached out, grabbed me by the hair and pulled me close, forcing me to look at her. "This is on *you*," he said, eyes flashing darkly. "She had a good life here before you came messing around. I *saved* her from hell down on that reserve."

"You steal girls and kill them," I said.

"No innocents ever died."

"Tell that to Emily Pike. And her father."

Danko shook his head. "You're the real cause. You were warned. I took your boyfriend's little girl, and you kept coming. You invade people's lives like a parasite—"

"We can save her, Paul," I said. "You didn't love and care for her all these years just to see her go like this."

His eyes went from me to Amber. Reaching over with one arm, he checked her neck for a pulse. In doing so, he released me enough that I could draw back and slam my elbow into his jaw, once, twice, three times. He grunted and let go. I rolled away, kicking at his legs and reaching for the hatchet. Danko's boot pinned my forearm just above the wrist. With my free fist, I cursed and pounded against his shin. I might as well have been hitting a tree trunk.

"Trap a coyote by one of its limbs," he said, "and most likely the beast will gnaw it off. People, too, will go to similar lengths if they have enough will to live. You don't have that luxury anymore."

I strained and closed my eyes, saw the Winnebago, heard myself scream. When I opened my eyes, beyond Danko's boot, I saw my sister holding both her dead children, watching with the same impassive stare as my captor. I blinked again and saw that it was Kaylee Green, barefoot in the mud, holding Eli in her arms.

"Katie," he said with measured calmness, "I need you to take Eli inside and clean him up. I've got to deal with some things in order to protect this family."

"She said my parents are looking for me," she said.

"She's lying, Katie, because she's crazy. I've shown you the documentation. Your parents are dead."

I made eye contact with her. "*He's* lying, Kaylee."

Pressing down with his boot, Danko ground my arm deeper into the muck. I cried out in pain. He told her again to take Eli inside, adding that she shouldn't be upset in her condition. She hesitated, looked at me for moment, before turning and disappearing back into the shed with the child.

A sudden blow jarred my entire body and sparks exploded behind my eyes. My head hit the earth and the last thing I remember was looking into Amber's glassy, lifeless eyes. I heard the familiar rattle and behind her, and just before I lost consciousness, I saw the yellow VW van pull up.

CHAPTER 64

MY EYES OPENED TO DARK CLOUDS AND A BLUR of shapes all around. Trees. Mounds of dirt. Crosses. A body.

Semi-focus returned, revealing Wayne on the ground nearby, bite marks on his arms and legs, face covered in blood. The jeans covering his right leg were shredded, and on the inside of his knee, bright red blood oozed from several puncture wounds.

We were in a clearing in the forest, next to a large hole dug into the earth. Staked into the ground nearby were two wooden crosses spaced about five feet apart. The cross on the left was considerably older, the wood weathered and warped. The other was topped with fresh dirt. Beyond the graves were more of the sensor sticks we had seen earlier. Remembering the collars worn by Amber and Kaylee, I now knew what they were for: the women would get electro-shocked if they crossed the barrier. Like animals.

Ten feet to the left, blocking a trail just wide enough to accommodate the vehicle, was the yellow VW van, its side door panel partway open.

Wayne's eyes fluttered open. *"Run,"* he croaked.

I crawled to him. Pulling off his belt, I cinched it high up and around his right leg.

"They're coming back to finish the job," he said. "Run. Get the fuck out of here!"

I grabbed Wayne, tried to pull him up. He pushed me away. A dog barked from the woods. Close.

"Get your ass up, Wayne," I said.

From behind came the distinct *chk-chk* of a shotgun shell being racked. I turned to see Lola aiming the weapon at us. Wound around her forearm was a leash connecting her to a brindle pit bull, its muzzle fresh with blood. With her buzzed head, faint moustache, and camouflage bandana around her neck, Lola looked more like a Marine awaiting deployment than the woman I remembered tending horses at the farm. She secured the mastiff's collar to the bumper of the VW van.

"Where's Danko?" I asked.

"He's coming," she said, her voice husky and strained.

"So are the police," I said. "They know about this place."

"Ain't true."

"It is. I told the cops in charge of the Emily Pike case. Our partner knows, too. You're a runner, right? Like me?"

She remained silent, finger on the trigger. Wayne remained very still as he watched through half-closed eyes.

"Well, when I head out into the woods," I said, "I always let someone know where I am."

"He found the GPS on your belt. It's gone now."

"But it'll still show that we were at the cabin. They're going to find this place, and they're going to be here soon. You should go while you still can."

"I can't."

"You *can*. You're a survivor. You've been running since you were fifteen. That's when Paul found you, right?"

"You don't know what the fuck you're talking about."

"Back then you looked like the others. He didn't realize you were trans."

Lola stepped in and raised the shotgun a foot in front of my face. He was shaking.

"You don't have to do this anymore, Loretta—"

"My name is Larry!"

"Larry," I said. "He manipulated you and brainwashed you like the others. He's sick. But you're not. You're not a killer. You don't have to do this anymore."

His eyes went panicky-wide as a tear raced down his cheek.

"What happened to Emily?"

"I didn't want to do—" Distracted by something over my shoulder, Lola looked up. I turned to see Paul Danko trudging around the van. His eye was roughly patched up with tissue and duct tape. His right hand held the hatchet, his left held my Enforcer.

"Cops are coming, she said," Lola said.

He shook his head as he examined the Enforcer. "No one's coming."

"You're delusional," I said, "if you think your connections to Travis Benoit will save you from murder charges."

"Anything remotely connected to him gets brushed aside. He's their number one boy."

"Not something like this," I said. "It's too big."

"You overestimate your own importance in the overall scheme of things. Maybe because you're batshit crazy, but it's unfortunate you had to drag others into the pit with you." He tapped Wayne's chest with the Enforcer and pressed the trigger. Wayne's back arched as he stiffened and twitched. When the current was released, he fell back gasping.

"Boy was playing possum," Danko said. "You get the keys off them, L? They didn't walk all the way up here. There's bound to be a vehicle around someplace."

Lola held her hand in my direction. "Hand 'em over."

I shook my head. "He drove."

Danko patted Wayne's pockets and my partner moaned in weak protest.

"The day of the dogfights at the ranch," I said. "That's where you saw Emily Pike."

He paused, blinking his one good eye at me, then looked over at the more recent grave. "Her dumbfuck boyfriend brought her there. She was so beautiful, wasn't she, L?"

Lola's eyes filled with tears as his jaw began to tremble.

"I don't know if you believe in destiny," Danko said, "but I do. Everything happens for a reason. Emma was meant to be there that day."

"Her name was Emily," I said.

"So much baggage in a name," he said. "Sometimes it's good to have a fresh start."

"What happened to her?" I asked.

"It was an accident," Lola said.

Danko reached a hand into Wayne's pocket. "Negligence," he corrected. "You left the news on TV, right when the girl's bitch moth—" His eyes grew wide as Wayne's hand latched onto his wrist. Danko raised the hatchet as Wayne booted him in the groin with his good leg.

I lunged for Lola, knocking the barrel of the shotgun away. He backpedalled, tripped, and went down with me on top. The shotgun fell to the ground. Lola kicked out, trying to buck me off. I struck out, hitting him in the throat several times. He stopped, stunned, and I used the moment to pin him down by the neck. He was crying. He wanted this to be over.

The pit bull barked and strained against his leash a few feet to my left, so close I could feel the dog's hot breath on my face, feel droplets of the animal's bloody saliva on my cheek. Ten feet to the right, Wayne and Danko grappled in the mud. Danko had released the Enforcer but he still held the hatchet and used his greater bulk to roll both of them into the pit. He raised the hatchet again.

I let go of Larry and groped for the fallen shotgun.

It wasn't there.

The weapon blasted from behind me. Danko flew off Wayne, ending up draped over the hole. Through his shredded shirt, his mid-and upper back looked like raw hamburger.

Amber Sebastian stood beside the grave, holding the shotgun, face bone white as she stared at her captor of the previous two decades. Pulling himself up, Wayne stood and gently pulled the weapon from her grasp. She collapsed sideways to the earth. I rushed to her, peeling off my jacket to staunch her abdominal wound. Reaching out with my free hand, I scooped up the Enforcer.

The pit bull broke free of its leash and launched itself at me. I raised the weapon to the dog's snout and pulled the trigger. The beast yelped and scrambled backward. Pressing the trigger repeatedly, the Enforcer crackled, and I hit the animal twice more before he bolted.

Wayne shouted something. I looked up to see him pointing the shotgun toward the forest in the opposite direction as Lola disappeared into the trees. He swore, then turned his attention to Danko, rolling him over and checking his pulse. "He's alive, but with the blood coming from his mouth, this bastard's got some suffering to do yet."

Amber Sebastian stared up at me, her eyes dulling.

"How is she?" Wayne asked.

"Not good."

He hobbled toward Amber, using the shotgun as a cane. "Go get Lola," he said.

CHAPTER 65

THE PATH THROUGH THE FOREST TWISTED downward in a haphazard zigzag, skirting boulders, dense second-growth forest, and massive fallen cedars. The rain had stopped but water dripped steadily from the leafy canopy above.

Ahead and to the left came faint and faraway sounds of something crashing through the brush. Lola had gone off-trail. Stepping over several fallen trees, I knocked branches aside and kept forging ahead. The ground ascended, becoming rockier, forcing me to use my hands on the steeper sections. Each time I heard a sound, I stopped to gauge the direction and distance and readjusted my course as necessary.

Sounds of trickling, then water rushing. A cry of pain. I stopped. Nothing. Only the water. Veering left, in the direction of the sound, I soon arrived at a fast-moving stream. Too wide to leap. Fifty yards upstream a tree had fallen across. Scrambling toward it, I spotted something partly submerged among the rocks on the other side. Using the fallen tree as a bridge, I balanced to the other side and bent to pick up a hiking shoe. The outside was wet from water, but the inside was sticky with blood around the ankle area.

Tossing it aside, I clambered up the embankment. The ground became boggy, making it easy to track the uneven footprints in the muck.

Picking my way through brush and bog, my feet made loud sucking sounds with each step. Speed was impossible here, and several times I came close to losing my own shoes. The footprints turned abruptly to the right, heading into the kind of deep brush where it became impossible to see any tracks. I kept going, until a sobbing sound at three o'clock made me change course again.

After several more minutes of bushwhacking, I heard the clatter of rocks ahead. Moments later I stood at the bottom of a steep and rocky rise. A stone clattered down, nearly clipping my shoulder. I looked up to see Lola's muscular body climbing, silhouetted against the dark gray sky.

Reaching up, I grabbed an outcrop and began climbing. About halfway, I glanced up again to see Lola standing at the top looking down at me. We made eye contact. He disappeared from sight for several seconds and returned, hoisting a football-sized rock.

"Oh, don't even—" I said, just as he dropped the rock. It crashed down the slope toward me, forcing me to hug the rock face as it bounced off an abutment two feet above.

Looking up to find him gone, I scrambled the rest of the way up. The top was an expanse of rocky bluff punctuated by stunted trees. No Lola. Drops of blood led obliquely across the bluff before disappearing over the edge on the other side. A warm breeze whistled through a stand of pines that looked wretched and exiled from the rest of the forest.

Beyond that, one could see the entire Fraser Valley, the river far below, a gray snake meandering its way toward the ocean. Mission. Chilliwack. All the way into Washington State.

The blood droplets ended at a cliff face. I looked down. It was a sheer death drop, the distance from where I stood to the tops of the nearest trees at least three hundred feet. Had Lola come all this way, only to make a dramatic exit?

Leaning further out, I saw a bloody foot dangling in space. Moving still closer to the edge, I saw him sitting on a ledge twenty feet below. I also saw the rusted climbing spikes that had been driven into the rock face at regular intervals.

"*Larry,*" I yelled.

No response. I called again, my voice echoing off the mountainside. His head lolled forward, like he was taking a nap. His leg twitched.

"*Can you hear me?*"

Nothing.

Dropping to my belly on the bluff's edge, I gripped one of the spikes and lowered myself backward down the rock face. If he had done it, so could I. A small, scraggly tree jutted out, its trunk nearly perpendicular to the cliff. Putting my right foot on it, I tested its strength, and finding it secure, used it to slowly lower myself down to Lola's perch, still having to jump the last two feet. My right foot landed on a loose rock on the ledge, and I nearly tripped and went for a final tumble.

Immediately I saw the blood pumping steadily from the sliced radial artery in his left wrist. A serrated blade pocket-knife hung slackly in his right hand.

Removing the bandana from his neck, I tied off his forearm just above the wound. I checked his neck for a pulse. It was very faint, but it was there. His eyes fluttered.

"Can you move?" I asked.

A low laugh. "What do you think?"

"C'mon, you can't just make me chase you all the way out here to have it end like this. Where's the winning attitude the night you made me dog you through skid row? Or how about the time you and Danko abducted and drugged my boyfriend's daughter?"

Holding up the knife, I added, "Come to think of it, maybe I should help you finish the job."

"Please do," he mumbled.

I flicked it off the cliff where it disappeared into the trees below. "You came all this way to die?"

"Found this place years ago. Thought about jumping lots of times. Turns out it ain't so easy to step off."

"Call of the void," I said.

"What's that?"

"Something a girl named Renay told me. She was a girl you and Danko tried to steal from Mission a few years ago."

"I remember."

"You knew this couldn't end well, right?"

"You're not taking me in."

I looked up. "That's the truth," I said. "So tell me what happened after Emily saw her mother on the news."

"She ran...grabbed a knife. I chased her and she fell and got cut bad. Paul was pissed. Made me stop her suffering. I strangled her. I can't stop thinking about her eyes." He began to sob. "She looked so scared."

"Seven years ago," I said, "the first time Paul saw Emily at the Benoit ranch—were you there?"

He shook his head. "Paul found out who she was, where she worked. He made me volunteer there. Had no idea they'd offer me a job."

"You fell for her, too. Bought her jewelry."

"I left it in her locker. I was too gutless to let her know."

"But not too gutless to help him steal her."

"He said he just wanted to see her again. We had no idea we were going to witness her and Oscar have a fight. When we drove by a second time, she was crying on the road. He told me to pull over."

"Police questioned you along with everyone else. They did a background check of all the employees."

"He had connections where I could get clean ID."

"Why did you stay all these years?"

"It's like those animals at the zoo, when they leave the cage open...the animals might wander out for a bit, but then they come back to what they know. That's what I felt like. In a weird way, I felt safe. I also felt like it was my job to take care of the girls."

"You never thought to go to the police."

"He told me that if he went down, I'd be arrested, and that he knew people who would kill me wherever I went. If I stayed and did what I was told, I got treated OK. Once he realized what I was, he didn't try anything with me, but he couldn't let me go either."

"Tell me about Amber?" I asked.

"He saw her at Mountain when she'd go visit her daddy. He knew her hitching route and we just picked her up. She was trouble from day one ... ended up being chained up in that basement so long..." His voice trailed off as he shook his head and stared off into the distance.

"Listen to me," I said. "Paul Danko is a monster. If he's not already dead, he'll never see the light of day again. He did this to you. Your story needs telling. Families need to know. It will help people heal."

"I'm going to die," he sobbed.

"No, you're not."

Somewhere behind us came the distinct *whup-whup* of a chopper. Lola's head perked up and he made a move to push off the ledge. Getting one arm around his neck, I managed to pull him back into a modified submission hold. For a few moments Lola thrashed against me, but in his weakened state I was able to restrain him. Eventually he went limp and hung his head and sobbed.

A few seconds later, a police helicopter came into view, circling around the cliff face, where it hovered before us.

CHAPTER 66

AFTER WAYNE HAD FAILED TO REPORT IN THAT day, Frank had promptly notified Mission R.C.M.P. that there was trouble brewing at the Danko cabin. At around the same time, Fiona Saddy had read my message and relayed it to Inspector Pryce Davis, who, to his credit, finally took action and mobilized the troops.

During the time I was chasing Lola through the woods, the police converged on the scene to find a hysterical and pregnant teenage girl, a sickly and caterwauling young boy, a frenetically-barking pit bull, and another woman and two men in varying stages of near-death.

A semi-conscious Wayne had managed to show his credentials before pointing to the forest. "Two more are out there. One of them is my partner."

A police chopper was called in, along with two air-medic helicopters to whisk away the wounded, Kaylee Green and baby Eli among them. In less than an hour, droves of cops and crime scene techs descended upon the cabin in the mountains. Hot on their heels, a dozen news crews soon choked the forestry road leading up to the police barricades, and by early evening, local and national news helicopters buzzed continuously overhead as the story broke, not just across Canada, but all of North America, before fanning across the globe.

Had Paul Danko not slipped into a coma just after his arrival at Vancouver General, maybe he would have enjoyed his week of worldwide notoriety as the prison guard who had abducted five women over a forty-year span, two of whom had died in captivity. His face made the front page along with the headline: EMILY'S TRUE KILLER. The article went on to say how the recently deceased Lucas Pike had been wrongfully set up for the crime of murdering his daughter. Despite an initial publication ban, the identities of Amber Sebastian and Kaylee Green were leaked. Given the public's fascination with long-term captivity cases, they would be approached with offers for exclusive interviews, even book deals. We had already been approached to tell our story, and while the blood was still fresh, Wayne had conducted a series of interviews from his hospital bed.

I spent one night in the hospital. My fight with Danko had resulted in a black eye and a low-grade concussion. After being dosed with IV-antibiotics as a precaution against infection from Amber's bite, I was released the following day. Wayne remained, receiving a barrage of shots for his dog bites, along with a blood transfusion and over a hundred sutures to his ravaged ankles, calves, and thighs. He spent the next three days hopped up on opioids and taking a weird, giddy pride when the vascular surgeon informed him that the only thing that saved him from bleeding out was the protective layer of fat on his inner thighs.

And then there was Lola. Following his attempted suicide, he too suffered blood loss and required a transfusion.

When interviewed, his subsequent memory loss was attributed to many years of exposure to a drug whose name the press absolutely adored: Devil's Breath. Hidden in a secret compartment within the Danko bunker, investigators found enough of the powder to keep a small army forgetting for the next millennia.

Lola was medicated and kept on suicide watch, while reporters camped outside the psychiatric wing of the holding facility in Burnaby, their telephotos trained on the mesh-enforced windows, hoping to get a shot of the trans man who had been stolen as a fifteen-year-old girl, before being used to lure the others. Photos of the ratty, yellow VW van were splashed over the nightly news, until the story became usurped by a movie theatre pipe bombing in the Midwest.

Amber Sebastian's wounds were severe, resulting in major external and internal bleeding. The surgeries were extensive, and after developing sepsis, she spent eighteen days in a medically-induced coma, her mother Dee-Dee at her bedside around the clock.

It was leaked to the press that Kaylee Green had been Paul Danko's "favourite wife". Despite being raped and impregnated by a monster, because she had been captive *only* a year, she had sustained by far the least amount of damage. Following a week of psychological observation, medical care, and multiple visits by police, Kaylee was reunited with her family.

CHAPTER 67

One week later

DURING A TELEVISED PRESS CONFERENCE IN front of Maddy Pike's townhouse, a scared, silent baby Eli rested in his grandmother's voluminous arms, before burying his face in the deep fissure of her armpit. Lilith hovered over her shoulder like a vulture, and Pryce Davis stood to the right, wearing a navy suit and a politician's smile. Fiona Saddy stood nearby, smiling tightly with eyes that looked several decades older than the rest of her.

The camera zoomed in on Maddy Pike, teary-eyed and kissing the top of Eli's head, while the boy's face ground deeper into her armpit, as though it were a cave into which he could escape.

"Jesus fuck," said Wayne, voice dopey from pain meds, "that kid's gonna suffocate in that bitch's pit before he's been free a week."

"Shush now," said Sally McGrudder, from her place beside Wayne in his hospital bed.

We watched Maddy on television, daubing her eyes with a tissue, and I thought back to the day she approached me outside HardKnocks. Seemed a lifetime ago.

She said, "I want to thank the police and the investigators involved for not giving up on this case and for locating my beautiful grandson, Matt."

"She changed his name already?" Sally said. "Given who the father is, I guess you can hardly blame her."

"So much baggage in a name," I mumbled, but no one seemed to hear me.

"'*Investigators involved!*'" Wayne shouted. He pushed himself up in bed, as Sally tried to restrain him. "Without us, in ten years, Hillbilly Eli there would be out there helping his daddy pull other girls into vans."

"You're going to rip open your sutures again, you stubborn man," Sally said, succeeding in tapping his hand-held morphine button. Several seconds later, Wayne's face went from splenetic to slackly serene. Sally wiped a little froth from his whiskers.

"Wait'll we get *our* press conference," he mumbled.

"It's not like you two haven't had your names all over the news and in the papers," Sally said. "Your phone must be ringing off the hook."

I took a sip from a water bottle filled with sauvignon blanc. "Mostly from my mother," I said.

"She must be so proud of you saving those girls and that little boy. And I hear Haley Cooper's people have been clamoring to turn it into a miniseries."

I took a bigger gulp from the bottle. On screen, the camera flashed to Emily's smiling face, then to a shot of a much younger Paul Danko wearing his corrections uniform. Then aerial shots of the cabin. A close-up of the pit, the graves. Everything seemed artificially arranged for effect; not the chaotic, blood-drenched tableau I remembered.

CHAPTER 68

M.J. BEAMED HER MISSING-TOOTHED SMILE and began strumming a far sprightlier version of "Stairway" than I'd ever heard. I smiled and tossed a ten into her ukulele case. Pepi the skunk stretched. M.J. stopped mid-chord.

"You better not let the hero complex go to your head, kid. Tossing me a tenner because you're famous now. Pfft. I hear you've been refusing big money interviews. It's only going to make your damn P.I. mystique grow in the eye of the public. Some might think that's a well-calculated ploy on your part, playing hard to get. But don't mess around; take the money and run, that's what I say. Or take it and give it to me, forget the misguided attempt at integrity. That ship sailed the moment you decided to make a living skulking around fleabag hotels photographing men dipping their shlongs in their secretaries."

"Quite the spiel, M.J. You take to the bottle again?"

"No, but you have. I could smell the booze on you from down the street. Not even noon yet." She pulled out a pack of gum and offered me a stick. "Take it. You got company upstairs."

"No more reporters, I hope."

"Uh, no," she said, gesturing with her head toward the black Escalade waiting down the block, Giller at the wheel.

Travis Benoit sat on the top of the stairs outside the door, wearing grandfatherly bifocals while reading an issue of *Spy Gadgetry* that had been delivered to our doorstep. He looked up at me as I climbed past. He handed me the magazine along with some bills and flyers that had been sitting by the door. I unlocked the door to the reception area and ushered him in ahead of me. No way was I turning my back on Travis Benoit.

"Interesting business you're in," he said, surveying the waiting room. "Once upon a time, I could've imagined doing something like this."

"Tough to get a license with your record."

"Therein lies the rub," he said, glancing around. "Is this room secure? Any recording devices whirring behind some clock face or an electrical outlet? I was just reading about the gadgets you people use. Interesting stuff."

"Had I expected you, maybe I'd have installed something ahead of time. With my voyeuristic partner, however, all bets are off." Opening the door to my office, I gestured him in. Once again, he appraised the surroundings before taking a seat facing the desk. I took a beer from the fridge and offered him one and he nodded. I sat down, and we opened our beers and sipped in silence. The evidence board to the right was stripped bare, all our case evidence turned over to the police. If Uncle Trav had paid a visit ten days prior, he'd have seen his face up there.

From the window came sounds of the street: trucks rumbling, horns, sirens screaming. It all seemed far removed, like I was living life through someone else's eyes.

"You're famous," he said.

"Hoo-rah," I said, gulping my beer.

"Pretty sick stuff up in those woods, that business of keeping those girls all those years, having babies with them."

"The drugs you supplied were instrumental in their abduction."

He just looked at me.

"Same stuff was also used to kill inmates at Kent," I said. "Before that, Mountain. Not merely inmates, but rivals of yours. I wonder why *that* didn't make the news."

Travis Benoit took another sip, crossed his legs, and picked a speck of lint off his jeans. "I was just glad to see justice done."

"Paul Danko came out of a coma a few hours ago," I said. "I just found out, but you probably already knew that. He isn't able to speak yet, but the doctors say his brain function is just fine. He'll stand trial, and given the nature of his crimes, it'll be a lengthy one. A great deal will come of it. No matter what investigations are under way, names will be named. This is too big."

His eyes didn't leave mine as his mouth gave the faintest of smiles. A contented smile of one who can see not just several chess moves ahead, but the entire game. "At the end of the day," he said, "everyone gets what's coming to them."

"Is that what you came here to say?"

He shook his head. "When you risked life and limb to talk to me in my home, I couldn't figure out if you were doggedly tenacious, or a couple cans short of a six-pack. Either way, you impressed me. I could use someone like you from time to—"

"You're offering me a *job?*"

"Strictly under the table."

"Of course."

"Does that mean you'll accept my offer?"

"Are you fucking kidding?"

He shook his head, then leaned forward and grabbed a tissue from the box on my desk. Holding it in his right hand, he reached inside his jacket. I grabbed the desk drawer that held my extra Enforcer, but he already had the gun out. The pearl-handled pistol he had relieved me of the night I showed up on his doorstep.

"Thought I'd return this," he said, wiping it down with the tissue before placing it carefully on my desk. "No bullets. Man in my position can't be walking around with a loaded firearm."

I placed the weapon in the drawer. He checked his watch and stood. "You did a good thing up there," he said. "You ever need anything—"

"Never going to happen, but thanks."

He smiled. "Never say never."

I followed him from my office and opened the frosted glass door. Travis Benoit turned to go down the stairs, then stopped and moved sideways to let someone pass. "Ma'am," he said, nodding politely to the diminutive figure of Dee-Dee Sebastian hobbling up the stairs. Her wizened face beamed a hard-earned smile, as two of the most incongruous people imaginable crossed paths, neither of them knowing how their lives were connected.

He nodded back to me, then turned and continued down the stairs.

"Dee-Dee!" I said, holding out my arms.

We embraced and Dee-Dee kissed me on the cheek. Tears streamed down her face. "You brought her back to me," she said, her voice a hoarse whisper. "You brought my baby back."

I couldn't speak. We remained in a silent embrace. At first, I thought the wetness on my cheeks was from Dee-Dee's tears, but it was from my own.

VANCOUVER SUN — OCTOBER 3
By Jerry Fifer, Staff Reporter

Former prison guard Paul Danko, charged with the murders of two women and the abduction and confinement of five women over a forty-year span, was found stabbed and beaten to death in a pretrial infirmary, where he was recovering from wounds sustained prior to his arrest on August 24. A trial date had been set for early next year. Danko's murder occurred when guards were mobilized during a fire alarm. Corrections Canada has announced that a full investigation is being launched. Authorities say that there are no suspects, though sources say that it is likely Danko made enemies during his eighteen-year stint working at Kent Institution.

Meanwhile, excavations are still underway in and around the Danko property outside Mission, to find possible remains of other potential murder victims. VPD Inspector Pryce Davis of the Serious Crimes Unit says, "Due to the scope of this case, the investigation will go on for some time, even despite Mr. Danko's demise."

CHAPTER 69

One month later

NUMBER 129, A TALL BRUNETTE, BOMBED PAST me on the steep downhill of the final stretch. Rocks and roots were slippery from torrential morning rains. The only thing I could hear was my own breath in my burning lungs. My hands and feet had been numb for the past hour.

Another runner passed me, a young, petite blonde. The bitch actually flashed me a smile that I read as: *nice try, old-timer.*

Pissed off, I cranked up my pace, passing the blonde and hurdling a fallen tree. Now I was flying, finding my stride. It had taken only sixty-five kilometres to do it.

A flash of white to my right. Glancing over, I expected it to be a white nightgown, but it was only morning mist lingering amid the trees. When my feet left trail and hit gravel road, I nearly stopped cold. The finish line was a hundred yards ahead. A cheering crowd, most people huddled under umbrellas. Panic surged in my chest and I felt the sensation of leaving my body.

Just kick and breathe, kick and breathe.

I felt myself slow.

"Sloane! Go, Sloane, c'mon, move your ass!"

Fuck off, Karin. I narrowed my vision to the road five feet in front of me. Lead seeped into my legs.

"C'mon, Donovan!" Wayne's deep voice. Of course, the one race he shows up to and I bomb out at twelfth place.

"Go, Sloane!" A shriller voice, almost a scream.

A child's voice.

No. I can't see them now. Not now.

Don't look.

Kick and breathe.

"Go, Sloane, go!" Familiar.

I looked up, saw Karin, Wayne, Sally, cheering and clapping.

My breath caught in my throat as I saw Sadie, clapping and waving her arms.

Sitting atop Jim's shoulders.

He smiled and shouted my name.

And I ran.

ACKNOWLEDGEMENTS

An author without people in their corner probably wouldn't be much of an author at all, and I'm fortunate to have many amazing people supporting and nudging me down the right path on this crazy journey.

Writing can be hard, but the phenomenal team at NeWest Press—Matt Bowes, Meredith Thompson, Carolina Ortiz, Christine Kohler, and Claire Kelly—makes the process of getting a novel from manuscript to print a joyful experience. What they do is considerable, and I am deeply grateful for all of it. Having Matt as editor means that there is little compromise in honing my vision into a finished product, of which I am truly proud.

I cannot imagine a better designer than Michel Vrana, and I feel honoured to have someone of that calibre working hard to prettify my babies. Seeing the cover magic he conjures up is one of the most exciting parts of the process.

To A.J. Devlin, my fratello and fellow crime author. If I somehow managed to get this far without him in my corner, it wouldn't be half as fun—or as good. #bros4life

To Sylvia Leong, long-time friend, author, and photographer, who never hesitates to give me the straight goods, whether I want them or not.

To my friend Tony Leong, for his computer wisdom, and his unrivalled skill in utterly grossing me out via a simple text message.

To Nicole Rigler, for her help in giving Danko a new first name that sounded appropriately creepy.

To the perpetually enthusiastic Magnus Skalgrimmson, writer, and promoter extraordinaire. Massive thanks for all the support, and for introducing Noir at the Bar to Victoria!

In terms of author inspiration and support, a hearty shout out to Sam Wiebe, S.M. Freedman, Frances Peck, Dietrich Kalteis, Niall Howell, Tara Moss, Iona Whishaw, Erik D'Souza, Winona Kent, R.M. Greenaway, J.G. Toews, and William Deverell.

To friends and loved ones Jack Kilgour, Corrie Bownick, Andy Wilkens, Kevin Spode, Chris Gallardo-Ganaban, Craig Watson, Chris Wells, Jess Lynn, John "Buzz" Barrigar, Daniela Sosa, and Naida Bertelsen.

To my mom and dad, for always letting me read whatever books I wanted at inappropriate times.

To Pulp Fiction Books, Book Warehouse, 32 Books, Western Sky Books, Munro's, and all independent book stores everywhere. They are the lifeblood of the book industry and deserve continued support in the same way that they support authors.

To Bill Selnes, Cozy Up With Kathy, Debra Purdy Kong, Mary-Ann Booth, Rosemary Keevil, and the book clubs that were so kind to host me.

My increasingly lovely and always supportive wife, Wendy, is the first to call out my many grammatical and punctuational blunders. Only with her approval does a manuscript go off to the publisher. Her attention to detail is unparalleled, and she never fails to bring out my best, as a writer, and as a man. I am forever lucky to have her at my side.

J.T. SIEMENS moved to Vancouver to become a personal trainer, but feels fortunate to have discovered his true love: writing crime fiction. After studying screenwriting at Capilano University, he followed it up with creative writing at the University of British Columbia and Simon Fraser University. *To Those Who Killed Me*, his first book in the Sloane Donovan series, was nominated for the Arthur Ellis Unhanged Award and won the inaugural Mystery and Thriller Book of the Year Award at the 2023 Alberta Book Publishing Awards. He lives in the West End of Vancouver with his wife and two cats.

Also by J.T. Siemens

To Those Who Killed Me

Praise for *To Those Who Killed Me*

"A scorching debut. Donovan is a sleuth to be reckoned with."
—SAM WIEBE, award-winning author of the Wakeland novels

"An exhilarating white-knuckled thrill ride that blasts out of the gates and doesn't let up for a moment. In his debut crime novel, Siemens brilliantly weaves together gripping tension and page-turning twists while showcasing a penchant for depicting the glamour and grit of Vancouver and introducing one of the most complex heroines I've ever read. Sloane Donovan is a compelling force not to be missed."
—A.J. DEVLIN, award-winning author of *Cobra Clutch* and *Rolling Thunder*